AUDREY ROSE

AUDREY ROSE

a novel by

FRANK DE FELITTA

G. P. Putnam's Sons, New York

COPYRIGHT © 1975 BY FRANK DE FELITTA

*All rights reserved. This book, or parts thereof, must not
be reproduced in any form without permission. Published simultaneously
in Canada by Longman Canada Limited, Toronto.*

PRINTED IN THE UNITED STATES OF AMERICA

For Eileen, my daughter

Acknowledgments

Daniel A. Lipsig provided thought and counsel. Dr. Donald Schwartz graciously gave of time, information and guidance. Dr. Jay L. Dickerson, Professor Irwin R. Blacker, Father Joseph Casper, Ivy Jones, Jeanne Farrens and Willard M. Reisz contributed instruction and encouragement. Dorothy De Felitta helped throughout with rare understanding and sympathy for the book she helped to form. William Targ, my editor, made it all possible.

I thank them all.

Pittsburgh Post Gazette, August 4, 1964

TWO-VEHICLE CRASH KILLS 2, INJURES 2

Harrisburg, PA (UP)—A woman and her young daughter were killed and 2 persons were slightly injured after their cars collided with each other on the Penna. Turnpike during a sudden hail storm.

Police have withheld the identities of the dead woman and child pending notification of relatives.

AUDREY ROSE

AUDREY ROSE

PART ONE

Bill and Janice Templeton

I

He was there again, standing among the glut of waiting mothers who arrived each day at ten to three and milled about in their separate worlds, waiting for their children to be released from school.

Until today he was merely a presence to Janice Templeton, just another parent standing in the cold, outside the Ethical Culture School, waiting for his sprite to emerge. Today, however, Janice found herself noticing him—a lone male in a sea of females—and wondering why it was always he who showed up, and not his wife.

He was standing now with his back half turned to her, gazing expectantly up at the big doors of the school building. Somewhere in his early forties, Janice guessed, and not at all bad-looking. He wore a thick mustache and carefully trimmed sideburns and had the lean, hard body of an athlete.

She wondered who his child might be and made a mental note to find out.

The school bell rang.

The parade of children tumbling through the doors was, each day, a bittersweet experience for Janice. It made her realize how quickly time sped by, how swiftly the child of yesterday was becoming the adolescent of tomorrow.

Tall, lithe, strikingly beautiful, ten-year-old Ivy Templeton possessed a feminine elegance that seemed out of place for her young age. A sweep of blond hair—pure to the roots—fell back past the line of her shoulders, framing a face of exquisite features. The delicate pallor of her skin formed the perfect background for the large deep-gray eyes. The shape of her mouth was clear-cut, a sensual mouth until she smiled, restoring childhood and innocence. Janice never ceased to marvel over the beauty of her daughter and never ceased to wonder about the genetic miracle that had formed her.

"Can I get a Coke?"

"I've got Cokes in the refrigerator," Janice said, kissing Ivy's hair.

Hand in hand, they started their walk up Central Park West when Janice stopped, remembering the man. Glancing over her shoulder to see which child's hand might be linked to his, *she froze*. The man was standing immediately behind them, close enough to touch, close enough to feel the plumes of his breath, and in his eyes a manic glint of desperate need—of inexpressible longing—directed exclusively at Ivy. At Ivy!

"Excuse me," Janice gasped inanely and in shock, her heart pounding as she clutched Ivy's arm and hurried up Central Park West toward Des Artistes, five blocks away, without once looking back to see if the man was following them.

"Who was he, Mom?"

"I don't know," Janice panted.

The thought of what might have happened had she not been there to meet Ivy brought Janice to a sudden stop at the corner of their street. What if she had given in to Ivy's persistent demands and had allowed her to walk home alone like Bettina Carew and some of the others in her class?

"Why have we stopped, Mom?"

Janice took a deep breath to regain control of herself, smiled wanly, and together, they crossed the street and entered the old building, Des Artistes.

The Fortress, Bill called it.

Built at the turn of the century at the whim of a group of painters and sculptors who purchased the land, hired an architectural firm, approved of the plans, and arranged for the mortgage, each level of the twenty-story building contained six master apartments of various sizes, featuring huge, high-ceilinged studios with galleries facing large floor-to-ceiling windows that offered a diversified selection of city views. A number of these windows admitted the northern light, a must for the painters. The decor of the apartments was lavish, imaginative, and fulfilled the esthetic and emotional needs of their owners. Some studios took on a baroque character, displaying vaulted ceilings replete with inset pediments and slavering gargoyles. Others went a more frivolous rococo route, featuring painted ceilings with rich, gilded moldings. A few apartments followed a somber Tudor pattern and were intricately paneled in darkly stained veneers.

A magnificent restaurant in the lobby of the building amply satisfied the artists' appetites and even delivered exquisitely prepared dinners to each apartment via a network of dumbwaiters scattered throughout the building.

During the Depression, Des Artistes was sold to a cooperative association, and the new people who purchased apartments began to remodel them. The space in midair was valuable to them and was quickly subdivided, providing a large living room downstairs and enough room for two or three bedrooms upstairs.

With all the changes and departures from the artists' original concepts, the one thing no tenant could ever alter was the inherent charm and grandeur of the building. Like the superb restaurant off the main lobby, the original atmosphere remained intact.

Janice's first act upon entering the apartment was to double lock and bolt the door. After pouring Ivy's Coke and sending her upstairs to do her homework, she poured herself a straight scotch. The man at the school had really rattled her. This was a new sensation for Janice. She realized that life was filled with pockets of danger, but thus far she had been spared.

She carried her scotch into the living room and sat in her favorite chair—an overstuffed antique rocker that had belonged to her grandmother. As she sipped the drink, her mind reformed the face, the expression in the man's eyes as he stood looking down at Ivy. There was nothing sexual in his look, or depraved; it was more a look that spoke of great loss—sad, hopeless, desperate. That was it, desperate.

Janice shivered visibly and took a large swallow of scotch. She could feel the spreading, soothing, warming sensation of the alcohol throughout her body as she rose and walked to the window. Her eyes ferreted among the antlike figures scurrying about on the sidewalks far below. Might he be down there? Watching? Waiting? She would tell Bill about it as soon as he came home.

Sipping the last of her scotch, Janice turned from the window and gazed at the long length of the living room in the soft, waning light of the autumn afternoon. The thirty-eight-foot expanse of dark-stained pegged floor led the eye to a huge stuccoed walk-in fireplace, a practical, wood-burning, marshmallow-toasting fireplace that warmed their souls on cold winter evenings. Next to the fireplace was a narrow flight of carpeted stairs leading up to two bedrooms and a small study. The banister and rail posts harkened back to the days of the artists and were fancifully carved; the newel post featured the bulbous head of a Viking chieftain.

Janice's eyes lovingly moved across the treasured corners of her world and, as always, finally came to rest on the pièce de résistance—the one item that had plunged them recklessly ahead on the perilous course of buying the apartment; the ceiling.

Deeply paneled in a variety of rare woods, varnished to a high luster, the ceiling was a magnificent work of art. Two large paintings, wrought by the brush of a true master, had been set into the woodwork, dividing the ceiling into two parts. Janice discovered, after much research, that the paintings were in the tradition of Fragonard, featuring woodland nymphs cavorting licentiously in cool, shaded glades. It was a stunning, breathtaking sight that literally startled new guests, and Bill and Janice loved playing it down, pretending to accept the ceiling as a matter of course, sometimes even expressing slight irritation at its gaudy vulgarity.

But alone, they would lie together on the hearth rug, holding hands and gazing spellbound at their ceiling museum, themselves stunned at the fantastic luck of having found and acquired such a treasure so soon after their marriage. They had rushed into buying the apartment just as they had rushed into marriage, impatient to get started on their lives together.

Devoted opera fans, Janice and Bill first met at a matinee of *La Traviata* in San Francisco. Both were in school at the time, Janice completing her senior year at Berkeley and Bill doing graduate work at San Francisco State. Each was potlucking for a single that blustery Saturday afternoon, hovering about in a throng of waiting enthusiasts for a cancellation. A second before curtain, a pair of the best seats became available. More expensive than Janice could afford, she quickly grabbed one ticket. Bill took the other.

Strangers, they sat together during the first act in perfect silence, drinking in the dolorous Verdi strains like two parched souls at a desert oasis. During the first intermission Bill offered Janice a cigarette. They smoked and talked opera. During the second intermission Bill bought Janice a drink at the Opera Bar. That night they had dinner on Fisherman's Wharf.

Seven days later they spent the weekend together in a motel in Sausalito and made love. They were married upon Janice's graduation and immediately went to live in New York.

Eleven years of perfection, Janice thought. In a setting unmatched.

Janice was feeling beautifully relaxed as she walked to the liquor cart and poured herself another scotch. She'd let Bill have his martini before telling him about the man.

She was dicing a carrot in the tiny kitchen when she heard the sound of a key fiddling with the lower lock. It was a tentative, groping sound. It wouldn't be Bill at this hour; it was much too early.

Janice stood rooted, clutching the small paring knife, hardly breathing as she heard the soft, scratching noises of metal against metal. She knew she was safe, really; there were two locks plus a chain bolt to protect her. Still, she felt vulnerable and in terrible danger. If the man had the nerve to sneak past Mario and the elevator men and find his way to their door, then he was capable of doing anything.

Suddenly, the tumblers turned with a noisy click. Janice froze. She heard the key move up to the second lock and find its way home with much less trouble. The tumblers turned. Janice took a step back toward the kitchen wall. The skin of her hand clutching the knife was white. The chain tightened across the narrow opening with a sharp clatter.

"Oh, c'mon, open up."

Bill's voice.

With a cry of relief, Janice sprang to the door, undid the chain, and flung herself into his arms as he crossed the threshold.

"What is it, hon?" Bill asked gently.

"Nothing," she whispered. "I'm just surprised to see you."

Then, pulling herself together, she smiled and added, "I've got a glass chilling for your martini."

Bill gently disengaged himself from her and in a voice that seemed to trip delicately over eggshells, quietly said, "Do . . . not . . . mention . . . that . . . word . . . please."

He and his assistant, Don Goetz, had entertained a new client at 21, and their lunch had been mainly liquid. The client, president of a thriving health food chain, obviously didn't practice what he preached and kept Bill and Don chugalugging doubles until they both could hardly stand on their feet.

Walking gingerly and with care, Bill started up the stairs to conk out for a while before dinner.

"You've got about an hour," Janice called after him with forced cheeriness. "And don't forget the Federicos tonight for bridge."

Bill's response was a groan of agony.

Janice returned to the front door and locked it again, including the chain bolt. She saw her empty glass on the butcher's block in the kitchen, picked it up, and carried it back into the living room. As she poured her third drink, soft, unintelligible voices penetrated from the floor above. Bill's gentle-gruff baritone. Ivy's light laughter. Loving, comfortable sounds.

"One club."

"Pass."

"Two spades."
"Pass."
Carole Federico studied her hand, biting her lips.
"Pass."
Bill laughed aloud, seeing her blunder. Russ Federico glared at his wife angrily.
"Are you out of your mind, didn't you see my jump bid?"
"But we've got a partial, and that gives us game," protested Carole.
"Damn it, I gave you a jump shift. I indicated we've got enough points for slam!" Russ threw his cards on the table. "Of all the goddamn stupid things to do!"

The Federicos took their bridge seriously, and the Thursday night sessions generally wound up in a fight. The game would get going at eight sharp but would never continue beyond ten. By that time, after a series of minor faux pas, Carole would always pull the granddaddy of them all, sending Russ into a towering rage and cuing Janice to put on the coffee.

The Federicos were slightly younger than the Templetons. Bill and Russ had come to know each other on the elevator, going down each morning. Occasional smiles and good-mornings had gradually ripened into conversation and then friendship. They would often walk to work together.

Russ and Carole had moved into Des Artistes in '70, having purchased one of the smaller apartments. They were married five and a half years and were childless. Russ owned a small sound recording studio on Fifty-seventh Street. Like Bill and Janice, they couldn't abide TV, loved bridge, and, best of all, were passionate about opera and owned a fabulous library of records, many of which were collectors' items.

Their first evening together was at the Templetons'. Janice had spent the entire day preparing a cold veal tonnato, celery aspic, and a creamy chocolate mousse spiked with Grand Marnier. The Federicos were impressed and adulatory, proposing toast after toast from the jeroboam of Mouton Cadet they had contributed to the meal. Afterward the relationship was firmed with one of Russ' rarest discs, a 1912 Victor recording of Alma Gluck singing selections from *Faust*, *Aida*, and *Manon Lescaut*.

The forceful combat of the lieder singers worked the opera toward its tragic conclusion. Janice sat in the rocker watching the others as they intensely savored the concluding strains. No one spoke, ever, during these musical sessions. Russ' eyes were half closed in an expression of deep appreciation. Carole stared at the floor. Bill lounged sideways in the big club chair, his hand covering his eyes in a keenly listening attitude; however, Janice suspected he was dozing.

As the clash of cymbals punctuated the final orchestral crescendo, Janice glanced up and saw Russ gazing intently toward the opposite end of the room, a glint of mischief in his eyes. She turned her head and saw Ivy coming down the steps, rubbing the sleep from her eyes. The effect she had on Russ was anything but subtle. Twice in one day, men had noticed her. Pained and puzzled, Janice wondered where the childhood had gone and why so fast.

"I don't feel well, Mom." Ivy yawned tiredly and walked across the room toward her mother. A floor lamp in the corner backlit her progress, turning the gauzy nightgown into a transparent veil.

Russ stood up and greeted her with a sultry smile.

"Hey, you're really getting there, kid," he said, his eyes shifting fleetingly to her breasts, peeking impudently through the sheer material.

Ivy smiled wanly at Russ and put her arm around her mother's waist. Carole joined them, having caught the byplay.

"Okay, buster." Her tone was mock serious and a touch too casual. "Take me home before you get into trouble."

Bill had been sleeping after all, for he remained in the same position, draped across the club chair, his hand shielding his eyes.

After the Federicos gathered their records and left, Janice gently shook Bill awake, then sent Ivy upstairs. Janice followed her with a cup of warm milk and took her temperature. It was normal.

By the time Janice undressed, creamed her face, and slipped into her nightgown Bill was sleeping soundly. His soft, rhythmic breathing, not quite a snore, enveloped the room. It was a safe, comfortable sound and often lulled Janice to sleep.

She turned off the lamp and crawled into bed beside him. Raising her nightgown to her waist, she gently snuggled up to him, fitting her body into the curvature of his warm nakedness.

Like everything else in their marriage, their sex life was perfect. Nothing between them was taken for granted. Both were experimenters, and every session brought with it something new and liberating. Bill bought books on the subject to widen their knowledge. "Bioloop," "biocurve," "mutual concentration," "intimacy spiral" were expressions they knew and used.

Janice smiled as she remembered the Orissan posture book that Bill had brought home one evening. It contained drawings of more than one hundred intimate positions practiced by sixteenth-century Arabians. Over the course of several weeks they tried a number of them, the more possible ones, which were mainly unrewarding. They were forced to give this up when Bill hurt his back trying the number seventeen, or cartwheel, position.

Her smile deepened with the memory of the joy, the fun, the perfect sweetness of their life together, high in the center of Manhattan, in the dreamy duplex they owned.

How perfect their life had been. How safe and protected. No frights, no miseries, no sudden shocks. Except for that spate of crazy nightmares that had come to plague Ivy when she was a toddler and that lasted almost a year, not sickness, or want, or fear, or desire for others had come to challenge the perfect order of their lives.

Until today, Janice thought, with an aching stab of regret. Until today—in front of the school.

Janice was certain, and had been certain since three ten that afternoon, that life as they knew it was coming to an end. That even now, as she lay beside the warm, breathing form of the man she loved, forces were gathering to shatter their dream. She didn't know how it would come about, or why. Only that it would happen.

That afternoon, in a flash of instant prescience, Janice had seen their doom reflected in the eyes of a perfect stranger.

2

Ivy awoke with a slight fever. It was just above normal, yet Janice thought it best to keep her home from school. With the weekend upon them, it would afford her three days' rest. She would call Dr. Kaplan only if the fever got worse. Janice rationalized the decision to her full satisfaction and felt a sense of relief at having made it. Or was it a sense of reprieve?

Whatever, three days had been granted her before the next confrontation with the man.

The morning was cold and sunny as Bill stepped through the big glass doors of the old building and started walking to the corner of Sixty-seventh Street and Central Park West. The weather was perfect for walking, and Bill would make it to the office in good time since he didn't have to take Ivy to school this morning.

He might even forgo the fast route down Central Park West and cut through the park directly at the Tavern on the Green. It took seven minutes longer; but the park was beautiful this time of the year, and Bill always enjoyed plodding across the soft golden carpet of crisp autumn leaves.

By the time the traffic signal had changed his decision was made. Bill crossed over to the Sixty-seventh Street park entrance and headed toward the famous old green and white clapboard restaurant.

As he entered the park gate, he casually glanced toward Ivy's school, six blocks down the traffic-clogged boulevard. He wondered what Sideburns would think when he and Ivy didn't show up this morning.

Bill plowed through a thick crunch of dried leaves which the wind had gathered together at the curb and proceeded on a southeasterly course through the park. The lanes at this point were wide and festooned with overhanging trees. The morning was still, and leaves drifted down gently around him under their own weight.

Bill had first become aware of the man on September 12, just four weeks and four days before. He hadn't really spotted him until the fourteenth, two days later, but the moment he realized he was being followed, his mind did some fast backtracking and eventually placed the first encounter at a specific moment in time.

It was on the Sixty-fifth Street cross-transverse bus. Bill had just finished an all-afternoon conference with a media representative from the Doggie-Dog TidBits account. They had conducted their business in the client's suite in the Hotel Pierre. As Bill left for home, it started to drizzle. He managed to make the four blocks up Fifth Avenue before the deluge began and happily found a bus parked there and taking on passengers.

As the loaded bus took off with its damp, surly cargo, Bill found himself wedged tightly in a mass of strangers, their breaths commingling intimately, their bodies swaying and jerking together in rhythm to the bus' staccato progress through the transverse.

The face closest to his was a woman's—middle-aged, care-worn, drained of joy or hope, with a pair of eyes that gazed vacuously into his, registering nothing. He couldn't see the person behind him, but knew it was another woman, as he could feel the soft, pliable form of her breasts snuggling into his back every time the bus came to a short stop.

The third face, only partially seen in profile, belonged to a man about Bill's age. What fascinated Bill here was the single perfect sideburn on the right side of his face. It was fascinating because of its perfection. Each hair was separate and distinct and seemed to have been trimmed by a draftsman. The thick crop of the man's sideburn was matched by his mustache, which was equally perfect. Still, there was something very wrong about them both. Bill puzzled over this halfway across the park before finally coming up with the answer. They were phonies. The guy's cheeks were nearly hairless; he could never have grown bushes like those on his own. Bill smiled with satisfaction at having solved the mystery when suddenly he realized that the man was looking at him. Bill quickly looked away and began studying an ad over the bus driver's seat.

By the time Bill got off the bus at the corner of Sixty-sixth and Central Park West, the rain was falling heavily. Tiny glistening explosions of water battered the wide street as Bill jogged the short block to Des Artistes. The man with the sideburns was totally forgotten.

Two days later Bill met him again. In the elevator of the building where Bill worked. He was standing in the rear of the car behind a group of people as Bill entered. He didn't look at Bill, and Bill pretended not to notice him. It could have been a coincidence, but Bill didn't think so.

Later in the day, to confirm his suspicions, Bill ran a tape in the big computer that Simmons Advertising used for its demographic breakdowns. He fed the machine all the data he could think of: population density, area of encounters, time elapsed, distance between two encounters, and even fed it their sexes, probable ages, and an estimate of their physical fitness. The machine came back with a probability of one in ten million that two such encounters could occur within two days.

Still, Bill was willing to grant the outside possibility that it *might* have been a coincidence.

Twice, yes. Three times, no.

One of Bill's accounts was a mutual fund with offices down on Wall Street. He and Don Goetz had spent an entire Monday morning presenting their spring ad campaign to the board of directors. The wrangling by the board would continue through the day, so Don and Bill escaped to a nearby restaurant for an early lunch.

They had finished their sandwiches and were sipping their second cups of coffee when Bill's eye caught the familiar sight of Sideburns floating in the rear of a mob of waiting customers near the doorway. The man was barely visible since people's bodies were blocking all but a fragment of his head. Yet Bill was certain he was the same person.

After they paid their checks, Bill pushed through the waiting mob clotting the doorway, keeping his eyes peeled for the man with the sideburns. But in the time it had taken him to pay his check and put on his coat, the man had vanished. Bill glanced back into the restaurant to see if he had been seated. He was nowhere in sight.

Bill was worried. He was obviously being followed. By whom? A cop? The FBI? And for what reason?

That evening, balmy with Indian summer, Bill strolled slowly up the path that flanked the small lake in Central Park. Swans and geese swam in gentle, patient circles in search of stray crumbs of popcorn or peanuts. Bill walked to an empty bench and sat down.

His was a logical, orderly mind. If he was being followed and if it *was* the FBI, then there had to be a reason. Sitting in the shadow of the Plaza Hotel which loomed impressively above the lake, Bill probed his memory for anything he might have done in college, any organization or club he might have joined, any donations he might have made, any lectures he might have attended that could possibly give the FBI a reason for being interested in him. He reviewed each episode of his youth, each small area of his school years, minutely scoured each miserable day of his one-year hitch in the Army, and still, he could come up with nothing. He was clean. Of that he was sure.

The man was obviously wearing a disguise. The mustache, the sideburns, the whole thing was amateurish. Maybe he wasn't a professional at all? Maybe he was just some nut. God knows, the city was filled with them. You met them on buses, in subways, in broad daylight, walking down Fifth Avenue, screaming, yelling, cursing, no cops around, and nobody daring to stop them. Yes, the city was infested with psychotics. And if you were smart, you never let them catch your eye.

Bill remembered what happened to Mark Stern. A promising career was cut short because of a nut. Mark and his wife had parked their car on a side street near Lincoln Center. They were members of the Metropolitan Opera Association and had lifetime seats in the Founders' Circle. After the opera they'd gone to where their car was parked and found this person pissing against the fender. Mark got angry and pushed him away from the car, so the man started pissing on Mark and his wife. Mark hit him in front of witnesses and knocked him down. The man suffered a small concussion but was out of Bellevue in two weeks. He got a lawyer and swore out an assault and battery complaint against Mark. The trial was by jury. Mark was found guilty. He did sixteen months in jail, lost his job, a vice-presidency with Gelding & Hannary, and the last that Bill heard, his wife was divorcing him.

Bill couldn't figure out why he was smiling. What happened to Mark was tragic, and yet he couldn't help wondering who wound up with the lifetime subscription to the Met.

He sighed and rose from the bench. Sideburns just had to be some nut.

The next day Bill was forced to reassess that opinion.

He and Don had spent the morning trying to land another agency's client—a client they had once represented but who had been snatched away from the Simmons agency some years before. Don felt encouraged by the reception they got, but Bill, a trifle older and wiser in the ways of the street, got a different message.

"They let us leave," Bill explained to Don as they rode back to the office in a cab.

"Well, they want to think about it," protested Don. "What's wrong with that?"

"If they have to think about it, we've lost them," Bill said with a note of finality.

Bill liked Don Goetz; he was bright, aggressive, loyal, and eager to learn. Bill had taken him as an assistant right out of Princeton three years before. He never regretted the decision.

Approaching his desk, the first thing Bill saw was the interoffice envelope. He glanced briefly at his phone messages before opening it. The envelope contained an eight-by-ten glossy photo of himself—an updated portrait he'd sat for last year at Bachrach's. It accompanied his bio, which was kept in a file case in Personnel. A handwritten note from Ted Nathan, personnel director of Simmons, was attached: "Forgot to include this with your bio. Sorry. Ted."

Bill shook his head foggily and tossed it aside.

He took care of several of the more important calls on his message sheet before dialing Ted's interoffice number.

"What's the mug shot for, Ted?" Bill asked when Ted came on the other end.

"What do you mean?" Ted said. "We always send them along with the bios."

"What bio?"

"The one you asked for."

"Hold on, old friend. Let's start at the beginning. You say I asked you for a bio on myself?"

"Yes, that's right." Ted Nathan's voice showed a slight nervous strain as he enunciated his words with care.

"All right, Ted," Bill said gently. "When did I ask you for it?"

"This morning. A little after nine. I had just gotten in when you called. You wanted it on the double, for your presentation. Don't you remember, Bill?"

"Sure, Ted, sure. Slipped my mind for a sec. Thanks, pal." And then: "Oh, say—by the way—you didn't tote it up yourself, did you?"

"Course I did. Nobody else is here at that time."

Cleared of any wrongdoing, Ted Nathan's tone became pointedly self-righteous. "I put it on your secretary's desk like you told me to."

"Yeah, that's right," Bill said genially. "Thanks, Ted."

Bill hung up the phone lightly. He sat back in his Eames tubular recliner and focused his eyes on the big Motherwell print that dominated the wall opposite him. His eyes burrowed into the soothing brown and black juxtapositions, drawn into the hypnotic spell of the artist's vision.

Sitting silently, immobile, Bill Templeton had real things to think about.

Somebody wanted to know all about him. Obviously. Somebody who had done his homework. Who knew that Bill's secretary didn't arrive at the office till nine thirty. Who knew that Ted Nathan always arrived shortly after nine. Who knew that on this particular morning Bill would go directly to his appointment and not come into the office at all. Who knew how to imitate Bill's voice well enough to fool a man whom Bill had known for more than nine years. Somebody with the training and resourcefulness to plan a break-in and accomplish his mission without getting caught. A person of talent and dedication—and daring.

One week later Sideburns showed up at school.

It was on the first Monday in October. There was a real threat of snow in the air. Bill, as usual, was taking Ivy to school on his way to work.

Their gloved hands clasped tightly together, they would jog down the length of a block, then, coming to a corner, swing suddenly about so that their backs would receive the frigid impact of the crosstown winds, whipping up the narrow side streets. It was a game they played and loved playing together each year at this time.

When they finally reached the school building, they both were out of breath and laughing in total delight at each other. Bill's eyes watered with the cold, and he could hardly see Ivy as she stood on her toes, kissed his cheek, then turned and scampered up the steps and through the big doors. As Bill turned to leave, he almost collided with a group of mothers, stationed at the base of the steps waving good-bye to their children.

Grunting an apology, he started to move past them when, suddenly, he stopped. Sideburns was standing directly in his path, staring at him. The look in the man's eyes gripped Bill tightly and seemed to push for a confrontation.

"My name is Bill Templeton," Bill said, and took a step forward. "I think you want to know me."

The man remained transfixed, gravely looking at Bill for a long moment, before quietly speaking.

"I don't know," he said. "I'm not certain. I'll let you know soon."

And without another word, he turned abruptly and hurried off down the windswept boulevard toward Columbus Circle.

Bill could only watch after him, staggered, replaying the words over and over in his baffled brain.

"I don't know. I'm not certain. I'll let you know soon."

A week went by.

Each morning Sideburns faithfully kept his rendezvous in front of the school. Bill would find him standing in his customary spot next to the steps, watching them approach from the distance. He'd watch them kiss good-bye, then turn and hurry off toward Columbus Circle the moment Ivy entered the building.

When, for two weeks, the pattern didn't change, Bill decided to go to the police.

The desk sergeant was paunchy, dyspeptic, and pushing retirement age. He listened to Bill's story in a bored, detached manner, then sent him upstairs to "Detectives" to see Detective Fallon.

Bill sat opposite a young, ruggedly handsome man in plain clothes and repeated his story to him. The room was large, painted a dreary green, and filled with an odd assortment of tables and chairs. The table where Bill and Detective Fallon were seated was deeply scored by years of use and mischief.

Detective Fallon listened attentively but without surprise or emotion. He made a few notes, flashed a quick look at Bill when he mentioned the man's disguise, but allowed him to finish before asking, "Did this person in any way batter you?"

"Batter me?"

"Did he come into purposeful bodily contact with you? Did he push you? Or hit you?"

"No, nothing like that."

Fallon's face softened somewhat. "Unless there's evidence of a battery, there's very little the police can do in a case like this."

"Isn't it enough he's been following me, spying on me?"

"What evidence do you have that he's spying on you?"

"I told you, he got into my office. He secured my bio-data sheet by impersonating me." Bill's voice steadily rose in indignation. "Isn't that enough evidence?"

"How can you prove that he did it? I mean, do you have real concrete evidence that *he* was the person who entered your office and did this?"

"Well, no, but. . . ." The energy in Bill's voice gradually flattened.

Fallon watched him a moment, almost regretfully.

"Officially, there's nothing I can do for you, Mr. Templeton, but tell me again, what time do you take your daughter to school?"

"The schoolbell rings at eight thirty."

"Okay. I'm on the nine-to-five this week. I'll stop by on my way in tomorrow and have a look at this guy for myself." And with a small, tight smile, he added, "*Un*officially, of course."

The next morning Sideburns didn't show up.

After Ivy had entered the building, Bill walked over to Detective Fallon, who had been hovering behind a mailbox trying to appear inconspicuous. When Bill informed him that the man had failed to show, Fallon grinned lightly, shrugged, and said they'd try again. The next morning the same thing happened: Fallon came; Sideburns didn't. The third morning Sideburns waited for them in his usual spot, but Fallon had given up.

The leaves crunched satisfyingly under Bill's feet as he approached the pedestrians' exit at Fifty-ninth Street and Fifth Avenue. Long lines of horse-drawn carriages were parked across from the Plaza Hotel, waiting for tourists to finish their breakfasts and start their day.

Bill waited in a small group for the light to change. In a way, he was glad that Ivy hadn't gone to school today. He'd have a three-day respite before having to face Monday morning.

Bill thought of the weekend ahead of him. It would be fun staying at home the entire weekend. Bill could do what little food shopping was needed. Maybe they'd have the Federicos up to dinner and some bridge Saturday night.

As he crossed Fifty-seventh Street and veered eastward to Madison Avenue, Bill sensed a light, jaunty bounce to his step. He was almost feeling good for a change. "Que sera, sera," he thought. "Whatever will be, will be." The next move is up to Sideburns. Screw him!

While the pressure on Bill had been tremendous over the past weeks, he prided himself that he had never once brought his worries home to Janice. She had been spared any knowledge of his little pas de deux with the man in disguise.

He had kept their fortress inviolate—secure.

3

The word was M-A-T-E-R-I-A-L.

Ivy giggled excitedly and pushed the letter *I* into place at the end of the *L*. Janice considered this deeply, then added a *Z* to the *I*. Ivy quickly completed the word with an *E*.

"There." She laughed triumphantly.

The time was only ten minutes past ten. The morning seemed endless.

Ivy had just placed an *X* beneath the *E*, starting a new word in the vertical line, when the telephone rang. Janice added a *C* beneath the *X*, pushed herself up from the floor with a funny little grunt, and quickly walked across the long, elegant room to answer it. It was probably Bill; he often called upon arriving at the office.

The telephone sat on a low table which formed the corner of a right angle connecting two black-covered sofas spiced by small bright pillows of green and lemon peel. A large stubby vase filled with autumn leaves spread a canopy of earth colors over the corner.

Janice picked up the phone on the fourth ring.

"Hello?" she said.

There was no answer.

"Hello?" she said again, in a softer tone, feeling a prickle of apprehension.

Janice was about to hang up when the voice finally came. Male. Quiet. Hesitant.

"Is she all right?" it said.

Janice hung up abruptly.

She stood there, eyes shut, steeling herself against the wave of utter panic about to overwhelm her. It was the man. She knew it was he. It could be no one else. He had found their unlisted number. Somehow. She felt herself trembling. *Control! Control! She must not let Ivy see her like this!*

A small, static smile affixed to her face, Janice gracefully squatted down to resume the game.

Ivy pushed an *E* under the *C*.

"Who was it?" she asked offhandedly.

"Secret Service," Janice replied with a light, controlled laugh.

Ivy giggled, knowing full well to what her mother alluded. Phone calls with no voice at the other end were a frequent occurrence in the lives of most city dwellers. Whether the calls were simply mistakes, the deviltry of children, or the pastime of seriously disturbed persons, there was no accounting for them and certainly no stopping them. One learned to live with the nuisance; it went with the territory. "Secret Service" became their euphemistic way of laughing off these unidentified calls.

As Janice moved an L under the E, the telephone rang again. Janice watched Ivy slide another L beneath hers. The telephone continued to ring. The word on the board had built itself to E-X-C-E-L-L-E-N before Ivy quietly asked, "Aren't you going to answer it?"

"Nah," Janice replied, forcing a cheery note into her voice. "I'd rather play this game than that one."

Ivy dropped the Y onto the end of E-X-C-E-L-L-E-N-C-Y with a cackle of merriment.

The telephone continued to ring.

"I really think we should answer it, Mom," Ivy said with concern. "It may be Daddy."

The same thought had occurred to Janice. She could visualize Bill sitting at his desk, worriedly listening to the phone ring and ring, wondering why no one answered it.

Janice rose quickly and started for the telephone when the ringing stopped.

"Aw!" said Ivy dejectedly. "Missed."

"If it *was* Daddy, he'll call again."

Janice reached down and felt Ivy's forehead. "How about some milk and cookies?"

"Sounds great."

The ringing started again, and Janice dropped the half-filled milk bottle, spilling the milk on herself and the kitchen floor. But this time the rings came in short, staccato sounds telling Janice that the house phone, which was situated in the hallway, near the door, was summoning her. If it *was* the man, she would refuse the call since all incoming calls were announced by the desk man in the lobby, Dominick. Still, she let it ring four times before she picked it up.

"Miz Templeton?" Dominick's rough, familiar accent was pleasantly reassuring. "It's your husband."

"Thank you, Dominick."

"Hey, what gives?" were Bill's first words. "I called you twice. The first time you were busy. The second time, no answer."

"I don't know," she lied. "I didn't hear the phone ring. Maybe you got the wrong number."

Bill made a small, thoughtful sound. Then: "How's my little princess?"

"Okay. She doesn't have a fever. It's probably just one of those one-day things."

"Well, keep her in anyway. I mean, don't go out—it was really freezing this morning."

"I wouldn't think of it," Janice said with a light dramatic flourish.

"I may be home early."

"Swell. Call me later and let me know," Janice said, trying to end the conversation.

"How about calling Carole to see if they're available tomorrow night for dinner?"

"All right."

A pause. Then: "Anything else doing there?"

"No." Why didn't he hang up?

The telephone in the living room rang again. Its distant, strident sounds caused every nerve in Janice's body to scream in protest.

"I've got to go, Bill," she heard herself sputter in almost a gasp. "The other phone is ringing."

"Answer it, I'll wait," Bill said.

Janice put down the phone, too brusquely, and hurried up the hallway to the living room.

By the time she got there Ivy had already answered it and was tailing off the conversation.

"Fine, thank you," she said with a small smile. "Good-bye." And softly returned the phone to its cradle.

Janice's heart pounded as she took several steps into the living room. Her voice was surprisingly casual as she asked Ivy who had called.

"A man," Ivy replied. "He wanted to know if I was all right."

"Did he mention his name?"

"No."

"Most likely a wrong number."

"Unh-unh. He called me Ivy."

Janice was amazed at her own control as she idly commented, "Maybe a teacher at school. They worry about you kids, you know."

"Hey, I'll bet it was Mr. Soames." Ivy broke into laughter. "He's always asking the girls how they are. He asked Bettina the other day, and she wasn't even sick."

Janice suddenly remembered Bill waiting on the other line.

"Why don't you go upstairs and lie down, dear? I've got your father hanging on the other phone."

"What about my milk and cookies?"

"I'll bring them up to you. Go now, run."

Ivy moved toward the staircase with some reluctance.

"Who was it?" Bill asked.

"One of the teachers wanting to know how Ivy is feeling," Janice replied without even pausing to think.

"Oh? Which one?"

"Mr. Soames."

Later, while Ivy was napping and Janice had a moment to collect her thoughts and calmly review each step of the ghastly situation, she wondered why she hadn't just simply told Bill the truth. She could think of no answer beyond a vague, foolish wish to preserve the peace and tranquillity of their coming weekend. Yes, that was it—she was seeking to protect their weekend, to permit them once more, perhaps for the last time, to savor the loving motions of togetherness before the ax descended, as she knew it inevitably must.

She was buying time.

The cab deposited Bill on the park side of Sixty-second Street, across from Gristede's Market. After a quick, instinctive sweep of the terrain, he jogged across the wide boulevard and entered the store.

Bill walked down the narrow aisles, filling the shiny aluminum shopping cart with cans and boxes and packets of beans, soups, kraut, bacon, hot dogs, milk, various kinds of breads and rolls, peanuts, chips, spreads, packaged cakes, ice cream, a veritable storehouse of provisions.

At the greens counter he selected three heads of iceberg lettuce and six bright-red hothouse tomatoes which he was shocked to find selling for a dollar five a pound.

Rounding the aisle of the meat counter, Bill thought he saw the fleeting image of a man disappearing around the far end in a big hurry. His suspicions roused, he trundled the cart at a fast gallop up the aisle and, panting heavily, turned the corner, fully expecting to see Sideburns fleeing down the aisle toward the exit. But all he saw were two elderly ladies eyeing him covertly in alarm. Bill grinned at them sheepishly and quickly steered his cart to the meat counter, where he ordered three strip steaks, a six-pound sirloin roast, and a dozen wafer-thin pork chops.

At the cashier's table, Bill wrote out a check for eighty-one dollars and fifty-six cents while the boxboy compactly packaged his order in three large paper bags. He had intended to walk home the five blocks, but the bags were too numerous and bulky to permit it. He suggested his borrowing the cart and returning it later and was politely refused. He would have to find a cab somehow.

Leaving the groceries behind in the store, which they graciously allowed him to do, Bill hurried to the Mayflower Hotel, a short distance up the street. He waited ten minutes before a cab arrived and discharged a passenger.

By the time Bill stepped into the elevator of the regal old building, along with Mario, the doorman, who carried two of the heavier bags of groceries, the time was four fifteen.

The weekend had begun.

4

From the moment Bill entered the apartment, the atmosphere seemed charged with a kind of hidden electricity. Each was overly aware of the other, each move, look, and gesture intensified and heightened beyond its worth. Janice's laughter was too full, overstated; Bill's humor, his display of ardor, too overdrawn. Each sensed the false note in the other but was unwilling to diffuse it. Each was determined that nothing was going to spoil their weekend.

Bill dashed upstairs to say hello to Ivy while Janice unpacked the food.

Ivy had spent the afternoon composing a poem for Bill. They sat together on the bed while Ivy recited it, wringing every drop of pathos from each cherished word:

> My dad is big, my dad is strong,
> He never does a thing that's wrong.
> His voice is firm, his laughter gay,
> I think of him throughout the day.
> Oh, how lucky 'tis to be
> A part of such a man as he.

Bill's eyes were moist as he leaned over and kissed Ivy's proud and smiling face.

"That's terrific, Princess." Bill's voice was husky with emotion. "I'll try to live up to it."

As Bill changed into his red velvet smoking jacket—last year's Christmas present from Janice—it occurred to him that he should have brought something home for Ivy: a small present or flowers. He was angry at himself for being so thoughtless. He'd make up for it tomorrow. Somehow.

Bill descended the last step into the living room and headed for the liquor cart, where he knew the ice would be waiting, when Janice suddenly appeared at the dining-room doorway, wearing a small, wondrous smile.

"Hey, come here." Her voice was soft, sensuous.

Bill went to her, and they kissed warmly. Then Bill felt the tears on her face.

"What gives, honey?" he asked her gently.

"I dig you, that's what gives," Janice replied, her face radiant with love.

Until this moment, Bill hadn't noticed the box in Janice's hand. It was a gift box, beautifully wrapped and ribboned, with a small card peeking out of the flap.

"Where did that come from?" Bill asked, puzzled.

Janice's free arm still clung to his shoulder. Her smile deepened as her eyes probed the tender, patient, mysterious face of the man she loved.

"Where you put it, darling." Janice smiled, continuing the game. "On top of the pork chops."

Bill was about to protest when Janice interrupted.

"Please sign the card, Bill. She'll be so happy."

The card was delicately designed, featuring an array of tiny flowers surrounding the etched legend: "Hope you're feeling better."

"What's in it?" Janice asked, fingering the box.

"What?"

"What did you buy her?"

"It's a surprise," Bill said.

Ivy and Janice's eagerness to undo the ribbon and find out what the box contained was matched by Bill's; however, with Bill, eagerness was tempered by doubt, worry and deep-seated fear. Someone had put the present in one of the food bags when he'd left the market to find a cab. Of that he was certain. *Who* that someone was also presented no great challenge to his deductive powers. It had to be Sideburns. But why?

"Oh, Daddy!" Ivy cried, producing a beautiful hand-painted purse from a nest of tissue. "Oh, Daddy, I love you, love you!"

She flung her arms around Bill's neck and squeezed him until he shouted with laughter, "Okay, okay, help, please, somebody!"

"But really, Daddy, it's perfect."

Ivy kissed Bill once again, then turned to study her gift.

Similar in style to the Fragonards inset in their living room ceiling, the illustration on the pale-blue satin purse featured a lovely French courtesan sitting on a flower-garlanded swing being pushed by a dashing swain. It was lush, excessive, and utterly romantic. Ivy hugged it to her breast.

"How did you know I always wanted it, Daddy?"

"I guessed," Bill said, the smile slowly fading from his face.

Now it was the demon's head—blunt snout, sunken eyes, stubby horns, lascivious serpent's tongue, a disgusting baroque horror leering down at Bill from the complex plasterwork of the ceiling plaque in the center of their bedroom. Small, circular, ancient, the plaque had once served as center base for a light fixture. A small chandelier, perhaps. Probably gas, from the age of the building, Bill thought, lying in bed, watching the constantly changing patterns appear, then recede, then alter into new forms all at the whim of his imagination. Forcing his eyes to shift focus slightly, Bill made the demon dissolve into shapeless fragments and, with a bit of concentration, brought back the soft, flowing, graceful lines of the woman running. She, too, was an old friend like the demon, and the man playing cards, and the ship's prow slicing through a sea in turmoil. All old friends, companions of the nights when Bill couldn't sleep.

It was after three, according to the luminous dial on the clock-radio. Janice's soft, rhythmic breathing beside him and the gentle whir of something electrical downstairs were the only sounds to be heard at this early hour.

At least *she* can sleep, Bill thought, feeling the warmth of her leg against his. The sleep of innocence. Of trust and faith and belief in the perfect order and certainty of their lives. He had not told Janice about Sideburns because he didn't want to shatter that belief. As long as Bill thought himself the target, the focal point of Sideburns' interest, why on earth drag Janice into it, especially since he hadn't the foggiest idea what the whole thing was about?

But now—with the coming of the gift—Bill knew that all his wishful thinking, his carefully organized conjectures and rationalizations would have to be drastically revised since it was obvious now that he was not Sideburns' exclusive target. The gift had thrust its way beyond Bill's life into the very center of his family's lives. Into the very heart of his home.

Sideburns knew a great deal about them. Knew of Ivy's illness. Knew just the thing that would please her. Knew more than Bill did, in fact.

"What the hell's going on here anyway?" he uttered aloud.

Janice stirred in her sleep, then turned over and snuggled into his side. Bill shut his eyes. Remained perfectly still.

What was it? Ivy had asked. "How did you know I always wanted it, Daddy?" The question now on Bill's mind was: "How did *he* know?"

Bill drifted into sleep gradually, fearfully, pausing on the edge of a deep jungle, reluctantly being drawn into its cloying fastness, its myriad color grades, its menacing refuge for fang and claw. Great coco palms reared toward the sky, blotting out the sun, surrounded by cascading liana vines, choking the trees and pathways. It was a sinister cathedral with the mold of a hundred years scattered along the ground, musky with decay. Bill looked around, not sure where he was or what direction he should take to get out. He finally selected an opening between two great trees and stepped through it carefully. One pace, two paces, three. . . . Suddenly, the bottom dropped out from beneath his world, and he began to fall. And fall. And fall. . . .

"Finish your breakfast before it gets cold."

Ivy smiled at Bill and nodded, glad to please him in every way she could this morning.

They were sitting opposite each other, across the narrow, shiny, polyurethaned dining table. The last to fall asleep, Bill had been the first to awaken and now sat bleary-eyed in robe, sipping coffee, smoking cigarettes, and observing his daughter slurping spoonfuls of some grayish substance he thought to be oatmeal, but couldn't be sure.

Ivy had awakened brimming with health and bursting with energy. What plans had they for the weekend, was her first exuberant query. Bill was thankful that Janice fielded that one, explaining to Ivy that she'd have to stay in for the weekend because of her recent illness.

"But I feel fine now, Mom!" Ivy protested.

"I know," Janice instructed. "But you don't press your luck after an illness. The rule is to stay indoors at least two days after a temperature returns to normal."

"Great." Ivy pouted. "I'll be just in time for school."

Bill watched Ivy tip the plate of cereal to gain the last mouthful. The satin hand-painted purse rested alongside her plate, where she could glance at it and lovingly contemplate its beauty between each spoonful. She obviously couldn't let it out of her sight.

"Is it really what you always wanted?" Bill asked, launching on a little fishing expedition.

"Oh, yes," Ivy said with a sincere smile.

"Or are you just saying that to please me?"

"Oh, no, Daddy. I've always wanted it, really."

Bill paused, mentally phrasing his next question with care.

"To want it so badly, you must have seen it someplace."

Ivy looked at Bill quizzically but made no reply.

"Did you see it in a store someplace?"

"No," Ivy said. "I never saw it in a store." Clearly, she was puzzled by this line of questioning and was seeking a clue to what answers Bill expected of her.

"Well, if you never saw it before, how did you know it was really what you wanted?" Bill demanded, his voice rising.

"I don't know, Daddy. I just knew."

"But to want something very badly has to mean that you know what it is you want? Which means that you have to have seen it someplace." Bill's voice had become strident.

Confused, Ivy observed him nervously.

"Well?" Bill shouted.

"Leave her alone, Bill." Janice said quietly.

Bill looked up and saw Janice standing at the kitchen doorway. He didn't know how long she had been standing there but long enough, obviously, to have taken in the gist of the interrogation.

"I didn't see it anyplace, Daddy!" Ivy cried, tears spilling from her eyes. "I guess I just wanted it because . . . because—" she picked up the purse and fingered the painting with a delicate caress—"because it's just like a part of our lives. It's like we are, in this apartment . . . like the paintings in the ceiling. . . . It's perfect, and I love it . . . and when I first saw it yesterday, I knew right away that I loved it . . . you know? Like you see something and it's so perfect that you know you've always wanted it, even though you've never seen it before. . . ." Having noted the long, silent exchange between her mother and father, Ivy realized that somehow she was the cause of what was happening and that even if she didn't understand it, there were fences to mend and she was expected to do it. "I loved it without knowing about it. Like you knew I would when you bought it for me." She opened the purse and took out a dainty handkerchief. As she wiped the tears from her cheeks, she looked across at Bill with eyes that begged understanding and offered love. "I'm sorry, Daddy, if I've made you angry."

Bill knocked the sugar bowl over in his eagerness to reach across the table to clasp her hand in his and assure his overwrought daughter that he was not angry at all, that he simply had a superanalytical mind that liked to dig and delve into the whys and wherefores of things.

His apologies humbly proffered, plus kisses, hugs, and a hundred tiny endearments, Bill excused himself and went upstairs to shower, shave, and dress, leaving a happy, fully restored Ivy to tussle over the morning's program in *TV Guide* and a frightened, totally confused Janice to clean up the spilled sugar and clear the breakfast dishes.

Janice sat in her rocker, immobile. She had the fixed, intensely vacuous look of a person caught in a witch's spell. Her eyes, unblinking, seemingly focused on a pinpoint of dust halfway across the room, were in reality turned inward, into the churning depths of her own stunned brain.
Bill had not bought the gift.
This single stunning thought was the sole subject of her entire concentration.

The sounds from above of smothered laughter and subdued girl talk between Ivy and Bettina Carew could not penetrate the tough shield of privacy she had built around herself. Not even Bill's softly querulous admonition to the children to "keep it down a bit" so that he could grab a couple of hours before dinner, managed to pierce the vacuum of her seclusion.
Bill had not bought the gift.
Janice could have known immediately if she had allowed herself. The air had been humming with signs and hints—a thousand little giveaways. Bill's odd, puzzled look when she showed him the gift. His eagerness to see what it contained as Ivy undid the wrappings. His strange, sullen behavior at dinner, hardly touching his steak. And pretending to be asleep when she crawled into bed beside him. He was in no mood for her, obviously. His mind was fully taken by other matters. Which kept him awake until almost dawn. And then the weird inquisition at breakfast, those paranoid questions, cruelly scaring the wits out of Ivy.

What she had considered abnormal behavior, totally alien to Bill's nature, was in actuality completely normal when put in its proper context. He was simply reflecting the concerns of a sane and reasonable parent, seeking the source of an unsigned gift his daughter had received, worried about who the sender was and how it had got into his food parcel.

Janice hated herself for not having told Bill about the man. She could have spared him all this anguish. For as certain as she was that Bill hadn't bought Ivy's gift, she knew who had.

She must tell Bill about the man.

Now. As soon as he awakened. Before the Federicos arrived.

Russ Federico did the honors at the liquor cart, measuring out exact amounts of gin and vermouth in a twelve-to-one ratio, while Bill still slept upstairs.

Janice, camouflaging her mood in a gay and festive ruffly-sleeved peasant blouse and evening skirt with flower appliqué, was in the kitchen. She finished basting the huge sirloin roast, then carefully peeled back the foil from chicken segments of Ivy's TV dinner to allow it to crisp. Ivy preferred dining in her room whenever the Federicos came, and Janice didn't mind. Opera talk bored Ivy almost as much as the music did.

Bill awoke to a crisp, ice-cold dry martini, lovingly placed in his hand by Janice.

"A Federico special," Janice said, kissing the tip of his nose.

Bill yawned deeply and took a sip of the drink.

"I'll be right down."

"Don't bother getting dressed," Janice advised as she left the room. "He's wearing a jump suit."

She would tell Bill about the man after the Federicos went home.

The dinner followed its usual familiar pattern. Like one of Russ' records, the conversation held no surprises as they tracked across the same wearisome grounds of opera, bridge, the charm of the old Met, and its graceless replacement.

After dinner, they decided to forgo bridge for Rossini's *Il Barbiere di Siviglia*, a recent RCA recording featuring Robert Merrill as Figaro, in excellent voice. Janice sensed it would be an early evening and was happy about it. Russ and Carole left soon after ten.

Usually, Bill helped Janice collect the dishes while she arranged them in the dishwasher, but tonight he excused himself. It would have been a good time for them to have talked. By the time Janice loaded the dishes, looked in on Ivy, and entered their bedroom Bill was already asleep. Or pretended to be.

Janice sat on the edge of the bed beside him and softly touched his face.

"Bill," she whispered, "I've got to talk to you. It's important."

His eyes remained closed.

"Dear," she said, a bit louder.

The rhythm of his breathing remained even, uninterrupted.

He really was asleep.

Janice's face was flushed and perspiring.

Eyes open, lips parted.

The dark silhouette of Bill's head and shoulders moved rhythmically above her. Playing peekaboo with the painting on the ceiling. Lush, heady, fulsome nudes cavorting merrily in the sparkling woodland stream. Ripe breasts. Rosy nipples. Wet, sensuous lips forming an O of ecstasy. Appearing and disappearing in staccato motion. Gaining in rapidity as the crisis nears.

Janice felt herself coming. Quickly veered her thoughts to neutral matters. Bridge. *Rigoletto*. It was too soon. Too soon. They mustn't let it end. Bill moaned softly and decreased his stroke. He was holding back, too. Good, Bill. Think, Bill, think! Consider. The essence here is not mere sexual gratification. It has a dimension over and above this. It is catharsis. An act of desperate necessity. The antidote to fear. Yes, fear. Think fear, Janice. Think the man. The man. . . .

She hadn't told Bill. There hadn't been the chance. He had come down late. Ivy plagued him with her math. All the morning. There had been no chance.

A pause. A shift of position. The pillow scratches the buttocks. Needlepoint pillow. Tiger-head pillow. Her artwork. Twenty-six dollars the entire set, including silk-screen canvas, varicolored yarns, and directions. It scratches during lovemaking. A statement of pure fact. There had been no time to improve matters. Bill had taken her on the floor at once, beneath the painting, the moment that Ivy left to play with Bettina. It was essential they sate their hungers at once. Both knew it. As birds know. There was no time. No time. Bill in robe, she in smock. No loveplay. No touching. In at once! An emergency operation. By royal decree. A command performance. The will of God!

He was coming. Damn, Damn! His moans were escalating with each deep, penetrating thrust. Yes, he was coming. It would soon be over. The end of sanity. The end.

The telephone rang.

Reprieved! They would stop. He would answer it. But no. Too late. He was past the point of no return. Panting, whistling, urging, pounding. . . . Too late for Bill. Too late for Janice. Too late.

The telephone rang.

Her fingers clutched his skin. Her tongue sought his. Their breaths exploded into each other's mouths.

The telephone rang.

Shrill, piercing, strident, jangling, jarring, merging, and mingling with their own percussive love sounds, tagging along with them on their swift, sweet leap into heavenly space, keeping them company each pulsating moment of their feather-soft fall back to earth. A *cavatina decrescenda* with bells. . . .

The telephone stopped ringing.

The sounds of their breathing dominated the room again. They clung to each other, on the floor, unwilling to concede an inch to the enemy. Bill played with her body. She followed in kind. Each strove to restimulate the other. Afterplay. Recommended by Allen & Martin. But somehow the nerve endings wouldn't cooperate. They kissed without passion and separated. Bill put on his robe. Janice went upstairs to shower.

He was standing in the far corner of the room, next to the ample autumnal spray. The telephone was at his ear, but he wasn't speaking. A slant of sunlight heightened the stricken expression on his face.

"What is it?" Janice murmured in a small, quavering voice as she took the last step down into the living room and came to a dead stop.

"There's no answer at Bettina's." Bill spoke the sentence almost dully —a stark statement of simple fact.

"What?" Janice could not quite take in the meaning of what he had said.

"I thought it might have been Ivy calling before. But there's no answer."

"That's impossible. They've got to be there." Janice felt her scalp tightening—the prelude to panic.

"Twelve rings, no answer."

"Dial again."

"I did. Get your coat."

Bill hung up the phone and propelled himself into action, while Janice remained rooted, dazedly watching Bill in rumpled Levi's and a black turtleneck pullover thread his tennis sneakers onto his feet. She was unable to move or think.

Bill glanced at her and crisply commanded, "Move, Janice!"

The words seemed to work. Somehow Janice found herself going through sensible motions in spite of her pounding heart and the floating watery sensation in her limbs. She was even surprised to find her purse in her hand as they charged down the dimly lit hallway to the elevators.

A sad, retiring widow, Mrs. Carew had resisted all offers of friendship, preferring a life of quiet isolation for herself and her daughter. Standing in the hallway, enveloped by the sound of a slowly ascending elevator, Janice recalled the image of Mrs. Carew's sweet, gentle face. Now there was a distinct malevolence behind the patient, kindly smile.

"Did you take Ivy down, Dominick?" asked Bill while the door was still in motion.

"Yes, sir," Dominick replied in his halting English. "Half hour ago. She went out with Mrs. Carew and her daughter."

Bill gripped Janice's arm and ushered her into the car.

A bright, warm sun had drawn the autumn chill from the air, bestowing a clear, springlike day on the city. Leaving the building, Bill and Janice hurried toward Central Park West, having agreed on a specific course of action while descending in the elevator. They reasoned that Mrs. Carew would have taken the children to either the park or perhaps the supermarket on Amsterdam Avenue, the only market in the neighborhood open on Sunday. Since the day was so perfect and the park the closest, they decided to look there first.

Waiting for the light to change, Bill began to feel a vague, fluttering vibration emanating from Janice's arm which he was lightly holding. She was trembling. Guardedly, he glanced at her face in a casual manner. Her eyes were pinpricks of intensity; a light film of sweat accented the pallor of her skin. She was truly terrified. Why? he wondered.

Crossing into the park, they all but ran up the narrow dirt path that led to the children's playground. The awkward surrealist play forms which had, in a spurt of unthinking generosity from the Estée Lauder company, replaced the swings, seesaws and jungle gyms, were literally dripping with children of all ages and races, gamely attempting to wrest a modicum of fun out of the odd, demented shapes.

Janice and Bill separated at the gate, striking off in different directions in order to increase efficiency. Janice covered the eastern perimeter of the playground while Bill took on the western side. They would eventually join forces somewhere on the northern end unless one lucked in on the objective, at which point he or she would communicate to the other by shouting.

Janice moved through a maze of children-ridden monoliths, her eyes darting swiftly about, focusing, refocusing on, past, around galaxies of screaming, laughing, upright, sideways, upside-down faces, seeking, searching, probing the nightmare world for a telltale sign, an essential clue: vanilla boots, faded jeans, golden hair. . . . Walking, stumbling, sidling, Janice felt herself drowning as she pushed through wee mad clusters along the western shore of Jabberwocky, hysteria rising, building, surging until screaming became the only possible antidote. . . .

"Janice!"
"What?"

"Janice! Here!"

It was Bill's voice, beautiful, powerful, strong, cutting through the mad, cacophonous wall, signaling success, coming to the rescue in the nick o' time, standing tall, waving to her from the other side of no-man's-land, and beside him, the smiling head of Mrs. Carew, floating, disembodied like a Dumbo balloon.

Janice collided with a gaggle of running children halfway across the playground and almost fell. Bill bravely ventured forth and collected her.

"Ivy and Bettina went for a walk up the bridle path," Bill whispered urgently to Janice while maintaining a façade of calm for Mrs. Carew's benefit. "I'll go find her."

Janice found herself shaking uncontrollably as Bill walked quickly away from her, leaving her standing beside Mrs. Carew, who smiled amiably up at her.

"You shouldn't have taken her out," Janice admonished in a taut, quavering voice.

"I *am* sorry, dear," replied Mrs. Carew. "I had no idea you'd be worried."

"You shouldn't have done it," Janice importuned. "She's been ill—"

"Yes, Mr. Templeton told me." Mrs. Carew smiled. "I had no idea. But it's such a warm, pleasant day. And we did call you. Apparently, you were out."

"Yes," Janice said.

They spoke no more.

In less than five minutes, Janice saw Bill's head bobbing distantly through a tangle of autumn growths, looming toward them. In the next moment, the bright, heart-clutching flash of Ivy's yellow hair beside him assured her that all was right.

Ivy was safe.

The rest of Sunday was given to Monopoly.

Bettina came back to the apartment, and they played until suppertime, all four of them, seated across from one another at the dining-room table.

Bill played a ruthless, impassioned game and won nearly everything worthwhile—Marvin Gardens, Boardwalk, a green monopoly consisting of Pennsylvania, North Carolina and Pacific avenues—collecting outlandish rentals on three houses and two hotels and winding up with something over twenty-seven thousand dollars.

They dined on pork chops with a tomato salad after Bettina left, watched television until nine thirty, saw Ivy to bed, and retired for the night to their own bedroom.

At ten twenty-six, Bill turned off the light. Lying on their backs, awake, under the green electric blanket, gazing up into the shadowy labyrinths of the plasterwork ceiling, their bodies separated by the width of their clinging hands, Bill and Janice finally talked.

Janice spoke first.

"Bill," she whispered, "there's a man out there."

"I know," Bill said, accepting the fact of her knowledge with no surprise and no emotion. "With sideburns and a mustache."

Janice's hand tightened in Bill's.

"How long have you known about him?"

"Tomorrow will be five weeks."

"He comes to the school each day."

"Yes. In the mornings, too."

"What does he want?"

"I don't know."

"He's going to harm us."

"Probably."

"It's Ivy he's after, Bill."

"Why do you say that?"

"The way he looks at her. And he called the other morning."

"Your Mr. Soames call, huh?"

"Yes. I lied. I'm sorry."

"That's all right."

Janice felt his hand relax slightly in hers.

"What does he want, Bill?"

"I don't know."

"We must call the police."

"I went to them. They can't help—until he makes some kind of move."

Silence, then softly: "Oh, God. What does he want?"

Bill sighed. "We'll know soon enough."

Like Hansel and Gretel, they held hands throughout the moonless, haunted night, sleeping in fits and starts, awakening and pushing onward, falsely guided by the pebbles which glittered like newly coined money, wandering, lost, deeper and deeper into the wood toward the terrors of an uncertain daybreak.

5

Monday.
October 21.
Temperature: 37 degrees.
Humidity: 98 percent.
Barometric pressure: 29.92 and falling.

A storm system that provided snow for the upper Mississippi Valley and western Great Lakes had moved during the night into New England and parts of New York, including Manhattan. A light film of refreshing white blanketed the dun-gray streets and buildings visible from the Templeton apartment. The weather would turn colder by afternoon. More snow was forecast.

The first assault came with the morning mail, delivered by Mario, the doorman, at nine twenty, thirty minutes after Bill had left the apartment with a warmly bundled, book-burdened Ivy in tow.

The letter was included among a pack of bills, advertising circulars, an invitation form to a Four-A's dinner-dance, and two magazines. The envelope was the standard white prestamped kind sold in the post office. It was addressed to Mr. and Mrs. William Pierce Templeton in a firm, bold hand, with no sender's name or return address. The "Pierce" was the giveaway. Whoever sent the letter had an intimate knowledge of Bill's private life, for Bill never used the middle name—his mother's maiden name—in any of his correspondence except his most personal legal documents.

Janice hefted the envelope in her hand, feeling its thinness with her fingers, to ascertain its contents. It felt so light that for a moment Janice thought it might be empty, but holding it up to the window for light, she saw a small grayish square contrasting with the white of the envelope. Denied sufficient liquid, the poorly sealed flap opened at her touch without scarring or tearing the paper.

Janice glanced sideways into the envelope—as a child watches a horror movie, through finger cracks—and saw a neatly clipped piece of paper covered with minute printing. She considered using tweezers to extract the paper from the envelope to preserve the fingerprints for later use as evidence, but settled finally on her long fingernails, which clutched the tissue-thin sheet by its edge. She read its contents with a self-control that amazed her before going to the telephone to call Bill.

"What's the matter?" Bill panted lightly, having been pulled from a meeting to answer the "emergency" call.

"He sent us his calling card," Janice replied dully.

"What? Say again," Bill stammered, trying to catch his breath.

"His name is Elliot Suggins Hoover."

"Yeah? How do you know?" Then, sudden concern: "Was he there? Are you all right, Janice?"

"A letter arrived!" Janice blurted, abandoning control. "With a printed slip of paper in it from *Who's Who* or the *Social Register* or something, telling about his life and background. . . ."

"Anything else come with it, a note, or—"

"No, just that!"

There was a long pause on the other end while Bill considered the situation.

"Listen to me, Janice." Bill came back briskly, resolutely. "Get the boys downstairs to find you a cab. Come down to the office and wait for me. This meeting should be over by twelve thirty. I'll have my secretary reserve a table at Rattazzi's. We'll have lunch and talk. Okay?"

He was doing what he did best—he was handling matters, Janice thought bitterly.

"If you want, I'll meet you for lunch, but I *can't* come down to the office."

"Fine," agreed Bill. "Twelve thirty, Rattazzi's, okay?"

"Okay," she said, then quickly added: "Bill?"

"Yes?"

"Was he waiting at the school this morning?"

"No. At least I didn't see him."

"Bill?"

"Yes, dear?" Bill was carefully maintaining the calm, conciliatory tone in his voice.

"I'm scared."

Janice checked the chain bolt on the door before going upstairs to shower and wash her hair.

It was ten fifteen, and she was fixing the damp conditioned locks around the heated rollers when the telephone rang. She let it ring. It rang fourteen times before stopping.

At eleven forty she stood before the door mirror in their bedroom surveying the finished product and was gratified by what she saw. Although the handsome blue and burgundy plaid pants suit was last year's purchase, it not only fitted her well, but did superb things for her figure. Her soft brown hair and lightly cosmeticized skin completed the portrait of a bold and, she had to admit, quite beautiful woman.

The sidewalk in front of Des Artistes had been swept clean of snow and was practically dry as Mario ushered Janice to the waiting cab and told the driver the address of Rattazzi's Restaurant.

At twelve twenty Janice paid the cabdriver and entered the narrow, dimly lit restaurant.

At twelve forty she ordered her second drink, still studiously avoiding the pernicious sesame sticks and butter plate that was set before her. By the time Bill arrived at one ten Janice was working on her fourth J & B with water and was feeling lightheaded and giddy. She saw Bill zoom toward her in a haze of apologies and heard him order their lunch immediately, since Janice needed to get to school by three in order to meet Ivy.

Only after Bill took a healthy sip of his frosty martini did he ask to see the letter.

Janice fumbled around in her purse, finally found it, and passed it across to him with a shaking hand. Obviously, Bill didn't have her concern about fingerprints, for he extracted the small printed sheet with a total disregard for the possible evidence it might contain.

Bill's eyes narrowed to slits as he strained to read the tiny print on the tissue-thin paper. His lips slowly mouthed the words but were submerged by the wall of chatter surrounding them:

> Hoover, Elliot Suggins (hoo'ver), corp. exec.; b. Pitts., Jan. 26, 1928; s. John Roberts and Ella Marie (Villatte); student Case Institute Technology, 1945-49, Dr. Engring (honorary), 1955; married Sylvia Flora, May 5, 1957; children, Audrey Rose. Asst. to v.p. in charge raw materials Susquehana Steel Corp., Jan.-Sept. 1959; v.p. in charge raw materials Great Lakes Steel Co. of Penna. 1960-62. Writer, lecturer on personnel administrn. and human relations. Trustee, mem. exec. com. Pitts. Community Chest. Health Fund Greater Pitts. Silver Beaver, Silver Antelope, Silver Buffalo Awards Boy Scouts Am. Member N.A.M. Clubs: HooHoo, Rotary, Harrison Country and Golf. Mem. Am. Iron and Steel Inst. Zeta Psi. Mason (33, Shriner, Jester) Home: 1035 Wellington Dr., Pitts. 29. Office: 1 William Penn Pl., Pitts. 30.

Janice was astonished to see Bill's smile grow as he slowly read through the short biography. She had found nothing funny in any of it.

"Well"—Bill chuckled—"you gotta admit he's an all-American boy."

"Why did he send that to us?" Janice asked measuredly, trying not to slur her words. "What does it mean?"

"Damned if I know." Bill shrugged. "He's dealing, Janice."

"Take it to the police. Show it to them."

"Is it enough? I mean, after all, what does it tell us? A couple of facts about his life, his work, his affiliations. . . . It says nothing about his motives, his intentions." Bill picked up the thin slip of paper and studied it intently. "It may not even be him. Maybe he just clipped any old bio out of *Who's Who* to test us. See what our reaction would be."

"Then you propose to do nothing?" Janice was conscious of a shrill note in her voice.

"What can we do?" Bill argued. "Right now the moves are all his. Until he does something that's overt or threatening, we have nothing to go to the police with. They wouldn't even consider this an act of mischief," Bill concluded, placing the slip of paper back into the envelope and pocketing it.

"I only hope," Janice stated in a soft, quavering voice, "that when he does decide to make his move, you don't live to regret it."

Her words scored. The firm, confident cut of Bill's rugged features slowly collapsed, fragmenting into small, vulnerable shapes of helplessness and despair. His eyes beheld her through a veil of hurt. Janice despised herself for having spoken.

Their meal arrived, and they ate in silence through the entrée, a veal marsala accompanied by a Bibb lettuce and rugala salad. Both finished all the food on their plates and even sponged up the delicious sauce with pieces of crusty bread, their anxieties failing to disturb their appetites.

"I'm sorry, Bill," Janice said after the waiter had cleared the table. "You're probably right. At this point, the police wouldn't know what to make of all this, no more than we do."

Bill reached across the table and took her hand in his. Their eyes embraced with compassion and understanding, reaffirming mutual trust and togetherness.

"Let me think on it," Bill said. "There may be a way to force the issue."

It was two thirty-one when Bill finally found a cab and deposited Janice into it. Even in the slush and misery of the traffic-clogged hour, there was still plenty of time to make the eight blocks to the Ethical Culture School before the three o'clock bell sounded.

Bill's storm boots sucked noisily into wet, grimy deposits, as he trudged the several blocks back to his office, his mind fully concentrated on devising formulas and elaborating plans of action to force Sideburns' hand.

Janice was right, he decided. Who could predict what his first real move might be? If he turned out to be a lunatic, and if Janice or *Ivy* were to fall into his clutches—Bill quickly maneuvered his thoughts away from such a horrible prospect and shifted back to ways and means of provoking a confrontation. By the time he reached his office building Bill was resolved that the very next encounter with Hoover would be the moment of truth for them both. He was finished pussyfooting around. Game time was over.

Ted Nathan was standing in the elevator when Bill entered. As the car whizzed up to the thirty-eighth floor, Bill turned to him and asked, "Do we keep editions of *Who's Who*, Ted?"

"Certainly," Ted replied. "We got 'em going back to sixty-nine."

Bill accompanied Ted back to his office and went through all three editions of the big red books. He found no Hoover, Elliot Suggins in any of them. This puzzled Bill. He had been certain that the clipping was pulled from a *Who's Who*. He compared the typeface and printing format of the clipping with those in the book and found them identical. Jotting down the publisher's name and address—The A. N. Marquis Company, 210 East Ohio Street, Chicago, Illinois 60611—Bill returned to his own office and asked Darlene, his secretary, to put in a call to them.

"Yes." Mrs. Ammons' voice returned on the other end of the line after a hold of nearly ten minutes. "Hoover, Elliot Suggins is listed in our 1960-61, 1962-63, and 1964-65 editions. He was dropped after the 1966-67 edition."

"Can you tell me why, Mrs. Ammons?"

"Well, I suppose because he was deceased."

Bill thought about this a moment, then asked, "How do you generally learn about a person's death, Mrs. Ammons?"

"We either read about it or we're informed by the family."

"I see."

"Sometimes we know when our mailings to biographees are returned to us unopened and with no forwarding address indicated."

"Thank you, Mrs. Ammons. You've been very helpful."

Bill slowly cradled the phone and began to probe the hypnotic patterns of the Motherwell across his desk.

Accepting the premise that Elliot Suggins Hoover was alive and that he and Sideburns were one and the same person, why then had he chosen to return the correspondence from *Who's Who* unopened and with no forwarding address?

Bill made two more long-distance calls.

One to the main office of the National Chapter of the Shriners, in Cleveland; the other to the Iron & Steel Institute, in Pittsburgh. Both corroborated the information he had got from Mrs. Ammons. The Shriners still had him listed in their inactive roster, although they presumed him dead since they had not heard from him in seven years. The Iron & Steel Institute had revoked his membership in 1968 after a one-year lapse in his dues payments.

Well, Bill thought, at least one thing was becoming clear.

Sometime around 1967, something happened to cause Elliot Suggins Hoover to wish to disappear from the face of the earth.

The noise was appalling. A bedlam of car horns and obscenities battered through Janice's wavering consciousness, pulling, tugging, wrenching her back to wakefulness. Against her will. She would have preferred the silent, restful nothingness to the tough, blasting cadences pressing in on her from all directions.

She was sitting on the curb in a puddle of wet slush, where the policeman had placed her after the accident, leaning against a litter bin with the legend "Use Me Please" hovering slightly above and to the right of her line of vision. A bevy of faces drifted in and out of focus around her, sympathetic, solicitous, rapt with interest and excitement. Beyond them, the indistinct figures of two men hurling foulnesses at each other strained to penetrate the barrier of blue-coated policemen separating them.

A voice suddenly descended to her ear, gently advising, "The ambulance'll be here soon, ma'am." Why these words filled her with dread, she couldn't define. She would have to think about it, in a methodical, orderly way, organizing each piece of information as Bill would, step by step.

She began with: The ambulance must not come. Which led to: Why must it not come? Because. . . .

And here she faltered.

Backtrack!
She had been . . . *where?*
With whom?
Bypass it!
She had been in an accident. Of that she was sure.

She had been sitting in a cab, going . . . somewhere. . . . A wire screen separating the driver from the passenger had impeded her vision somewhat. Even so, she could see what was going to happen fully a minute before it did. The corridor between the traffic on the left and the Number 5 bus on the right was much too narrow to slip through. Certainly, the cabdriver must have realized it. If he attempted it, the cab would be sandwiched between them and crushed. It was inevitable. Janice reenacted the scene in her mind, reprising the same shock of terror she had previously felt as the cab lunged madly forward at full speed, plowing ahead in total disregard of the consequences. She recalled the metal scraping against metal sounds as the cab skidded bouncingly off traffic from left to right, the crunching collision against immovable forces, and the sudden, jarring halt that sent her hurtling forward into the wire screen . . . into blackness.

There was a fraction of a second, just before she fell into the soft cushion of darkness, when Janice experienced a fear, no, it was more a terror, so overwhelming that she thought her heart would stop beating.

Sitting on the curb, sorting about the hazy corridors of her memory, Janice had the distinct feeling that the terror she had felt in the minuscule moment of time related to something quite apart from the accident. Some other issue, not the accident, was involved. Some issue or duty that the accident was preventing her from completing. Duty. Yes, it *was* a duty.

"Keep it movin'," a policeman was saying. "Give her some air."

A gauzy parade of faces milled sluggishly past her in double images, a grotesque montage of mixed genders; painted eyes; scarlet lips, pursed, smiling; the head of a man, bristling with red facial hair; a child, a girl, gawking wide-eyed down at her— The girl! Janice's eyes widened in alarm. The girl!

"Oh, my God!" Janice stammered aloud and struggled to her feet, clinging to the litter bin for support. Ivy! She'd be out of school! She'd be waiting! Alone! With the man! What was his name? Oh, God!

"Take it easy, ma'am," the policeman was saying to her. "The ambulance'll be here soon. . . ."

Janice clutched her shaking hand to still it as she strove to focus her vision on the small, numberless Lucite wristwatch, trying to decide whether the hands were pointing at the two fifteen nubs or the three fifteen.

"Please, what time is it?" Janice sobbed, grasping the policeman's jacket and spinning him around.

"Easy, ma'am," the officer urged. "It's just a little past three o'clock."

"Oh, my God! I've got to go!"

"Now, now, you just take it easy—"

"But I must go, Officer!" Janice was shouting into the young Irish face. "It's an emergency!"

"Oh? What kind of emergency?"

"It's my daughter. Ivy. She's been let out of school. She's alone, waiting for me!"

"She'll be all right, ma'am," the policeman soothed. "They'll keep her in the office till you get there."

"No!" Janice shook her head at him in a crazy, wild way. "I must go now! Please!"

Her tears and hysteria were beginning to score points with the policeman. After a moment's thoughtful consideration, he asked, "Don't you think you should have a doctor look you over, ma'am?"

"No." Janice wept. "I'm all right, really. Absolutely all right. Please, help me find a cab! Please!"

"Well— If you think you'll be all right—"

"I'll be fine. Thank you."

Janice swayed only slightly as the policeman led her through the circle of faces, clearing their path with shouts and threats. He halted a cab with his whistle and opened the rear door. A man was seated in the back.

"Please leave this cab, sir," the policeman ordered, using the proper Delahanty-approved words. "I am a police officer, and under Section One Hundred and Fifty of the Penal Code of New York, it is necessary for me to use this vehicle."

The flabbergasted occupant of the cab quickly emerged, and Janice climbed in.

"Remember the name Donovan, Twenty-eighth Precinct, in case you need me," the policeman shouted as the cab pulled away. Janice heard him, but her mind did not record the information.

A strange and invigorating feeling of buoyancy was working itself through the various levels of Janice's body as the cab skittered and swerved through the maze of slippery streets, selecting the least encumbered route to their destination. She found her dizziness a distinct comfort as it mitigated orientation and reduced awareness of the terrors that lay in wait at the end of their journey.

The time was three thirty when Janice, maintaining a frail hold on consciousness, counted out four dollar bills, which included the ejected passenger's fare as well, and shakily turned them over to the cabdriver. He had plotted his course so that Janice would be discharged directly in front of the school building, which, she noted with a sinking heart as they approached it, was totally deserted.

A few flakes of new snow were falling on the cleanly swept sidewalk as Janice left the cab. She started toward the school entrance, but the moment she did, she saw the sidewalk slide away from her and felt as if consciousness might depart at any moment. A nearby fire hydrant became her support, and she stood, stooping over it, clinging hard for several minutes, commanding her vision to cease whirling and her heart to stop pounding.

A sharp, rapping noise emanating from somewhere within the precincts of the school building guided Janice's eyes back to the red stone façade and up to a tall window, behind which a woman, wearing horn-rimmed glasses, stood watching her with concern. Janice recognized the face but could not think of her name.

"Are you all right, Mrs. Templeton?" The woman had opened the window slightly and was shouting down at her. "Do you need help?"

"Yes, I'm afraid I do." Janice laughed helplessly.

The woman vanished instantly and in the very next moment was clambering down the icy steps, her hands extended toward Janice in a helping gesture.

"I suddenly felt faint," Janice explained, allowing the woman to take her arm and cautiously walk her across the pavement and up the concrete steps.

"I came to pick up Ivy; a bit late, I'm afraid." Janice dreaded asking the next question. "I hope she waited for me in the office?"

"No," the woman said. "There's no child in the office."

She sat Janice down on a hard oaken bench just inside the registrar's office and went to fetch aspirin and water.

The room was deserted. The copper nameplate on the desk said Mrs. Elsie Stanton. The wall clock read three forty-one. Janice saw a telephone on a nearby table and lunged at it, swaying slightly as she dialed her home number. There was no answer. She let it ring ten times, then hung up and dialed the desk number in the lobby of Des Artistes. Dominick answered.

"This is Mrs. Templeton, Dominick. Is Ivy in the lobby by any chance?" Janice made the words sound light and casual.

"Just a minute, Miz Templeton."

Janice felt the cold sweats and the feelings of dread encroaching subtly as the seconds swept by on the Western Union clock above her.

"No, Miz Templeton," Dominick said regretfully upon his return. "She ain't in the lobby or outside on the street."

"Thank you, Dominick. If you should see her, please keep an eye on her until I arrive."

"Sure thing, Miz Templeton."

Janice stood there, shakily readjusting the belt on her raincoat, which had become twisted somehow, concentrating on straightening it out, in a futile effort to forestall the consideration of topics of greater importance. But her mind would not cooperate, kept fielding the darts of anxiety battering through the frivolous defense. Ivy was not at school! Ivy was not at home! What alternative was left? None! She had been met by the man! He had taken her! It was that simple, really. Simple? Oh, my God! Janice felt a scream begin to well up from somewhere deep within the core of her despair, felt herself yielding to a blinding impulse to run screaming from the building.

"Take them with the full glass of water," Mrs. Stanton prescribed, placing the aspirin and glass in Janice's trembling hands. "They'll work faster that way."

As Janice swallowed the pills, refreshed by the cool liquid which eased her parched throat, she knew what her very next step must be.

Without asking permission, Janice picked up the receiver and dialed Bill's office number. She was put through to his secretary, who told her that Bill was at an important outside meeting and would not be returning to the office.

It was while she was listening to the secretary's full-bodied, authoritative voice that Janice remembered something that sent a sudden surge of renewed hope coursing through her. Once before, less than a year ago, Janice had been delayed and Ivy had waited for her across the street in the park. Of course, it had been a beautiful spring day then, but still, perhaps the snow had worked its own kind of spell on Ivy and she was there right now, waiting for her, just beyond the wall, building a snowman.

Mrs. Stanton's cautionary recommendations scarcely registered as Janice desperately propelled herself toward the exit doors and out into the cold afternoon. The concrete steps were covered by a layer of slippery snow, forcing Janice to descend slowly and cling to the frigid metallic railing for support. The snow was falling densely now, in large quarter-sized flakes. At the curb Janice strained hard to see across the sluggish traffic, seeking a glimpse of Ivy on the park side of Central Park West. But the thick wall of white made it impossible to see beyond the center of the street. With single-minded objectivity and total disregard for personal danger, Janice plunged ahead into the heavy traffic and crossed the wide boulevard in the center of the block. Squealing brakes and blasting car horns followed her fool's march across to the other side.

In the brief time it took to reach the edge of the low rock wall which separated the promenade from the park, the snow had turned to frozen sleet. Tiny pellets of ice were stinging at Janice's face; still, she found herself perspiring as she daintily picked her way through drifts of crusting snow which had gathered along the wall's edge. With the aid of her hands, cupped tightly around her eyes, Janice scoured the immediate area of the park, squinting hard to penetrate the opaque shield of wind-whipped ice falling madly about her. Once, when the wind shifted slightly, she thought she saw the figure of a girl gamboling amid the falling snow on a hillock a short distance away. But she couldn't be sure and decided to climb over the wall in order to gain a closer vantage point. She felt a number of things ripping as she straddled the wall and gradually lowered herself down on the other side, her hands clinging to the slippery ledge. Hanging there, her feet seeking purchase and finding none, Janice had the sinking feeling that her body was dangling over a gaping hole and would be swallowed into the earth if she ever let go. She would have remained fixed in this position had not her fingers lost their hold on the frozen concrete. Her feet met the ground a few inches below her, but the slant and slickness of the terrain upset her balance and sent her plunging sideways down a gentle embankment, rolling uncontrollably down the crusted snow to the edge of a pathway. Janice sustained the ordeal in total silence, accepting it as the next logical step in the day's insanity.

The sleet was descending in hard, twisting sheets all around her as she rose unsteadily to her feet and gently flexed the muscles of her body, briefly checking for possible injuries. She felt stupid and foolish and was thankful that the impenetrable curtain of sleet had obscured her mad antics from the prying eyes of any passersby. It was then she realized that her purse was missing, but she couldn't take the time to look for it now.

Turning toward the hillock where she thought she had seen the child romping, she cupped her hands around her mouth and shouted, "Ivy! Ivy! Can you hear me, Ivy?"

But the wind-driven sleet threw the words back into her face, forcing her to trudge on ahead through wet clumps of ice-blistered snow.

"Ivy!" she shouted, hurling the word forth at the top of her failing voice. "Ivy! It's Mother!"

"Ivy is at home," said a man's quiet, courteous voice beside her. "She waited for you until three twenty-five, then left."

The voice spoke at Janice's left side, close enough for her to see plumes of steam accompany each word. She must not look at him, Janice commanded herself, her bruised body shivering. Above all, she must not look at him or acknowledge him in any way.

"She's quite all right," the voice continued softly, factually, and with no sign of aggression. "She's waiting for you in the lobby."

Janice stood rooted, feeling the flush of terror rise within her, hearing her respiration coming faster and faster. She would not look at him, nor would she enter into conversation with him.

"Here," he said. "You dropped it when you fell."

Janice's purse entered her frame of vision, slightly below and to the left, hovering there, disembodied among crumbs of whirling ice. If she took it, she would acknowledge his presence, motivate an encounter, lay the groundwork for discussion. Yet how could she not take it? It was her purse. *He had trapped her.*

Janice accepted the purse without a word.

"We must talk," the man said. "I'm certain now, and we must talk. Tell your husband."

Janice's eyes remained steadfast on a small patch of brown earth which had somehow resisted the encroachments of snow and sleet. She tried to concentrate on the ultimate cause of this phenomenon in an effort to obliterate the sound of the man's voice, but his words persisted in coming through.

"I mean you no harm, understand. But we must talk."

Janice's eyes shifted to her purse and saw it shaking in her hand. She was trembling all over, visibly, violently, clearly betraying her fear to the man, admitting his power over her. She tried to will the trembling to stop, but it refused to obey. She must move, she thought. She must find the energy to walk away from the man before he noticed the shaking and took advantage of her weakness.

The sleet stung her eyes as she found herself in motion, taking mincing steps down the slick pathway. She walked on her toes, as Bill had taught her to do on icy pavements, for to slip and fall now would be disastrous, encouraging a further relationship with the man, who would naturally rush to her assistance.

"Tell your husband that I'll call him tonight."

The man's words were fading behind her, which meant, she was thankful, that he was not following her.

Janice thought how proud Bill would be to learn that she never once looked at the man, or said a word to him, or acknowledged his presence in any way.

"Come." Janice spoke the word with all the heat and force of a rebuke.

Ivy quietly gathered up her books and outer garments and followed Janice into the waiting elevator. Ernie, the relief elevator operator, gave Janice's soaked, mud-spattered garments a fleeting once-over as they rode up in silence. Ivy cast nervous, surreptitious glances up at her mother, knowing full well the cause of her anger and dreading the moment of confrontation which was only three floors away.

"I waited till three twenty-five, Mom," Ivy said the moment they were alone in the ninth-floor corridor, keeping her voice at a soft, ingenuous level, striving to crack the armor of her mother's hostility. "I didn't know what time you'd be there, so I walked home. A man helped me cross the streets," she added proudly, innocently.

Janice opened the door of the apartment and, grasping Ivy's arm, ushered her across the threshold with a sharp tug. After slamming the door shut, Janice spun the frightened child around to her own lowered face and shouted, "You do not leave without me! You do not go with a strange man! You sit in the office and wait! And wait! And wait! And *wait!* Do you *understand me?*" Janice was screaming and shaking the sobbing child with all the force she could muster.

"Yes, yes!" shrieked Ivy. "Mom, you're hurting me!"

Janice quickly let go of Ivy's arms and took a step back, appalled by her own cruelty, as she saw red welts begin to form on the delicate white of her beautiful daughter's skin. Oh, dear God, she thought in utter anguish. I am truly going mad.

"Go upstairs, please," she told Ivy in a small, stunned voice.

Choking, racking, tormented sobs assaulted Janice's ears as the child dashed down the narrow hallway and rounded the bend of the living room, the sobs gradually fading as they followed the route of her escape up the staircase and into her bedroom, where they lingered distantly.

"Oh, God. Oh, God," Janice mumbled again and again as she staggered into the living room and fell crying across the sofa, vaguely aware of the soggy, muddy garments staining the black silk upholstery, and not giving a damn, letting it all pour out over the expensive Schumacher fabric, all the pent-up feelings, the hidden fears, panics, hurts, horrors of the past three days— Dear God, has it only been three days?

The telephone rang.

Janice's first reaction was to let it ring. But then the knowledge that their bedroom extension was susceptible to Ivy's curiosity forced her to pull herself, sobbing across the sofa, to pick up the receiver.

"Janice?" It was Bill's voice. "Darlene says you called before. What's up?"

Bill's steady, assured voice finally broke the dam.

"Oh, God, Bill!" Janice cried, unleashing the full torrent of hysteria. "Oh, God, come home!"

"Leaving now," Bill said crisply and hung up.

Somehow Bill made all the right connections and arrived home in less than ten minutes. After quickly surveying the wreckage and spot-checking its seriousness, he immediately commenced to put his house back into order. He drew two steaming bubble baths and put both his women into them to soak. He divided himself between the two bathrooms, allowing each equal time to sob out her story to him.

From Janice, he learned the incredible details of each grisly experience that had befallen her upon leaving him outside Rattazzi's, with special emphasis on her encounter with the man, recalling every word he said to her, including intonation, inflection, and possible intent behind each sentence.

"What time did he say he'd call?" Bill asked.

"He didn't give a time; he simply said tonight."

"He told you he took Ivy home?"

"No, she told me that. He said that she was in the lobby, waiting for me, and that she was all right."

Bill hesitated, then asked, "You're sure it was the man? I mean, mustache, sideburns?"

"For God's sake, Bill," Janice shouted.

"Okay, okay," Bill placated. "I suppose it had to be him."

"Well, I didn't see him. I didn't look at him or acknowledge him in any way. I thought you'd be pleased by the way I handled it."

Bill placed a comforting hand on her soapy shoulder and grinned.

"You did great, Janice, just great." Then, soberly: "I want you to know that I've had it with him. I'm through playing games."

Bill found Ivy even more overwrought than Janice. She had never seen her mother behave like that; she was absolutely freaky, shaking her and shaking her till she almost vomited. And for what? All the girls her age walk home from school alone. "Bettina's been doing it since she was nine! What's so special about me?"

"You're our beautiful child," soothed Bill, holding her wet hand. "That's what's so special about you. We love you and want to protect you."

"Protect me against what?"

"Against lots of things that happen each day in this city, Ivy. So far we've been lucky; they've happened to other people. People who are willing to take risks, take chances with their children. We're not willing to do that."

The warm bath, Bill's tender touch and mollifying tone gradually eased Ivy's tensions and gently guided her back toward understanding and forgiveness.

"Well, it's really the first time I ever did a thing like that. And I wouldn't have if that man hadn't offered to help me cross the streets."

"Tell me about the man, Ivy," Bill asked in a disarming voice. "Did you ever see him before?"

"Sure. He waits in front of the school every afternoon." Ivy looked up at Bill suddenly. "You *must* have seen him; he's there in the mornings, too."

"Oh, yes—mustache, sideburns?"

Ivy nodded. "He was really very nice. He walked me to Sixty-seventh Street and waited till I crossed."

"Did he say anything? I mean, did you talk at all?"

"Nothing special. It was starting to snow again, and he said he liked winters better than summers. I said I like them better, too. Then he said that his daughter liked winters better, too. Things like that."

"Did he ask any questions about me or Mother?"

"No." Ivy studied Bill with a look of suspicion. "Do you know him, Dad?"

"No, dear, we don't know him."

"That's funny—"

"What is?"

"I felt as if he knew us. Or at least he knew me."

After their baths, relaxed and warm in the king-sized bed, with the electric blanket turned to "Hi," mother and daughter were left to repair their shattered relationship while Bill went down to the kitchen to fix dinner.

When he returned, carrying a huge tray filled with thinly sliced roast beef sandwiches with the crusts removed, a pot of steaming beans, two kinds of pie, and milk, he found Janice and Ivy bundled together in a warm embrace, playing Actors and Actresses.

Bill spread a tablecloth across the coverlet, and they ate their picnic dinner on the bed. By seven thirty, when the call came, love and togetherness were firmly reestablished.

Ivy snatched up the phone from the bedside table on the first ring.

"Yes?" A short pause, then: "It's for you, Dad."

Bill signaled Janice to take the receiver, then hurried out of the room to take the call on the downstairs extension. Janice kept the phone at her ear, but covered the mouthpiece with her hand. In a moment Bill's voice came on the other end.

"Hello?"

"Mr. Templeton?"

"Yes."

"My name is Elliot Hoover."

"Yes."

"I think we should talk."

"All right."

"May I come to your home?"

"No. How about my office tomorrow morning?"

"I think we should talk right away. I'd also like Mrs. Templeton to be present. How about meeting me downstairs in the restaurant bar?"

"Impossible. We can't leave our child alone."

"Carole Federico might be willing to sit with Ivy for an hour or so."

Janice could well understand the long pause that followed this remarkable statement. She could sense Bill's shock at the scope and depth of Hoover's knowledge of the most intimate corners of their lives.

"I'll see," she heard Bill stammer at last.

"Say, eight thirty?"

"I'll see."

The phone clicked twice before Janice placed hers back on its cradle.

Ivy broke into a giggle. She had picked up a Snoopy book and was browsing through it while they talked on the phone. Inwardly, Janice reacted harshly to the laughter, felt it was all wrong, inappropriate, totally out of place—like someone laughing at a funeral.

PART TWO

Elliot Hoover

6

EXCEPT for two functioning tables and a lineup of tuxedoed waiters, silently manning their posts at strategic peripheral intervals, patiently awaiting the nine thirty closing time, the Des Artistes Restaurant seemed poised on the precipice of sleep.

Bill and Janice quietly made their way through the hushed, somber atmosphere, en route to the barroom, which lay just beyond the restaurant in a small, partially enclosed niche.

Kurt, the bartender, gave Bill and Janice a smile of recognition as they stood on the threshold of the darkly paneled room, searching among several faces for a sign of Hoover. There were only five customers present.

"Mr. and Mrs. Templeton, I'm Elliot Hoover."

Janice jumped, startled; Bill swung about, too fast, betraying his surprise. Hovering before them was a face they would have sworn they'd never seen before.

The hairless pale skin, clear and unwrinkled, belonged to a man of twenty. The smile, sweet and ingenuous, disclosed two rows of small white teeth sandwiched between colorless thin lips. On closer inspection, the light-brown hair was somewhat sparse and receding, yet could this be the forty-six-year-old man they had read about in *Who's Who?*

Hoover noted their surprise, and his smile deepened, as he suggested, "There's a quiet table over there in the corner."

Bill and Janice followed him like a pair of sheep being escorted by a Judas goat to the killing room. They sat together, against the wall, at the wave of Hoover's hand, while he took the chair opposite them across the table.

"I want to thank you both for agreeing to see me tonight," Elliot Hoover began, in a low, soothing voice that seemed to dicker over the selection of each word. "I truly appreciate it."

Marie, the pretty barmaid, appeared at their table, smiling inquiringly.

"Would you care for something, Mrs. Templeton?" Hoover politely asked Janice.

"No, thank you," she replied.

"I'll have a scotch and water," Bill said.

"Do you have Chinese gunpowder tea?" inquired Hoover.

"I think they may have some in the kitchen," Marie ventured.

"That'll be fine for me, thank you," he said, dismissing Marie and turning his attention back to Bill and Janice. "I also want to apologize for the mysterioso behavior these past few weeks," he continued with a small, embarrassed chuckle. "I know how frightened you must have both been, and I'm sorry, but it was necessary. You had a perfect right going to the police, Mr. Templeton; under the circumstances I probably would have done the same thing myself. But all the subterfuge, the clumsy disguise were necessary steps that had to be taken before this meeting could be arranged." Hoover paused a moment to allow the words to sink in before he continued. "Actually, the preparation for this meeting has taken seven years to arrange. Seven years of travel, investigation, and study, calling for a total reconditioning, you might say, of my spiritual and intellectual perspectives. . . ."

Bill felt Janice's cold hand steal into his, beneath the table, as Hoover continued to talk, the words tumbling out of his mouth in quick, short, explosive bursts that, Bill decided, sounded labored and prearranged. Many phrases he used were stilted, uncomfortable, as though he'd read them in a book and had memorized them.

He was in the midst of telling about the seven years he had spent traveling, how Pittsburgh, his home, could not provide him with the proper background for his investigations, and how his search had taken him to India, Nepal, the frozen reaches of Tibet, where in the sanctuaries of certain lamaseries he first began to glean ("glean" was his word) the light of truth, when Bill interrupted him in midsentence.

"Er . . . excuse me, Mr. Hoover, but what the hell is this all about?"

"It isn't easy saying what I've got to say to you," Hoover spluttered. "It requires a certain foundation of knowledge, of understanding. . . ."

Hoover's hand shook as, obviously flustered, he gratefully reached for the tea Marie placed before him. Bill had drained half his scotch before Hoover was able to go on, groping for words.

"I can't tell you how many times I've placed myself in your position and how unbelievable what I'm going to tell you sounded to me. I've done many things since arriving in New York—committed many bizarre acts, indeed—which are totally alien to my nature. I mean, the bio in *Who's Who* should have given you some insight into the kind of man I am. . . . I'm not the kind of person who would do these things for no reason, you must believe that."

Hoover flung the disjointed sentences across at Bill in a quavering, impassioned barrage. He met his cup halfway and took a sip of the strong black tea, which gradually brought his shaking hand under control.

"Before I go on, I must ask you both a question. Does either of you know anything about"—here he paused a moment before measuredly pronouncing the word—"reincarnation?"

The tension in Janice's grip on Bill's hand relaxed a bit as she slowly shook her head in the negative. Bill, convinced he had heard "green carnation," could only stare dumbly at Hoover and wait for further information.

"My entire upbringing," Hoover continued, "has always steered me away from a serious belief in Karma. . . ."

The statement was utterly baffling to Bill, it didn't connect with his train of thought. What the hell was Karma, and what did it have to do with flowers?

"But after seven years of seeking and meditating, I began to experience the reality of reincarnation and now believe, as the Koran tells us, that 'God generates beings and sends them back, over and over again, till they return to Him.'"

"Did you say 'reincarnation'?" Bill suddenly asked, finally linking into the drift of Hoover's words.

"Yes, Mr. Templeton," Hoover replied warily, "the religious belief of nearly one billion people on earth, a doctrine accepted by some of the greatest men our world has produced, from Pythagoras to Schopenhauer, from Plato to Benjamin Franklin. . . ."

"Oh," Bill said lamely, swallowing the last of his drink.

"Understand, I don't expect you to accept or believe in the ethics of Karma, any more than I did at first. What I am asking is that you keep an open mind to the things I'm about to tell you. You will doubt them, of course. You may even think I'm insane. Quite natural. I accept your skepticism beforehand. But do hear me out."

"Okay," Bill said. "Go ahead."

"Ten years ago"—Hoover began his story on a note of solemnity—"there was an accident. And in this accident my wife and daughter were taken from me. It was very quick, very sudden. For a long time it left me paralyzed mentally. For a year I did nothing, went nowhere, avoided people. The vacuum they left in my life was unbearable." A quick mote of brightness flecked his eyes. "And then, one day, I had this distinct feeling that they were near me. I felt as if my daughter, her name was Audrey Rose, was very close to me. I had never believed in life after death or the supernatural; I thought it was probably an aberration of my mind brought on by the painful loss, as if my mind were trying to compensate—to fill in the gap. But it was a good feeling, and I didn't reject it. In fact, the sense of Audrey Rose's closeness gained in intensity as time went on and served to put me back on my feet, brought me to the point where I could deal with life again and with people—"

"Would you care for something else?" Marie had sidled up to their table, unobserved, causing Janice to jump slightly.

"I'll have more tea, thank you," Hoover said.

"Do it again," Bill said, handing her the empty glass. "Make it a double."

Janice remained silent.

After Marie cleared the table and left, Hoover shut his eyes, composed his thoughts, and continued.

"About a year and a half after the accident I was at a dinner party and—now, please bear with me—one of the guests was a woman who claimed she could read minds. It's called psychometrize. She'd take your ring or some other personal possession and, through it, tell you things about yourself, as psychics do, about your past, present, and future—like one of those magicians you see on the stage. I thought it was stupid, silly; people can't do these things. Anyway, the friend who brought me to the party persuaded me to give the woman my ring, and she began telling me things about myself—very accurate things—about my past that only I knew. And then she started describing my daughter, as if she were a child of about two, and I got very upset. I started to leave when she stopped me and asked why I was so reluctant to talk about her. I told her that Audrey Rose had died in an accident and that the memory was still very painful. She laughed and shook her head." Hoover's voice rose in pitch slightly as he attempted to duplicate the woman's speech. "'Your daughter is alive,' she said. 'She's come back.' And she went on to describe my daughter as being a lovely blond child, living in a beautiful home in New York City. She gave Audrey Rose your daughter's name, Ivy, and combined them so dramatically that they were the same person, they were one and the same, and I thought, Oh, this is impossible! It was very shocking, upsetting, and so I left. . . . It was a very disturbing feeling when she told me all this. . . . And I told her she was crazy, she was wrong, and I took my ring back, and I left. . . ."

The words were spilling forth at a rapid rate. Bill felt himself wince under the viselike grip of Janice's hand as she increased pressure apace with Hoover's incredible statement.

Hoover filled his cup from the pot of tea and continued his story in a quieter, more controlled voice.

"Almost a year went by. I couldn't help thinking about the incident, of course—it was natural to want to believe in such things—but I considered myself an intelligent, rational person and tried to push the whole thing away from me. But I couldn't really. The things she said, the way she described Audrey Rose, the accuracy, it was all too convincing, and so I clung to the hope that perhaps she might not be just another fraud. But I did nothing about it."

After another slight pause, Bill thought to heighten the dramatic effect, Hoover picked up the threads of his story.

"The year was 1966; the month was December. I happened to be in New York on a business trip when I saw an ad in the *Times*, announcing a lecture appearance of a famous psychic at Town Hall—he was a well-known expert on paranormal phenomena and a clairvoyant as well. For some overpowering reason, I felt I had to attend. I remember giving up a ticket to *Hello, Dolly!*, which was the hottest show on Broadway at the time.

"The weather that night was miserable; it was almost impossible to find a cab, but I finally did and arrived at the hall as the lecture was in progress. I walked down the aisle as quietly as possible and had got to my seat when I realized that the speaker had paused in his lecture and was looking at me—studying me, actually, with a look of amazement. It took him a couple of seconds to recover his poise and continue with the lecture, which mainly centered on ESP and thought-transference experiments."

While Hoover took a sip of tea, Bill sneaked a glance at Janice. Perspiration glazed her perfect skin; her eyes were riveted exclusively on Elliot Hoover, scrutinizing him with all the awe and uncertainty of a scientist on the brink of a fearful discovery. Bill squeezed her hand reassuringly, but the tenseness remained.

"After the lecture," Hoover continued, "as I was about to leave the hall, he pointed his finger at me and indicated that he wanted me to wait. I joined him in his dressing room, where he immediately apologized for staring at me and told me about an aura, surrounding me, that had first caught his attention—"

"A what?"

"An aura. A kind of halo of light that emanates from certain persons and can be apprehended only by a specially attuned consciousness."

"Oh."

"Like the woman at the party the year before, he told me things about myself, very accurate things about my past, about my daughter, describing her as if she were alive and referring to your daughter as my daughter, all very detailed—descriptions of the kind of clothes she wore, and the friends she had—but it was my daughter, in your daughter, born again. He told me of the home she lived in, describing the living room with a large white fireplace and a lovely paneled ceiling with paintings set into it . . . and the room upstairs, where Ivy slept . . . the yellow and white gingham curtains, the bright terry-cloth bedspread . . . the dresser drawer that always sticks, second one from the top. . . ."

Janice flinched. She remembered well the checkered gingham curtains which she had made from a magazine pattern just before Ivy's birth. And the terry-cloth bedspread that Aunt Wilma had sent them, discarded years ago. And that awful drawer, second from the top, that still defied the strongest, most patient attempts to pry open.

Janice spoke for the first time. "How old was your daughter when she . . . died?"

"Audrey Rose was just five, Mrs. Templeton. She and her mother were driving to Harrisburg on the turnpike. They were in a storm. The road was slick. The car skidded and smashed into another car and went down a steep embankment." Hoover's eyes reflected the painful memory of the tragedy. "They died before help could get to them."

Janice bit her lip in hesitation, before asking the next question: "When . . . did it happen?"

Hoover didn't answer at once. For a long moment, his eyes probed across the table, first into Janice's face, then Bill's, measuring his audience, pacing himself with care, before softly replying, "August 4, 1964, a little after eight twenty in the morning, a few minutes before you gave birth to Ivy at New York Hospital."

Janice remained sitting, immobile, locked in the grip of Hoover's penetrating gaze. Bill coughed and rose to his feet.

"Well, Hoover, this is certainly a lot of information you've given us. Give us a couple of days to think about it."

Elliot Hoover stood up, flustered, as he saw Bill clutch Janice's arm and begin to assist her to her feet.

"Y-you do understand what I've told you, Mr. Templeton?" Hoover stammered, placing himself in their path in a futile attempt to delay their departure.

"Sure," Bill replied genially. "Your daughter died and was reincarnated in our daughter. In effect, you are saying that our daughter, Ivy, is really your daughter, Audrey Rose."

"Well . . . yes," Hoover said, attempting to gauge Bill's sincerity. "I think we should talk more and come to some kind of . . . understanding. I don't want to hurt anybody. I know that legally there's nothing I can do about this. And even if there were, I wouldn't do that to you. I know what it is to lose someone you love."

"Yeah, sure." Bill steered Janice purposefully past Hoover toward the restaurant archway. "We'll think about it, see if we can't come up with some answers."

"May I call you tomorrow?" Hoover directed his words at their backs as they moved rapidly away from him.

"Call my office," Bill flung back over his shoulder; then, with a trace of sarcasm: "I think you know the number."

Carole Federico, sitting at the dining-room table playing solitaire, rose to leave as Bill and Janice entered the apartment. Their parting exchanges were brief and friendly: Did they have an interesting evening? Ivy went to bed soon after they'd left; there were no phone calls, how about dinner with the Federicos Saturday a week?

After Carole left, Janice looked in on Ivy, while Bill prepared himself for bed. They hadn't spoken of their meeting with Hoover, nor would they, Janice knew, until later, in the darkness of their bedroom.

Gazing down at the lovely blond innocence of her sleeping child, Janice felt suddenly chilled throughout by the terrible prescience. Incredibly, they had met the enemy, had estimated his forces, had learned of his objective—Ivy.

A soft, fretful moan from Ivy, a flinching, her sleep disturbed by some dream. A wave of dread swept through Janice as she recalled the year of the nightmares. Pray God they never return. . . . Janice felt her child's head. Cool. Normal. A good sign.

The warmth of her own bed felt good as she slipped between the paisley-print sheets and geared her troubled mind to the silences of the night.

Soon Bill would join her, and they would talk.

Having removed his robe, Bill turned off the bed lamp and crawled into bed beside her. His hand groped for hers beneath the sheets. Janice waited to see which of them would speak first. But as the seconds ticked by and Bill's breathing rhythm began to extend itself into even patterns, Janice realized that if she didn't speak, he would soon be asleep.

"Bill, *talk* to me!"

"For God's sake, Janice, relax." Bill sighed deeply. "We're in good shape. The man's a nut. There are places for nuts. They're called nut houses."

"He knew you'd say he was crazy. He predicted it and was even willing to accept it."

"Sure, because that's how their twisted minds work. They tell you what you're going to think in advance to put you off guard. They hook you that way, don't you understand?"

"No, Bill, I don't understand. I'm scared to death."

"That's reasonable. Nuts are scary people."

"That's not why I'm scared. I'm afraid he *isn't* a . . . nut."

"You believe his story? You buy his Karmas and auras?"

"*He* believes it." Janice put all the force and feeling she could manage behind the quietly uttered phrase. "*He* believes what he said, sincerely. I could tell by the way he looked. . . ."

"How did he look? Pale face, weird, empty eyes—is that the look of a normal, healthy man?"

"But why would he do it? Why would he come to us with such a story?"

"The answer to that is locked up in his crazy brain, Janice, and I'm no mind reader."

"I can see that you've decided not to answer any of my questions in a rational manner."

"Tell me one question you've asked that I can answer rationally."

"All right. What if he isn't crazy? What then?"

Bill smothered a yawn. "If he isn't crazy? Well, then"—Bill considered his choices— "it's possible he's doing it for money. He's an extortionist. He's come up with this elaborate scheme to get our money."

"What money?"

"That's not the point. The extortionist theory makes good sense to me."

"You mean, he spent seven years traveling around the world just to come back here and take our money, which doesn't exist?"

"How do you know he traveled anywhere? Because he told you so? I say he never went anywhere. He's always lived in New York. He's got a racket. He pulls names out of the phone book. He finds his marks and zeros in on them. Disprove it."

"What about *Who's Who?*"

"A borrowed identity. Can the real Elliot Suggins Hoover stand up and identify himself? No. Because he's dead."

"You don't know that for a fact."

"No, Janice. The only thing I know for a fact is that he isn't from the FBI, the CIA, or the IRS, and that takes a hell of a load off my mind. Anything else I can handle."

Janice heard his final words dribble off into a deep yawn. He was edging off into unconsciousness.

"Bill?"

"Hmmm?"

"How are you going to handle this, Bill?"

"Depends," Bill mumbled, half asleep. "I'll talk to Harold Yates tomorrow. Whatever this guy is, psychotic or extortionist, Harry'll know what to do." Another yawn, followed by a barely audible "Night. . . ."

"Good night," Janice said, and thought to herself: But what if he's neither?

For a long time, sleep eluded her.

The storm had passed over the city, leaving a clear, cold night in its wake. Tomorrow would be a beautiful autumn day.

7

AND so it was.

Crisp, cold, bracing, a pollution-defeating gift from the northern reaches of Canada.

Bill and Ivy lucked in on a cruising cab at the corner of Sixty-seventh Street. As they drove down the broad, slushy avenue toward the Ethical Culture School, a fine spray of mud freckled the cab's windows, drawing a somber gray curtain across the vivid day. Ivy loved cabbing it to school, even though the ride took less than a minute. It lent a note of elegance to the start of her day.

Watching her bright and smiling morning face—open, innocent, trusting—Bill felt a quick constriction in his chest. How utterly vulnerable she was. How helpless. How dependent and needful of his care and protection.

He watched Ivy half turn at the big double doors, smile and wave him a kiss, then enter the school building. He waited a few seconds to make sure she was safely inside before giving the cabdriver his office address. Bill knew Hoover wouldn't be there this morning. Now that he had made his move, had his foot in their door, his Sherlock Holmes days were over, Bill thought with a grim smile. Exit Hercule Poirot.

The cab skidded slightly as it took the sharp left down Fifty-seventh Street and barely missed sideswiping a standing bus. Bill hardly registered the event. His mind was on Hoover.

He'd talk to Harry. Harry would know. Harry was his link to all legal remedies. Meanwhile, there was one wheel he could put into motion: The part about Hoover's child's death occurring at the precise moment of Ivy's birth could be checked out. Either Pittsburgh or Harrisburg newspapers would have covered the accident, if true, or the state police would have a report on file. He'd ask Darlene to start checking immediately.

By the time the cab deposited Bill outside the sterile black monolith that contained his office he was like a boxer waiting for the bell to sound—primed, tense, and ready for action.

The first punishing jolt occurred just outside his office when Don

Goetz signaled to him from the opposite end of the hallway and slowly approached wearing the face of doom.

"Jack Belaver had a coronary last night," he glumly informed Bill.

"How is he?" Bill stammered, quickly evaluating the myriad significances of this stunning piece of news.

"He'll live, they say. But he'll be out of action three months, at least."

Jack Belaver was senior vice president at Simmons and handled its largest accounts, the most impressive being Carleton Industries, a diversified giant whose corporate fingers reached into every nook and cranny of the electronics industry. Its account represented a tidy two and a half million per annum to Simmons. Its yearly sales convention would start this coming Thursday on the beach at Waikiki. Jack Belaver played a key role in prepping and staging the sales show. Simmons could ill afford to lose Jack at this critical juncture.

"The old man would like to see you," Don said in the same subdued voice.

Sure, Bill thought, knowing damn well why.

"Okay," he said aloud, and entered his office, whereupon he received his second jolt of the morning.

Sitting at Darlene's desk was a sec-temp replacement, a swarthy girl with stubby figure and eyes that were slightly crossed behind thick tortoiseshell glasses. Darlene, she told him nasally, was at home with the flu. Wow! He was really fielding them this morning.

Her name was Abby, and she couldn't quite get the drift of what Bill was asking her to do—couldn't understand what newspapers he wanted contacted and what accident he wanted verified.

Bill made legible notes on a yellow legal pad and hoped.

Stepping out of Pel Simmons' office an hour later, Bill had the hunched-over, totally drained look of a man carrying a hod of bricks. Not only had Pel asked him to sub for Jack Belaver on the Hawaiian adventure, but he had instructed him to stop off in Seattle on the way back and look in on another of Jack's accounts, DeVille Shipping, which was making funny noises of late.

"Sorry to load this on you, Bill, but with a backstop like Don, you're the only man who's sparable."

"Sure, Pel," Bill said. "I'll plan to leave on Friday."

"Make it Thursday. You'll need the time there to brief up."

Back in his own office, his message sheet told him that Hoover had called twice during his absence. Sinking wearily into the Eames recliner, Bill heaved a sigh of profound hopelessness and softly uttered, "Shit." A box of paper clips was close at hand. Singly and with studied deliberation, he extracted them one by one and shied them across at the Motherwell, aiming at the black deltoid shape in the center. Of all the rotten luck. Of all the rotten times to be leaving town. How would he break the news to Janice? She was in semishock as it was. Oh, by the way, honey, I'm going to Hawaii for a week, how does that grab ya? Probably send her over the edge. . . .

Unless! Unless!

Yes, why the hell not? They'd all go. They could take Ivy out of school for a week and fly to Hawaii as a family. The trip would do them all good. He'd be on the company's expense account. They could manage the rest of the money. It would, of course, be unique, a man in his position, taking his wife and child on a ball-buster of this kind, but hell! The alternative of leaving them alone and unguarded. . . .

His spirits buoyed by pleasant thoughts of sun, surf, and safety for all of them, Bill quickly rose and walked across to the Motherwell, reclaiming the paper clips scattered over the sofa and floor. When Abby stuck her head into the room, she found Bill down on his knees, picking "things" out of the carpet.

"I'm sorry," she stammered, "but I flashed. . . ."

"What is it?" Bill said sternly.

"Mr. Hoover is on the line."

"I'm at a meeting and won't be back till late this afternoon."

"Yes, sir."

"Wait," Bill ordered, as she was about to duck out. "What about the Pittsburgh newspapers?"

"They're checking. They'll call back later, collect."

"Okay. Call Mr. Harold Yates, that's Y-A-T-E-S, you'll find it in the Rolodex, and ask him if he's free for lunch."

"Yes, sir." Abby gulped and disappeared.

Harry, as it turned out, was in court and wouldn't be able to see Bill until three o'clock, please confirm. Bill did, then put in a call to Janice through the Des Artistes house line. Janice answered after a great number of rings, and Bill listened as Dominick announced him.

"Anything new there?" Bill asked.

"No," Janice said.

"Any phone calls?"

"A couple, on the other line. But I didn't answer them."

"Good."

Bill was about to tell her of their impending trip to Hawaii when Janice suddenly remembered: "A package came."

"A what?"

"A package. Mario brought it up a few minutes after the mail. It was delivered by hand."

"Well, what's in it?"

"I don't know. I haven't opened it."

Bill paused a moment, then quietly asked, "Why not, Janice?"

"I don't know. I guess I'm afraid."

"All right." Bill softly sighed. "Why don't you open it now?"

"Just a minute."

The light on Bill's number two line flashed, then stopped, remaining alight, as Abby took the call at her desk. In a moment, it went dark. Hoover again, Bill surmised, knowing that Abby would hardly have hung up that quickly were it anyone else.

The sound of paper tearing preceded Janice's voice. "It's books. Four of them."

"Who from?"

"I suppose from Mr. Hoover. They seem to be religious books. Very old. One is called *The Annotated Koran*. Then there's the *Upanishads* —I don't know if I'm pronouncing it right—*A Modern Translation*. There's also a diary."

"Is there a letter? A note or something?"

"There's an envelope in *Dialogues on Metem . . . psychosis*, by J. G. von Herder. . . ." Again the sound of paper tearing as Janice opened the envelope. "It's from Hoover, a list of page references for each book, handwritten and signed, 'Sincerely yours, E. Hoover.'"

"Okay," Bill said after careful consideration. "Keep them. They may be useful as evidence."

"Has he called there?"

"Yeah, a couple of times, but I'm not taking his calls till I've spoken to Harry Yates."

There was a pause.

"Bill?" There was a childlike tremor in her voice.

"Yes, honey?"

"Will he be at school when I pick up Ivy?"

"No. He wasn't there this morning."

"What if he is?"

"If he annoys you, call a cop."

"Oh, God," she whispered in a choked voice.

A few minutes after Bill hung up the phone, he remembered he hadn't told her about their Hawaiian fling. He considered calling her back, then decided against it. It would only add to her state of confusion. He'd tell her tonight in bed.

The books, partially exposed in their torn wrappings, remained on the dining-room table the entire morning. Janice walked past them at least a dozen times but conscientiously refrained from noticing them. The little game was self-defeating, however, for at ten past two, after having loitered over her hair and clothing far too long to justify the simple expedition to the school and back, she still found herself with better than thirty-five minutes and nothing to do.

Fully dressed in coat, rain boots and white fake-fur hat, she fixed herself a cup of instant coffee and stood drinking it in the kitchen, the edge of the books, sliced by the frame of the doorway, just within range of her vision.

Standing above the stack of books, cup in hand, her fingers tracing the battered embossed cover of the one on top, she had no memory of having walked up to them, nor could she stop herself from turning back the cover and revealing a hardly legible inscription at the top of the frontispiece. Handwritten in a pale mauve ink was the inscription "R. A. Tyagi, '06," and beneath it, in a brighter, bolder hand, "E. Hoover, '68." The book's title, printed in a delicate floral design, was *The Bhagavad-Gita—An English Translation*. The publication date was: "1746—London."

Janice gently grasped a sheaf of the yellowed pages and allowed them to riffle slowly through her fingers, causing a small eruption of powdery dust to drift upward from the heart of the ancient volume. The pages seemed to fall in clumps, signifying the more studied portions of the text. At one such point, she read: "As a man, casting off worn-out garments, taketh new ones, so the dweller in the body, casting off worn-out bodies, entereth into others that are new. . . ."

On another page, she read: "For certain is death for the born, and certain is birth for the dead; therefore over the inevitable thou shouldst not grieve."

Janice shut the book decisively and stepped away from the table, feeling very much a traitor for having so easily capitulated to the enemy. Bill was right. It was nonsense.

Janice picked up the pile of books and carried them to the hall closet, where, standing on a chair, she consigned them to a shadowy corner on the top shelf, next to several volumes of Bill's more graphic pornography.

She joined the waiting mothers in front of the school, and at three o'clock sharp the bell rang and the exodus began. Less than five minutes later Ivy appeared at the double doors and smiled her way down the steps toward Janice. Hoover was nowhere to be seen. Bill had been right. No doubt, he was right about everything, Janice thought, her confidence in her husband's judgment growing by leaps and bounds.

For the first time in nearly a week Janice found herself heading north at a leisurely pace instead of in a panic. Ivy chattered continually. Janice laughed unreservedly. It was like old times for both of them.

"I don't know if he's an extortionist or a nut or let's say he's a man who believes this to be so. We're talking about an area that a lot of people don't know anything about. . . ." Harold Yates paused a moment to organize his thoughts and place them in their proper legal perspective.

Bill sat on the couch, adjacent to Harold's Barca-Lounger, from which, in a semisupine position, Harold conducted all his business. There was no desk in the office. A low cocktail table immediately to his right sufficed to accommodate two telephones, a cup of pencils, and several legal pads.

"But regardless of whether he's a . . . nut, as you say, whatever the definition of that is," Harold continued in a slow, pedantic manner, "regardless of whether he's an extortionist, you're really concerned about what you can do to protect your family from being bothered by this person. Now I have a question to ask you. Did he make any demand upon you?"

Bill considered carefully. "He didn't come right out and make a demand, except to say that he wants to see us again and that we have to come to some kind of understanding."

"What understanding? Does he want Ivy?"

"No. He said he doesn't want to claim her or take her away, that he couldn't legally, and in any case wouldn't, since he knows what it is to lose someone you love. Don't you see, Harry? It's a pitch. We're being primed for a shakedown."

Harry mulled on this. "Is your question: What are your legal rights?"

"My question is: How do I get him off our backs?"

"Well, when you say off your backs, if he continues to intrude on your privacy, in terms of following you wherever you go, calling you at home, asking to see members of your family, he has no legal right to do that. If the amount of attention he is paying your family is bothersome or a nuisance, you can go to court and apply for an injunction restraining him from harassing or annoying you and your family. If he violates that injunction, he is in contempt of court and will be punished by the court. Punishment for contempt of court is subject to imprisonment."

Bill's eyes remained staring across at the lawyer.

"If we do take him to court, how do I prove that all this actually happened?"

"There are ways you can obtain proof. For example, next time he calls and wants to come to your house to talk, have a witness present."

"Isn't Janice a witness?"

"Certainly she is, but it would be better if you had an unrelated person present. Conceivably, you might get this Hoover to write you what he wants and proposes to do, or perhaps secretly tape his conversations. . . ."

That was it, Bill thought with a quick surge of elation. He'd tape him. Surely, Russ Federico would lend him the equipment and even help him set up the living room and work the machine. Russ could be the unrelated witness at the same time. Bill heard Harry droning on in the background of his thoughts and quickly shifted his concentration back to what his friend and lawyer was saying.

"The tape, while probably inadmissible, could certainly be used to convince the police that this man is bothering you and enable you to avail yourself of their legal restraints and powers."

"I think I can arrange to tape our next meeting," said Bill, rising.

"Not so fast. Where are you going?"

"To set things up." Bill glanced at his watch. "I haven't got much time."

"You intend to do this that soon?"

"I intend to do it tonight."

"In that case, there are some questions I will want you to ask him." Harold's stubby hand reached for a legal pad and sharp pencil. "A few simple bedrock questions, the answers to which will have some legal force and validity in a court of law, if indeed that is the course we select to pursue."

Bill slowly sat back down on the couch and watched Harold bring the rubber end of the pencil up to his thick semiparted lips and begin mentally formulating the substance of his first question.

"One," he said.

The meeting with Russ had gone as expected; he was not only willing, but eager to help Bill. They agreed to rendezvous at the apartment at six thirty and, as Russ put it, rig the place for action. Bill hadn't gone into great detail with Russ, only that he was being preyed on by a shakedown artist and that he needed Russ' expert help to nail the bastard. They discussed the kind of equipment Russ would use and its deployment. Hiding the wire connecting the mike and recorder would pose a problem, he felt, unless he used a wireless mike, which was kind of temperamental and not as dependable as a direct hookup. Russ finally decided to bring a variety of systems and test them all before Hoover arrived.

Bill felt a growing excitement as he saw each step of his plans dropping neatly into place.

Before leaving Russ' studio, he had called Janice, told her what they were up to, and suggested she arrange with Carole for Ivy to spend the night there.

"He called this afternoon, Bill."

"Did you talk to him?"

"No," Janice said. "I let Dominick take a message. He left a phone number."

"Okay, let me have it."

"Just a sec." Janice was back almost immediately. "555-1771."

Bill dialed the number and was surprised to hear a woman's voice say, "Good evening, YMCA."

"Good evening," Bill said. "I'd like to speak to Mr. Elliot Hoover, please."

"One moment, please." A sharp click, followed by a buzzing sound and then by a subdued male voice: "Fourth-floor dormitory."

"Elliot Hoover, please," the woman said.

"One moment, please."

Bill put his hand over the mouthpiece and quietly asked Russ, "Nine o'clock okay?"

"Nine thirty," Russ whispered back.

Bill could hear the echoing sound of footsteps approaching. Then Hoover's voice said, "This is Elliot Hoover."

"Bill Templeton here."

"Oh, yes, Mr. Templeton." The voice held a note of eagerness.

"I'd like to get together with you tonight, at my apartment, say, nine thirty?"

"That will be fine. Thank you."

Yes, Bill thought, jumping over a dirt-encrusted snow drift at the corner of Fifty-ninth and Central Park West, it will all work out fine.

"A girl named Abby called. She said that the Pittsburgh *Post-Gazette* confirmed the information you wanted: that Sylvia Flora Hoover and her daughter, Audrey Rose, were killed in a car accident on the Harrisburg Turnpike a little after eight thirty on the morning of August 4, 1964."

No kiss, no hello, no chance to take off his coat and boots; Janice assaulted him with the information the moment he pushed open the door.

"Okay," Bill said quietly, edging his way around her into the apartment.

"Okay?" she shrilled back.

"Take it easy, baby. Let me take off my coat and make us a drink," he said soothingly, although the rich winy odor on her breath informed him that she hadn't waited to be asked. "We can talk about this thing reasonably."

"Oh, God," she moaned softly.

"Janice!" Bill's voice sharpened. "I don't know what you're building here. But I want you to know that I do not believe in spooks, ghosts, haunts, auras, Karmas, or any of that crap. There's got to be a simple, real-life explanation to all this."

Janice took a quick step back.

"All right, give me *one!*"

"Okay, off the top of my head. The guy picks his mark, finds when their child was born—the exact minute of birth—then does research on what child died at that very same time. He's got the whole country to pick his child from. And once he matches them up, he simply steps into the character of the dead child's father and makes the hit. Reasonable?"

Janice stared back at him without saying a word. He could tell by the softening lines in her face that his explanation had scored with her. Not entirely, but enough to permit him to take her into his arms and kiss her lost and haunted eyes.

"And that's off the top of my head." Bill smiled. "Believe me, Janice, we're gonna get to the bottom of this thing and shake ourselves loose from this creep. I promise."

He kissed her lips and felt her mouth open and her body lose most of its tension. But for Ivy upstairs, zealously packing her overnight bag for her sleep-over date with the Federicos, Bill might have made love to her then and there.

Russ showed up at six twenty-five with a mountain of sound gear. Mario and Ernie helped him lug it off the elevator and down the corridor to Bill's apartment.

For the next hour, Bill's voice intoning, "One, two, three, four, five, six . . . do you read me? Do you read me? Six, five, four, three, two, one . . . come in, Russ, do you read me?" filled the apartment and filtered through to Janice, in the kitchen, preparing sandwiches and dressing a large salad of mixed vegetables, lettuce, and tomatoes. Ivy had left on her overnight journey a few minutes before Russ had arrived, toting a much too heavy suitcase and her favorite TV dinner under her arm.

At eight fifteen, Russ, Bill, and Janice were seated around the living room, finishing the last of the sandwiches and beer and surveying their handiwork. The wireless mike hadn't worked, compelling them to string a wire from the microphone, concealed among the autumn leaves and flowers in the vase next to the sofa, clear across the long living room, hidden under a series of carpets and up the staircase wall to their bedroom, where Russ had set up his Nagra recording equipment. It would be up to Bill to get Hoover to sit in precisely the right spot on the sofa in order to guarantee a usable signal. Janice felt the whole thing was too complicated to work. The men were not discouraged by her skepticism and continued to work with enthusiasm, perfecting the setup, until nine twenty-five, when the phone rang.

Bill lifted the receiver gingerly and said, "Yes?" Then, after a pause; "Okay, send him right up."

Bill signaled Janice with a quick motion of his finger. She heard Russ' footsteps ascending the stairs to their bedroom to man his post, and she quickly moved to her own prearranged position at the far end of the sofa adjacent to the one intended for Elliot Hoover. She would be the decoy, Bill reasoned, to lure Hoover to that part of the room.

A pronounced hush settled over the apartment, a conscious, collective stillness such as one experiences in a theater, just as the houselights dim and the curtain goes up.

8

THE doorbell rang.

Janice heard Bill and Hoover mumble something incomprehensible to each other as they walked down the long, narrow hallway toward the living room and assumed it to be some form of salutation. There was a sense of madcap, Janice thought, in the act of two men, undoubted enemies, observing the gentle amenities prescribed by a rigid upbringing—like two opposing generals shaking hands before a slaughter.

Bill's face was stern, set, ungiving, as he preceded Hoover through the carved doorway and into the living room and attempted to guide him toward the area of the sofa with a slight wave of his arm. But Hoover stopped on the threshold and remained standing, critically surveying the room, his doleful eyes filled with great awe as they slowly took in each detail of the walls and ceiling. The soft pink light of the sconces accented the clear, unlined pallor of his face, lending it a youthful, priestlike placidity.

Bill had turned quickly when he realized that Hoover's attention was elsewhere and now stood impatiently waiting for their guest to make a move.

"It's exactly as he described it," Hoover said in a small, incredulous voice. "The fireplace . . . the white stuccoed walls . . . the ceiling paintings"—his eyes found the staircase—"and the staircase, with the carved-head newel post. . . ." He walked to the staircase and placed his fingers on the Viking's head in a delicate, tentative gesture, as if he were seeking tactile corroboration to confirm the fact that his eyes were not deceiving him. His gaze slowly drifted up the banister to the top of the staircase, and his eyes became pinpoints of curiosity.

"The bedrooms . . . upstairs"—his voice was hushed with emotion—"three of them . . . Ivy's to the left of the stairs. . . ."

Bill girded himself for action. If Hoover took one step up the stairs, he would charge across the room and tackle the son of a bitch.

But Hoover held his ground and turned his attention to Bill.

"Am I right?" he asked with a smile that Bill decided was smug.

"Umm . . . yeah . . ." Bill said, shifting about nervously. "I . . . er . . . think we'd better get this thing started, if you don't mind."

"Certainly," Hoover replied, and quickly crossed the room, taking in the slipshod arrangement of carpets concealing the microphone wire. He sat on the sofa where he was meant to sit, and Bill took the seat immediately to his right.

"Uh . . . I wonder, Mr. Hoover," Bill began, groping, "if you'd mind going through the . . . highlights again of what you told us last night? We were kind of hazy, and . . . you hit us with so much. . . ."

Hoover thought a moment. "Is there any particular part that you would like me to repeat?"

Janice was sure that Hoover knew he was being recorded.

"No, no," Bill said. "Just a general summary of things, you know, starting, say, with the death of your wife and child."

Elliot Hoover took a deep breath and shut his eyes. There was a sense of ritual in the gesture, a rallying of inner strengths to muster support for a time of trial. When he spoke, it was in short, well-organized, fact-filled sentences.

"My wife and child died in a car accident on August 4, 1964. About a year later, I met a woman, a psychic, who told me that my daughter had returned to life, in the body of another person, and was living in New York City. My tendency was to scoff at the notion, but I did find it intriguing. A year later I attended a lecture given by a well-known parapsychologist, and he told me substantially the same thing the woman had a year before, that my daughter was living in the body of a child named Ivy, and he went on to describe her home, which was identical to the environment I now find myself in."

The simple, direct manner of his delivery gave Janice the chills. He really seemed to believe this.

"Who are these people?" Bill interrupted.

"I beg your pardon?"

"The two psychics? What are their names?"

"I never knew the woman's name. The man was Erik Lloyd."

"Erik Lloyd?"

"Yes, he"—Hoover's eyes lowered in respect—"died several years ago."

"Uh-huh," Bill commiserated. "That's too bad."

He could have predicted both answers. Hoover obviously thought he was dealing with novices.

"All right," he continued, his eyes fastened on Hoover, "at that point, we're talking about 1965 to '6. You say that two people, psychics, told you your daughter was alive and living in New York and that her name was Ivy, is that correct?"

Janice thought Bill was overplaying it. Still, Hoover answered forthrightly and without seeming concern.

"Yes," he replied. "That's correct."

"Well, why didn't you come here then and claim her?"

"It was never my intention to claim her. Nor is it now."

"Well, why didn't you at least come and look us up, as you're doing now? What took you, was it, seven years to decide whether or not she was really your child?"

"Mr. Templeton"—Hoover's voice was soft with patience—"as I explained last night, my entire background, my religious upbringing, the sum and substance of all I was and believed in, were strongly opposed to such ideas. I was a scoffer and a disbeliever, as you are now."

"So you went to India to discover the truth?"

"I went to many places, Mr. Templeton, met and stayed with many families, many teachers; learned of a way of life that was totally alien to mine; joined my life with theirs; embraced their customs; shared their poverty; partook of their beliefs and their philosophies; and, in time, with the help of God, and the wisdom of Siddhartha Guatama, their Buddha, came to know the reality of their religious convictions."

Hoover turned to Janice.

"Might I please have a glass of water, Mrs. Templeton?" he asked.

As Janice rose and walked toward the kitchen, Bill's next question faded off in the background.

"Understand, Mr. Hoover, when it comes to reincarnation and things like that, I'm at ground zero. Tell me. What are these religious convictions you're talking about? And what convinces you that they're right and that you are right in what you're doing?"

Janice wondered if Hoover took ice in his water and decided finally to serve the ice separately. The thought of Russ, upstairs, listening to this strange conversation, brought a fleeting smile to her lips. Somehow Hoover didn't seem so frightening tonight. He had no doubt been through a very bad experience and was a tortured man, willing to believe in anything. Janice almost felt sorry for him.

When she returned with the tray, Hoover was speaking in a voice charged with passion.

"The ego in man never dies. It keeps coming back over and over again, having gained in wisdom during each sojourn spent on other planes of being between the incarnations. Therefore, some souls are older in wisdom, have enjoyed more stages of spiritual and intellectual evolution, so that a great teacher may be an older soul than, say, a bricklayer or a savage. . . ."

"Ummmm, yeah . . ." Bill said as Janice put down the tray.

"I didn't know if you wanted ice," she said unsurely, placing the glass of cubes on the table next to Hoover.

"No, thanks," he said with a quick smile. "I take it straight."

"What did you do for money, Mr. Hoover," Bill asked, "for sustenance during all this time? I mean, you quit working back in sixty-seven. How did you support yourself during all those years?"

Janice was sure this was one of Harold Yates' questions.

Hoover finished drinking his water and answered simply. "A great deal of money came to me from the death of my wife and daughter. A double indemnity policy amounting to more than two hundred thousand dollars has more than provided for me during these years."

Bill did a quick mental calculation: At eight and one-half percent interest, two hundred grand would net him seventeen thou per year, which, if true, was enough to support him on any number of truth searches.

"While the money, on the one hand, was abhorrent to me," Hoover continued, "I did make positive use of some of it. There's still a great deal left as my needs are very simple."

"When did you come to New York?"

"This year, on the twelfth of July."

"And you used a disguise?"

"Not until I was pretty sure I had . . . found the right people."

"You mean us?"

"Yes."

"How were you sure we were the right people?"

"A process of elimination. I had only three real clues: She lived in New York City; her hair was blond; her name was Ivy. That, plus the time of her birth, which had to be soon after Audrey Rose's death. I went to the boards of health in all five boroughs and checked the birth records. I found six girls who were possibles: two in Queens, one in the Bronx, one in Brooklyn, and two in Manhattan. All had been born within a year of Audrey Rose's death. But only one was born at the moment of her death. Your daughter."

His words settled deeply into the atoms of the room. Janice licked her lips, which had suddenly become parched. Bill cleared his throat.

"Isn't that a little unusual," he ventured, "a person coming back so quickly? I mean, I always heard it took . . . uh . . . a long time to come back. I mean, people who believe in it, always speak of having lived during the time of Caesar and Davy Crockett, you know? Isn't it unusual for someone to die one second"—Bill snapped his fingers—"and be born the next second? I mean, you tell me—"

"In my experience, Mr. Templeton, I have found that those who die an early or violent death and are interrupted from experiencing the full opportunities of their mental, physical, and spiritual growth often return sooner than those who die in peace at a ripe old age. Oftentimes a soul may return at the instant of death. In Tibet each Dalai Lama is the immediate incarnation of his predecessor. When a Dalai Lama dies, Tibetan notables immediately begin a search for the new incarnation."

"And they always find him?"

"For five centuries they have never failed."

"How do *they* do it?"

"By interpreting certain portents. After the thirteenth Dalai Lama died, they placed his body on a throne, facing south. After several days, they found that his face had turned to the east, where curious cloud formations were also seen in the vicinity of Lhasa. High lamas and notables went to all parts of Lhasa in search of the newly born Dalai Lama."

"And they found him?"

"Yes. In the village of Taktscr, they found a boy of two, living in humble surroundings. When the leader of the party, Lama Kewtsang Rinpoche, entered the house, the little boy went to him immediately and sat on his lap. Around the lama's neck was a rosary which had belonged to the thirteenth Dalai Lama. When the child saw it, he recognized it and wanted it. The lama promised to give it to him if he could guess who he was, and the boy said, *Sera-aga*, which means, 'A lama of Sera.'"

Bill coughed.

"Okay, so *you* found *your* girl. Why the disguise? Why all that Secret Service stuff, following us around, scaring the hell out of us?"

"I apologize for that," Hoover replied with a look of regret. "But I had to be sure you were the right people. That Ivy was the right child. The times of death and birth, although pretty remarkable, were still not convincing proof. It might still have been only a coincidence. . . ."

"And your research convinced you that we were the right people?"

"Try to understand, Mr. Templeton. In the Buddhist belief, death becomes a mere incident in life, a change of scene, a brief journey in which the soul wanders in search of a new life, selecting the parents to whom it wishes to be born. Audrey Rose would naturally have sought out a life and parents similar to those she knew and loved in her previous life. It was no accident that she chose you. The kind of people you are, the depth of love and understanding, the quality of intellect, the way of life you offered made you the perfect family in which to be reborn."

"What if Audrey Rose hadn't died?" Bill interjected. "What would our daughter have become, an empty shell?"

"She would have become the receptor of another soul."

Bill shook his head. "You would think, if that were the case, that she'd remember some of her past lives."

"Such remembrance would only complicate her present life, Mr. Templeton. Hindus consider it tragic if a child remembers a former existence, for this, they believe, signifies an early death."

Bill heaved a deep sigh, as if catching his second wind.

"Okay," he continued, his mind ferreting among the questions still left to be asked, seeking the proper, logical successor to the last. "So you came to New York, and using a disguise, started observing our family. . . ."

"No, not immediately. As I said, there were others, but for one reason or another they didn't fit. I started observing *your* daughter a little over a month ago, and almost at once I began to see little things in Ivy that did indeed remind me of Audrey Rose. . . ."

"Like what?"

"The way she walks, for example. Her tendency to get lost in a daydream whenever she walks. The funny habit of licking her lips just before she starts to speak. Her sudden laugh; the way she throws back her head when she laughs; the gentle sadness in her eyes when something painful occurs—like that day, Mrs. Templeton, when you both stopped to help that injured pigeon. . . ."

Janice felt her soul turn white as he went on to describe the myriad, lovely, subtle gestures and qualities that were Ivy's exclusive property—those rare, tenuous nuances of movement, style, and nature that Janice thought she herself had only been aware of. She was suddenly thankful that Ivy was not around, that she was safely tucked away with Carole downstairs, beyond the proximity of Elliot Hoover's strange and terrible insight.

"All these things, these little idiosyncrasies were Audrey Rose's, Mr. Templeton. In so many ways, the two of them are one and the same person."

"Do they also resemble each other?"

"No. It is only the spirit which passes from life to life; the physical you is new with each birth. Here"—Hoover reached into his pocket and removed his wallet; he carefully extracted a small photograph from its Plasticine container and handed it to Bill—"a picture of Audrey Rose, taken about a month before she passed on."

Bill studied the picture. The face he saw staring back at him was round, flat-featured, and plain. Her hair was straight, light brown, and resembled her father's, as did her eyes. Bill passed the photograph to Janice, who glanced at it briefly and quickly thrust it back at Bill as if it were something diseased and contagious. Bill offered the photograph back to Hoover, who gingerly reinserted it into its protective covering.

"Well, Mr. Hoover," Bill said, flashing his best street smile, "we seem to have come to the point where I'm supposed to ask you what it is exactly that you want from us?"

Hoover smiled back. "Nothing more or less than you and your wife are prepared to give me."

"Well, like what?" Bill urged. "You tell *us*."

Hoover's eyes became distant, serene. "The chance to see Ivy occasionally, to watch her grow, to be of help, if needed. . . ."

"That might be difficult to arrange."

"Not if I became your friend. Your neighbor. I intend to settle in New York and take up my professional life once again." Hoover saw the stiff lines of resistance on their faces and quickly added, "Understand, I'll make no demands on your time or expect any special privileges or considerations. . . ."

Yeah, sure, Bill thought hotly, in a pig's ass you won't.

"And, of course, Ivy would never know about our . . . relationship. As I said before, it would be dangerous for her to know. . . ."

Bill held up his hand. "Okay, I have a question. Since, by your own admission, your presence does present a danger to Ivy, and since you say you care about what happens to her and that you wish to be of help to her, why don't you just step out of the picture? That would be the greatest help you could give her, as I see it. Right now, our daughter is a normal, healthy child. Aren't you interested in seeing that she stays that way? I mean, say that there is a little bit of your child mixed up in her somehow, why take a chance on destroying them both?"

The question was a good one, direct, simply expressed, to the point, and Janice was proud of Bill for having thought of it. There was no way Hoover could answer without betraying his own selfish interest. She watched Hoover press the bridge of his nose with his thumb and index finger and knew that behind the bland gesture was a mind that was racing.

"You are right, of course," he finally said. "It would be the simplest thing for me just to walk away. And it's quite possible it may ultimately come to that. But put yourself in my position, Mr. Templeton. . . ."

He was interrupted by the sudden ring of the house telephone—a strident, continual ring that signified danger. The last time it had rung like that was when the building was thought to be on fire.

Bill jumped up and dashed down the hallway. Janice rose, as did Elliot Hoover, startled and confused by the sudden activity.

Bill snatched up the receiver and heard Dominick's tense voice say, "Go ahead, Mrs. Federico."

"Bill?" Carole's frantic whisper stung his ear. "Bill, get down here! Something's happening to Ivy!"

"What is it?" Bill snapped.

"I don't know . . . she's . . . she's running around the room, crying. . . ." Carole's voice heightened with panic. "She's having some kind of nightmare. . . ."

"Coming!" Bill said, slamming down the receiver and turning to Janice, standing white-faced behind him. "It's Ivy! Get Kaplan's number!"

The fleeting look between them raised the shroud on a memory shared, yet abhorred. Janice felt a chill sweep through her veins as she pulled the leather-bound telephone book from the kitchen drawer, then found herself floating, featherlike, through the service door and down the fire stairs in pursuit of Bill. She was unaware of her feet as they sped her down the iron and concrete steps to the floor below, transporting her to the Federicos' door, where Bill stood, knocking lightly and quietly calling, "Carole! It's Bill!" An anxious heart pounded in Janice's ear merging with the noise of the chain as it slipped off its track and the door opened inward. Carole stood on the threshold, her tense face white as a sheet.

"Upstairs," she cried faintly and hurried after Bill, who pushed past her through the archway into their small living room and up the short flight of stairs.

"Everything was fine," she panted frenziedly. "She had dinner . . . went to bed on time . . . then I heard these noises . . . I was in the kitchen . . . I went up . . . and . . . you'll see . . . it's . . . it's frightening . . . I mean . . . she's sleepwalking or something . . . and crying . . . I tried to wake her up . . . but I couldn't. . . ."

The door to the spare bedroom was partially ajar. Bill waited before entering, listening to the terrified little sounds emerging from the room: the scampering of bare feet on the carpeted floor; the light impact of a body crashing into objects; the soft, mouselike weeping of infantile anguish, desperately repeating the same pleading litany of strung-together words, "*Mommydaddymommydaddymommydaddymommyhothothothotmommydaddy* . . . ," they had heard on certain other nights more than seven years before.

As Janice quietly entered the room behind Bill, the bizarre, incredible memory of that distant time, sapped of reality for seven long years, sprang back to sudden and pulsating life.

Totally oblivious of their presence, Ivy's eyes shone wildly; her feverish face was swept with a thousand nighttime terrors as she fled about the small, cluttered room this way and that in random disorder, knocking into furniture, chairs, sewing machine, desk, climbing over the larger pieces in order to gain some unknown, desperately sought objective. As before, the tiny, babylike, fretting sounds, "*Mommydaddymommydaddyhothothotmommydaddy* . . . ," underscored her tortured necessity to succeed.

Each time she'd get by an obstacle and seem to approach the door or window—her hands flailing, groping, reaching toward the glass— she would draw back suddenly in pain and plunge back into the helter-skelter circle of confusion, weeping, crying, mewling her plaintive lament, "*Mommydaddymommydaddyhothothothotmommydaddymommydaddy*. . . ."

Janice's hand grasped Bill's tightly as they stood rooted, just inside the room, helplessly watching the macabre spectacle, knowing, from past experience, how ineffective they both were during these crises.

"Ivy, it's Daddy," Bill pleaded, stretching out his arms to embrace her as she passed him, her eyes blazing lights projecting out of a feverish face, as she drew away from him and fled to a far corner of the room.

"Call Dr. Kaplan, Janice," he whispered huskily.

"*Wait!*"

The voice was Elliot Hoover's, speaking from the doorway directly behind them. Janice turned and saw him looking intently at Ivy, rushing about the room at a quickened pace, totally driven by the acute urgency of her nightmare. Hoover's eyes were fixed on the tormented child, critically observing every movement and gesture she made, listening to the rasping, thoroughly exhausted voice repeating, "*Mommydaddymommydaddyhothothotmommydaddymommydaddy*. . . ."

Janice felt Bill's hand stiffen in hers as he, too, turned and planted a stern, warning look on the interloper.

But Hoover ignored them both, his eyes and mind wholly devoted to their daughter, trying to define the meaning of the terrible hallucination in which she was caught. And then a look of inexpressible sadness swept across his face; his eyes grew large and haunted as he uttered, "My God," in a barely audible breath.

He quickly stepped past them into the room and worked his way closer to Ivy, who was reeling about dizzily, near the window, her hands seeking the glass, reaching for it, gropingly, each time pulling back in pain and fear, as if it were molten lava.

"*Audrey!*" The word burst out of Hoover like a shot: sharp, clipped, imperative, holding promise, offering hope. "*Audrey Rose! It's Daddy.*" And he took another step toward the agonized child fretting at the window, waving her thin arms at the glass despairingly, pleading with the demons without in the high-pitched, sorrowing voice of a child half her age, "*Mommydaddymommydaddyhothothothotmommydaddymommydaddy. . . .*"

"*Audrey Rose! I'm here, Audrey! Here!*"

Janice's knuckles turned white in Bill's hand as she watched Hoover take still another step toward Ivy, who gave no indication that she heard him or was aware of his presence.

"*Over here, Audrey! It's Daddy! I've come!*"

Bill's hand sought release from Janice's grip, and she knew he was about to move, about to seize Hoover and throw him out of the room. She saw the murderous intent in Bill's eyes and flashed him a look entreating patience.

"*Audrey! This way, darling! Audrey Rose! It's Daddy!*"

Suddenly, Ivy swung about from the window and turned her flushed, fear-ravaged face to Hoover, gazing up at him like a suppliant asking for mercy, the beseeching babble of words shifting to "*Daddydaddydaddydaddydaddydaddydaddydaddy. . . .*"

"*Yes, Audrey! It's Daddy! It's Daddy! This way, darling!*" he desperately urged in a breathless voice. "*This way, Audrey Rose! This way! Come!*" And taking a step backwards, he extended his hands to the startled child, offering direction, inviting trust. "*This way, darling! This way!*"

Slowly, the anguish and panic seemed to drain from their daughter's face; the rapid, feverish intensity of the words seemed to relax, to space out and become more defined, "*Daddy, daddy, daddy, daddy. . . .*"

"Yes, darling, this way," Hoover coaxed, bending down and extending his two arms fully to her. "Come, Audrey, come!"

"*Daddy . . . daddy?*" Her eyes remained fastened on a point just beyond the image of Hoover, squinting hard to penetrate the opaque veil of the all-engulfing nightmare.

"This way, Audrey Rose! COME!" His voice rose to a command. *"COME, AUDREY!"*

A prickle of fear coursed up Janice's spine as she saw the face of her own child begin to soften with recognition, begin to lose the ravaged and brutalized look of terror. Teardrops hanging on her eyelids—the great blue eyes which now shone so large and brilliant out of her white and worn face—she slowly extended her hands to Hoover, in a tentative, testing manner. *"Daddy?"*

"Yes, Audrey Rose! It's Daddy!" Hoover encouraged, in a subdued voice charged with emotion. *"Come, darling. . . ."*

"Daddy?" And with a smile that seemed to answer him, she scampered forward into his arms, clutching him in a deep embrace. And thus they remained, clinging to each other, like a pair of lovers finally meeting after a long and wearying journey.

Bill stook like a man in a trance, his shadow thrown vague and large upon the two of them by the hall light behind him. His face was pale; his eyes were wet and glistening; his mouth quivered with parted lips. His whole being seemed absorbed in the anxiety and tenderness at his feet.

"What the hell do you think you're doing?" he sputtered hoarsely, in a voice Janice hardly recognized. He stood, waiting for an answer, the lines in his face continuing to move, to speak, though his voice had stopped.

Elliot Hoover rose slowly, lifting Ivy up with him in his arms. When he turned to Bill and Janice, they saw that she was asleep, breathing normally, her lovely face now calm and composed in restful slumber. The man who had released her from her bondage took a step closer to Bill and gently conveyed the precious burden into its rightful arms.

"It was the accident," Hoover said starkly. "There was a fire . . . the windows were closed . . . she couldn't get them open, and there was no way of getting her out of the car . . . I was told that it lasted for some minutes. . . ."

A strange stillness seemed to close all around them. The very air seemed hushed and solemnized.

A cough behind Janice made her aware that Carole had been witness to the entire drama. She had forgotten about Carole, had forgotten about Russ, still upstairs in their bedroom.

"I'll be leaving now," Hoover said, a look of profound concern in his eyes. "There's a great deal I must think about. You were both very kind to see me. Good night."

With a token smile, he excused his way past them and left the room. Janice could hear his footsteps fade away through the lower regions of the apartment and finally disappear. Bill heard nothing. His entire attention was caught up in the subdued and peaceful cadence of Ivy's even breathing, as she slept, satisfied and calm, in his arms.

Russ was still in their bedroom, breaking down the sound equipment and packing it, when Bill carried Ivy past their door to her room.

"Everything okay?" Russ asked Janice, who had paused at the open door.

"I think Carole needs you," she said wanly.

"Oh, yeah? What's up?"

"There was some trouble with Ivy— She'll tell you."

Russ nodded and picked up his recorder. "I'll go right down."

At the door he turned to Janice with a parting shot. "By the way"—he grinned, placing the reel of tape down on the bureau—"this guy's bananas!"

"I'm sorry, Janice, I just don't buy it."

"Okay."

"I mean it, I don't buy it."

"Okay." Her voice was soft, bereft of passion, past caring any longer what he bought or didn't buy.

The darkness of the room seemed darker than Janice ever remembered it. Each lay awake, their bodies separated, hands disconnected, dwelling on their own private islands of despair.

"Suggestive hypnosis? Isn't that what Dr. Vassar called it?"

"I don't remember," she said.

"Well, that's what it was. It worked for her, it's worked for him. Suggestive hypnosis."

"You mean he's a psychiatrist?"

"Or a hypnotist."

Janice suddenly felt sorry for Bill. He had been through a bitter, emasculating experience and was desperately trying to regain some semblance of mastery over the situation.

"You don't believe it's possible?" he asked.

"That he's a hypnotist? No."

"All right, then, what *do* you believe?"

He was forcing her to think.

"All right," she said quietly. "I do not think he's a hypnotist. I do not think he's a nut. I do not believe in reincarnation. I believe that Elliot Hoover is a dedicated, persuasive man with a single purpose in his life. For some reason, he wants our child. With all his sweet, poetic, religious talk, he's got a fire burning inside him that won't let him quit till he gets what he wants." She heard her voice quiver and felt tears sting at her eyes. "So you'd better stop him . . . before he destroys us all. . . ."

Janice turned her head into the pillow and let it all come out. Bill was there at once, holding her, caressing her body, kissing the tears from her face.

"It's a hell of a thing, isn't it?" he whispered huskily. "But don't worry, he's not about to get what he wants . . . I promise you that!"

His hand moved to her breast, kneading its soft and pliant goodness, finger tracing the corona of her nipple, feeling the gravel begin to ripple and rise along with his own passion. Her sobs were stifled by the depth of his lingering kisses. They made love. Afterward they both slept.

Janice awoke abruptly at three ten, having heard a sound from Ivy's room. But when she looked in, Ivy was sleeping peacefully in the arms of her stuffed panda. Janice felt her head. It was hot. If the pattern of seven years ago persisted, her fever would grow by morning.

She tiptoed from the room and returned to bed. Neither she nor Bill slept the rest of the night.

9

Even after a long shower and a lingering shave, Bill looked haggard and spent, and he spoke in a voice that was gritty with weariness. He told Janice about the trip to Hawaii as he stood in the kitchen doorway sipping coffee.

"Goody for you," Janice replied. The flippancy of her remark failed to camouflage fear and accusation.

"I'm planning to take you and Ivy with me."

"Really? How will we manage that, rent a hospital plane?"

"She's not that sick, Janice."

"She will be. Give her time."

"Maybe Dr. Kaplan can give her something."

"For God's sake, Bill," Janice said, with a sort of wild fatigue, "you know what course these things take! By afternoon she'll be burning with fever . . . and there's not a damn thing Kaplan will be able to do about it beyond aspirin and bed rest."

Bill drew a deep breath and said, "Well, we'll see," then told her about Jack Belaver's heart attack, why he couldn't turn down the assignment, and how it would be pure hell going without them. But Janice scarcely heard him through the noise of the water tap whipping up a froth of suds on the breakfast dishes, forcing him to raise his voice in competition.

"I don't know why you're acting like this—"

Janice turned off the water and looked at him with quiet intentness. "You *really* don't?"

His answer was to stride purposefully away from her into the living room and pick up the telephone. She heard him dial a number, then say in a voice loud enough for her to hear, "Extension 7281." A pause. "Don Goetz, please, this is Mr. Templeton." Another pause. "Hi, guy. Listen, Don, I pulled something in my back and gotta go to the bone man. Cover for me today, will you? . . . Yeah? What else is cooking? . . . Well, you can handle that. . . . Get hold of Charlie Wing if you get into trouble. . . . And, oh, Don, tell that girl of mine to get me three good seats on tomorrow's flight to Hawaii. . . . Yes, three. Janice and Ivy are going with me. . . . And Don, tell her to make it the last flight of the day that gets there before midnight." A chuckle. "Pel said Thursday, and Thursday, it'll be. . . ."

Bill didn't return to the kitchen. Janice heard him go upstairs, where he spent several minutes before presenting himself at the kitchen door, dressed for the street and carrying Russ' tape recorder.

"You really believe she'll be well enough to travel?" Janice said with gloomy skepticism.

"I'm not ready to predict anything, Janice. If she's okay, your tickets are there; if not, I'll cancel them." His voice shifted to a more lethal register. "One thing I will predict, though, it's the end of the line for Mr. Hoover—we won't be bothered by *him* again." He held up the tape recorder for emphasis. "If you need me, I'll be with Harold Yates."

He left without kissing her.

Janice puttered in the kitchen another ten minutes, then fixed Ivy a large glass of orange juice and carried it upstairs.

Ivy was sitting up in bed, alert and active, cutting figures out of an old *Vogue* with Janice's sewing scissors. Except for a slight headache, she was gay, buoyant, talkative, and, as in the past, seemed to have no memory whatever of her nightmare.

"I'm making a family," she said with a lovely smile as Janice reached out and felt her head. It seemed a bit cooler. Perhaps Bill was right after all. Perhaps they would be able to make the trip.

Thoughts of the warm, clear, multicolored waters, the soft rain showers with their incredible rainbows, the balmy, sensuous nights beneath an impossibly yellow moon gradually quieted Janice's restless spirit.

Ivy had to tell her, "The doorbell's ringing."

Janice descended the steps with a racing heart. The mail had been delivered earlier. No one came to the front door without first being announced—unless it was Carole.

"Who is it?" Janice asked through the bolted door.

"It's Dominick, Miz Templeton," came the muffled reply. "I got a delivery."

It was a potted plant, a hothouse chrysanthemum with two large white blooms. The pot, a Mexican ceramic, was encircled by a red ribbon with a small envelope bearing the florist's name attached to it. Janice thanked Dominick and brought the plant into the kitchen. She paused a moment, gazing grimly at the gift, before opening the envelope and extracting the card.

Tiny, precise handwriting covered both sides of the stiff cardboard, forcing Janice to seek a patch of sunlight in order to read it. The message was in quotes, and said:

> Take the flowers. The blossom perishes as completely as if it had never existed; but the roots and bulb hold in subjective embrace the most minute details of that flower. When the cycle, the basic law, is fulfilled, the subjective entity thrills, expands, clothes itself again with the specimens of cells and reproduces the plant in all its former perfection and beauty. Thus do flowers reincarnate and express the same elemental soul of the plant. How much more reasonable is it that the intense individualization in man should also be conserved by subjective periods in his life history?
>
> And below it was the credit line: *"Esoteric Astrology,* by Alan Leo."

A shudder of superstition and fear went through Janice as she tore the card into small pieces and threw them into the trash can. Next, with a set face and trembling hand, she picked up the plant and all its green tissue and, holding it away from her body as if it were something loathsome, carried it out to the service hall incinerator and dropped it down the chute. It was the only thing to do, she thought, sensing a sudden power and mastery over her destiny, a perfectly normal, healthy reaction to a foe's sneak attack.

The house telephone was ringing as she reentered the apartment. She closed the service door and bolted it, before taking up the receiver.

"There's a Mr. Hoover on the line, Miz Templeton," came Dominick's high-pitched voice. Janice felt a leap of panic and was about to refuse the call when she abruptly changed her mind. She had acted resolutely and correctly with the flowers; what then had she to fear from the man who had sent them? He was enemy, and enemy must be dealt with.

"Connect him, please," she said as her quivering hand went to her head and brushed a wisp of hair away.

"Hello, Mrs. Templeton?" Hoover's voice bore a distinct note of anxiety.

"Yes," replied Janice tremulously.

"Good morning, thank you for talking to me. I just called to find out how your daughter is."

"*Ivy* is much better," answered Janice very gravely.

"But not well enough for school. You're very wise to keep her home."

The statement required no answer, and Janice made none.

Hoover picked up the slack with: "I wonder if you'd mind my dropping in? I think we have a great deal to talk about."

"You'll have to ask my husband about that."

"Would you put him on, please?"

"He isn't here."

"Oh?" Hoover seemed surprised. "His office said he was home ill."

"He's gone to see the doctor."

"I hope it's not serious." Then, shifting mood: "By the way, have you had a chance to look at the books I sent you?"

"No. I haven't the time for books. Besides, I'm not interested in the subject."

"Oh?" said Hoover quietly. "I thought, after what happened last night, you might want to know more about . . . the subject."

"You're wrong, Mr. Hoover." Janice was finding a new strength in her voice. "Nothing happened last night to increase my interest in your books."

"I don't believe that, Mrs. Templeton. I saw the look on your face when"—he paused, seeking the right words to express his next thought —"when Audrey Rose sensed my presence nearby and made contact with me through Ivy. You had the look of a person who had just witnessed a miracle, as it surely was. Your husband was too overwrought to perceive it, but you certainly did."

"The look you saw on my face, Mr. Hoover, was the look of a mother in despair over the health of her child. It is a look I often wear, as my daughter often experiences these attacks."

"She does?" Hoover said, as if stung.

"Yes, Mr. Hoover, several times a month over the last nine years," Janice lied. "What happened last night was not unique, nor was what you did to calm her. Her psychiatrist uses a similar technique to bring her out of these trances. It's called suggestive hypnosis."

"I didn't know Ivy was under the care of a psychiatrist," Hoover replied, as if berating himself for having failed to discover this fact in his research on them.

"Well, she is. And the cause of her problem has been fully defined and is well known. It relates directly to an accident she had when she was an infant—a milk bottle that was too hot burned her fingers and made a lasting impression on her mind. The 'hot, hot, hot' she babbles refers to the milk bottle and nothing else." Janice could hardly believe the words were her own.

"Your psychiatrist approves of this theory?"

"Yes, she does."

"I think she's wrong," said Hoover in a voice deflated of energy. "I think your daughter may be in far greater trouble."

"You may think that, Mr. Hoover, but we do not. We believe in our doctor, have confidence in her training and experience, and trust her completely. Furthermore," Janice continued, socking it home to him, "we believe in medical science, not in superstition."

Hoover was silent a moment, then spoke in a tone that was quietly respectful, and even sympathetic.

"Do you have a religion, Mrs. Templeton?"

"No, I don't believe in religion."

"Were you always an atheist?"

"Yes, always. And I'd really appreciate it if you'd stop sending me your religious books, your flowers, your sayings, or anything else regarding your beliefs, as I have absolutely no interest in the subject, nor do I have the time to continue this conversation, so good-bye, Mr. Hoover. . . ."

Janice quickly lowered the receiver onto its cradle without giving him a chance to say another word. She was trembling with the fevered excitement of an athlete who has just won a race, her heart fluttering, but her soul uplifted by success. A drink, she thought, would be marvelous. She had never drunk liquor this early in the morning, but this was a morning like no others.

Sipping the neat scotch, seated in the rocker, vaguely hearing the television upstairs, Janice wondered why she had lied to Elliot Hoover about the history of Ivy's nightmares. It was fear. He was seeking a wedge into her mind. He was the enemy. One doesn't share truths with the enemy.

Actually, the nightmares had struck only once before—beginning one night soon after Ivy's second birthday and persisting for nearly a year.

Dr. Ellen Vassar, whom Bill promptly nicknamed Brünnhilde, had swooped down into their lives like an avenging angel, her strong, heavily accented voice and razor-sharp Freudian mind probing, questioning, analyzing, and finally succeeding in casting the demons out of Ivy's dreams.

Janice recalled the strong, humorless face of the German psychiatrist at their last session and her parting words to them.

"Your child was expressing some special fears of separation from you, Mrs. Templeton, and she appears now to have mastered those fears, which children do as they grow older. However, do not treat her as though she were in any way special and fragile. Simply treat her as any three-year-old. You should have no further trouble."

And now, seven years later, the demons were back, with a renewed and murderous fury. . . .

Janice felt a glacial chill rise within her and quickly swallowed some scotch to dispel it.

Suggestive hypnosis? That was Bill's theory. It had worked for Dr. Vassar. Why not for Elliot Hoover? Well, why not? His explanation was too self-serving and convenient to be believed.

She was less certain of why she had lied to Hoover about her religion.

Born a Catholic, she had gone through all the rituals of that somber faith and had actually enjoyed being frightened by the nun's talk of death and resurrection when she was a child. The church, St. Andrew's, was hewn out of ancient and silent stone, covered with fungus and stained with bird droppings. Entering its massive, silent mustiness was like walking into Dracula's castle. Yet she had truly believed in all the lovely, improbable promises of heaven, the sick, terrifying threats of hell.

She had stopped believing even before high school. She went to mass each Sunday to please her parents, as a matter of rote. The Latin words and rites had been reduced to a meaningless jumble by then. In her third year of high school she left the Church. Her parents never said a word. They were pained by her decision, but they never said a word. In the back of her mind, Janice feared a terrible retribution for her sin of inconstancy. She knew that when the time for death came, she would wish to have the last blessed sacrament read over her and receive extreme unction.

Maybe *this* was God's retribution, she thought—the empty glass dangling from her fingers—sent down to her in the form of Elliot Suggins Hoover.

Harold Yates lay stretched across the Barca-Lounger like a reclining Buddha. His damp features were screwed up in a curiously bemused smile as the tape came to an end.

"Boy, when you bump into 'em, you sure bump into 'em." He chuckled softly.

"He's gotta be a kook, right?"

"I don't know, Bill. That's hard for me to say. He seems to know what he's talking about. I mean, he certainly puts his case forth in a logical manner. He's not a ranting hysteric. He's a calm, reasonable person who seems to believe what he's saying."

"What the hell are *you* saying, Harry?" Bill's voice was unsteady. "You telling me I've got to honor this guy's demands?"

Harry held up the flat of his palm in Bill's face.

"Whoa, Bessie! Back up! I said nothing about honoring his demands. I said you can't stop him from believing what he wants to believe in. When it comes to honoring his demands, you certainly cannot give in to him, for then you will have taken another member into your family. So regardless of what he wants, you must take steps initially to protect yourself and your family, and the law will help you in doing this."

"Okay, give! What steps?"

"Well, initially you might adopt a less vigorous attack. You might tell him, next time he calls, that whatever he believes, thinks, or feels about your daughter sheltering the spirit or soul of his daughter, you do not subscribe to his thinking, you don't feel that you can permit him visitation privileges, nor can you allow him to interfere with the normal course of your family life. And then you tell him, if he's going to persist, that you'll take legal steps to restrain him from bothering you."

Bill thought about this, a look of uncertainty on his face.

"Is there some special way, some special legal language I should use to tell him these things?"

"If you want, I could write you a letter," obliged Harry. "You could send it to him, registered mail, or even have it hand-delivered, return receipt requested, telling him to cease and desist from doing this objectionable act and, if he does not stop, that you are authorized to seek whatever legal remedies are available. The effect of this letter is of no real legal significance, except it is evidence to the court, should you seek injunctive relief, that Hoover was advised that what he was doing constituted a nuisance and was objectionable to you and your family."

With a slight strain of tension in his face, Harry advanced the Barca-Lounger to the sitting position and depressed the button for his secretary. "It's the best way to proceed, Bill; we find ways to discourage him, ways short of hauling him into court or a police station. I mean, we try all kinds of peaceful ways before we bring down the majesty and the awesome force of the law."

The secretary, a tall woman in her early sixties, had silently entered, taken her chair, and, pencil poised over memo pad, was waiting.

The "majesty and awesome force of the law." The words had a fine, comforting ring to them, Bill thought with a tinge of emotion as he entered the elegant elevator and smiled his routine hello to Ernie.

Harry had written a strong, solid letter, couched in all those intricate, fearsome phrases that lawyers use to strike terror in the hearts of their opponents. They had sent it via special Red Arrow messenger to Hoover's YMCA address, to be delivered into his hand, and with signed receipt to be returned to Harry's office for safekeeping.

Having opened both locks with his two keys, Bill still had to ring, as Janice had kept the chain bolt on the door.

She seemed gayer, her mood lighter, as she took the tape recorder from his hand, placed it shakily down on the floor, then rose on her toes to kiss him, losing her balance in the process. Bill held her arms to steady her and chuckled, "Well, well, somebody's been juicing it up."

Janice grinned. "What the hell—"

It was just after three o'clock—a bit early in the day to be potted but, "What the hell," Bill agreed and went to the kitchen for ice.

Janice told him the good news as he knocked ice cubes into the martini shaker. Ivy's temperature was down to absolute normal, and Bill was an absolute genius for having predicted as much, at which point she started humming "Isle of Lovely Hula Hands" and doing sensuous things with her hips. Bill hummed along with her as they hulaed their way to the liquor cart in the living room, where Bill filled the shaker with gin and refreshed Janice's drink. Oddly, the crisp, cold jolt of pure alcohol had a sobering effect on Bill, and a moment of seriousness ensued as he told Janice about Harry's letter, trying to recall the specific words and phrases: "harassing, molesting, invading . . ." and "an ex parte order shall be issued . . ." and "the majesty and awesome force of the law. . . ."

"*He* called this morning and sent me a plant," Janice told him, spacing her words out with care to keep from slurring.

"Sent you what?"

"A plant—with a note saying that even flowers do it—reincarnate, that is."

"The bastard."

Janice's face screwed up in a sly and wicked smile. "I dumped it in the incin . . . erator," she said falteringly. "Pot, plant, flowers, poem, the works—"

Bill grinned and clinked his glass to hers. "That's my gal." They sipped their drinks and looked at each other approvingly. Then Bill asked, "He called, you said?"

"Yup. Right after the plant came—and *went*."

"What'd he want?"

"Wanted to come up, what do you think?"

"What'd you say?"

"Told him to . . . *bug off*, mister . . . go peddle yer karmers up the street!"

Bill burst out laughing. "You didn't?"

"Or words to that effect." Janice winked with pride and nodded her head. "He got the message all right."

Putting down his drink, Bill reached out, drew his brave, besotted wife into his arms and kissed her soundly.

The telephone rang.

Each felt the other flinch. They drew apart.

Bill took a deep breath, then picked up the receiver.

"Yes," he said, brusquely, then relaxed and offered the phone to Janice. "It's Carole, for you."

Janice's face fell; it would be a long and weary siege, but there was no way to refuse the call.

Bill picked up drink and shaker and went upstairs to visit Ivy, whom he found sitting on the floor, Indian-style, surrounded by elements of Clue. Her eyes shone with a healthy glow as she reached up, took his hand, and placed it against her cool face.

"One game, Daddy, please?" she begged, gazing up at him with her impossible-to-refuse smile. "Mom played terrible," Ivy complained. "I beat her without even trying."

Bill could well understand why.

By the time he had finished the last dividend in the shaker they had played two games, which they split, and were on the final lap of the third. The time was ten to five, and good odors were wafting up to them from the kitchen.

Bill wondered if Hoover had received the letter. There was a way to check that. He made two purposeful blunders, allowing Ivy to take the third game. Her victory whoops followed him into the bedroom, where he put in a call to Harold Yates.

"Letter delivered, signed receipt returned, currently stashed in my file case," Harold informed him with a deep rumble of satisfied laughter.

"Great," Bill said. "He hasn't tried to call me."

"Nor should he! He's on notice. From this point on, if he bothers you or your family in any way, we go to court and file for injunctive relief."

"Yeah," Bill said, then added, "We leave for Hawaii tomorrow, Harry. It's business, but I'm taking Janice and Ivy along."

"Excellent. Your timing couldn't be better. If you want my opinion, you've heard the last of Mr. Hoover, so relax and enjoy your trip. Call me when you get back."

They ate as a family, around the dining room table, at six fifteen. Janice had whipped up a Mexican gala out of cans and packages: a cold gazpacho, allowed to thaw to room temperature from its frozen state, small tamale pies, and bowls of spicy chili, with hot biscuits substituting for the missing tortillas, and topped off with lime sherbet and sesame cookies. Bill and Janice drank Cold Duck with their meal; Ivy drank milk.

Ivy went to bed at eight fifteen, kissing Janice five times and Bill ten, before drowsily snuggling up to Panda for the night. Janice remained with her until she was sound asleep, then went in search of aspirin. The hours of tippling had had their effect on her, producing a dull headache and a logy feeling of depression.

Entering the bedroom, Janice found Bill half packed, moving swiftly and expeditiously between drawers and suitcase, whistling softly as he worked. Janice sank wearily into a chair and gazed at her empty suitcase, unable to cope with the chore ahead of her. Bill flashed her a smile of encouragement, went to her bureau and opened the top drawer for her, prompting her into activity. Janice smiled wanly, struggled out of the chair, and had just taken her first limping step when the house telephone rang downstairs. The ring was normal, noncontinual, routine, yet for Janice in her debilitated state it had the effect of the bells of hell heralding the demon host.

She felt Bill's hand in hers, and saw the calm smile of assurance on his face, and heard him confidently say, "Pack," before hurrying out of the room and down the stairs to answer it.

"It's Mr. Hoover, Mr. Templeton." The voice belonged to Ralph, the night desk man.

Bill was hardly surprised, yet his heart was pounding.

"All right, put him on."

"He's here," corrected Ralph. "He wants to come up."

Christ, Bill thought, the prick has nerve.

"Tell him we're in bed, Ralph," Bill said harshly. "No, wait! Put him on the phone . . . I'll talk to him."

"Yes, sir."

Bill could hear Ralph mumbling directions to Hoover and could visualize the thin, wiry body making its way across the lobby to the alcove containing the house phones.

"Mr. Templeton?" The voice echoed desolately in the instrument. "May I come up and see you?"

"No," Bill said. "We've just gone to bed."

—*A sound from above reverberated on the ceiling . . . Janice must have dropped something. . . .*

"I got your letter—the one your lawyer sent. I'd like to discuss it. . . ."

"There's nothing to discuss, Mr. Hoover. The letter is self-explanatory and clearly states my position."

—*Footsteps running across the ceiling . . . a heavy door slam . . . what the hell was Janice doing?*

"I don't see why you felt the need to go to a lawyer. It's a matter we could have discussed between ourselves. . . ."

"Look, Mr. Hoover, I do not wish to have any further discussions with you on this or any other matter. The letter is intended to sever our relationship once and for all. Understood?"

—*Was that sobbing? Or laughter? It was hard to tell through the thick paneling and inset paintings. . . .*

"Please, Mr. Templeton, if you'll just let me speak to you, I think you'll agree that you need my help as much as I need yours—"

—*"Bill! For God's sake, Bill!" It was Janice! Shouting!*

"Listen, Hoover, if you don't hang up and leave the premises of this building forthwith, I will call the police!"

Bill slammed down the receiver and dashed around the archway into the living room.

—*Rat sounds . . . pattering across the ceiling . . . a chair falling . . . directly overhead . . . Ivy's room!*

Bill's feet took the steps two at a time to the upper landing, stopping short at Ivy's open door, almost stumbling over Janice sitting on the floor, sobbing, childlike, staring up at him with a hypnotized horror, shaking her head plaintively, choking out words: "S-she's . . . she's . . . looking for him. . . ."

"Stop it!" Bill shouted, seizing her by the arms and pulling her roughly to her feet.

"*Daddydaddydaddydaddydaddydaddydaddy*. . . ." the high-pitched clutter of words spilled out through the open door beside them.

"S-she's looking for her . . . daddy!" Janice sobbed with rising hysteria.

"Janice!" Bill shouted again, louder, and shook her hard. "*Stop it, Janice!*"

The sharpness of his voice was therapeutic. The sobs suddenly abated, became dry heaves in a face that was pale and filled with terror and confusion.

"Call Dr. Kaplan! I'll take care of Ivy! Go now, hurry!"

Janice faltered, glanced about like a person caught in the middle of her own nightmare. She started to move, then stopped as the squealing, beseeching "*Daddydaddydaddydaddydaddy* . . ." grew stronger and more demanding; the sound of furniture toppling and things spilling—books, dolls, games, balls—grew more pronounced.

"Go, Janice!" Bill commanded.

Janice looked at Bill with eyes that fought for composure; then, pulling herself together with obvious effort, she began to edge furtively away toward their bedroom, glancing rapidly back toward Ivy's room, as if fearing the sudden emergence of something monstrous.

Bill waited till Janice had entered their bedroom before turning to the lilting voice and the desperate sounds of his daughter's room.

"*Daddydaddydaddydaddydaddy*. . . ." The piercing staccato became more frenetic as the slight body jumped upon the bed and started kicking at the bedsheets which impeded forward momentum, finally forcing her to fling herself, headfirst, onto the floor to escape their tangling grip. Bill shuddered at the sound her forehead made as it connected solidly with the corner leg of the pink and white dresser. He charged forward to grasp her, to help her, to comfort her, but she deftly eluded his arms and, oblivious of injury or pain, continued her madcap roundelay uninterrupted. Her hair, newly washed and dried, was frizzed up in a bouffant halo around her face, making it seem smaller than normal and lending a note of insanity to the dainty, flushed features and bright saucer eyes roving constantly in search of "*Daddydaddydaddydaddydaddy*. . . ." Bill could see a red welt begin to appear on her forehead directly above her left eye. She had hurt herself terribly. A sudden rush of fear swept through Bill. He had to do something to stop her from disfiguring herself.

"Ivy!" he shouted, taking a step toward the child, now climbing over a chair that had toppled over. "Ivy! It's Daddy! I'm here, Ivy!" Consciously or unconsciously, his voice had taken on the same tone and timbre as Hoover's voice. *"Ivy! I'm here, Ivy! Here, darling!"*

Ivy seemed neither to see him nor to hear him, as she clambered to her feet and tripped across the room to the window and started to make grasping gestures at the glass, drawing quickly back from the cold pane whenever her flexing fingers got too close, her fierce and frightened voice reverting to its former plea of *"Daddydaddydaddymommymommymommyhothothothotdaddydaddydaddy. . . ."*

Bill took several steps closer to her and sank to his knees. *"Over here, Ivy! It's Daddy! This way, darling!"*

Suddenly, as if his words had got through to her, she spun about and stared at him with large, questioning eyes.

"Daddydaddy, daddy, daddy. . . ." The panic in her voice lessened; the pitch descended; the big eyes sought, searched, probed through some invisible density for a glimmer of light.

Bill was encouraged. He was making contact. She had calmed down noticeably. She seemed to be hearing, listening. He raised two arms to her and stretched out beckoning fingers and in a strong, hopeful voice offered her the sanctuary she seemed to be seeking.

"This way, Ivy! Come! It's Daddy! Come!"

Even as he spoke, the waxen pallor of her feverish cheeks increased until she looked like a corpse with living eyes.

"Ivy! THIS WAY, IVY! COME! IT'S DADDY!" His voice rose with fierce excitement. His fingers clutched at her nightgown.

At his touch, she drew back sharply as if struck and spun about toward the window, seeking escape, her voice rising in pitch and hysteria, *"Daddydaddydaddydaddydaddydaddy . . . ,"* her two hands slamming against the frosted glass in desperation and panic, then pulling away with a terrible scream of pain, *"HothothothothothothothotHOTHOTHOTHOTHOT!"* over and over, holding up her hands before her tearful, anguished eyes, studying the burned and blistering flesh.

Seeing the awful redness of his child's hands deepen and a blister begin to form on the middle finger of her left hand, Bill feared he would collapse and faint. This wasn't possible, wasn't reasonable. The glass was cold, frosted over. . . . Somehow he managed to raise himself to his feet and stood like an automaton, hovering helplessly above the weeping form of his darling child, who was rocking back and forth on her knees, softly crooning, *"Daddy, daddy, daddy, hothothothot . . . ,"* licking the scorched fingers of her hands, the high, melodious whimpers and sobs commingling with the sharp hiss of the radiator directly behind her.

The radiator!

Bill's eyes widened with suppressed excitement as the simple, factual, logical culprit stood before him, beneath the window, its scalding cast-iron panels releasing jets of steam through a nozzle designed to relieve the awful pressure of its boiling interior.

"Oh, God—her hands!" Janice's stark voice came from the doorway, causing Bill to jump and spin about. She stood in the doorway, backlit by the hall light, staring down at Ivy, rocking pitifully back and forth in a paroxysm of sobs and lamentations, *"Daddydaddydaddyhothothothot . . . ,"* licking and sucking her burned fingers.

"What happened?" Janice gasped, taking a step into the room.

"The radiator—she fell against it and burned her fingers."

Janice began to sway unsteadily. Bill reached out and held her. "Have we got something in the house?"

"There's . . . there's some ointment in the kitchen cabinet."

"Stay with her. I'll get it." Bill gently forced Janice to sit on the edge of the bed and started to leave. At the door he turned.

"What about Kaplan?"

"He's coming. . . ." The voice was dull, lackluster.

Bill left the room, closing the door.

Expressionless, Janice could only sit and watch the moaning, weeping, rocking bundle of misery across the room, the pink tongue licking furiously at the welting fingers, the squealing voice intoning, *"Daddydaddydaddydaddy. . . ."*

Ivy! Dear God! It was Ivy! Her Ivy! Her baby! Alone, abandoned, hurting! Needing! Locked in the steel vault of her nightmare. Unable to get out. Struggling to survive—to stay alive till help came. Help? What help? What combination was there to open the door—to release her from her terrible bondage? For Ivy, there was none. No combination. *None. For Ivy, none. But!*

"Audrey! Audrey Rose! Come!"

The voice was soft, barely a whisper. Gentle. Humble. Begging.

". . . *daddydaddydaddydaddydaddyhothothothot. . . ."*

"Audrey Rose! I'm here, Audrey!"

Inviting. Entreating. Insisting.

". . . *hothothothotdaddydaddydaddydaddy. . . ."*

"AUDREY ROSE! COME!"

Strident. Compelling. Commanding.

"... *daddydaddydaddyhothothothotdaddydaddy*...."

But the door remained shut.

"I'll look in tomorrow; meanwhile, keep using the cold compresses to reduce the fever and keep her hands outside the covers. Those burns are nasty, and even the light pressure of a blanket might irritate them. Let her stay in your bed where you can keep an eye on her. The Nembutal suppository should make her sleep through the rest of the night. By the way, Bill, if I were you, I'd get in touch with that psychiatric clinic first thing in the morning. They helped her once, I recall."

Lying there, inert, folded into the trembling form of her child, Janice heard the doctor's words.

The quarter moon forced a wan path through the venetian blinds onto the flushed and quivering face lying on the pillow next to her. Caught in the twilight of her own sedated brain, Janice tried to penetrate beyond the flesh life of the lovely face, beyond the glazed, half-open eyes, the two windows, the pair of light and air holes, that must surely lead into the dungeon where the restless soul of Audrey Rose, bound as with a seven-fold chain, lay captive and alert.

10

"Dead?" It was not so much a question as a shocked reiteration.

"Yes, I'm sorry." The voice coming through the telephone belonged to Dr. Benjamin Schanzer, director of the Park East Psychiatric Clinic—a name totally unfamiliar to Bill. "Dr. Vassar passed away more than two years ago."

"Oh. . . ." Bill paused, redirected his thoughts. "My daughter was a patient of Dr. Vassar's . . . about seven years ago."

"I see."

Bill found himself groping. "She had a problem and . . . Dr. Vassar helped her. The problem seems to have returned."

"Let me see . . . that would be in 1967 . . . a bit before my time, I'm afraid."

"Yes, I believe a doctor . . . Wyman was director of the clinic then."

"Dr. Wyman is still a practicing member of the clinic. Why don't I put you through to his office?"

"Thank you."

"Not at all."

Bill was seated in his own office. It was just after nine o'clock, and the floor was still deserted. Abby wouldn't arrive until nine fifteen. Don usually dragged himself in around ten. Bill was the early bird this morning and with reason. There was a lot to do and fewer than five hours in which to do it; a lot of loose ends to tie up before takeoff time. That, plus another reason, one that he hated thinking about. For the first time in their marriage he had felt the overwhelming need to escape this morning. Immature, irrational, inconsiderate, cruel—the fact remained that he had to get away.

Ivy's tears had awakened him; normal tears, a natural reaction to the pain in her hands. As usual, she remembered nothing of the nightmare and was willing to accept Bill's explanation of the accident with only one question.

"If I burned them on the radiator, going to the bathroom, how come I didn't wake up?"

"Because we put ointment on quickly, and burns only hurt later on."

"Oh, yes," she remembered. "Like when I got sunburned on the beach last summer." Though terribly hurt and feverish, she still managed to bring a smile to her lips, a smile of acceptance, of a willingness to start the day off on a positive, hopeful note.

Janice, however, awakened into a vacuum.

Mute, unresponsive, unapproachable, she went through her morning chores as if she were a wind-up toy. Neither Ivy's complaints nor his own gentle probings seemed to get through to her.

"Sorry to have kept you so long." Dr. Schanzer's voice came back on the line. "It seems Dr. Wyman won't be coming in for the rest of the week. But Dr. Perez, who was interning here at the time, may have some memory of the case."

"Well, may I speak to Dr. Perez?"

"Hold on, please."

The first hint of apathy showed when he told Janice of his decision to scrub the trip to Hawaii—that he'd sooner quit than go without them. Her response was to make none. Then, when he asked if her silence signified that she wished him to go, she still said nothing, simply continued squeezing oranges. Finally, and with some heat, he asked her what the hell it was she wanted him to do? To which she replied, "I think you should go." The words were fine, but the spirit behind them left much to be desired. When he suggested they keep her and Ivy's tickets in abeyance, to be used the moment Ivy's temperature eased off, she said, "Okay." Again, the content of the reply was acceptable, but not the force and feeling behind it. When he asked her if she was afraid to be left alone, afraid that Hoover might annoy her or that Ivy might have a relapse, she said in the same bland, listless tone, "Why should I be afraid? The majesty of the law will protect me against Hoover, and Dr. Kaplan's suppositories will help me with Ivy."

It was at this point that he felt the need for some fresh air. He suggested they both meet with Dr. Vassar later in the morning and make immediate arrangements to get Ivy back into therapy, to which Janice replied, "If you wish." And that was it. The sum and substance of their morning dialogue—the totality of their exchange.

"Hello, this is Dr. Perez speaking; to whom do I speak?" The voice was thin; the accent South American.

"My name is William Templeton, Dr. Perez. Our daughter, Ivy, was a patient of Dr. Vassar's some years ago. . . ."

"Dr. Vassar died two years ago. . . ."

"Yes, I know, Doctor, but there are some questions I would like to ask you since I understand you were at the clinic during the time my daughter was being treated."

"Please ask. . . ."

"First, I'd like to know, do you still have Dr. Vassar's records pertaining to my daughter's case?"

Dr. Perez answered without hesitation, seemingly without thinking.

"Yes, we are a group practice at Park East, and all physicians' case records are kept in a master file room. That would include Dr. Vassar's case records as well."

"Might I have access to those records?"

"Yes, you must sign a request for them, and we will be happy to turn them over to any other physician."

"That's another thing I want to discuss, Dr. Perez. My daughter's problem has recurred, and we have no other physician at this time. Would it be possible for you to take on this case?"

"Yes, it is possible. One moment, please." There was a short pause during which Bill heard Perez breathing. "Mr. Templeton?"

"Yes, sir."

"I have here a space in my book on December 14, at one o'clock. . . ."

"No, Dr. Perez, perhaps I haven't made myself clear. My daughter is quite ill; she requires attention immediately. . . ."

"Then it would be impossible for me to take your daughter's case. Perhaps another doctor in the clinic might do it."

"Fine, fine. My wife and I would like to come to the clinic this morning and make some kind of arrangement. Whom do we see?"

"Dr. Schanzer would be the person to see."

Bill then called Janice and told her that Dr. Vassar had died, and she asked, "What from?"

"I don't know," Bill said peevishly. "I didn't think to ask. What the hell's the difference?"

"None, I suppose," was her reply. The apathy persisted, deep-grained and enduring.

"I made an appointment to see the head of the clinic at ten thirty. Do you think Carole would be willing to stay with Ivy?"

"I'll ask," she said.

"We can have lunch afterward. I don't have to check in at Kennedy till two fifteen."

"Fine."

The anteroom of the Park East Psychiatric Clinic had undergone a few minor alterations but essentially corroborated the image Bill had held in his memory for seven years. The wall of undraped windows exposed the same lovely knoll of park, although the trees then were as yet untouched by snow. The character of the paintings on the opposite wall had, however, made the transition from European Impressionism to American Modern, relying heavily on Nolan and Robert Indiana.

Five people were seated in the anteroom when Bill arrived at ten forty-five. Janice was not among them. He gave his name to the receptionist and was told to be seated. At eleven o'clock Janice had still not arrived. Bill was considering calling home when a young, pretty girl appeared at the far end of the room and addressed herself to the entire group.

"Mr. Templeton?"

Bill followed her down a corridor to a long, windowless room containing a large conference table with more than a dozen chairs ranged around it. A file folder had been placed on the table.

The girl smiled at him and said, "Dr. Schanzer's schedule is quite tight this morning. He hopes to be able to pop in from time to time to talk with you."

When the girl left the room, Bill took off his outer coat and placed it over the back of a chair. He loosened his tie somewhat, as the room was oppressively warm. His eyes gravitated to the legal-size manila folder with the word "Templeton" boldly printed in black ink on the tab. It seemed thinnish to Bill, considering the time Dr. Vassar had spent with them: those multiple in-depth family and individual sessions, held either in her office or at the apartment, some lasting as long as five hours, depending on the need and circumstances.

Bill stared at the folder and wondered what Dr. Vassar had discovered about them: what secrets that sharp, intuitive brain had managed to ferret out; what conclusions she had come to concerning Ivy's strange and terrible illness that she hadn't shared with them. He had only to open the folder and look.

His fingers extended to the manila cover and stopped. The German woman's wide, formal face and deep, penetrating eyes seemed to float above it.

Bill slowly drew back the cover.

The top sheet was a scrap of yellow, lined paper with strong handwritten notations. The writing had a foreign character about it; some of the letters such as the S's and L's were difficult to make out. She even wrote with an accent, Bill thought, as he slowly picked out the words.

Differentiation of disturbances of consciousness of epileptic origin from those of psychiatric origin is frequently very difficult—there is no prior history of epilepsy in this case—no temporal lobe disturbances indicated through physical examinations. . . ." And below it, the name "Cullinan, 555-7751."

Cullinan had been the doctor who had run electroencephalographic tests on Ivy just prior to her treatment at the clinic.

The next page was written on the back of a letter, a circular listing psychiatric pamphlets for sale. It seemed that Dr. Vassar made her notes on anything that came to hand.

"Hysterical phenomenology—???" was the question written across the top. And then a longer paragraph below:

> Patient shows symptoms of somnambulistic state. Parents describe movements as being in response to the manifest content of the dream. The meaning may be an escape from the temptations of the bed; however, this would be unusual in the case of a child not yet three. Yet possible—since parents report child possesses ability to portray images and carry out complex actions during dream state. . . .

And below it: "Will arrange to be present during next seizure."

Bill remembered the call he made to Dr. Vassar that night seven years before. It was two in the morning, and he wondered if he should disturb her, but she answered the phone on the first ring and said in a clear alert voice, "I will come." She arrived soon after and spent the entire night with Ivy, alone, behind a closed door. There were many such nights that followed in the next year.

Bill quickly skipped over two scraps of paper, each containing the brief notations "See Kretschmer" and "See Janet," and came to a small, thin notebook with a pebbled cover of imitation leather. It was a diary, an eyewitness account of her sessions with Ivy during the seizures, written in a fast, shaky hand, as though she had made the notations as the actions were happening. The first entry was dated 1/18/67, and read:

> Purposive action . . . trying to get out . . . touching things and pulling back as though they were hot . . . complicated

motor actions . . . strange . . . bizarre . . . most uncommon at this early age . . . at times during spell she seems to be shrinking back from things not visible to anyone else . . . tries to climb over the back of a chair—and succeeds! Appears well coordinated and shows a degree of muscular coordination and skill of an older child. (Test subject's ability to climb over chair during wakened state.) She tries to reach the windowpane, then pulls her hand back whenever she is about to touch it . . . then reaches for it again, in continuous dramatic posturing episodes . . . accompanied by weeping, fretting, trembling . . . babbling . . . "Hothothotdaddydaddy—" Seizure continued until five twenty at which time subject succumbed to exhaustion and fell into feverish sleep. Body temperature: 103.6 degrees.

Bill turned to the next entry, dated 1/25/67.

At first, subject seemed to be trying to get away from something . . . possible traumatic episode relating to incident of isolation . . . locked room? . . , but now movements seem to indicate less escape behavior, less trying to get away from something than trying to go toward something. . . . her motions grope toward things, not away from them. . . . approach behavior which is suddenly stopped by. . . . imagined thermal barrier . . . painful . . . hot . . . "Hothothothotdaddydaddydaddy . . ." babble may relate to traumatic event experienced in the past, yet early age seems to negate this possibility . . . possible event relating to prenatal trauma? Difficult birth? Discuss with obstetrician. Possible event relating to very early age . . . stove? . . . fire? . . . possibly hot sun? . . . beach? . . . somewhere in summer where surfaces were very hot? metal frame of perambulator? . . . accidentally touched? . . . doorknob in direct sunlight might have been too hot . . . (discuss with parents). . . .

The heat in the room was becoming unbearable. Bill stood up and removed his jacket. His shirt was stained with perspiration. He folded his dark suit jacket over the back of the adjoining chair and rolled up his shirt sleeves. Then he turned the page of the diary to the next entry.

2/20/67 . . . results of chair-climbing test during wakened state disclosed subject unable to climb over chair successfully without falling . . . but within dream state is able to climb over chair and appears to show much greater creative muscular skill and coordination than one would expect in a child of two and a half . . . particularly striking: although the child has the typical speech pattern of a two-and-a-half-year-old, with the somnambulistic state, she appears to be talking with the enunciation and speech patterns of a much older child, perhaps five or six years of age . . . "Hothothotdaddydaddydaddy . . ." display clear, precise enunciative dexterity even during rapid, staccato bursts. . . . (Test subject's speech competence during wakened state.)

The next page contained a brief note:

Dr. Osborne, attending obstetrician, disclaims any untoward or unusual event during fetal development or birth of subject. Perfectly normal in all respects. Air conditioning in nursery normal—no record of malfunction—no accident with heat—hot glass—surgical instrument.

Bill smiled as he recalled the joyous August morning of Ivy's birth. Janice had opted for the Read Method, without fear and without drugs. She had remained fully alert as Ivy slipped into the world at exactly 8:27.03, clocked in by Bill's stopwatch. She was born with her eyes open and seemed fully aware of her world and the people in it. Even unwashed, her awesome beauty was clearly evident. There had been no problem whatever.

Bill sighed and turned the page.

4/3/67 . . . results of speech-dexterity tests during wakened state disclosed subject unable to enunciate staccato word pattern with same degree of skill as within dream state . . . subject tends to slur words, loses "t" sound altogether in rapid word stream, "Hothothothot . . ." and has difficulty in coping with the "d" and "m" sounds in words "daddy" and "mommy" word streams. . . .

4/21/67 . . . the window seems to be her main goal—an unattainable goal, the glass pane presenting a barrier of prodigious heat . . . the fires of hell? . . . attempts to approach

> glass unsuccessful as heat too intense . . . stumbles back . . . falls . . . weeps . . . corneal and pupillary and deep tendon reflexes are present . . . patient does not bite her tongue or urinate . . . she becomes red in the face rather than blue or white . . . bodily temperature increases evident whenever approach behavior takes her to window. . . .

Bill rubbed his eyes a moment. Drops of sweat had flowed into them from his forehead. He took his handkerchief from his pocket and mopped his face. He then looked at his watch. It was only ten past eleven. He put it to his ear to see if it hadn't stopped. He felt certain he had been in the room longer than ten minutes. But the watch was ticking normally. He thought about calling Janice. There was a phone on a table at the end of the room. He decided to give her another ten minutes. He wondered if Hoover had tried to call the house. His eyes traveled down to the notebook, spread open before him, beckoning. He could think of no other matters to delay his turning the page.

> In summary, what we have here is a child who, at age two and a half, appears to have developed, much earlier than one usually sees it, a somnambulistic form of hysteria . . . she appears to be reenacting some earlier traumatic experience in which heat or fire is the motivating force . . . there are very peculiar circumstances which have come up during treatment —namely, that within somnambulistic state, both language and motor activity show a degree of maturity greater than what the child shows normally, which is a most striking and unusual thing. . . .

The next page read:

> Treatment: somnambulism is a manifestation of hysteria . . . hypnotherapy indicated, yet not possible because of early age of child . . . suggestive therapy applied with some positive results . . . strong authoritative suggestions during dream state—strong insistence and pressure to give up the symptom— found some response indicating child is a very susceptible somnambulist . . . hence, using the suggestibility of the child in order to command the traumatic experiences to go away, positive results were achieved over a period of forty-one sessions of varying durations. . . .

The next page of the notebook was blank. Bill riffled through the rest of the pages, expecting to find nothing more and was surprised to see another entry on the last page.

> We are dealing here with something of which limited knowledge and information preclude full diagnostic evaluation. Jung's concept of archetypes . . . possible relation to behavior here . . . possibly child is reenacting an experience which is not her own, but is in her mind, without having happened to her, lends some credence to possible Jungian interpretation . . . may be event not expressing child's own experience, but something from the collective unconscious??? . . .

Bill turned over the black-pebbled cover and closed the notebook. The perspiration on his neck had turned to an icy chill. He sat still, emptying his mind of all thought, for thought at this moment was an enemy, challenging reason, encouraging doubt. He could almost see the German woman's face grinning at him.

The door pushed inward. Dr. Schanzer's secretary held it open for Janice.

"Your wife is here, Mr. Templeton," the secretary said cheerfully, and quickly left.

"Come join the fun," he said, pulling out the chair next to his. Janice looked very pretty, he thought: cool, fresh, and wearing an outfit he didn't remember seeing before. She had obviously taken pains to please him, which was a good omen.

"Better take off your jacket," he warned. "This place is a steam bath."

"I'm okay," she said, sitting down beside him.

"How's Ivy?"

"Much better. Her temperature is down to one hundred. Dr. Kaplan stopped by and changed her bandages. He doesn't think the burns will leave a scar."

"Thank God," Bill said strongly, then asked, "Carole with her?"

Janice nodded. "They were watching Let's Make a Deal when I left."

"Anyone call this morning?"

"No," Janice said, knowing to whom he referred.

Bill sat down and tossed her the folder. "Dig in," he said.

"Anything interesting?" Janice opened the folder and started reading the first scrap of yellow paper.

"A lot we already know; a lot I don't understand."

Bill rose, put on his jacket, and excused himself to get a drink of water. Walking down the long corridor, looking for a water fountain, he almost collided with a young, swarthy man emerging from a brightly lit office on the right and wondered if this might be Dr. Perez. He found a men's room hidden inside a small alcove and went in. The water felt cold and bracing against his face as he bent his head down into his cupped hands and even drank some of it. He gave Janice enough time to finish reading before returning to the conference room.

Dr. Schanzer was with Janice when he arrived, the folder clutched in his hand possessively. Janice looked decidedly paler than when he had left her.

"Forgive me for keeping you waiting, Mr. Templeton." Dr. Schanzer's dark-brown eyes twinkled at him. He was a stocky white-haired man with powerful arms and chest. "I was telling Mrs. Templeton here that Dr. Noonis, one of our associates, might find a slot for your daughter later this week. He has five thirty on Friday afternoon open; if that's convenient, we could set up an appointment for a family interview."

"I don't know," Bill hedged. "We were planning a trip. . . ."

"My daughter and I will be here, Doctor," Janice interposed. "Friday will be fine." The statement was uttered in the same dull monotone he had heard that morning: impassive, indifferent, apathetic.

"Fine," Dr. Schanzer intoned. "Then I'll make the appointment for you." He rose to leave.

"Doctor—" Bill's voice stopped him. "Can you tell me what archetypes are?"

Bill noticed Janice's quick, grave look through the corner of his eye. The doctor shut the door and formed a small smile on his face. He seemed almost amused by the question.

"Jungian archetypes. The word is a contrivance of Dr. Jung's. It refers to what he called the collective unconscious. In his work with schizophrenics, he was struck by the frequent appearance of images which were remarkably similar for patients of widely varied backgrounds. The evidence suggested to him that the mind of man as well as his body bears traces of his racial past, that his longings, expectations, and terrors are rooted in the prehistory over and above his experiences as an individual."

"Do people in your profession subscribe to this theory?"

Dr. Schanzer chuckled. "Let me say, Mr. Templeton, that people in my profession attempt to keep an open mind at all times. Dr. Jung was a brilliant man, but something of a maverick—a lot of his theories are pretty explosive, yet there is merit in a great many of them."

"Do you believe that people can remember things that they didn't personally live through?"

The smile on Dr. Schanzer's face lessened somewhat.

"I, for one, do not believe in a racial unconscious, Mr. Templeton, or in memories inherited from the collective prehistory of an individual's background."

"Thank you," Bill said.

"Ten days without the two of you—it's gonna be pure hell, you know that."

They were back in Rattazzi's, sitting, Janice thought, at the very same table. It was a few minutes before one o'clock, and the room was filled with people and noise. Everyone seemed to be shouting, Bill included.

"I mean," he continued, a touch too sorrowfully, "you don't even leave the hope that you might join me in a day or so."

His face was flushed; his eyes were beginning to glaze. The straight gin was having a decided effect on him. Janice had resolved to stay sober. Since she would be alone now with Ivy and an uncertain future lay before them, a clear head was essential.

"I don't believe there is a hope that we can," Janice answered quietly. "Considering what's been happening to us lately, do you?"

"I think you're taking this whole business too seriously."

Janice looked at him, unbelieving.

"What amazes me is that you don't."

"Okay, I left myself wide open for that one. Let me rephrase. The health and happiness of my family are of prime concern to me. Your depression, Ivy's problem, I take very seriously. I am trying to do something about them." His sentences were spaced out and slightly tipsy. "To you, I can only offer love, understanding, and extreme patience. To Ivy, I offer the additional benefit of expert medical help, which she will receive. The business I do not take seriously is all the business with Hoover and archetypes, and all the crazy mumbo jumbo that's been going on in our lives, lately. . . ."

"For God's sake, Bill—" Janice exploded. "You honestly think that what's been happening to Ivy is nothing more than a simple illness like . . . like the flu? And what you read in Dr. Vassar's book—you don't see a connection to Hoover—you consider her opinions and conclusions all a pack of mumbo jumbo?"

The waiter brought Bill's martini.

"Do it again," he mumbled and, picking up the fresh drink, quaffed half of it in one gulp. He focused bleary eyes across at Janice and continued in a low, husky voice.

"I don't think that a D-r in front of a person's name necessarily makes them infallible. You know, there are a lot of dumb doctors in the world—"

"Oh, wow! You really believe that?"

"Yeah. And since you bring it up, let me tell you a little more about what I really believe. I'm a firm believer in things as they are. Not what they seem to be, but what they are. Dig? I may not like some of those things, but I know damn well I can't change them, and I sure as hell ain't gonna try. . . ." He raised the glass and finished the drink down to the olive. "I believe that up is up and down is down. I believe that if I stood on this table and dived off headfirst, I'd probably break my neck. There'd be no guardian angel around to cushion my fall. I'd be taken either to a hospital or to the morgue. If I died, I would either be cremated or planted in the ground, and it would be the end of me. No harps, no wings, no pitchforks, no nothin'. Finis!" He paused to allow the message to sink in. "I do *not* believe that I would ever find myself floating around some maternity ward, waiting to sneak into the body of some unsuspecting infant as he came popping out. I'm sure he would resent it, and I know I would be horrified. . . ."

Janice suddenly found herself laughing, in spite of herself.

"No, don't laugh!" he cautioned, raising his voice. "I'm not kidding, and I'm not finished!"

The laughter departed Janice's face as she saw the look of intense sincerity in his red-rimmed eyes.

"I believe that *hot* is *hot* and *cold* is *cold!*" He picked up a book of matches from the table and struck one. "I believe that if I hold my finger to this flame, it will burn and cause a blister!" His finger approached the flame and remained there.

"Bill, don't!" Janice put out her hand to stop him.

Bill blew out the match and held his reddening finger up to her.

"See it getting red," he said with absolute seriousness. "It will form a blister—as it should!"

He picked up the glass of ice water with his other hand.

"Now, if I place my finger against this frosted glass of ice, it will cool it, for ice does not burn! And no power on earth can make this ice burn my finger!" The words were spilling out of him, compulsively, and he was shouting, attracting the stares and side glances of people around them.

"Ice doesn't burn! No matter how long I hold my finger to the glass, it will not burn or form a blister!"

It slowly came to Janice that what she was hearing was not a man's drunken ramblings, but the anguished cry of a man whose sense of reality had been sorely tested and who was fighting to hold onto the last shred of sense and reason left to him.

"Fire burns! Ice cools!" he continued, loudly. "Now if that isn't a law of Copernicus or Galileo, let's just call it the law of fucking Templeton! Accepted? Fire burns! Ice cools! And never the twain shall produce the same effect! Accepted?"

The room had quieted noticeably. People were looking directly at them. Tommy appeared with Bill's drink and genially asked if they cared to order.

"Sure," Bill said, "what the hell—"

But the force and energy were gone from his voice. The earthquake had subsided. He ordered for them both, mechanically, Janice nodding in agreement to his first suggestion.

Watching Bill raise the drink unsteadily to his lips, seeking to allay his turmoil and confusion in its numbing effect, a gust of pity and dread swept through Janice. The frosted glass had been the giveaway. Ice is cold. Fire burns. The cold and frosted window had burned Ivy's hands, not the radiator. He had seen, with his own eyes, the groping, seeking hands press against the pane of frosted glass, then pull away, reddened and scorched. "Fire burns! Ice cools!" The hot, fiery radiator had been the logical culprit, not the cold, Jack-Frosted pane of glass directly above it. To a mind as well ordered and rooted in reality as his, this could be the only possible, the only acceptable explanation.

Oh, Bill, Bill! Janice's heart reached out to him. Sweet, confused, beset darling! Her eyes, moist with tears, gazed across the table at the dear face, lowered over the plate of food, scooping forkfuls into his mouth, chewing, tasting, or perhaps not tasting.

Toying aimlessly with her own food, Janice felt a further pang of hopelessness. While she had resented Bill's purposive obtuseness, his unwillingness to buy all the "mumbo jumbo," she had found a certain comfort in it, too. Whatever the facts were, his rigid, doubting-Thomas attitude had lent a certain balance to their lives, had brought a note of sanity to their world suddenly gone mad. It would be missing now, this leveling force, this good, solid, healthy skepticism. From now on, there would be two of them to corroborate insanity, to galvanize the atmosphere of fear and tension in their home.

Outside on the street, Bill and Janice waited for a cab. The day had turned gray again, and the air had a smell of rain in it. Bill waved his arm toward cabs as they proceeded sluggishly down the street, but the gesture was useless; the cabs were either filled or unwilling to stop. Still, he continued to wave at them, while Janice insisted that she really preferred to walk home. The food had sobered Bill somewhat, and his face held a slightly guilty, sheepish expression as he bent down to her and kissed her lips. Holding her tightly, he softly apologized for his behavior and told her that he would phone her at nine in the morning, her time. Tears stung at Janice's eyes as she clung to him, loving him, wanting to comfort him, wanting to tell him that she knew of his terrors and confusions, and not knowing quite how to say it.

He gave her a slip of paper with his itinerary typed on it: the times of arrival in LA and Honolulu, the name of the hotel where he was registered, and several phone numbers at which he could be reached. It also contained Harold Yates' office and home phone numbers in the event she might need him. He begged her to call him in Honolulu at any time and for any reason.

"And if things work out," he added, "get in touch with my secretary, and she'll have your tickets validated in less than an hour."

Janice nodded and told him to put a Band-Aid on his finger, which had formed a small blister. They kissed again and whispered, "I love you," to each other, standing in front of Rattazzi's; then Bill left her and started to walk toward Madison Avenue. The tears in her eyes blurred her vision as she stood watching his tall form mingle and merge and finally get lost in the crowd.

A sharp gust of wind swept up the narrow side street, chilling Janice to the bone. She drew her coat collar tightly around her throat and walked briskly toward Fifth Avenue. Her thoughts remained with Bill, gently reiterating the image of his kind and generous face, smitten now by shock and bewilderment, challenging the evidence of his eyes, defending his reason, struggling to survive.

The heavy-laden clouds were reluctant to commit themselves as Janice walked up Fifth to the corner of Fifty-first Street and waited with an army of people for the light to change.

Looming above her, across the street, stood St. Patrick's Cathedral—its Gothic lines plunging upward, springing like a fountain at the leaden clouds. The weird transplant from the Middle Ages, nestled incongruously in the midst of Manhattan's steel, glass, and pollution, seemed to Janice less an anachronism than a monstrous joke that the Catholic Church had played on the city.

Walking past its complex gray stonework and carved metal portals—several of which were open and draped with purple velvet bunting—Janice had the sensation of walking past a colossal genie, squatting imperiously with his fly open, inviting the world to enter and partake of his magic and miracles.

Groups of tourists were entering the church through the open doors at the southern end; at the same time other tourists were emerging from the doors at the northern end, maintaining a constant equilibrium within the church. Janice walked up the steps and merged with the stream of people going through the doors at the southern end.

Entering the nave, she sensed a stillness that absorbed the hollow sounds of shuffling, pushing, whispering humanity as it sluggishly circled around the cavernous hall. Just inside the doorway was a marble font of holy water, the basin stained with greenish rings of sediment denoting various water levels throughout the years of its use. The couple in front of Janice, an elderly man and woman, dipped their fingers into the water and crossed themselves. Janice walked by it without partaking of its solace.

There in the semidarkness Janice was moved counterclockwise down the side aisle along with a group of tourists craning their necks toward the various points of interest. To her left was the central apse of the cathedral, ringed by lines of stained glass windows caught in the upward drive of buttressed walls that seemed to rise to the very heavens. The main altar and sanctuary dominated the center of the cathedral, with long rows of pews falling back from it. Except for several prayerful people occupying the pews, there was no service in progress at this hour.

To the right of the side aisle were a series of lesser chapels, each devoted to a particular saint. In the chapel of St. Joseph was an open coffin, draped in purple, with the body of some church dignitary lying in state and solitude. Janice saw the tip of the corpse's nose peeking out of the coffin and was momentarily mesmerized. The people behind her gently, insistently pushed her onward.

Soon Janice found herself alongside another small chapel. A few candles burned at the altar, shedding a gloomy light on the carved inscription in the marble balustrade: SAINT ANDREW. Janice's face grew warm, her eyes and mouth hot. She stepped out of the path of those moving along behind her and took a step into the chapel.

At first, in the dim light, she thought she was alone. But when her eyes adjusted, she realized that a man was standing in a far corner, his head bowed in meditation.

Janice stepped up to the altar. She felt her hands shaking as they reached out to the cold marble railing. She wondered what it would be like, kneeling again, after so many years. Slowly, she descended to the platform, feeling a shock of pain as her knees pressed into the hard surface. A wave of guilt swept over her for feeling pain. It was a sign of her apostasy.

St. Andrew looked down at her with forgiveness, but Janice wasn't deceived. The face was made of plaster; the forgiving eyes were formed by an artist's hands. God's face, she was certain, would not be so forbearing and understanding. Thinking of God brought the face of Father Breslin to her mind. He had been the monsignor of St. Andrew's parochial school, which she attended as a child. His stern, wrinkled, flushed face had been the terror of the classrooms. His commanding voice, booming down a hallway after some hapless child, was like a preview of God's wrath. Janice shivered in remembrance and turned her attention back to the face of St. Andrew. She recalled how the nuns' expressions would soften when they spoke of him, telling the students of his humility and modesty and lack of pretensions as he roamed across the lands preaching the Gospel of Jesus. And how, when he was sentenced to death in Achaea, he insisted on being crucified on an X-shaped cross so as not to duplicate the passion and death of Our Blessed Saviour. How easily they spoke of death, the sisters, and how easily the children had accepted it.

She reached out for a taper, but her hand shook so, she could hardly gain a light from a burning candle. When she did manage to light the taper, she found it impossible to bring it to the wick of the new candle. It remained in her hand, trembling before her eyes transfixed by the bright and leaping flame.

Ice cools; fire burns, she thought, as she watched the sputtering fire travel down the length of the taper toward her waiting fingers. It would cause a blister to form. And well it should. *For fire burns.*

A hand covered her own—strong, yet gentle. A voice said, lightly and with humor, "You certainly have an *ardent* devotion to St. Andrew."

The trembling of the flame was stilled as the hand—a man's hand, the wrist encircled by a white French cuff held together with black button links—swiftly and surely guided the flaming taper to a new candle and lit it. A breath blew out the taper.

Janice felt herself trembling anew as the hand disengaged itself from hers. Staring at the floor and the black wing-tipped shoes, glowing under ages of wax, her eyes moved up the black worsted trousers shining at the knees, to the breviary held under the same arm as the straw hat, and up to the face. Like Father Breslin's, it was wrinkled and flushed, but not stern, and the voice was not booming or frightening.

"St. Andrew is my namesake." He smiled. "I never visit New York without stopping in and having a chat with him."

Janice could only stare at the elderly priest, into the helpful face that seemed to be offering. He had taken her hand. Suddenly, he had taken her hand. It had been as if God's hand had closed over hers. A flood of faith rose up in her. Was this man sent to her? The sisters had always said that God never forgot His own. . . . Was it possible? It was no less possible than all the other mysteries that surrounded her life in recent weeks.

Janice felt the wet of tears on her face and saw a disturbed look enter the priest's eyes.

Smiling, she stammered, "I went to St. Andrew's Church when I was a child."

"And where was that?"

"Portland."

"You're a long way from Portland." He noticed that her hands were still trembling uncontrollably, and Janice saw that he noticed.

"Is there any way of getting back?" he asked gently.

The next thing she knew, she was weeping like a child into her hands. The priest seemed disquieted and looked around nervously to see if they were being observed. He removed his neatly ironed handkerchief from his pocket and offered it to her, but Janice quickly took her own from her purse and tried to smile.

"I'm sorry, Father," she apologized.

The old priest paused as he considered, then asked, "May I be of service to you?"

Janice attempted to rise, but her knees were frozen. The priest saw her dilemma and took her arm. Needle-sharp pricks of pain coursed through her legs as she tried to stand on them, and she swayed uncertainly. The priest continued to support her and slowly guided her toward a bench in the corner of the chapel.

"Shall we sit down?"

Janice allowed herself to be seated, grateful for the positive act of assistance he was offering, yet knowing that any possible conversation with the priest was unthinkable.

"Father, I don't know if I have any right to be asking for help. I've been away from the Church for a long time, and I'm not a practicing

Catholic—I"—her mind sought the correct words—"I haven't been to the sacraments for many years. . . ."

"How long?"

"Fifteen . . . sixteen years. . . ."

The priest was pained. "And why are you here now?"

"I'm in trouble."

His eyes softened. "Isn't that the way of it? Trouble always brings us to our knees."

"I don't know *how* to tell you. I don't even know how to say these things to myself, Father." She thought of Hoover and the difficulty he had in saying them. "It seems so ludicrous when you put it into words. . . ." She paused and shook her head. "But then . . . I see what it's doing to us . . . my daughter, my husband . . . turning us around in all kinds of circles. . . ." Her eyes sought the priest's eyes. "Father, may I ask you?"

"*What* is it?" There was a strained, fearful note in the old man's voice.

"I know our faith doesn't believe . . . in reincarnation . . . and yet things have happened that cause me to wonder if it may not be so."

The priest measured her closely. It was the last thing he had expected to hear.

"What things?"

"My daughter . . ." Janice started, then stopped, and replotted the direction of her thoughts. "A man"—she began again—"has come into our lives. He . . . he has told us—my husband and me—that our daughter is . . . the reincarnation of his daughter who has been dead for many years."

The old man shut his eyes and lowered his head, as in prayer. After a moment, he softly asked, "Is your husband a Catholic?"

"No, Father."

"Your daughter, was she baptized?"

"No, Father."

"How old is she?"

"Just over ten."

He looked up at her through eyes that were incredulous—that had seen so much, yet apparently knew so little, and attempted to penetrate the mask of tears, seeking insight into the mind and soul of the strange, tormented woman before him.

"And you believe what this man has told you to be true?"

"Things . . . strange things have happened that convince me that it may be true, Father."

Again, the priest shut his eyes and placed his hand over them, feeling bewildered, under pressure to give earnest attention to a matter that struck him as entirely absurd.

"You must know the texts. The Gospels do not substantiate such a belief. We don't hold with such beliefs. We believe in endings, and beginnings, and middles. A life doesn't travel around in circles. There's a movement, there's a drive to our life, there are goals . . . we're going *somewhere!*"

Janice wept. "I know, Father, and yet this has come into our lives . . . and I'm troubled. . . ."

The priest looked at her suddenly with eyes that had hardened.

"You're so troubled," he said sternly. "Do you think you would be in this trouble if you had held onto what you were given? To what God gave you? Christ promised from the very beginning that His spirit would be with the Church. And the Church has reacted wisely for two thousand years—the only human institution to have withstood time and spaces and revolutions—and has given us something solid to hold onto."

"I'm all mixed up, Father."

"Because you've been listening to the world. You're floating here, you're floating there, you must stop listening to all these alien forces; you've got to get hold of yourself, get back to basics, get back to what God has given you . . . you have to get back to home." The priest's face had reddened, and his hands were shaking. "You must get meaning into your life, a point!"

"Until this man came, there was a point to my life, Father." Janice sobbed into her handkerchief.

"You can't entertain these alien thoughts . . . they're evil thoughts. . . . Our Lord said, 'If your eye scandalizes you, cut it out.' So this man has come into your life, he is evil! You mustn't pay attention to him! You must cut him out of your life! He is a danger to you—"

"It's my daughter, Father . . . she is the one in danger . . . she has these terrible dreams, dreams that punish her . . . and he is the only one who seems able to relieve her."

The priest raised a halting hand to her tearful face.

"You must return to the institution that Christ dwells in. It will help you ward off the powers of error, to withstand lies and deceits and all the snares of the evil one."

He gazed at the woman sitting next to him, weeping bitterly, and his voice softened. "As a girl you were told to avoid the near occasions of sin, and you have let this man and his force invade you. You must turn your back on him; you must give yourself to the truth, the one Holy Catholic Faith."

The priest rose, concluding the interview.

"I would suggest you go to your parish priest and make a confession and throw yourself on God's mercy. Open your hand to Christ."

He reached down to the bench and picked up his breviary and straw hat, but did not leave. He seemed unable to escape the strange and disagreeable situation and remained gazing down at the weeping young woman, who could only nod her head in agreement to his parting advice. He tried to put it from him, to simply walk away from it, but could not. A feeling of profound failure seized him. What did he know of the matters she had brought up, the problem she had laid at his feet? Reincarnation? A never-ending cycle of lives? It was childish, if not wicked. And yet how implicitly *he* believed in the miracles recorded in the Bible, how carefully he regulated his life by their messages. The old priest suddenly felt very confused and . . . useless.

"My dear woman, let me bless you," he said with heartfelt compassion, gently pressing the palms of his hands against the sides of Janice's wet face. "May Almighty God bless you," he intoned, drawing the sign of the cross in front of her eyes, "in the name of the Father, and of the Son, and of the Holy Spirit, amen."

Janice didn't watch him leave. She stayed there alone, in the shadow of St. Andrew, waiting for her anguish to abate and her mind to compose itself before quietly rising and joining the stream of tourists circling the cathedral.

At ten minutes past three Janice left the protective sanctuary of the church and stumbled through the portals back into the bleak and alien world without.

11

THE long walk home from St. Patrick's Cathedral in a driving rain was a revivifying tonic for Janice. The sharp spears of rain striking her face had a cleansing, therapeutic magic to them, and Janice held up her head to receive them. They were reality: cold, stinging, painful, shocking her into a full and sudden awareness of herself and the world around her—the real, present, only world there was in her particular speck of eternity.

Drenched, she arrived at the corner of Sixty-seventh Street and stood a moment gazing up at the massive stone and glass façade of Des Artistes, glistening wetly in the faltering autumn light. Bill's fortress, she thought with a grim smile. Their bulwark of defense against the enemy without had been useless against the enemy within. Somehow, in planning the building, the artists had failed to provide against intruders from the spirit world. Garlic and wolfbane should have been mixed into the mortar.

She found Carole and Ivy playing checkers on the living-room floor. Ivy's cheek felt cool against her own. Carole remained to finish the game, then picked up her needlepoint and went to the door, flashing Janice a high sign to accompany her.

"He insists on seeing you tonight," Carole whispered in a kind of delight. "He said he knows that Bill is away, but that you and he gotta talk for Ivy's sake." Her face twisted into a funny fright mask. "Gee, hon," she tremoloed, "why don't you call the cops? Like Russ says, this guy's bananas."

Janice smiled wanly and said, "I may do just that if he keeps it up."

"If you need help, give a yell. We're having dinner with Russ' brother, but we'll be home by eleven."

"Thanks, Carole, for everything," Janice said, meaning it, but glad to see her friend leave.

Janice had failed to shop for food and had to scrounge together a supper for them out of odds and ends. She found a half-filled box of spaghetti in the cupboard and prepared it with butter and Parmesan cheese. They ate it with gusto at the dining-room table, along with canned Bartlett pears and glasses of milk. Afterward they watched television until eight thirty, then went upstairs.

While Ivy sat up in bed, reading her newest Nancy Drew mystery, Janice went about *preparing* the room.

"What's that for?" Ivy asked, referring to the large four-panel screen Janice had brought in from her own bedroom.

"It's for the window; there's an icy draft coming through the edges of the panes. We'll have to have them resealed."

"I don't feel it."

"It's there," Janice said, spreading the screen to its fullest extension and raising it above the radiator. For some minutes, the sheer bulk resisted all efforts to force it behind the radiator, causing Janice to swear softly and Ivy laughingly to admonish, "Watch your language, Mother; there are children present." But the screen finally found its way past the various pipes, and now a Chinese red and gold motif totally obscured the window.

"Hey, that looks nice," Ivy said, surprised. "Can we keep it there?"

"We'll see," Janice said, as she packed layers of blankets around the offending radiator. "I don't want a repeat of what happened last night," she explained, moving about the room, tidying up, but mainly pushing the bulkier pieces of furniture off into corners, out of harm's way, and setting the stage for possible action.

At ten minutes past nine, after tucking Ivy in with Panda and kissing them both, Janice turned off the light and left the bedroom, closing the door behind her. She then walked into her own bedroom, opened her little phone book to the letter K, and placed it facedown next to the telephone. Her mind briefly reviewed all she had done, and only after having assured herself that she had forgotten nothing did she allow her head to seek the softness of her pillow. She would rest. Not sleep, she hoped. She would remain dressed, and keep the light on, and just rest, as she waited.

A sound woke her. She keened her ears, listening. She heard the rain, very softly, against the window. And even softer at first, the faint patter of feet—mincing, tiny steps, and the terrible twittering voice: "*Daddydaddydaddyhothothothot—*" rising, fading, then rising again, louder: "*Hothothothot!*"

Janice shook the sleep from her eyes and looked at the clock. Ten five. She had dozed off after all.

The voice suddenly rose to a shriek, became chambered, "*HOTHOTHOTHOTHOT!*" reverberating, grating across the corridor into Janice's ears. She covered them with her hands and heard the rush of blood and the pounding of her own heart. The telephone!

—*Fists pounding, beating at—something!*

Her hands shaking, Janice turned over the directory and sought "KAPLAN." Her fingers had trouble staying in the holes as she dialed.

—*Scratching, ripping sounds—tearing at—what?*

"Dr. Kaplan's service, hold on, please—"

"Damn!"

Seconds passed, then a minute.

"HOTHOTHOTHOTHOT!" *The screaming shook the house.*

"Dr. Kaplan's service, thank you for waiting—"

"Dr. Kaplan, please!"

"Is it serious?"

"Yes!"

—*Pounding, tearing, beating—*

"Name?"

"Janice Templeton."

"Phone number?"

"555-1461."

"The doctor will call you shortly."

"Hurry, please, it's an emergency!"

—*Scraping, bruising, scratching, shouting—*

Janice dropped the receiver on the cradle and pushed herself off the bed and made her way to the door. . . .

"HOTHOTHOTHOTHOT!" echoing, rebounding, filling the hallway with madness and terror, lashing out at Janice with shattering impact, rushing to meet her as she stumbled past the staircase and across the corridor to the bedroom door still closed as she had left it. She paused, panic growing in her, then pushed it open and stared into the sound-consumed darkness.

"HOTHOTHOTHOTHOT" blasted into her face, pitifully sobbing out the words in choked, agonized, throat-rasping bursts!

Vague outlines appeared in the darkness as Janice's terrified eyes sought to adjust. The specter was at the window, flailing white sleeves and bandaged hands digging, scratching at the Chinese screen, prodded, impelled by the continual, unabating "HOTHOTHOT!"

"Oh, God—the screen!" Janice heard herself gasp and, reaching for the light switch, illuminated the room.

Her hands jerked up to her eyes. "No! Oh, God!" she said, nearly voiceless, her eyes blurring with dizziness. "Oh, dear Mary, Mother of God, No!" she cried, feeling a deep nausea rising within her.

For at the window stood her child, screaming, beating, tearing at the Chinese screen, ripping at the varnished and painted canvas with the nails of her hands, now bandageless and exposed, the scorched and blistered fingers bleeding from her superhuman efforts to tear through the barrier and reveal the thing she both craved and hated, desired and feared—*the window*, her symbol of hope and despair, of horror and salvation, the fires of hell, the doorway to heaven—*her unattainable goal.*

"*Ivy—dear Mary!*" Janice tried to say the names—to link them together in a cry of desperate appeal to the powers above, to seek the intercession of the Mother of Jesus in this her moment of severest agony—but her voice wouldn't work, refused to obey her brain's command, and all that emerged was a soft and abject sob.

"Help me," she cried to herself. "Dearest Mary, help me to help my child!"

Her hands clenched and unclenched, the nails of her fingers biting deeply into the flesh of her palms, as she struggled to keep from fainting.

"Dearest Mary, Mother of God," she whispered chokingly.

The telephone rang, barely audible beneath the sounds of hysteria surrounding her. She felt something that was dying inside herself flicker back to life, energize her numbed, inert body into action. Finding her legs, she turned and stumbled out of the room and headed for the telephone in her bedroom, where the bellowing screams followed her with increasing intensity.

"Has the doctor reached you, Mrs. Templeton?" the woman's voice asked.

"What? No!" Janice snapped back.

"Well, he's en route from the hospital and will call you the moment he gets home—"

"*HOTHOTHOTHOTHOT!*" The screaming voice suddenly grew stronger, and the patter of naked feet emerged into the hallway, running—

Janice froze. *The door! She had left the bedroom door open!*

There was a flicker of silence—a heartbeat's suspension of all sound—followed by the awful noise of the small body tumbling down the staircase, descending to the floor below with a scream that coincided with Janice's scream as she dropped the phone and plunged headlong into the hallway and up to the railing. Her hands clutched the fanciful balustrade to steady her weak and trembling body.

The child had landed in a light, crumpled ball of flesh and flannel and was just getting to her feet as Janice forced herself to peer over the railing. Miraculously, the fall seemed not to have injured her seriously, for she was up in a flash, scampering and twittering about the living room, reviving the same plaintive diatribe: *"Hothothothotdaddydaddydaddyhothothot—"* Driven by the same desperate need to escape the torments of the all-consuming flames that still burned hot and bright in the foreground of her unconscious, she rushed toward the long bank of windows overlooking the rain-soaked city and began making her fearful, fretting obeisances at them.

"Daddydaddydaddydaddydaddydaddyhothothothot!"

Janice descended the stairs, clinging to the railing, feeling her way down with her hands, unable to tear her eyes away from the frightening apparition below.

Ivy was now standing before the near window, in profile, whimpering in terror, her bleeding hands making undulating, praying-mantis motions toward the dreaded glass, seeking, yet repelled by its proximity. Descending closer to her, Janice could see that she had not escaped from her fall entirely unharmed. The left side of her face was badly bruised, and a thin line of blood trickled from her nose.

A sudden misstep. Janice fell down the remaining three steps, descending to the wooden floor and landing heavily on her hands and knees. The clatter and noise of the fall and the accompanying scream elicited no reaction whatever from the child, whose agonized and haunted eyes remained totally locked in the grip of her own terrible plight at the window. *"Daddydaddydaddyhothothothot!"*

Spears of pain shot up through Janice's legs, drawing sobs from her lips, yet she did not seek to rise from her knees.

—*It was correct that she be on her knees, for wasn't this the attitude of penance, of contrition and confession, and acts of reparation?*

Forcing her body upright, so that her full weight might be brought to sustain itself on the points of her sore and aching knees, Janice heard the words come tumbling out of her in a torrent of passion. Clear, bell-like, plucked intact from the forgotten halls of childhood, her voice spoke out to the God of her one and true faith.

"Oh, my God! I am heartily sorry for having offended thee, and I detest all my sins because I dread the loss of heaven and the pains of hell, but most of all because they offend thee, my God, Who art all-good and deserving of all my love. . . ."

"HOTHOTHOTHOTHOTHOT—!"

The child's voice rose to a shriek as she drew back from the window in horror and, spinning about, went stumbling across the room toward the far bank of windows, climbing desperately over chairs and other pieces of furniture as they got in her way.

The voice in Janice continued without interruption as she tracked across the room on raw and smarting knees in pursuit of her tormented daughter.

"... *Holy Mary, Mother of God, pray for us sinners, now and at the hour of our death. Amen!*"

"*Daddydaddydaddydaddyhothothot—*" She was on the sofa, seeking to stand on the soft and giving cushions, losing her balance, falling to the floor. . . .

"*Lord, have mercy on us.*
"*Christ, have mercy on us.*
"*Lord, have mercy on us.*
"*Christ, hear us.*
"*Christ, graciously hear us.*
"*God, the Father of Heaven, have mercy on us.*
"*God, the Son, Redeemer of the world, have mercy on us.*
"*God, the Holy Ghost. . . .*"

—*Rising; whimpering; climbing back on the sofa; standing; swaying; falling.* . . .

"*Holy Mary, pray for us.*
"*Holy Mother of God,*
"*Holy Virgin of virgins,*
"*Mother of Christ,*
"*Mother of divine grace,*
"*Mother most pure,*
"*Mother most chaste. . . .*"

—*Struggling to her feet; panting; weeping; climbing; falling; striking her head against the table edge; bleeding.* . . .

The telephone rang.

The voice in Janice stopped. A wondrous look came into her eyes. *The doctor!*

She clambered to her feet and fell forward onto the sofa, as her legs gave way beneath her. She reached across to the phone and snatched it up. A hum. A long, steady hum. Still the phone kept ringing. It kept ringing distantly. Humming and ringing at the same time. With Janice poised at the fulcrum of both sounds. Her mind could not take it in, could make no sense of it.

The house phone! It was the house phone that was ringing! In all the hysteria she had forgotten to hang up the receiver upstairs, and the doctor was contacting her through the house line.

"DADDYDADDYDADDYHOTHOTHOTHOT!"

—Bruised; bleeding; climbing back onto the sofa; on her knees; swaying precariously to and fro in genuflection before the altar of her despair. . . .

Janice rose, pulled the cocktail table out of harm's way, and plowed across the living room and into the hall corridor, hands grasping at furniture and walls to keep her upright, and finally falling to her knees just within reach of the telephone. With a pained cry, she grabbed at the receiver and pulled it down upon her.

"Doctor!" she gasped.

Dominick's voice answered. "Miz Templeton, there's Mr. Hoover down here in the lobby."

Janice's tearstained face blanched, stiffened, then quieted. Her stark eyes became impassive, while the house around her shook with the cries and bleatings of her one and only child. She had asked for God's help, and He had answered.

"Miz Templeton?"

"Yes!" she said inaudibly.

"What'd you say, Miz Templeton?"

"*Yes, send him up!*" Janice cried, dropping the phone.

Holding onto the doorknob, Janice pulled herself painfully up to her feet. She felt dissociated from her body and swayed dizzily. She shut her eyes to steady herself for a moment, then directed her shaking hand to the chain bolt.

The elevator rose with a hum.

A panel of light and a clang of doors announced Hoover, dramatically spotlighting his exit, as he stepped out of the suspended vehicle and paused, hat in hand, staring down the long, dark hallway toward Janice. As the elevator descended behind him, plunging him into silhouette, he took a step forward and stopped again, testing the mood and temper of the enemy, probing the terrain for hidden pitfalls and booby traps before daring to advance further. Janice remained at the door, watching him, waiting for him to approach, but he didn't move.

Suddenly, the shrieking voice pummeled at Janice's back and spilled out into the hallway.

"DADDYDADDYDADDYDADDYDADDY!"

Hoover took a tentative step forward.

"*Hurry!*" Janice screamed at him.

Her senses absorbed the events of the next minutes in the abstract—fleeting images, some vague, some clear, with little continuity and no particular order of importance: the smell of wet wool as Hoover sped past her through the door; his stance as he paused on the threshold of the living room, recalling the circus lion tamer she had once seen as a child; her tripping over the telephone, still on the floor, as she hesitantly closed in on Hoover's back; her skinned knees leaving bloodstains on the hall carpet; Hoover's booming voice dominating her own sobs of pain and the screams of her child.

"*Audrey Rose! It's Daddy! Here, darling! I'm here!*"

"*Daddydaddydaddydaddy!*"

"*NO! HERE, AUDREY ROSE! DADDY IS HERE, DARLING!*"

A delirium of sound—mad patterns of movement—approaches, denials, entreaties, rejections—a lunatic kaleidoscope of sight and sound—leading finally and inevitably to the first startled suspension of disbelief—the bright look of recognition—the heart-stabbing smile of pure joy on the blood-smeared face—the quick scamper into waiting arms and the unifying embrace, bringing with it the sudden, blessed absence of sound—the descent of calm—sweet, languorous, settling peacefully on the torn air, mending the breaks, renewing silence.

Hoover remained kneeling, cradling the child in his arms, comforting her, quieting her with gentle strokes and soft whispers. Almost immediately, her wet eyelids began to flutter and close in sleep.

Janice stood, tightly clinging to the back of a chair to keep from falling, watching through tears, as Hoover rose with the sleeping child in his arms and slowly, so as not to waken her, carried her up the stairs and into her room.

Janice was scarcely aware of following them; her bruised and aching body seemed to move under some automatic compulsion. She only knew that somehow she had arrived at the bedroom door and was silently observing Hoover as he gently removed her child's pajamas and placed her naked and sleeping form on the bed. Then, moving rapidly between bedroom and both bathrooms, Hoover assembled his makeshift clinic of towels, Bactine, Solarcaine ointment, Band-Aids, a basin of warm, soapy water, and several washcloths.

He worked on Ivy's wounds with a sure and practiced touch, washed the encrusted blood from her face and hands, then sterilized and bandaged the cuts. He spread ointment on the raw and blistered fingers and wrapped them loosely in two towels. Janice's numbed brain took in each motion and gesture, accepting it all without question.

"Fresh pajamas!" He flung the words crisply over his shoulder. It was the first time he had addressed Janice that night.

She stumbled to the bureau and removed a flannel nightgown. As she turned to deliver it, she found Hoover standing behind her. His eyes probed the dazed, ravaged face with a look of great sadness, then glanced down her messy, torn dress to her blood-smeared legs. He sighed deeply and gently took the garment from her hands.

After easing Ivy's flushed body under the covers, he turned to Janice and, taking her arm, softly whispered, "Come, let me help *you* now."

The warm water felt soft and soothing against Janice's bruised, chafed skin as Hoover cleansed her knees and legs with the soapy washcloth. She sat where he had placed her on the edge of her bed and watched him as he knelt at her feet, deftly maneuvering the wet cloth around each cut, carefully avoiding direct contact with any open wounds. It vaguely occurred to her that she should be resisting these intimate ministrations, but at the moment she had neither the energy nor the mental capacity to do anything about it.

As Hoover worked on her legs, words tumbled out of him in quick whispers which, for a long time, Janice failed to hear. Her ears received his intonations as simply another sound in the room along with the clock and the water trickling into the basin each time he wrung out the washcloth. When her fractured brain did finally begin to absorb the content of his words, she discovered that he was lecturing her in the gently condescending tone of a teacher instructing a student.

"I know you don't take the responsibility of a child lightly. I see the guardrails on your windows. I've seen the way you hold Ivy's hand when you cross the street. But we're dealing here with something far greater than Ivy's physical welfare. We're dealing with something that's indestructible. Her soul. And that's what we must help and try to save —the soul of Audrey Rose which is in pain and torment. . . ."

His hands were manipulating her legs with the towel, drying the excess water with soothing, mopping motions.

"A pain and torment as real as the actual physical torment that took Audrey's body out of this life. Ivy is experiencing the same anguish that Audrey experienced in that terrible fire, and Audrey will continue to abuse Ivy's body until her soul is set free."

His words throbbed dully in Janice's head.

Dear God, what was he saying?

"She will keep pushing Ivy back to the source of the problem; she'll be trying to get back to that moment and will be leading Ivy into dangers as tormenting and destructive as the fire that took Audrey's life."

The softly uttered words oscillated in and out of Janice's blurred consciousness, chaotic, distorted, a medley of terrifying catchwords and phrases. Soul. Harmful. Ivy. *Danger.* Audrey Rose. What was he saying?

Shut it out!

"And now I can no longer just leave. It might have been simple once, when your husband so rightly asked, well, why if we're doing such a good job with the child, why don't you just go away and leave us to raise her? Fine! There was nothing I could say to that. He had the justice of man and God on his side. Why do you come here and upset our lives? Why do you come into my home and bring your turmoil with you? What can we do for you, man? We don't know how to help you! But! Look what happened! The very first night I entered your home...."

He was massaging her legs now with the baby oil in long, kneading, provocative strokes, replacing weariness with euphoria.

"That very first night, *there* was Audrey Rose! Wanting! Needing! Crying out for help! For *my* help! Saying, here, Daddy! I'm here. I need you, Daddy. And making her presence known to me."

The stroking action of his hands eased off somewhat.

"You lied, Mrs. Templeton. I know you lied. Your daughter didn't have these attacks all through her life as you told me. Isn't that true? She never had these nightmares before I came, did she?"

"Once before," Janice blurted huskily, "when she was two and a half. They lasted nearly a year."

Hoover looked stunned. "Two and a half?" He slowly rose to his feet, wiping his glistening hands on the towel. "That would have been in 1967—the very time I was here in New York City, doing a series of articles for the *Steelman's Quarterly—*"

He remained standing before Janice's wavering vision, his eyes pinpoints of intense concentration as his mind reviewed the awesome connection of the two events.

"My God," he whispered in a kind of benediction. "That far back?" He turned to Janice. "Even then she was pleading for my help!" And seizing her arms with a strength that astonished her, he raised her up to the level of his eyes. "Do you understand now, Mrs. Templeton? It's the cry of a soul in torment! Can you bear to hear it? I cannot!"

"Then get out of our lives!" Janice snapped back at him. "This only happens when you're near. Ivy has been fine and healthy all these years."

"No, you're wrong! Your daughter's health is an illusion. As long as her body shelters a soul that is unprepared to accept its Karmic responsibilities of earth life, there can be no health, not for the body of Ivy or the soul of Audrey Rose. Both are in peril!"

Janice shook her head, as though ridding herself of hearing him.

"I don't know what you're saying—"

"I'm saying that Audrey Rose came back too soon."

Too soon? Oh, dear God, what on earth was he talking about?

"After World War Two, many children came back too soon. Victims of bombings and concentration camps, bewildered, confused by their own untimely deaths, these souls rushed to get back into a womb, rather than the new astral plane they should have gone to."

He was a nut. Bill said he was a nut. Bill was right.

"And, like them, so did Audrey Rose move from horror back to horror, instead of remaining on a plane where she might have meditated and learned to put together her past lives before seeking a new one." There were tears in his eyes, and his voice was choked with emotion.

"She came back too soon, Mrs. Templeton, and because of it, Ivy is in great danger."

His eyes, moist and limpid, fixed themselves on Janice's drawn and frightened face. "Do you understand what I'm saying?"

"No," Janice shouted, staring at him in unblinking incredulity. "I don't know what you're talking about!"

"That's because you know so little, and there is so much you need to know. Because your fear keeps holding you at arm's distance from what you have seen and heard and know within you to be the truth."

"What truth?" Janice struggled to free herself from his grip, but Hoover's hands held fast to her arms. "My husband says that you're crazy! That you're a nut and belong in a nuthouse, and I think he's right!"

Hoover's grip relaxed somewhat. He gazed at her deeply, sadly.

"That's your fear talking, Mrs. Templeton."

"No, damn it, it's me talking!" Janice sobbed. "Now please go!"

For a fleeting instant, in the midst of Janice's sobs, Hoover seemed to lose his poise, but he held on and softly replied, "I've frightened you. I've been clumsy, and I'm sorry."

His hands continued to hold her arms, to support the sagging weight of her bruised and weary body.

"I know you love your daughter," he continued in a very gentle voice, "and are seeking what is best for her. Love tries, love is so desperate to help, but it must also question and take chances until no more cries are heard. How do you think a man like me, accustomed to a life of credit cards and soft mattresses, could spend seven years with cows and rice? Come on, Mrs. Templeton, I'm no nut. I didn't give up a fine career and a position in life for no reason. A story, an incredible story that two people told me, grabbed my heart and made my heart search.

That's God, Mrs. Templeton, that's love, when your heart moves faster than your fear."

His lips were inches from Janice's face; she could feel his breath on her cheeks.

"Will you open your heart and try to understand what I'm saying?"

"I don't know," Janice murmured uncertainly through softening tears. "I don't know what you want of me."

"I want your help and your trust. The soul of a child is crying, Mrs. Templeton. She is crying over a pain that occurred more than ten years ago, and she will keep suffering this pain unless we can help her."

Janice turned to him in woebegone confusion.

"Help her . . . soul?"

"Yes," Hoover said brightly, sensing contact. "We must form a bond to help her get through this ordeal. A bond that is so tight and so filled with all the love you have, and all the love that I have, that we can carefully mend her, patch her, get rid of the scar tissue, wipe it out so that Audrey Rose's soul may be put to rest once again. We are all part of this child, Mrs. Templeton. We have all had to do with the making of her, and only we can help her. You and I. Together. You will help Ivy. I will help Audrey Rose."

His voice held a hypnotic power, lulling, gently tugging at Janice's defenses.

"How?" she heard herself softly inquire. "How will you help her? You say she's trying to kill Ivy. How can you or anyone stop her?"

"I must try," Hoover asserted. "I must be with her, close to her, to pray and do good for her soul. Audrey was only five when she died. In her brief time on earth she was just coming to an awareness of the beauties of life." His voice cracked with emotion. "I must return her soul to that awareness of God's manifestations, the beauty and oneness of the earth life she knew and loved before the fire seared her soul with its destructive force."

Janice felt his hands tighten on her arms and herself being drawn closer to him. He was crying openly, without shame.

"Not for me and for the fact that I miss her, but to quiet her spirit, which is the right of every one of us. Please, please allow me to help her!"

Janice began to weep, holding her face away from him, avoiding the sting of his passion.

"Don't shut the door on me, Mrs. Templeton," he cried breathlessly. "Please allow me to come into your life. Allow me to serve you, and Ivy, and Audrey Rose." The tears overflowed his eyes and were coursing down his smooth cheeks. "This is why I'm here tonight. This has been the meaning of my journey. All those years of seeking and searching, of questioning and doubting have been a prelude to this one moment in time and space."

Pausing for emphasis, he drew Janice closer to him.

"Can you now just push me aside, Mrs. Templeton? Can you do this now? Reasonably?"

"No," Janice cried weakly, feeling the wet of her own tears on her face.

"Thank you." Hoover exhaled, grateful for her understanding. "Forgive me. I'm not an evil man. I'm not a saint. What I am is a man who now knows that God sent him on a journey of absolute necessity. And there must be no further talk of separation between us. For we are so connected. You. Your husband. Your child. Audrey Rose. And I. We have come together by a miracle and are now inseparable." He paused, for emphasis, then went on in a stronger, more urgent voice. "Say *yes*, Mrs. Templeton. *Please!*"

"Yes." Janice wept, feeling her breath commingling with his, as his hands continued to grip her tightly.

His face softened, and she thought he would kiss her, would not have found it extraordinary, nor would she have resisted, but he did not.

His hands relaxed and slowly withdrew.

Unsupported, Janice took hold of the bedstead as she felt she might fall. Her legs were like water.

Hoover's eyes remained fixed on her, but the tension had left them. He smiled in a kindly way and said, "Get some rest, now. I'll let myself out. We'll talk again in the morning."

At the door, he turned and again smiled. "Good night, Janice," he said, pronouncing her given name with all the confidence and assurance of a conqueror.

She heard his footsteps trailing off through the apartment, then the distant click of the front door closing. Still, she remained standing, listening to all the old familiar noises of night reassert themselves: the clock, a distant siren, a car horn, and, added to them, another sound—unexpected, intrusive, demanding.

Janice groped about the room, tracking the wildly buzzing sound to its source, and discovered the telephone, still off its hook, on the floor where it had fallen. Her head reeled as she bent down and replaced the phone on its cradle. The moment she did, it rang, causing her to jump.

"Mrs. Templeton—" It was Dr. Kaplan's voice. "I've been trying to reach you for the last hour, but your line's been disconnected."

"It's all right, Doctor," Janice stammered. "Everything's all right, now."

"Is the child all right?"

"Yes, Doctor, she's fine. She's sleeping quietly now."

"Good. Keep her on aspirin and plenty of liquids. I'll stop by tomorrow."

"Thank you, Doctor."

The rain, buoyed and driven by ocean winds, lashed against the long row of windows overlooking the night city. From where Janice sat in the rocker, the beads of water glistening in the foreground of a thousand lights appeared like diamond pendants tracing their mysterious paths down the glass panes. The tumbler of scotch in her hand was freshly filled from the half-empty bottle of J & B on the sewing table beside her. Liquor, fortunately, had an energizing effect on Janice, heightening her perceptions even as it dulled her senses and quieted her alarms.

The time was one ten. Two hours earlier Elliot Hoover had left, and now Janice sat in the nearly dark living room beneath the cavorting nudes, waiting for morning to come.

She had decided to consider five o'clock as heralding dawn, at which time she would awaken Ivy. She had ordered the VIP limousine for five thirty. The sharp chill in the room had forced her to slip into her fur-lined raincoat, so that now she sat in the rocker fully dressed, with two packed suitcases on the floor beside her, sipping scotch and waiting.

There had been a jungle of decisions to pick her way through, and Janice prided herself on having been able to thrust emotion aside and channel her thoughts down a fairly straight and practical path.

Her first move had been to the telephone, to call Bill and throw the whole thing at him. She had actually placed the call and was waiting to be connected to the Reef Hotel when she changed her mind and canceled it. Bill would simply tell them to come to Hawaii and might even convince her, but Janice knew that it was too late for Hawaii—too much had happened that night to be remedied by a Hawaiian tranquilizer.

It was then that Westport came into her mind, and the dreamy month they spent on the Sound the summer when Ivy was six years old. They had rented a cottage right on the water. Sound-Side Cottages, the colony was called. They'd probably be closed this time of year, but remembering that their cottage was equipped with a fireplace and wall heaters, Janice placed a call to the Stuarts, in Westport.

Mrs. Stuart, the owner's wife, answered after the fourteenth ring and was less angry at being disturbed than Janice expected she'd be. Although the cottages were indeed closed until late spring and there was some hesitation, arrangements were finally made with Mr. Stuart to let Janice have one of the cottages the following day, but only after twelve noon, since it would require a full airing and cleaning.

In less than an hour she had packed two bags with a week's worth of clothing for both of them, plus Ivy's schoolbooks, Clue, Scrabble, WordKing, and medicinals; checked the balance in her checkbook; and counted her cash, fifty-eight dollars and ninety cents—enough to pay for the VIP limousine and lunch in Westport. She'd decided to splurge on the cab ride to Westport in deference to Ivy's fever, which persisted even though she was sleeping soundly. She packed her electric blanket and would pack Ivy's when she awakened.

The idea was to vanish for a time without trace, clue, or scent. Janice needed time to think, away from the pressure and hysteria of Elliot Hoover. If, as he insisted, Ivy's life was in danger, and past history could be trusted, the danger was more acute with Hoover nearby than when he was far away. There had been no nightmares in his absence.

"We are so connected. You. Your husband. Your child. Audrey Rose. And I. We have come together by a miracle and are now inseparable."

He had invaded their home, planted his stake, and established his right to be there.

Janice shook her head dazedly and wondered which was the more incredible: that it could all be true, or that she was willing to accept it as being true? She was not a gullible person, had never been a believer in the occult or the supernatural. But this was different. She was directly involved, an eyewitness, a participant in Audrey Rose's little game of spiritual hide-and-seek.

She took a large swallow from her glass and thought how good if, in the end, Bill was right, and Elliot Hoover turned out to be just another crazy person shattered by his loss, unable to cope, employing magic as a means of compensating for the brutal blow that life had dealt him.

But deep inside, she knew differently. And Hoover knew that she knew.

". . . your fear keeps holding you at arm's distance from what . . . you know . . . to be the truth."

He was right.

Her fear had steadfastly veered her mind away from a direct confrontation with the logic of all she had seen and heard.

"... *you know so little, and there is so much you need to know....*"

Janice rose and, swaying unsteadily, minced her way to the hall closet, where, standing on a chair, she foraged about the dark corner of the upper shelf until she finally brought forth the book she sought.

Seated once again in the rocker, Janice pulled the floor lamp closer to her side, and gazed down at the large leather-bound diary in her lap.

Scuffed, worn, abused by time and the elements, it bulged with swollen pages and paper clips, fastidiously directing the reader's attention to the more cogent passages in the seven-year hegira of Elliot Hoover.

Flipping through the segmented pages, Janice immediately recognized the small, dainty script. The earlier portions were clearly written in black ink; the later pages, many of which were stained and discolored, in barely legible pencil. This, in itself, seemed to trace the route of Hoover's quest for the truth, from the comforts and niceties of Western civilization to the hardships encountered on his journey through India.

There were no datelines, printed or otherwise, and each page was crammed to the margins with a spillage of words, writing as he spoke, in staccato bursts of information.

The first page contained his name and the date, which was April 17, 1968. And, just below it, two words, hand-printed in large block lettering: "I START!"

And, turning the page, so did Janice.

12

I left my ticket upstairs. Had to find the landlady to unlock the door and bribe the cabdriver to wait. Already the whole thing is too hard to handle. . . .

Air India is terrific. We have a hostess named Suman and a pilot named O'Connor. Next to me is this elderly lady who keeps touching Suman's outfit. A sari in pink and purple. My companion's name is Mrs. Roth, and she said she's "in woolens." Suman doesn't seem to mind, so I told her I was "in woolens," too. . . .

I'm feeling a little weak. We've been in the air almost a day and that means a lot of martinis. Also double Lassi.

Suddenly, I'm scared, like I'm the new kid in school and they're not going to like me. . . .

Dumdum Airport. I think that's the whole reason I chose Calcutta to land in. Just to look at that sign.

Took a cab to the hotel where I'll rest before starting the railway tour in the morning. Indian State Railways. I'll travel light. A few changes—some shirts, ties, slacks, a pair of shorts —and my credit cards can take care of anything that might come up. At all times, I'll have my notebook, my $10.95 "Travel to India" fact book, and a book on reincarnation which, by the way, I cover with a brown paper bag.

It's hot, and I think I just saw a dead man lying on the street.

My hotel overlooks the Maidan. It's like Central Park.

I cross Chowringhi Road, which takes awhile to do. At the southern end of the park is the Victoria Memorial, very marble, with a statue of Queen Victoria herself. Leaning on the statue right now is a skinny Indian boy about seven, selling something in a little bag to a group of people watching a performance of the *Gita*. I'm surprised I recognize it. I remember something about . . . "between us, lies the difference . . ." you know, like, I remember about past lives, and you don't. . . .

I buy a bag from the boy and find it is grain. Am I supposed to eat it? I pass student meetings, prayer meetings, and I see dancing bears and a fortune-telling monkey. I give the monkey some grain, and I eat some, too. That monkey could have all my answers. . . .

The first paper clip in the diary secured a thin sheaf of pages representing days, weeks, months—of what adventures Janice was excluded from knowing—which led her eyes to a page bearing the printed caption "Benares."

I'm walking and many things are coming at me. First is the smell of jasmine, very sweet. Then the smell of smoke, and that's not so sweet. And the crowds—the crowds of people—wedding processions, crowds of cows, buffalo, and there are men with long Biblical beards who are nude except for loincloths, and pilgrims on foot, and streams of camels, and children yelling, laughing, squalling, and bells, I hear bells all over, and then I see corpses wrapped in white silk or linen. They're on bamboo stretchers, and they're being marched to the Ghats, where they will be deposited and await their turn to be cremated.

I talk to a man who cannot understand me, nor can I understand his language. Later another old man approaches me, and he speaks English with a British accent but is still difficult to understand. He tells me that his ambition has been to visit Benares once in his lifetime, and that now he has realized this ambition and, if possible, he would care to remain here to die. He tells me that the waters here hold the powers of salvation. All the waters do in India, but the main sanctuary is Benares. The old man tells me that people who have never in their lives walked out of their villages will come and make a pilgrimage to Benares. And they'll take about a week to do so and are absolved of all their sins and stand a good chance for spiritual salvation. He also tells me that if he could have his ultimate goal attained, it would be not to be reborn at all.

Right now, there is smoke twisting up in the sky, and it is from the burning corpses in the Ghats, and I'm half afraid to investigate further. I do not understand my fear, unless it has something to do with the fiery deaths of my wife and child. . . .

I watch the bodies being removed from the bamboo stretchers, with the families in attendance, as they prepare the bodies for cremation. The Ghats are over three miles in length, three miles of steps that lead down from a very steep bank into the sacred river. And these stone steps wed this great Hindu city to the Ganges.

Water, flowers, smoke, fire—all are forces of divine meaning to these people. In the Ganges are bathing bodies, while in the Ghats are burning bodies. Life and death, the living and the dead, moving onward together in close proximity and in perfect harmony.

Kids. Young children, watching bodies being burned. Flesh being burned. And they're smiling and handing out flowers. They're even giving funeral cakes called *pindas* to the dead. Imagine that! Cakes. Pastries. To the dead. . . .

I think of Sylvia and Audrey Rose, their ashes mingled with those of the '62 Impala, sealed together in copper cylinders, consigned to the great forgettery in Mount Holyoke Mausoleum. I think of the quick Baptist service . . . words read from a book . . . postures, posings, the regulated silence, a tear shed, a brief exchange of grief—all over in less than an hour. No cakes. No *pindas*. In lieu of flowers, the family requests a donation be made to your favorite charity. No ritual offerings of prayer, daily, monthly, yearly, or otherwise.

Janice flipped past a thicker group of clipped pages to the next entry Hoover thought essential for her education.

There is a fact of life here that means everything we do each day is potentially a pious act. I'm grasping, I think, either a truth about the way these people live, or I'm imagining a very wonderful way to live. I must learn more. And that's not going to happen in forty five days.

That, perhaps, is the most important thing I discovered in Benares—that time is unimportant.

The way that woman launders her clothes is as pious an act as that man who hasn't stopped looking at the sun. I don't know, I might be getting far afield of reality. Perhaps it's just a poetic way of seeing a life-style that is totally new and different to me. Or maybe there is indeed that poetry here in the sounds and vibrations of work and religion. . . .

Reincarnation here seems a fact of life.

Destruction, which confused me at first, which caused me to wonder why there was a temple for a goddess who was the consort to the god of destruction, is an equal fact of life.

Destruction and creativity go hand in hand. As I look around me, I see temples and homes that are lopsided, I suppose from the floods during the monsoons, and practically falling into the river, held up by the river. And once again, the idea of destruction—of life persisting, of life continuing, of life fighting on in the midst of all this destruction—seems to pull me toward an understanding of a basic truth, as yet unclear to me. And in trying to define this basic truth, I'm brought back to all the reading I did back in the States. The reading that didn't make sense there but that now, in view of all that I see around me, must become a whole new education.

I will start by staying here in Benares, the seat of the Hindu religion, using my knapsack as a pillow if I must, and continue to watch these cremations to understand why death can be considered a holiday. And what they are celebrating. If it is the final death, if, as that old man said to me, he is not to be reborn again, then what he is celebrating is God. Union with God. But if he has not yet got to that point, then what he is celebrating is another chance toward union with God, a closer step.

It was here that Hoover forsook pen for pencil, which made the going extremely rough.

I've come across a student who speaks little English and whom I am now fortunate enough to share my thoughts with. He explains to me that in Buddhism the problem of true knowledge arises as a personal problem, and this is why Buddha sat and meditated and finally arrived at the truth. This is very important for me to understand because it is just that which compelled me to come to India. To personally find the way to truth.

So much of what I'm saying now began in conversation back and forth between my new friend Sesh and myself. A little corny, perhaps, but he teaches me some of his language, so I will teach him some of mine. He wears a *safa*, a cloth head covering that is wound around his head loosely to protect him from the sun's heat, since he remains outdoors most of the time. He also wears the *lengha*, the trousers that look like pajamas, and he has given me a shirt called the *paharen*. When I tried to thank him for it in my effusive Western way, he became very upset and walked away, and I didn't see him for at least an hour. I thought I had lost my friend Sesh. He returned then and told me that to thank someone for something is to take away part of the act of giving. I am learning so much each day.

As I think of the noble truths, the Eightfold Path, I am chaotic in my joy, yet even that joy must be pushed in a direction, an order, a balance toward evolution.

In a way, the destruction of my wife and child was almost a reconstruction of me. The fact of their death, of Audrey Rose's death, in all her beauty and her joy, set me into a dying cycle and forced me to reexamine our lives together. If I believe in God, as these people do, then I must believe that somewhere along that noble Eightfold Path, I failed. I failed and, in doing so, polluted the environment around me. In some way or another, I destroyed the order, and so the imbalance made something as lovely and wondrous and bright as Audrey Rose's spirit incapable of surviving around it. Am I accepting blame? I don't know yet.

When I look at Sesh and the time he's taking with me, I realize that what these people want is to do good. And if I can prove God and reincarnation to myself here, as Buddha did to himself, if I can find a creative way of life, then it is because I want to do good. If the souls of Sylvia and Audrey Rose are in pain, then I must do good for their souls. If I can do this little, I will have done a great deal toward getting them closer to the cycle of bliss which is their right. . . .

The small, thick writing swam before Janice's eyes, and she was forced to rest them a moment before continuing. Flipping to the next entry, she found that matters hadn't improved; if anything, the shape of the words were even more blurred.

Sesh and I walk to Sarnath, the center of the Buddhist world, because it is at Sarnath that Buddha preached his first sermon, and we are going to see where it is partially recorded on a stone. It is here that he revealed the Eightfold Path that leads to the end of sorrow, the attainment of inner peace, enlightenment, and ultimately, Nirvana. It is here that he established his doctrine of the middle way, which is the golden path between extremes of asceticism and self-indulgence.

He came upon four great truths. Suffering is universal. Cause of suffering is craving or selfish desire. Cure is the elimination of craving. And the way is to follow the middle way. A path of practical action. To do this, we have the Eightfold Path which is: Right knowledge. Right intention. Right conduct. Right means of livelihood. Right effort. Right mindfulness. Right concentration. And the five precepts: Abstaining from the taking of life. Abstaining from the taking of what is not given. . . .

The writing at this point was indecipherable, and Janice could not continue. Flipping past several similarly difficult segments, she came to an entry written in pen, and her eyes felt suddenly cleansed.

> I look at Sesh; no Hindi comes to mind: no English comes to mind. I see a tear in his eye, and it doesn't even fall down his cheek. We know we have to part. We have rededicated ourselves to the need for finding truth. For we have shared a desire for life, a need for absolution, a need to understand reincarnation in order to love God. We have given each other that gift.

And a few pages later, still in pen:

> I walk for many days. I walk because I know I have made a commitment now to live out something in daily deeds that before was just an ideal.
>
> I find something else, too. I find that in walking, I am becoming very aware of my body, its needs, what I can do without. I can now go without food for a while, but I cannot go without truth and faith. That is my joy right now. And I am hurting my feet, and my back is tired. I am not used to this, but it's forcing me to become very cognizant of this flesh that is carrying me through God's world. To figure out why I am housed inside this flesh, to understand the idea of the soul

occupying the body, rather than the soul having a body, which is what I used to believe. And in this walk I'm learning that we are in eternity. Eternity is here with us now.

And a page later:

As I walk, I see in front of me a small girl with long black hair, almost to her ankles, pulled back in a braid, huge eyes, a bit downcast, a tight little white shirt, and a bright, bright shawl, green and orange and pink, over her. She has a basket with her, and as I get closer, I see there is nothing in the basket. I have half an orange left. I give it to her, and she gobbles it up.

She says, "Prana," which I know to mean "breath." So I take it to be her name. I say to her, "Prana ji," which I have learned is the endearing suffix to add to a name. As we walk, she sings. I can't tell if there are words to the song.

She leads me to her family's house. As we are nearing the house, I see buffalo, I see the water tank which is in so many villages. The water tank, artificially built, looks like a pond. I see a very old lady walking with a brass pot on her head, walking to the tank, and I see a robust man with a curly black beard. He has two chairs on his head. They stop what they're doing, and they look at me. The man puts the chairs down. I don't know what I'm going to say, and he leads me into the house. As he does, I'm glad that I remembered to take my sandals off. I'll probably never put them on again. The man, who seems to be Prana's father, says to me, "Amdhu," and holds out his hand. I take it and we shake, and I say, "Elliot," and he says to me, "*Atcha,*" and I say, "*Atcha,*" with a laugh, *atcha* meaning "okay."

The woman of the house scours the floor with sand. She rises when we enter and draws her shawl up over her head. Her hair is just like her daughter's hair, long, in a braid, parted in the middle, and she wears a huge ring in her nose, as well as earrings and big silver bracelets on her ankles. Prana has sweet gold earrings in her ears, and there is a lovely jewel that falls from the long sari that the old lady wears over her head.

The woman's name is Rama, and she looks to be having another baby.

The old lady enters the house, and her hair, long like the other women, is absolutely white. Her name is Shira, she seems to be the grandmother, and she wears the *kabja*, the blouse which covers the top of the body, and a loose-fitting petticoat, the *chania*, and over all is the eternal sari. She still has the brass pot on her head, but now she removes it, and we all sit on the floor where there is a meal. We eat chapati, the bread. It has been freshly baked for this meal and is served hot.

At the meal, too, are Uncle Chupar, Aunt Kastori, and Shakur, their son. These Indians live like many Indians in the villages, in what they call joint families. Almost like a miniature commune. All the property is communally owned, and the earnings of all the individual members are thrown into a common pool. There is great emotional security, and there is great economic security. If we think it does not offer much privacy or solitude, we must think only of their religion and how it invites them to go into themselves for privacy and solitude.

And later:

The family Pachali's day begins at 4 A.M. We bathe in icy cold water, and prayers are begun. The women join in the meditations but soon get down to household chores, churning butter, making buttermilk, leaving the men to continue with their meditations and prayers.

There are daily rituals which are accomplished by every member of the family. The first is *Bhuta Yajna*, an offering of food to the animal kingdom, symbolizing man's realization of this obligation to less evolved forms of creation. In this way we come to understand instinctively that the weaker animals are also tied to a body identification as we are, but they do not have the quality of reason that we have. So as we help those that are weaker than ourselves, we can feel sure that we will be comforted in like manner by higher unseen beings. That is the first form of daily worship. The second form is a ritual of silent love, silent love for nature. This is the way we surmount the inability to communicate with earth, sea, and sky. The other two daily *yajnas* are *Pitri* and *Nri*, these being offerings to ancestors so that daily we may acknowledge our debt to past generations, since it is their wisdom that has brought the light on us today.

I observe Amdhu and Rama and the real bond of love that exists between husband and wife. They treat each other with great gentility, although they are not openly affectionate in public or in front of their children. Rama sacrifice, at all times, for Amdhu and her children, keeping them the center of her universe and serving them at all times. She is concerned for Amdhu's religious progress, feeling that the deeds she carries out for him will help him progress toward God. There is also a very close attachment between Amdhu and his daughter, Prana. Until puberty, she is allowed to accompany him on all male gatherings. With the knowledge that she will be sent to another home at marriage, she's treated with indulgence by her father.

Arun, like all boys his age, spends more and more time outside the women's quarters, in the vicinity of the men, in the company of his father and uncles who indulge him. But Amdhu always maintains a certain formality with him. The desire for sons is great, for only a son can adequately perform the death rites and the annual ceremony that assures peace to his father's soul.

And so at all times death is looked upon quite openly with a sense of responsibility, planning, and a knowledge that every day lived leads toward that death which, in turn, will ensure a worthy progression to the next life.

And then:

I see great poverty, pain, sickness, drought, famine. Yet, in the midst of calamity, I see life progress with joy and love, with great care, and with great reverence.

The family is a microcosm of God's world. . . .

Two large paper clips were necessary to fasten the thick group of pages that led to the next entry, which, surprisingly, found Hoover in a different part of India—in the forests of the south. For some reason he had left the Pachali family and either did not think it important enough or did not want Janice to know why. The two paper clips were all that barred her from learning more. Without hesitation, she flicked them off and renewed her relationship with Amdhu, Arun, Prana, and the rest of the family.

The drought continues. Failure of the monsoon to arrive on time makes the difference between abundance and blight. The entire village suffers. What few food stores are left are carefully divided between all the villagers.

Rama's twins, who are just over a year old, cry a great deal, the girl more than the boy, since Rama favors him, nurses and feeds him first while the girl gets the leftovers, which is very little. . . .

The boy, Khwaja, cries, but the girl, Sarojini, no longer cries. Prana, too, is ill from hunger, as is Rama, since the greater portion of what little food there is must go to the men. There is no hostility in this seemingly callous act of willful deprivation. It is simply part of a deeply ingrained tradition. In every village family, the women are fed last. . . .

Things are critical. . . .

On hands and knees, we all scour the parched fields for vagrant roots and seeds. . . .

A child in the village has died, and two others are soon to die. The family left this morning with the child's body for the Ghats at Benares, eighteen kilometers to the north. Wrapped in white linen, the tiny form of the dead girl seemed to tremble with life as the cart trundled over dry clods of earth. The entire family pulled and pushed the cart. It will take them all day and all night to reach Benares. . . .

Prana has stopped speaking. Her large eyes can only stare at me. I must try to rehabilitate her and the village with whatever I possess. For two years now, I have not thought of the money or any of the ways and means of the life I left. But now I must think about it. And act!

Benares. Heat at 118 degrees. Sidewalks and streets covered with prostrate bodies, sacred cows chewing on coconut husks.

I have been here five days now, living in the transients' settlement down by the riverbanks. Rejected air-conditioned hotel. Should have rejected American meal (Southern fried chicken and apple pie, first in two years). Made me violently ill. . . .

I am waiting for Barclay's Bank to receive a wire from their correspondent in New York City approving my credit. I have contacted a man—shifty fellow—regarding grain stores which are black-market. He promises me vans will deliver supplies immediately that money, in American dollars, is received. I put my faith in him, reluctantly, but what choice have I? I have bargained for eight vanloads of rice, flour, and food grains for planting. They will be distributed among our own village and the neighboring villages, stretching the food as far as it will go. It will take all the money from the accident benefit to accomplish this. I like to think that Sylvia and Audrey Rose would approve. . . .

Strong ocean winds, lashing rains, and an extreme drop in temperature. The monsoon has come. With the suddenness and force of an avenging god. In minutes, the streets of Benares are flooded. The river is forced hundreds of yards beyond its banks. I hear that some of the villages to the south have become mudholes in the space of a day. There is no traffic, trucks, carts, cows, or people, as the roads are impassable. . . .

Barclay's Bank has received a wire from their correspondent in New York. It seems my credit cards are not sufficient identification to satisfy my Pittsburgh bank. Forms will have to be filled. Signatures compared. A delay of at least a week. . . .

All is lost. . . .

The monsoon is in full flood. Every day it rains and rains and rains. The Ganges covers the land to each horizon in a vast, swirling grayness. Treetops protrude from the water, and now and then the bloated carcass of a cow or a human corpse is carried across my vision. . . .

All over the floods are spreading across the land. Men, women, and children labor to stem the water's fury, but cannot. I wonder about my village and think about Amdhu and Rama and the children and how it is with them. . . .

The flood control officer attached to the Rescue Commission in the third sector told me today that most of the villages to the south are under water. He said that all India is suffering severely and that it's one of the worst monsoons in memory. . . .

The flood tide has retreated, leaving the land dark and loamy with death and decay. Good for planting. But where are the people?

Arriving at my village, I see it all but deserted, and there are no dwellings left. It's as though a huge trowel had smoothed the land. . . .

I find Jafar Ali and his two boys trudging among the muddy runnels. He tells me they were away when the water came. He also tells me that Aunt Kastori is somewhere about but will say no more. He seems dumbstruck. . . .

The settlement stretches along the left bank of the river. Water still. Intense sun.

A few bodies of drowned dead are laid out in beautiful symmetry along the base of the rocky piles. Aunt Kastori and I forage about for Pachali faces, but terribly bloated features make it difficult to recognize Amdhu, Rama, Prana, Shira, Arun, the twins, Uncle Chupar, Shakur. . . .

Aunt Kastori joins another family in their search as well as ours. They are friends from a neighboring village. Even in her grief, Aunt Kastori cannot help being what she is—a busybody. She had been visiting neighbors on high ground when the flood tides swept across the village, taking people, dogs, cows, houses, everything. Her busybody ways saved her life. . . .

I secretly wish not to find any members of my family here among the rescued dead. I prefer to think of them now as part of the river, which Sesh once told me contains chemical properties that can dissolve a human body in less than a day, flesh, hair, and bones. . . .

We find Prana's body. Bleached. Puffed. Her belly distended as though she had eaten a great meal. . . .

First Audrey Rose. Now Prana. . . .

Aunt Kastori wails her grief, which will be short-lived, as Indians do not brood over death. I shed no tears. I find I can look upon Prana's death and no longer feel the need to cry, which was not true of Audrey Rose's death.

The Ghats are working at full tilt day and night. . . .

The sweetly acrid smoke infiltrates every pore of Benares' ancient skin. Long lines of carts, rickshaws, and bamboo stretchers exceed the city's limits as families progress in sluggish clusters toward the steps leading down to the sacred river. Since death is defiling, all are anxious to cremate their corpses quickly so that the spirits of the dead may be purified.

There is bargaining and bribery going on with the police, who keep the lines in order. Some of the wealthier families are escorted to the front of the line. . . .

I wait my turn, along with Aunt Kastori and the slight linen-clad form lying across the seat of the rickshaw wallah I hired. . . .

Flowers in water-filled vases cover the floor of our rickshaw. Freshly cut this morning, they are beginning to wilt in the unsparing humidity. . . .

Aunt Kastori carries the ceremonial tray of *pindas*. . . .

Although I am neither family nor blood relation, I will light the cremation fire, but that is as far as I will go. I will not remain for the offering of the *pindas*, nor will I perform the annual ceremony for the spirits of Prana or her family. I am neither worthy nor prepared for that responsibility.

In the midst of all this death I cannot keep my mind from dwelling on life. Not life past or life future, but life present—full, sweet, beautiful, bursting with promise. . . .

In the presence of Prana's ruined beauty, I experience no enlightenment. I sense no lesson to be learned from her wasted and emaciated body or from the final anguish of her cruel death. I can foresee no consequence of good being derived from all of the terrible suffering I have witnessed. . . .

I do not understand any of it. . . .

Standing now within sight of the Ghats, watching the bodies burn, I know that these steps I take to the river will be my last, for in the morning I shall depart this city, never to return. . . .

I know not in what direction I will go, or why. . . .

I am hopelessly lost. . . .

Janice's eyes blurred with strain and emotion as she raised them from the small, difficult pencil scratchings of Hoover's diary and glanced at her wristwatch. Four fifteen. There was much left to read, but she would have to stop now and think about waking Ivy. The limousine would be arriving in an hour.

After replacing the diary on the upper shelf of the hall closet, she went to the kitchen to prepare breakfast.

Watching over the witch's caldron of bubbling oats, Janice's mind reeled with a dizzying jumble of thoughts. While she understood only some of what she'd read, the sheer passion of Hoover's words had made a profound and powerful impression on her.

All at once Janice felt herself in the grip of nausea, her body shuddering uncontrollably in huge, lumbering waves. She shut her eyes and tried to will it to stop, even tried to find humor in her own pathetic weakness, but she was finally forced to rush upstairs to the bathroom to vomit. Afterward, she felt better.

Ivy was surprised to be leaving the house in the dark, but was so tired and feverish she hardly questioned it. She allowed the chauffeur to bundle her up in robes and almost immediately fell asleep.

Dominick, too, was slightly mystified at the early departure and asked Janice if they were joining Mr. Templeton.

"Yes," Janice replied. "Look after our mail."

The rain had slackened to a fine drizzle. A silvery luminescence slid between a stream of dark and roiling clouds above their heads. Autumn leaves, sodden, had collected at the curbside, and the wind blew bitingly off the Hudson River, lashing their faces with the sting of winter.

It was five twenty-six when the limousine pulled away from the building and plunged smoothly ahead into the morning mist.

13

Sound-Side Cottages were not, after all, designed for winter use. Situated as they were on an unsheltered knoll of land fronting the storm-swept Sound, their flimsy, clapboard façades creaked and groaned under the onslaught of the wintry gale. Lacking insulation of any kind, the sievelike walls admitted icy drafts of wind and moisture.

Janice and Ivy sat by day directly in front of the fireplace, bundled up in electric blankets, reading books, and feeding logs onto the sputtering fire. The first vestiges of the storm had greeted their arrival nearly a week before, starting with a gentle rain and steadily burgeoning into a full-fledged nor'wester, bringing snow, wind, and driving sleet in continual cycles.

They would have moved out after the first day (there was a snug inn just outside town) had not Mr. Stuart shrewdly insisted on the full two weeks' rent up front.

Janice had come to Westport to think—to sort out her alarms and confusions and attempt to tidy her mind—but now, a week later, she was in as great a state of mental upheaval as when she had left New York. Hoover's diary, that simple, deeply felt chronicle of death and despair, had only served to reinforce his sincerity, and validate his dark assertions. ". . . *the soul of Audrey Rose . . . will keep pushing Ivy back to the source of the problem; she'll be trying to get back to that moment and will be leading Ivy into dangers as tormenting and destructive as the fire that took Audrey's life.*" His words, like portents flung ahead, clung like amulets before her eyes.

Ivy's temperature had returned to normal soon after their arrival, and her hands, which Janice scrupulously medicated and bandaged each morning and evening, were beginning to heal. Thus far she had been spared the ordeal of the nightmares, which, to Janice, was a mixed blessing since this only confirmed Elliot Hoover's theory of their origin.

Possibly the biggest shock was Bill's reaction when she called him that first morning. He accepted each of her bombshells calmly and quietly, making no real protest, but probing her on every detail of her evening with Elliot Hoover: what he did upon entering, how long it took for him to quiet Ivy, what he said to Janice afterward, how long he remained, and what his parting words were. He thought her decision to flee to Westport was a good one; was glad they hadn't come to Hawaii since it was hot, sticky and dull; told her to stay put until he arrived, which would probably be just after the weekend as he was cutting out the trip to Seattle, and screw Pel.

Monday, the day before Bill was to arrive, the storm drifted out to sea and, like a curtain being drawn across a child's painting, disclosed a big, yellow, make-believe sun in a sky of azure blue.

The morning was a special gift for Ivy.

As they trudged along the water line, gingerly sidestepping the larger breakers, Janice rejoiced to see a faint tint of pink return to Ivy's pale cheeks and hoped her appetite would return as well. They walked barefoot down miles of beach, seeking treasure given up by the sea during the storm. The booty presented itself to them in a continual line at the water's edge, like a long counter of goods at the dime store. Shells, crustaceans, rocks, pebbles, sea plants, bits of driftwood, punctuated by larger set pieces—cruciforms of tree limbs, massive pilings, acres of bubbly seaweed—a variety of manufactured oddments: sea-weathered boards, bricks, and sundry bottles and rusted cans, their labels and messages obscured by tides and time.

"Look, Mommy!" Ivy called. "It's dead!"

Janice, who had been lagging some distance behind, now approached to find her daughter squatting at the water's edge over a large dead fish. Huge bites had reduced its flesh to the skeleton. A small shell had found a home in its eye socket.

"Come away from it," Janice gently ordered and, taking Ivy's hand, quickly led her past the mutilated carcass.

"It looked so—*dead*," Ivy said, incredulous.

"Dead is dead," Janice lightly replied.

"Is that how people look when they die?"

"People look like people, not like fish."

"I mean, all stiff and—broken?"

"Sometimes. If the death is violent."

"Like in a car accident?"

Janice felt her heart leap.

"Yes," she replied, her voice faltering slightly. "Like in a car accident."

"It's awful dying like that."

Janice said nothing.

"Sometimes I have dreams about it," continued Ivy.

Janice bit her lip. Then: "What kind of dreams?"

"Oh. Dying dreams."

"In a car accident?"

"Sometimes. Sometimes I dream I'm dying in my bed. And everybody's standing around me and crying. Bettina says the living suffer more than the dead. Her mother still suffers."

"Do you have these dreams a lot?"

"No. Just sometimes."

They walked a bit in silence.

"Will you mind very much?" Ivy asked wistfully.

"Mind?"

"Dying."

"Yes." Janice's voice was heavy, stark. "I'll mind very much."

"I suppose I will, too," Ivy said simply. "Especially if it's in a terrible car accident."

The conversation ended, leaving Janice to battle the rattling crash of the breakers with her own pounding heart.

There could be no doubt.

No doubt at all.

Audrey Rose's terrors were beginning to leak into Ivy's waking thoughts.

For a week, her daughter had been free of nightmares. . . .

The week away from Hoover. . . .

Audrey Rose sensed her father's presence. . . .

—*"Wanting! Needing! Crying out for my help! For MY help!"*

His proximity alerted Audrey Rose, brought on the cruelly punishing nightmares. . . .

Away from Hoover there would be no nightmares. . . .

She must do everything in her power to keep Elliot Hoover away from her child. . . .

Somehow, she must think hard, and find a way to keep them apart . . . *forever—*

On their return to the cottage they passed a group of uniformed girls about Ivy's age, sifting and sorting among the sea forms. A nature study class, Janice surmised, private, probably parochial, and very expensive. A middle-aged woman, not a nun, was seated nearby on a camp chair, attending her brood. There was an exchange of smiles between Janice and the woman as each paid tribute to the glorious morning, while Ivy squatted among the girls and became part of the class.

The scene was idyllic, restful, secure, an obvious and perfect answer.

"No!"
"Why not?"
"No discussion, Janice, I'm not buying—"
"Why not?"
"I'm not going to let this guy break up my family, that's why not."

Bill had rented a car at the airport and had driven directly to Westport, arriving just after 10 P.M. With Ivy safely asleep, they stood on a tuft of knoll a few paces away from the cottage, within sight of the moon-speckled waters of the Sound.

"I happen to like our life the way it is," Bill continued hotly. "All of us together under the same roof. I'm surprised to hear you suggest such a nutty idea. Correction: I'm not that surprised. You're really sold on this guy."

"What does that mean?"

"You let him in, didn't you? You let him help you—wash your wounds, take care of things, isn't that what you told me?"

"I did it because I had to do it—"

"You didn't *have* to do it—you could have waited for Kaplan!"

"I couldn't— For God's sake, I was there, you weren't! Ivy was going crazy, I was afraid she'd kill herself—I had to let him in because only *he* could help her! Is it possible you still don't understand that?"

"Right, Janice—on that point we part company. To me, Elliot Hoover is no miracle man. To me, he's a misguided nut who seems to have made a hell of an impression on my wife!"

Janice shut her eyes and flexed her hands. Her voice, kept soft, was filled with shocked disbelief.

"You're right, he's made a hell of an impression on me. He's scared me half to death; that's what he's done. Most of the time I'm so scared I can't think straight. He's got me talking to myself when I'm not talking to priests or screaming to God on my knees. He's got me drinking in the mornings and stealing off in the dead of night to escape from him. Not because I'm afraid he's a nut, but because I know he's sane. Because I believe what he believes is true. Because I accept the fact that our child is the victim of some cosmic screw-up, and as long as she is near him, she's in terrible danger of losing her life."

Janice was trying not to cry, but could not stop the tears from coming.

"But the most terrible and frightening thing of all is that I'm completely alone in all this . . . that with all you've seen and heard, with all the evidence clearly stated before your eyes and ears, you still choose to ignore it. Bill, we're in trouble! Sooner or later you've got to come out from under that fig leaf of yours and face it!"

Janice was sobbing now, but Bill made no move to hold her or soothe her. His face took on a masklike appearance.

"Okay, you've had your say. Now let me have mine." The voice was grave, subdued. "To begin with, what you believe, I can never believe. Even if Hoover took me on a personal tour through St. Peter's Gate and gave me a point-of-sales pitch, I still wouldn't believe it. It's not my reality. Although I will admit the day I left you and went to the airport my head was twisting and turning in every direction. I was glad to be leaving the whole mess behind me—you, Ivy, Hoover, all the sick bullshit we've been going through. Imagine. Me, model father, glad to be getting away from my own wife and child, whom I love more than life itself. But that's the way I felt—glad and guilty, glad and guilty, glad and guilty, halfway across the country.

"I tried to remove the guilt with many applications of gin and vermouth, but it didn't work—the glow grew, my head hurt, but the pricky feeling remained. I tell you, it was pure agony, but there wasn't a thing I could do about it. Until, somewhere over Kansas, I happened to look down and saw the nation going by, forty thousand feet below me, and I started to focus on life and all its problems from that vantage point, watching cities, plains, mountains, the Rockies, the miracle of America going by from sea to shining sea—and me, encased in another miracle, a massive hunk of steel hurtling through space at the speed of sound. And it suddenly dawned on me that these were the miracles that really meant something—not Hoover's miracles, but the miracles that living men made: taming lands, building incredible machines. These were the *real* miracles!

"And then I began to get the glimmerings of an answer. It was raining at this point, you see—we were in the clouds and rain was streaking against the window—and I said to myself, 'Into each life a little rain must fall.' A helluva cliché, but that was the answer. Hoover was the rain in our lives, like heart trouble or cancer, and thinking of him in this way, as a disease, he became less ominous and more manageable. I mean, you take cancer to a doctor, and if he can't help, you go to another doctor and then to a specialist, and you keep on fighting and fighting to the bitter end . . . you don't give up. Same with Hoover . . . you take him to a lawyer, and if that doesn't help, you go to the police and ultimately to court, and quite possibly that may fail too, but you don't give up—you don't cut and run, you don't hand in your ticket, give up your job, your home. . . . You don't break up your family, Janice—you stick it out together and fight with guns, rocks, clubs, anything that comes to hand in order to keep what you've got and love. If all else fails, we've got to be the minutemen: you, me, Ivy, together as a family. And as long as we remain as a family, we've got a chance to beat this son of a bitch. . . ."

". . . *of a bitch, a bitch, itch* . . ."

His voice came to a discordant halt, sending the final word echoing across the expanse of water like a rock skimming its surface. In the silence that followed, the soft wave sounds reestablished themselves. Janice stood motionless, letting the gentle noise wash over her boggled, benumbed brain. He wouldn't understand, couldn't understand, and she suddenly felt too weary to care any longer whether he did or not.

"So forget about boarding schools for Ivy. Tomorrow morning we're going to return to our home. *As a family.*"

The words were uttered softly, but with Biblical obstinacy and determination, closing off all channels of discussion.

So be it.

"All right," Janice said.

They returned to the city in the late afternoon of November 13, a Wednesday.

Janice's eyes quickly scanned the solitary, shadowy parts of the street as the car pulled up in front of Des Artistes.

Bill, she noticed, did the same, though less obviously.

There was no sign of Hoover.

Janice watched Ivy kick listlessly at the curbside drift of blackened snow as Mario and Ernie helped Bill carry the suitcases into the lobby. There was a swiftness to Bill's movements that betrayed his anxiety to get off the street as quickly as possible.

"Better get her inside," he told Janice, and climbed into the car to return it to the Hertz people.

Janice complied.

The bottle of scotch was where she had left it, open and half consumed on the sewing table next to the rocker. The cork was nowhere in sight.

The entire living room seemed slightly tipsy, furniture, draperies, pillows, askew or out of place—victims of the nightmare.

Janice restored order while Ivy watched TV.

Upstairs, the basin of water was on the bedroom floor, a sediment of brownish grit formed on the bottom. Janice thought of Hoover's hands washing her legs as she emptied the soiled water into the toilet and rinsed the basin clean.

Ivy's room was at the epicenter of the cyclone—furniture upended, blankets and bedsheets coiled together in twisted, knotted balls, the Chinese screen, still at a slight angle, covering the window, the subtle motif of the center panel torn and mutilated beyond recognition.

Janice spent the better part of an hour returning the room to its normal state, but could do nothing with the screen since it was stuck solidly behind the radiator. She and Bill together finally pried it loose and carted it back to their bedroom.

Upon first seeing the screen, Bill had asked her what the hell had happened. She told him. His face blanched.

They ate sandwiches from the Stage Delicatessen (Bill had picked them up on his way back from the car rental), along with beer and milk. As they were finishing their meal, the house telephone rang.

Bill calmly ate the last of his sandwich before rising to answer it. His composure was too calculated to pass for indifference.

Russ. Mario had told him they were back. Did they need anything? Carole had baked a large lasagna and they were welcome. Bill thanked Russ and told him they had just finished dinner and were making an early night of it as they were all beat.

Which was partially true, Janice thought worriedly, observing Ivy's heavy-lidded eyes and drawn, pale face—she seemed ready to flake out at the dinner table. Her milk glass was empty, but her sandwich had been hardly touched. Janice reminded herself to make an appointment with Dr. Kaplan in the morning. Unless, she bleakly reflected, we have need of him sooner.

The bath forgone, Janice tucked Ivy into bed just shy of eight o'clock, and almost immediately she fell asleep. She stayed with her child for a long time, listening to her soft, even breathing, before leaving the room and quietly closing the door.

She found Bill in their bedroom, lethargically unpacking his suitcase, lingering over the disposition of each item as though reluctant to complete the task. Janice snapped open her own suitcase. There was only one exchange between them.

"Is she asleep?" he whispered.

"Yes," she whispered back.

They both continued to unpack in a silence that was charged with tension and expectancy.

They didn't have long to wait.

Audrey Rose arrived at eight fifteen.

"*Mommydaddymommydaddymommydaddyhothothothot—*"

Bill snapped his finger at the telephone . . .

"Kaplan!"

. . . and dashed out of the room.

Janice dashed to the telephone. (teamwork)

—snatched it up and, the number burned in her brain, quickly dialed it from memory. . . .

"HOTHOTHOTHOTHOT hothothot—"

Agony rose and fell as the bedroom door opened and closed. . . .

"Yes?" Kaplan, thank God!

"Doctor, it's Janice Templeton, please come right away!"

"I'll be right over."

Janice stumbled forward into the hallway, zooming toward bedlam—

"Hothothothothotdaddydaddydaddy—"

—opened the bedroom door—

"HOTHOTHOTHOT—"

—saw Ivy, head thrown back, howling up at Bill, standing staunchly between her and the window, arms akimbo, legs outstretched, the Colossus of Rhodes, the human barrier to her ravening need—

"HOTHOTHOTHOT—"

—bandaged fists flailing and pelting him, ripping at shirt and trousers with a strength that brought beads of sweat popping to his face—

"Kaplan's coming!" Janice encouraged.

"HOTHOTHOTHOTHOT—"

—Ivy's face a raging mask of fear and anguish, fists pummeling Bill with maniacal force and accuracy; thudding impacts collecting him in sensitive regions of belly and groin, causing him to wince in pain and seize the thin arms to stay the vicious hammerblows—

"HOTHOTHOTHOT—"

Janice gasped as Ivy's teeth sunk into the soft flesh of Bill's arm.

"Janice! Help me!" he croaked, wrenching his arm from her bloodied lips.

Janice charged toward her daughter's back, arms extended, and threw herself at her legs, engulfing them in a viselike embrace.

Bill grabbed Ivy's arms.

Wriggling, struggling, squirming, they carried her screaming to the bed, eased her down, and lay upon the small, convulsing, jerking body to still it.

Gradually, the volcano abated, the body relaxed, the screaming imprecations became soft, plaintive cries, childlike: "*Mommydaddymommymommydaddyhothothot—*"

Gently conveying the relaxed arms to the strong grip of his left hand, Bill grasped the sheet with his free hand and quickly bound her wrists. His face was dripping sweat, and he was breathing hard. Clinging to the legs, Janice watched the shocked face of her husband as he tied the end of the sheet to the scrollwork of the carved headboard, then rose to repeat the same process with her legs.

Shortly, their daughter, in all her pale perfection, lay trussed and suspended between the two corded sheets firmly secured to the bed. Both sheets were bespeckled with Bill's blood.

For a long time, neither spoke. They stood by the bed gazing down at the gently twisting body, in mute horror.

"My God," Bill groaned hoarsely.

The doorbell rang.

Kaplan!

"Stay with her," Bill ordered brusquely, and bounded out of the room and down the stairs, flicking on light switches in living room and hallway . . . twisting two locks . . . removing the chain bolt . . . opening the door to—

Hoover. Standing pale, smiling nervously, hand extended in a semi-offering gesture, noting the bleeding arm and the sweated face filled with shock—

"Hello," he ventured unsurely.

"H-how the hell did you get up here?" Bill choked out in a haggard whisper.

"I—" Hoover began.

"Who allowed you up?"

"I . . . live here."

Stunned, stupefied silence.

"What?" breathed Bill.

"I sublet a small apartment on the fifth floor—while you were gone. We're neighbors."

A film of red drew a veil across the pale face as Bill felt the throb of blood in his temples and a spasm of rage gorge his throat. . . .

"You son of a bitch!" Bill exploded, and thrust his hands at the thin neck, seeking to enclose it, to squeeze it, to tear it apart—

"No, please—" the face begged, falling away from Bill's grasping, flexing fingers, falling backward, downward, floatingly—causing Bill's hands to grapple with air, a mirage, unattainable. A foot in Bill's groin, assisted by his own forward momentum, sent his hulking body into the air in a gentle arc, suspending it in space for a fleeting instant, then dropping all one hundred and eighty-two pounds of it onto the hard tile floor with a sickening, brain-rattling thud.

Bill felt his head bursting and knew there were broken parts inside him. Tricky bastard, he thought in his agony, vaguely aware of doors opening and closing down the hallway.

"I'm sorry, Mr. Templeton." Hoover's voice came through an echo chamber. "Here, let me help you—"

Bill felt a steellike grip on his arm, as Hoover assisted him to a sitting position. The sight of Mrs. Carew's round face, watching solicitously from a distance, completed the indignity, sending a jolt of adrenalin pumping through his damaged body, rekindling energy, recharging rage.

"I'll kill you, you prick," he groaned, and with a sudden lunge and cry, grabbed Hoover's legs, wrenched him off his feet, and pulled him down on top of his own body. Rolling about on the floor, Bill's arms encircled the lean, hard waist in a tight hammerlock and started to apply pressure, when a sudden electrical shock coursed up his spine, immobilizing his body and sending star bursts shooting across his darkening vision. He sensed Hoover's strong fingers digging into the nape of his neck, impinging on a particular artery. Totally paralyzed, Bill felt himself slipping from consciousness, as Hoover's agitated voice begged, "Please, Mr. Templeton—I hear Ivy—"

"DADDYDADDYDADDYDADDY—"

Her shrieks, tunneling their way through the apartment and down into the hallway, were partially obscured by Janice's frantic scream: "Bill, my God!"—all vaguely apprehended, as was Janice's drained, shocked face staring down at Hoover in unblinking disbelief and hostility.

"Let go of him!" she screamed, and began tugging at Hoover's arm with a strength that was fierce.

"DADDYDADDYDADDYDADDY—"

"Yes, yes, I'm coming," Hoover answered, releasing the artery in Bill's neck and plunging toward the open door.

Blood gushed back into Bill's head, causing his vision to pulsate with reds and blacks, as the life force slowly returned to the stunned brain.

"Bill, Bill!" Janice cried, on her knees beside him, cradling his thickly throbbing head against her breast.

Other doors opened, other people emerged, some in robes—faces Bill didn't recognize—remained watching mutely, as Bill coughed and gasped for breath and tried to bring his eyes to focus on the door of their apartment, *which was now closed.*

"Get a cop!" he shouted in a rasping voice. "That son of a bitch's got my kid!"

A movement of neighbors, complying, as Bill struggled to his knees and, with Janice's help, stood up on legs that seemed to belong to someone else.

His face ashen and wild, he stumbled forward toward the door, using Janice's body as a crutch, and tried the knob, needlessly since he knew the door would be locked, then started to pound on the metal facing with both fists.

"Son of a bitch, bastard! Open the door, you goddamn bastard!"

The stream of obscenities overflowed the banks of reason, punctuated by battering blows against the door, sending shuddering waves rebounding down the length of the hallway.

"Somebody get a passkey!" he hurled back over his shoulder. "The guy's a kook, a psycho, *hurry!*"

Mrs. Carew detached herself from the small knot of onlookers and quickly waddled down the hallway toward the elevators.

Janice could only watch helplessly, attempting to keep her own hysteria from bursting loose, as Bill continued shouting, cursing, and pummeling the door with his fists.

"Bill, darling," she pleaded, trying to keep her voice under control. "It's all right. He won't harm her."

Bill spun a ravaged, sopping face around at her—eyes bulging, trickles of spittle at the corners of his trembling mouth (a face she had never seen before)—and bellowed in a harsh, accusing voice, "Keep the hell out of this! I've had enough of your bullshit, too!"

Janice flinched, reeled away from him, her heart pumping wildly, in rhythm to the pounding fists resumed and intensified, as was the voice issuing forth, horrible and coarse, from the face she didn't know.

The distant clang of the elevator door.

Dominick, with keys, white-faced and grim, trotting up to them, selecting from the tinkling bunch first one key, then two, inserting—twisting—opening—SNAP!—the chain bolt flexing—

Bill pressed his mouth into the narrow slit.

"Open up, Hoover," he shouted a bit more reasonably. "The police are coming!"

Silence from within—deep, ominous.

"What's the trouble?"

Two young police officers had approached, unseen, their winter blues exuding a frigid breath.

"A man's in my house with my child, Officer! He assaulted me, then locked us out!"

"Do you know this man?" the shorter of the two officers asked.

"His name is Elliot Hoover," Janice answered when Bill failed to.

The taller officer stepped up to the door and, raising his nightstick, beat a quick, sharp tattoo against the metal panel.

"Mr. Hoover!" His voice was shrill with authority. "I am a police officer! Open the door!"

He waited the prescribed interval of time for a reply, then turned to Bill.

"Is there another entrance to the apartment?"

"Of course." Bill slapped his head, angry at his own stupidity. "The service entrance, around by the fire stairs!"

They were running—Bill, the policemen, Dominick (fiddling with his keys), and Janice, loping after them in great awkward strides, the sound of neighbors' whispers and buzzings closing fast behind her.

It was all useless, Janice knew, and as Bill surely must know, the chain lock was never left unhooked on the service door.

Dominick inserted the key, twisted, and pushed. The door opened inward, unencumbered.

Janice froze. A thought too awful to contemplate tantalized her mind. He would not be there, nor would Ivy; he would have left and taken with him—Ivy? No, not Ivy. Audrey Rose, his child.

A deep sigh rumbled out of Bill as he led the policemen and Dominick through the door on the run. Janice lagged behind, in no hurry to confirm her suspicions. The neighbors remained in the service hallway, eagerly curious, wishing to enter, but questioning the propriety of doing so.

Janice heard Mrs. Carew solemnly call after her, "I do hope Ivy's all right, dear."

Janice arrived in the living room in time to see the file of men clumping grimly down the staircase. Bill's face was chalk white.

"They're gone!" he informed Janice flatly, then raised his voice. "He's kidnapped Ivy!"

Without breaking stride, they hurried through the living room and to the front door, Dominick advising the policemen, "If you're talking about Mr. Hoover, he just sublet Mr. Barbour's suite on the fifth floor."

As they approached the elevator, the door of the second elevator slid open and discharged Dr. Kaplan. Janice noted his startled expression as the human stampede bore down on him.

"Ivy's been kidnapped, Dr. Kaplan!" Bill yelled at him. "Come with us!"

"Yes, certainly," the doctor murmured in complete bewilderment and allowed himself to be swept up in the tide of bodies plunging ahead into Dominick's elevator.

As the door clanged shut, Janice saw the covey of concerned neighbors, led by Mrs. Carew, pile into the other car.

The trip down was made in tense silence. Janice's head throbbed painfully as her eyes critically studied the dry, scuffed leather of Dr. Kaplan's medical bag, worn and battered from years of faithful service, not unlike the binding of Elliot Hoover's diary.

What happened then was to be forever recorded in Janice's mind as a series of flickering images—a speeded-up old-time movie, with the nightstick rapping sharply against Mr. Barbour's door the curtain raiser.

"Mr. Hoover, I am a police officer! Open this door!"

No verbal reply, yet the sound of scurrying footsteps within, clearly heard by all.

"Mr. Hoover, I will ask you once more to open this door!"

The belated reply, distant, muffled: "No."

Bill shouting, "Open up, you son of a bitch!"

The shorter policeman cautioning, "That'll do, sir." Then turning to Dominick and nodding.

—Inserting the key—
—Opening the door—
—Chain bolt snapping—
—Revealing a thin slice of foyer and Elliot Hoover, partially seen, standing by a Grecian column, grim-faced, resolute—
—The policeman thrusting his badge through the opening—

"Will you please open this door, Mr. Hoover?"

"No. There's been enough insanity for one night."

—The policeman turning to Bill: "What's your name, sir?"

"William Templeton."

—The policeman addressing Hoover: "Do you have Mr. Templeton's child secreted on your premises?"

—Hoover, flustered, replying angrily: "They tied her to the bed—!"

—The policeman simplifying: "Is there a child on your premises?"

"A child is sleeping upstairs—peacefully."

"Does the child belong to Mr. Templeton?"

—A pause, Hoover's gaze holding theirs implacably. Then: "No. It is my child who is sleeping."

—The policeman, confused, whispering to Bill: "What does he mean?"

—Bill spluttering: "He's a nut! Break down the door!"

—The policeman consulting Dominick: "Does Mr. Hoover have a child?"

—Dominick shaking his head: "He didn't have any yesterday when he moved in."

—The policeman's stentorian voice booming through the slit: "I will give you thirty seconds to open this door. If you do not comply, I will send for the riot squad to break it down!"

—Mrs. Carew's sharp intake of breath—

—Ten seconds—

—A smothering hush of anticipation—

—Twenty seconds—

—Another moment of dogged resistance; then Hoover giving way, slowly approaching the door—

—Twenty-five seconds—

—The door closing—

—The chain disengaging—

—The door opening gradually—

—A sigh of relief, generally exhaled—

—Hoover standing mutely in defeat, in the center of Mr. Barbour's Grecian spa—

—Bill pouncing through the door with an animal cry, pushing Hoover roughly aside, running up the narrow staircase, followed by the shorter policeman—

—The taller policeman guarding Hoover, watchfully, his right hand near his gun holster—

—Bill descending, carrying Ivy (thank God), sleeping soundly, freshly cleaned, her hands rebandaged—

—Dr. Kaplan's knowing hand feeling Ivy's forehead—

—The shorter policeman stalking up to Hoover, sober-faced: "My name is John Noonan, police officer first class, Badge number 707325. I am placing you under arrest for the suspected felony of kidnapping."

—Hoover's eyes seeking and finding Janice's, probing them sadly and with accusation—

—The taller policeman removing the handcuffs from his belt, as his partner produces a booklet and reads from it: "You have the right to remain silent. If you give up the right to remain silent, anything you say can and will be used against you in a court of law. You have a right to speak to an attorney and have an attorney present during question-

ing. If you cannot afford an attorney, one will be appointed for you, without charge, during questioning. . . ."
—Applause—
Was it really applause Janice heard in the surrounding hubbub of neighborly approval, as Elliot Hoover was led, manacled, down the hallway to the elevator, in the grip of the two policemen?
Applause?

PART THREE

Ivy

14

"You have been a practicing Catholic all your life, Miss Hall?"

"I go to church on Sunday." The pretty blonde smiled.

"And what is the name of the church you currently attend?"

The lean, sparrowy figure of the young defense attorney listed at a relaxed, somewhat rakish angle toward the young woman.

"St. Timothy's in the Village," she replied.

Brice Mack's boyish, ingenuous smile maintained the precise degree of harmless innocence as he carefully selected and put his questions to the twelfth prospective juror, constantly aware of the danger of antagonizing the other jurors by any word or gesture that might be construed as being offensive.

For three weeks the process had continued as the lawyer for the defense and the lawyer for the people delicately scoured among the impaneled veniremen for a jury as prejudiced to its own side of the case as possible.

For Bill, it was a time of sheer hell.

For Janice, it was simply one more episode in the same seemingly endless nightmare. Quite often, as a day wore on, the softly uttered questions and answers would lose the character of speech, become a pleasant, mesmerizing drone, whisking her off into soothing thought-free dream states from which she often didn't return till the hard sound of the gavel brought the day's session to an end. They were a looked-forward-to blessing, these happy flights from the stodgy and wearisome goings-on in Part Seven of the Criminal Courts Building in downtown Manhattan.

For the duration of the trial—five weeks at the outside, according to Scott Velie, the deputy district attorney in charge of the case—the Templeton routine was fixed and unchangeable. Weekday mornings at nine, arms linked in a show of mutual support and confidence, Bill and Janice would take their seats in the second row of the nearly empty courtroom and await Judge Langley's appearance. The front row of seats was set aside for the press, only two of whom were ever present at one time. This morning, there was the man from United Press International and the elderly woman from the Long Island newspaper. On one occasion the woman had turned suddenly around in her seat and, in a sympathetic, motherly way, tried to question them about the case. Bill had simply ignored her, but Janice could not and had responded with the set speech they had been instructed to give to the press: "We have been asked not to discuss the case." A few days later the woman reporter asked Janice how Ivy was faring at the school up in Westport, which startled her, since they had kept their daughter's whereabouts a top secret. Still, Janice was able to smile and reply that Ivy was doing well and was happy, which was the truth. The school had been a success from the start. Janice could see this in the pink and healthy glow of her daughter's face, in the bright and shining eyes that greeted them each Saturday morning upon their arrival. Best of all, the nightmares had stopped.

Bill had been forced into agreeing to the school in Westport since the district attorney had insisted that both parents be in court each and every day of the trial, but Janice knew he was unhappy about sending Ivy away even though they did not discuss it.

Ever since the night of the kidnapping she and Bill maintained a relationship that could, at best, be described as strained. Always polite, considerate of each other, they were like two strangers on a plane, forced to share each other's company. Their conversation was limited and noncommittal, each saying no more to the other than was necessary to convey the basic substance of a question or answer.

Bill's hatred of Hoover and his ambition to see him put away for the full count burgeoned with each passing day. Whenever Janice sought her own feelings about Hoover, a switch in her brain would click off the thought and veer her mind in other directions.

For weeks now, at precisely nine four, Janice's eyes would drift to the side door leading to the prisoner's holding room and watch as Elliot Hoover was ushered into the courtroom by a uniformed guard, who always, she was constantly surprised to see, held Hoover tightly by the arm.

Janice would always shift her gaze away from Hoover as he was led to his seat at the defense table because once at the beginning of the proceedings Hoover had caught her looking at him and had returned a nod and smile in her direction. Bill, sitting beside her, had noticed, for Janice could feel his arm tense and his breathing rate escalate. She wondered what Hoover thought about during the long days in the courtroom and the even longer nights alone in his prison cell. He had not tried to communicate with her since his arrest. She had half expected he would and had steeled herself to repel any such attempts, but she was thankful he hadn't tried. Looking back on their evening together, fraught with its odd commingling of terror and intimacy, she wondered if Hoover considered her a traitor.

As on every other morning, Brice Mack would rise at Hoover's entrance, smile, and shake his client's hand in an open display of affection and confidence. After which they would both sit and briefly confer. That is, Brice Mack would do the talking, while Hoover, betraying no emotion whatever, would sit imperturbably, a vast cathedral calm within him, pencil in hand, entering notations on a legal pad as his lawyer engaged in a clearly one-sided conversation. For two weeks Janice had watched, fascinated, as Elliot Hoover filled page upon page with notes during the course of jury selection and, remembering his diary, wondered what deeply felt thoughts and emotions he must be expressing on those yellow legal pages. Then, late one afternoon, after court had adjourned and Hoover had been ushered out of the courtroom, she purposely passed the defense's table and glanced down at several pages he had left behind. They were filled with neat rows of nearly perfect circles.

"Do you believe in the resurrection of Christ?" Brice Mack gently queried the pretty blonde in the jury box.

"Well, I used to when I was a kid," she responded with a vague smile.

Brice Mack wasn't sure that her answer was entirely acceptable. He begged the court's indulgence while he conferred with his client. Since no objection was registered by the prosecution, Judge Langley banged the gavel and declared a five-minute recess.

Brice Mack leaned across to Hoover, his arm draped loosely around his shoulder, and spoke in a hushed tone.

"We have one more challenge left. I'll use it if you wish; however, I think this juror is going to be okay. What do you think?"

"Fine," Hoover replied, "I have confidence in anyone you select."

It had been this way between them from the first day they met. In Brice Mack's mind, the luckiest day of his life.

He had been sitting in the courtroom of Judge Ira Parnell when he happened to glance up and notice a prisoner, flanked by two bailiffs, standing in the rear of the room, looking over at the section beyond the railing where he and several other lawyers were sitting. The prisoner seemed to be sizing them up. None of the other lawyers had noticed him, but Mack did. Their eyes met, whereupon the prisoner marched forward with his two bailiffs and, halting in front of Mack, said, "My name is Elliot Hoover. Will you be my lawyer? I can pay." Although there had been no great ego satisfaction in having been picked at random, Mack welcomed a case where, for a change, somebody could afford to pay him and without hesitation said yes.

However, his first conversation with his new client sent a ripple of current dancing up and down his spine. For here was a case to sink one's teeth into. This had angles. All kinds. Oblique, obtuse, bizarre, the stuff that galvanizes courtrooms, magnetizes the press, draws in the eyes and ears of the world.

Reincarnation? Hot damn! If the man wasn't psycho and the court could be prevailed upon to accept the evidence as a competent defense, who knew where it could lead to, and where it might end?

During the first meeting with Hoover, Mack had tentatively offered his client the possibility of a defense based on temporary insanity. He felt it his duty as a lawyer to do so, but the notion, fortunately, was rejected by Hoover.

During subsequent meetings Brice Mack was filled in on all the events that occurred before, during, and after the abduction at 1 West Sixty-seventh Street, and each new disclosure was more delicious than the last. Mack was delighted to find Hoover a willing client who forthrightly maintained that he was simply trying to help Ivy Templeton and, through her, his deceased daughter, Audrey Rose, and who related substantial eyewitness testimony that his daughter's soul was crying out to him through the vehicle of Ivy's body for help and that in abducting Ivy, he was simply doing what any concerned father with the capability of helping his ailing child would do. On this point, Hoover made his position perfectly clear; he had the right to take Ivy, he felt, under the circumstances.

Somehow a defense would have to be formulated to convince a court and a jury not only of the sincerity of his belief, but of the reality of reincarnation.

The next stunning event was Hoover's refusal to be released on bail, contending that he found the accommodations in the detention cell block of the Criminal Courts Building perfectly adequate to his needs. When Brice Mack pressed him to accept bail, Hoover resisted strongly, stating that his religious principles decreed that all mortal suffering is natural and necessary to purify the soul on its cyclic journey through earth life. Mack accepted this reasoning with a large grain of salt and informed his client that he had sources who would be willing to arrange for bail to be posted and also provide the necessary collateral. Hoover seemed genuinely offended at the suggestion.

"I don't need help of that kind. I have plenty of money."

Brice Mack felt the same tingle of electricity prickle up his back as he casually asked, "How much do you consider plenty?"

"Oh," Hoover replied, "by now it must be a quarter of a million at least."

Mack felt his throat go dry. "Where is it?"

"In a Pittsburgh bank. The First Fidelity Savings."

Mack managed to swallow a thickness of dry phlegm. "Would you be willing," he gently put forth, "to spend some of it on your defense?"

"All of it, if necessary," Hoover stated instantly.

That tore it. Every which way.

By some miracle of sheer luck and Buddha's special grace, the case of the decade had dropped right into Brice Mack's young and inexperienced lap. A fear of his ability to handle it properly briefly assailed his confidence, but he quickly suppressed it. With enough money to pursue evidence, gather information, call in expert witnesses from around the globe, the trial would become a classroom seminar. Here was a case that was precedential, textbook, a once-in-a-lifetimer, permitting the imagination its fullest range, opening avenues into legal terrain previously uncharted. The kind of case Darrow would have relished, that Nizer and F. Lee Bailey would drop everything to defend, free of charge. And here it was, all his, punk kid just out of law school.

His mind boggled. At age thirty-two, penniless, unmarried, struggling to survive in a cruel and alien profession, with two suits and one pair of shoes to his name, Brice Mack was suddenly plunged into the center of the winner's circle. *He was made.*

Still, his antennae for danger, keened by the proximity of fame, kept a tight rein on his enthusiasm, cautioned him to proceed slowly and with care as there were hurdles ahead, dangerous road slicks and sudden, unmarked dead ends. Three of which were identifiable. The first, and least important to Brice Mack's long-range game plan, was the jury itself. By a process of careful selection, he would have to requisition jurors of compassion and sensitivity whose minds would be open to fresh concepts and whose imaginations would permit them to take the plunge into the penumbra of the occult and whose religious backgrounds would not cause them to discount the supernatural as entirely unthinkable. He knew he would have to be careful in his questioning, since his adversary, Deputy District Attorney Scott Velie, was certainly no fool and represented to Brice Mack the second and most dangerous hurdle to overcome.

Scott Velie was an old-timer in the trade. A mild man with a soft manner and a sleepy face, but a killer. Brice had studied Scott Velie in law school. His lethal string of convictions were classroom exercises.

Long before a court convened, Velie would have learned from the Templetons of Elliot Hoover's religious beliefs; hence, he would be privy to the defense's strategy and would be waiting in the wings to counter any move they might make in the direction of reincarnation.

This, the third hurdle, was the toughest—that of getting the court to accept reincarnation as a feasible defense. Velie could be expected to pull out all stops to discredit such a defense, and the odds were in his favor, unless Brice Mack lucked in on a sympathetic judge or was clever enough to convince an unsympathetic judge of its feasibility.

The assignment of the trial to the court of the Honorable Harmon T. Langley was a break of mammoth proportions.

Elderly, silver-maned, a political appointee from the days of Carmine De Sapio and the O'Dwyer landslide, Harmon Langley, having come to the end of a long and unspectacular career, poised, so to speak, on the edge of the great forgettery, would not be the one, reasoned Mack, to shun the mantle of sudden fame this baby offered.

In less than a day a group of prospective jurors was impaneled; the court clerk revolved the large drum of cards, and the business of selecting a jury got under way.

During the three weeks it took to select eleven jurors, Brice Mack gradually came to learn one disconcerting fact: Scott Velie was allowing him to pick the jury he wanted.

At no point did the district attorney register objection to any question Mack put to the jurors, and very often he agreed to seat a juror acceptable to the defense on the barest minimum of information. That he could be so sure of himself discomfited Brice Mack, but even more discomfiting was the thin, bemused smile Velie wore as he sat back relaxed, listening to his opponent's deeply probing examination of a juror's religious beliefs and biases. Either Scott Velie put little stock in the defense's ability to build its case on the reincarnation angle and was thus permitting him a free hand, or he was waiting for a more opportune moment to smash him.

"Your Honor"—Brice Mack rose from the defense table and faced the bench—"the defense finds no reason to dismiss this juror." Then, smiling vividly at Miss Hall, he added, "In fact, we welcome her addition."

Judge Langley turned to Scott Velie.

"Mr. Velie?"

Velie didn't bother to stand or move, merely shifted the direction of his vision past the eleven seated jurors to the juror under examination.

"Miss Hall, do you believe that criminals should be pampered?"

"No, sir."

"Have you ever been arrested?"

"No, sir."

"Are you acquainted with anyone who has had trouble with the law—say, a relative, or friend?"

"No, sir."

These were Scott Velie's standard opening questions to each prospective juror. The prosecution could ill afford to take on a juror who at any time in her life might have looked on the law as an enemy.

"Tell me, Miss Hall, if someone takes a child who doesn't belong to him and removes that child from her legitimate premises and takes her to other premises without consent of the parents, and indeed against the strong objections of the parents, even if that person believed he was committing no wrong and, in fact, the law could prove he was wrong and liable for his actions, would you have any difficulty in finding that person guilty?"

Miss Hall thought it best to give the question a considerable amount of thought before replying, "No, sir."

Bill's eyes stole past a row of heads to where Hoover sat, composed and serene. The hated face was like alabaster, its equanimity insufferable. With the slightest shift of focus, Bill brought his vision to rest on the gentle and cherished face of his wife, sitting beside him. The perfect, exquisite profile remained immobile, her attention seemingly fixed on a time and space beyond the present. Bill wondered what thoughts lay on the other side of the glazed and vacuous eyes. He recalled those eyes on another occasion—reflecting a look of shock, revulsion, betrayal, a look that was fleeting, yet one he would never forget. He had deserved it, God knew he had deserved that look—letting go like that, pulling her into the caldron of his anger, pointedly accusing her, practically branding her a traitor. Yes, Bill sadly reflected, in that moment he had lost his most precious possession, more dearly prized than love—the confidence and trust of the only person on earth who really mattered to him.

They ate, they conversed, they made love, by rote and necessity. They smiled a lot. Bill constantly found himself presampling and censoring each word and thought before uttering it. And when the need was upon him and he was able to muster the courage to reach out to her, he never failed to sense the momentary, slight stiffening of her flesh, the small sigh of resignation, the dutiful submission. It was all false. Both knew it. And in that knowledge the full measure of his loss was most painfully realized.

Their days and nights became computerized. Court from nine to four, cocktails and dinner, out mainly, from five to nine, the long walk home, and bed by ten. Weekends were spent in Westport with Ivy. They would drive up in a rental and stay at Candlemas Inn, the three of them.

Bill had agreed to the boarding school, but he didn't like it. He hated seeing Ivy in uniform, her beauty camouflaged, shorn of individuality. Yet she seemed to love it. She had been readily accepted by the other girls and in three weeks had already made two "best friends."

To date, newspaper accounts of the case had not traveled much. After the initial arrest and booking, which earned a second-page spot in the New York *Times*, the courtroom progress received minimal attention from the press. What coverage there was of the jury selection generally found itself in the back end of both the *News* and the *Post*. The *Times* printed an occasional squib. Connecticut papers ignored it entirely.

The time would come, Bill knew, when the case would rip its way into the headlines of newspapers around the country. For there was no doubt in Velie's mind of the defense's intention to put the issue of reincarnation into the record, although he would try to convince the court to rule it inadmissible as a viable defense. But by then the harm would have been done; the floodgates of publicity would have been opened.

Knowing what lay ahead of them, Bill had leveled with Sister Veronica Joseph, mother superior of Mount Carmel Parochial School for Girls, the day they had admitted Ivy, thus preparing her for the avalanche of publicity to come. While her bland expression had undergone a slight constriction of anxiety, she was quick to find the strength within her faith to cloak her shock and temper her misgivings with mercy. Bill saw her hand go instinctively to the large silver crucifix attached to a rope of black beads which fell from her habit as she softly intoned, "The poor child. We shall do everything possible to shelter her from the calumnies of the outside world." Which, Bill thought, was a quaint, yet certainly correct way of putting it for all of them.

It occurred to him to speculate on what calumnies he might expect from his colleagues at the office when the bombshell burst. Pel Simmons had been genuinely concerned and more than fair in letting him take a leave of absence for the duration of the trial and with no disruption in the flow of his semimonthly paychecks. It was an indication of his faith and trust in Bill, a lovely way of saying, "I like you, I want to keep you in my company." Of course, Pel wasn't aware of anything beyond what he had read in the newspapers and what little information Bill had vouchsafed him, which was precious little.

Soon, Bill glumly reflected, there would be one hell of a jarring note, one diamond-bright cog in Pel Simmons' quietly purring nondescript machine to fuck up the works. It would mean his job, ultimately. Not quickly—there'd be no pink slip stapled to the paycheck—it would take a year or so to phase him down and *out*. Don Goetz would move into his slot, reluctantly, of course, hating like hell to depose the master, flushed and angry at the injustice of it all, at the same time feeling the soft leather of the Eames recliner edging closer while his eyes sought the restful and mysterious silences of the Motherwell.

And that would be it. He'd be out! On the street! Pounding the pavement, avoiding dogshit. *Thump! Thump! Thump!* His heart was playing handball against his chest. Pods of perspiration glistened on his forehead. Was he having a coronary? That would cap it. To drop dead, right here in the courtroom, in the presence of the nearly picked jury. He wouldn't mind. It would help Velie's case. Elicit sympathy. Guarantee a conviction. Put the prick away for the limit.

Bill studied Hoover through a haze of sweat droplets clinging to his eyelashes, rendering an image that was blurred, distorted, and malevolent. Like a jungle animal, the son of a bitch had padded into his life and had quietly devoured all he possessed and prized—family, career, the love and respect of his wife, all that really mattered.

He could feel the flexing of his skin at the corners of his mouth and knew he was smiling. It always happened when he hit bottom, when his depressions and despondencies became intolerable. It was then some inner survival mechanism switched on, and a smile came to the rescue. And with the smile, an accompanying thought: If I'm destroyed, so will you be, you bastard!

Scott Velie wheeled around to the bench.
"This jury is acceptable to the State, Your Honor."
"Very well," Judge Langley said, keeping things moving. "The bailiff will swear in the jury."

Janice saw Hoover look up from his pad and turn to the twelve men and women, who rose in a body and faced the bailiff at the far end of the courtroom.

Reading from a sheet of paper, and in a voice that was low and grave, the uniformed man tremulously intoned the prescribed litany.

"Do you solemnly swear that you shall well and truly try and true deliverance make, between the people of the State of New York and the prisoner at the bar, whom you shall have in charge, according to the evidence and the laws of this State. . . ."

Hoover's face radiated purity and innocence as his twelve peers, whose duty and responsibility it would be to decide the guilt or innocence of one Elliot Suggins Hoover "beyond a shadow of a doubt" of the charge of "feloniously, willfully, and with malice aforethought" kidnapping one Ivy Templeton, were sworn in.

Watching Hoover watching the jury, the bland exterior enveloped by a will of tempered steel, pursuing the ends of his own self-interests with no apparent care or awareness of the mischief and malice of his acts and no shred of concern for the irreparable harm he was doing them, Janice knew that with all of Velie's confidence and Bill's assurances, it would be Hoover's single-minded obstinacy that would prevail in the end.

It was at this sepulchral moment that Janice knew they would lose the case.

15

". . . So help you God?" The bailiff looked up from his paper toward the jury.

The organlike chorus of "I do's" vibrated throughout the partially filled courtroom.

"Be seated," Judge Langley instructed the jury and, turning to counsels' tables, asked, "Are both sides ready to proceed?"

As Velie and Mack affirmed that they were, Judge Langley's eyes flicked up at the wall clock. "It's ten past eleven, Mr. Velie," he said in an offering voice. "If you wish a continuance until after the lunch break before making your opening remarks—"

"Thank you, Your Honor," Velie interposed. "I'm sure I'll be able to conclude what few remarks I wish to make to the jury well before the noon break."

"Very well," Langley said, somewhat nettled. "Proceed."

Scott Velie commenced his prepared speech as he sat, holding in abeyance his moment for rising, which was timed to occur at the delivery of a key sentence halfway into his brief statement. He began by swinging his chair around to the jury box and facing his twelve fellow citizens with an air of easy confidence. His voice was subdued, conversational, aimed at alleviating whatever tension might exist among them and putting them at their total ease.

"You know, folks," he began, "there are few crimes committed today for no reason. Sometimes somebody'll do something that's against the law and either not know why he did it or be unable to distinguish between right and wrong. In many such cases those people are deemed by the law to be suffering from a mental disease and are often adjudged insane. But in the great majority of cases people commit crimes for a reason. And these reasons are many. Hatred, fear, jealousy, the desire to appropriate what doesn't belong to them. You name it, the court records are full of reasons why people commit crimes."

He hunkered forward, hands clasped, arms resting on knees, and went on, confidentially. "Now you know, there are reasons behind reasons for committing crimes. Take hatred. There are many reasons why people hate other people—and some of these reasons are strong enough to cause a man to rob, maim, batter, injure, and even kill another person. Sometimes these reasons behind the reasons are the only hope a man who is proved to have committed a crime has to keep out of jail. His lawyer will often build a defense based on this reason behind the reason and call it an extenuating circumstance. Now this is what I'm getting at and, please, listen to me good. In any crime, and especially a capital crime, there can be no reason behind the reason, no extenuating circumstance to absolve a man from accepting the full responsibility of his lawless act; there can be no reduction of his liability for that lawless act; there can be no condoning, forgiving, forgetting, and no acquitting him from paying the full legally prescribed penalty for his lawless act. Not in the name of extenuating circumstance, not in the name of mercy, mother, or God in heaven!"

On this dramatic note, Velie shot to his feet—a move so sudden and unexpected as to cause several jurors in the first row to flinch—and pointing a finger at the bench, he shouted, *"Not in a court of law!* Which is where *you* are sitting today! A court of law, ladies and gentlemen! Not a church, which is constituted to dispense God's forgiveness. But a court of law, which is constituted to dispense *man's justice!"*

Scott Velie's eyes traveled slowly across the courtroom toward Elliot Hoover, sitting motionless beside his attorney.

"Today, in this courtroom," the district attorney continued, "a man stands accused before us of a crime so heinous and offensive to society as to be, along with willful and premeditated murder, categorized a capital crime. For there can be no more despicable act of lawlessness, outside of the taking of another human being's life, than the taking of another human being's child. . . ."

There were several choice moments in Velie's cracker-barrel sermon when Brice Mack might have objected, but he restrained himself. Juror Number Seven, Graser, Mack had noticed, seemed singularly unimpressed by Velie's approach and, at one point, during his admonition that God's forgiveness was to be found in church and not in court, even antagonistic. Juror Number Three, the carpenter and devout Catholic Mr. Fitzgerald, wasn't buying either. But Velie plowed ahead, scourging the courtroom of God's mercy and setting the stage, Mack realized, for the confrontation with the reincarnation issue, the mainstay in the defense's case.

"And we will further prove that it was a carefully considered and premeditated act. Through eyewitness testimony, we will demonstrate the care and planning that went into the engineering of this depraved and heartless crime. We will develop eyewitness testimony to show how many times Elliot Hoover lurked outside the child's school, in disguise, stalking his victim; the number of times he visited the apartment house in which the child lived, for the purpose of casing it; how he ultimately moved into the apartment house to be in a better position to steal the child; how he consciously, knowingly, and intentionally created an incident, a diversion: a brutal attack on the child's father which enabled him to gain access to the apartment and take the child; how he sneaked out the back door and secreted the child in his hideaway...."

Brice Mack glanced at the wall clock. Eleven twenty-five. Velie, he knew, would continue his harangue until just short of the noon hour, at which point he would wrap it up with a dramatic denunciation of his client's *execrable* and *depraved* act and call for the full penalty allowable by law. Then, following the lunch break, some two hours in the future, the moment would finally arrive when the defense of Elliot Hoover would formally begin. When two months of hard, round-the-clock, frantic activity would all be risked on a single throw of the dice: proof of the existence of reincarnation.

"... and for the damage he has done this family in his unwarranted attentions, leading up to the perpetration of"—instead of "execrable" and "depraved," as Brice Mack had predicted, Velie resorted to—"this *degenerate* and *evil* crime of kidnapping, and the incalculable damage he might have done to the child, the State demands that Elliot Hoover be found guilty of kidnapping in the first degree, and that the court assess upon him the maximum penalty allowable by law."

The courtroom heaved a long and weary sigh as Scott Velie nodded to the bench that he was through. The time was eleven fifty-seven. Judge Langley rose.

"We'll take our noon recess now. Court will reconvene at one thirty."

A murmuring hum accompanied jury and spectators to their respective exits.

Janice remained standing while Bill and Scott Velie exchanged friendly smiles topped off by supportive winks, expressions of confidence, as each knew the moment of truth was upon them. Janice saw Brice Mack speaking animatedly to Elliot Hoover as they slowly gravitated toward the prisoner's door in the company of the armed guard. They would all eat lunch now, Janice thought, partake of sustenance, renew their energies for the ordeal ahead. The condemned would eat a hearty meal. All of them.

It would be a four-martini lunch for Bill, Janice calculated, since he'd just finished his second, and they hadn't ordered as yet. She, too, had relented on this day and was nursing a double J & B with water.

Pinetta's was located in an alleyway just east of Foley Square, within easy walking distance of the Criminal Courts Building. Featuring a Tudor façade with South-of-France striped awnings, the restaurant was the happy marriage of two stores with upper lofts merged into a Dickensian fantasy. A collection of small paneled rooms, authentically furnished and decorated in the tradition of the Cheshire Cheese offered quasi-private dining rooms on three levels. Staircases went up and down in the least expected places. A charming and totally unexpected treat to have discovered in this rather bleak and monotonous part of town.

Catering almost exclusively to a clientele made up of the more affluent members and guests of the Criminal Courts Building, it was possible, during ongoing cases, to reserve a luncheon table for the duration. Bill and Janice's table was located on the second-floor balcony, not too noisy, and well serviced, but with one serious drawback. Below them, visible from every angle of their table, was Brice Mack's long deal table, around which his "team" gathered each day: five, sometimes six men of varying ages and social backgrounds eating, drinking, smoking, and jabbering their reports and opinions to the "boss," Brice Mack, who sat at the head of the table.

Twice Bill sought another table from the manager and twice was put off with the polite promise: "Soon there will be plenty of tables, sir. The case in Part Four goes to jury any day now." The "any day now" stretched into three weeks.

A week before—it was a Monday, and Janice had skipped lunch to run some errands—Bill had invited Scott Velie to join him. Over tankards of beer and short ribs steeped in creamy horseradish sauce, Velie had identified each of Brice Mack's cohorts for Bill and filled him in on their backgrounds.

"The two young guys are lawyers doing research and general legwork in the courthouse. The dignified old duffer with the rimless glasses and the goatee is Willard Ahmanson, professor of religious studies at NYU. The thin pimply guy is a legal secretary, name of Fred Hudson; he used to work as a court clerk. The old disreputable-looking character drinking whiskey neats is an ex-cop named Brennigan." Velie smiled and winked. "Private eye." Then, after chewing a forkful of meat and washing it down with beer, he added, "they're all on run-of-the-trial retainers, which, when added up, comes to quite a piece of change."

"Hoover's got plenty."

"Really? Well, that's not all he's paying for. They've got a Hindu maharishi stashed away at the Waldorf. A man named Gupta Pradesh, reputed to be one of India's leading yogis. Flew him in all the way from Calcutta."

Swallowing the rich food, Bill had experienced a momentary nausea as the full breadth and scope of Hoover's defense suddenly struck him. There were no lengths or extremes the son of a bitch wasn't prepared to go to prove his fucking point.

"Why is he paying a detective?"

"To get a line on your daughter's nightmares. Brennigan's been nosing around Dr. Kaplan's office. With no luck, I'm pleased to say."

Bill felt a quick surge of warmth for Kaplan and for all doctors in general. They were like priests. Tight-lipped. Under the Hippocratic Oath to betray no confidence.

"Can Mack bring him into court to testify?"

"Certainly. But that doesn't mean he's going to be able to get answers to all his questions."

"What do you mean?"

"Any communication between patient and doctor is privileged in the State of New York and, as such, cannot be elicited except under certain conditions. For example, if the patient should consent to the doctor's testifying. Which she certainly is not about to do."

Hoover and his attorney were seated at the defense table when Janice and Bill entered the courtroom at one twenty-six. Typically, Brice Mack was engaged in an animated one-sided conversation while his client doodled furiously on his pad, engrossed in his own mysterious labors and betraying no sign that he was the least interested or even heard what his lawyer was saying.

The spectators' section of the courtroom was less than a quarter filled, and only one reporter, the woman, occupied the long row reserved for the press. The man from UP had not bothered to return. On the basis of all that had been heard and what meager coverage it had received in the press, the trial held little promise of being anything more than another routine, predictable, open-and-shut case. Thus far the proceedings had augured no slight hint of the drama to come; hence the house was definitely no sellout.

A few seconds before one thirty Scott Velie and two assistants ambled up to the prosecution's table, where they remained standing and chatting quietly. In another moment what few people there were in the courtroom rose to their feet as Judge Harmon T. Langley swished past the flag of the State of New York and nestled his black-robed bulk behind the altar of justice. His acolyte with shining sidearm and badge accompanied his progress with all the rigidity of a papal guardsman.

Up until the very second it took for the bench to settle in, gather its thoughts together, bring the court to session, and ask the crucial question of the defense, Brice Mack had serious doubts about its answer. Only two were possible. Either, "Yes, Your Honor, the defense is ready to proceed with its opening remarks." Or, "No, Your Honor, the defense wishes to postpone its opening remarks until it commences the presentation of its case."

The former answer would bring about a quick confrontation on the reincarnation issue and create a sudden-death situation; however, the jury would have been made privy to the defense's contention and would hear the testimony of each witness for the prosecution in the light of that knowledge. An important consideration, since it would tend to soften and compromise the prosecution's case in the jury's mind.

The only benefit in the latter answer was to buy more time. It would postpone the reincarnation issue for at least a week since the state's roster of witnesses was considerable—twelve according to Velie's office—and allow them to continue their investigation of Ivy Templeton's nightmares. Until now Brennigan had been singularly lacking in success in tracking down any leads or information. Dr. Kaplan, who certainly was aware they existed, remained closemouthed. The friends of the Templetons, the Federicos, were totally unapproachable. Still, the nightmares were a fact. They existed. They had come to plague the child twice in her life. Both times when Hoover was present in the city. His presence, Hoover contended, triggered these deeply disturbing experiences that never varied in content or degree.

As Elliot Hoover had described the nightmares to him, and if his accuracy could be trusted, they constituted the one direct link between the Templetons' child, Ivy, and Hoover's daughter, Audrey Rose—or, at least, his daughter's *soul*.

Brice Mack felt a light film of sweat appear on his face. It always happened at these times, when his most serious concentration was directed at the basic issue in the case and he found himself giving sober credence to such concepts, actually employing detectives to match a living child to the soul of a dead child, that his face became moist and clammy and the ground began to shift under his feet. It was at such moments of weakness, when the mind-boggling enormity and effrontery of such a defense suddenly struck like a whiplash, that the placid, sincere, and assured face of Elliot Hoover would come to his rescue. After all, he would tell his quaking heart, a lawyer's duty is not to question the validity of his client's beliefs or to render a judgment on his competency to entertain such beliefs. A lawyer's duty is only to represent the legal interests of his client and see to it that he receives a fair and just hearing under the law. But his quaking heart knew better.

Born and bred in a tradition of reality in a tough Bronx ghetto, harsh and uncompromising, put through school by the sweat and toil of a working mother, gaining his Ivy League degree via the indignity of a change of name (their quota on Jews, he had heard recently, had gone up one-half percent in the last five years), Brice Mack, né Bruce Marmorstein, knew the difference between what is and what ain't. Or, as Walt Whitman more fancily put it, "He could resist the temptation to see what a thing ought to be rather than what it is."

And he also knew a *meshuganeh* when he saw one.

"Yes, Your Honor." Brice Mack rose and addressed the bench. "We are ready to proceed with our opening remarks."

Janice sensed a palpable stiffening in Bill, a girding of inner resources for the blow about to come, as Brice Mack slowly pressed forward toward the jury box, smiling easily, his hand extended confidently.

"Ladies and gentlemen of the jury," he began in a somewhat stilted and formal manner, "what I am about to tell you will take some time and will require your absolute attention, for what you are about to hear is unique in the annals of Anglo-Saxon jurisprudence. By the time this trial is over and this honorable court is adjourned; by the time the final words of the prosecution and the defense have been uttered and written into the court record; by the time you have returned to your seats in the jury box with a verdict which I am sure will be fair, just, and well considered; by that time, ladies and gentlemen of the jury, you and this court and the world at large will know that what took place in this courtroom—Part Seven of the Criminal Courts Building—will forever be memorialized in the history books and records that assiduously follow the progress of mankind's most important steps on earth." He stopped, carefully sustaining a dramatic pause before continuing. "What you will hear may shock you. May elicit an initial response of disbelief. May even bring smiles of derision to your faces. But I promise you, ladies and gentlemen of the jury, that before this trial is over, your shock will be replaced by understanding, your disbelief by total acceptance, and your derisive smiles will become smiles of pure joy and hope, for not only will the many proofs and testimonies we have amassed convince you to liberate a human being and free him from the fearsome punishment of imprisonment, these very same proofs and testimonies will serve to liberate each and every one of you sitting before me from the most fearsome and dreaded punishment known to man, the legacy we all inherit at birth and which hovers, shroudlike, above us through every day and night of our lives: the sure and certain knowledge of our own impermanence and our own personal oblivion."

Brice Mack paused here to let the weight of his message sink in before continuing.

"Before going on, however, if you will bear with me in a small digression, I should like to tell you, since Mr. Velie failed to do so, just what precisely the law in this state regards as first degree kidnapping. . . ."

Scott Velie had come to his feet halfway through Brice Mack's statement and was waiting patiently with arms folded for the proper moment to object, which was now.

"Objection, Your Honor! Defense counsel knows that only the bench has the authority to instruct the jury on the law and that it is improper for either counsel to assume such an authority; besides which, this is not a proper statement to be made in an opening address anyway. . . ."

"Your Honor," Brice Mack retaliated with equal force, "the defense contends that the charge of first degree kidnapping is inept, inappropriate, and improper as it applies to the defendant; that, if any charge had pertinence in this case, and the defense is confident of its ability to disprove even that, it would be the lesser charge of custodial interference in the second degree. . . ."

It was coming. Janice's hand groped for Bill's, found it tense and clammy. The woman reporter seemed suddenly revitalized, her attention riveted on the dueling lawyers. Even Judge Langley was leaning forward in an attitude of renewed interest.

"Custodial interference, Mr. Mack," the judge instructed, "as I'm sure you know, implies the existence of a direct blood relationship between the litigants in an action. Can you offer such proofs?"

"Yes, Your Honor. Through the development of testimony based on the knowledge and experience of expert and learned witnesses, the defense will clearly demonstrate that the most conclusive and strongest possible familial relationship does indeed exist between the defendant, Elliot Hoover, and the child known as Ivy Templeton—"

"Objection, Your Honor," Velie cut in. "This is totally improper in an opening address. Again, defense counsel is attempting to discuss the law; if he felt the charges were inappropriate, there were motions he could have made before the trial commenced to have the charges dismissed. Further, the state can offer substantial proofs and documents to refute any earthly claim of a direct blood relationship between the victim and her abductor."

"Well," said Judge Langley somewhat dryly, "it would seem that both of you are aware of a good deal more than I."

"Your Honor!" Both lawyers spoke at once, but Velie's booming voice overpowered and outdistanced his opponent's.

"Your Honor, lest this hearing become polluted with wild and unfounded assertions, may I beg the court's indulgence for a conference in chambers out of earshot of the jury?"

Judge Langley, his curiosity piqued, was quick to agree. "Very well, court will stand in recess. Jury will be ushered back to the jury room until summoned."

Janice heard a sibilant sigh slowly escape from Bill as the pent-up tension within him was gradually released. He turned to Janice and smiled nervously.

"Velie's round, I'd say," he murmured.

Janice smiled back encouragingly. His hand clasped hers tightly, as would a child's about to enter a haunted house.

"Why wasn't I advised of this earlier?" Judge Langley said, his irritation showing. "Not a word about reincarnation in our pretrial conference. Why wasn't this matter brought to my attention?"

"The only matters that are important in this case, Your Honor, are the hard, earthbound facts," Velie said in a sulky, aggrieved tone of voice. "It doesn't matter whether Hoover believes in reincarnation or believes that the moon is made of green cheese. The fact is he committed a crime by taking someone else's legitimate offspring, removed her from her home, secreted her in his own home, and then interfered with the performance of a government function. No matter what his reasons were for doing this act, he is liable to arrest and prosecution under the law."

Judge Langley fixed a cold stare on Brice Mack.

"All right, Mr. Mack, let's have it."

"Very simply, Your Honor," Brice Mack said, holding his voice to a discreet and reverent level, "we believe that the question of reincarnation is relevant and material to this case."

"On what grounds?"

"On the grounds that it provides the defendant with a perfectly valid defense."

Langley's voice fell like a hammerblow. "You mean, just because your client happens to believe this poppycock, you are prepared to turn my courtroom into a three-ring circus?"

"Your Honor," Brice Mack quickly interjected, "please, sir, it is certainly not our intention to in any way compromise the dignity of your court. However, my client stands accused of one of the gravest charges on the books, and I'm sure you will allow that he does have the constitutional right to defend himself against such a charge."

"Your client is entitled to a *reasonable* and *proper* defense under the law, Mr. Mack. Nothing more and nothing less. Do I make myself clear?"

"Yes, sir, perfectly clear. And we believe that a defense based on reincarnation is entirely reasonable and proper under the circumstances."

"Have you done any research?" growled Langley. "Can you cite sources, give me any legal precedents for such a defense?"

"No, Your Honor," said Mack in his most disarming little-boy voice. "We have found no legal precedents to support this defense."

Judge Langley appeared stunned. "And you expect me to instruct the jury that if they find your client took the child in the belief she was his reincarnated daughter, they must find him not guilty?"

He gazed at Scott Velie with a twinkle of a smile and shook his head. Velie, sunken deeply in his chair, grinned back. Brice Mack waited until their exchange of looks was completed before continuing.

"It is not my client's belief in reincarnation that's important, Your Honor. What's important is whether reincarnation is a fact. I believe, in order for my client to be found guilty, the jury must make a finding that there is no such thing as reincarnation and that it is impossible for Ivy Templeton to be Elliot Hoover's child. We have experts who will testify to the contrary, and regardless of Your Honor's predilection or predisposition to believe or not to believe this, *we* believe the court owes the defense the opportunity of presenting this evidence. We believe it is material and relevant and competent, and we should be permitted to convince the jury that this is so; because if we are able to do this, then the kidnapping charge is not a viable charge."

During the soft-spoken, slowly articulated statement, Judge Langley felt himself retreat into the soft burnished leather of his ancient chair as a sick, oppressive weight bore down on his chest. He had had a prescience when he awakened that morning, after having passed a restless and mainly sleepless night, that it would be one of those days. Looking across at the unlined, eagerly bright, and rapacious face of the young attorney, Judge Langley suddenly felt very, very old.

Scott Velie was quick to catch the momentary flagging of attention, the diminution of intensity in the judge's eyes, and knew it was his cue to step in. The old hypocrite's intellectual range and judicial acumen were obviously being sorely tested.

"Your Honor," he said, removing a document from his inner pocket and passing it across the desk to the judge, "this is a Xeroxed copy of Ivy Templeton's birth certificate; physical evidence that Ivy was born to William and Janice Templeton and was the issue of Mrs. Templeton's womb. So, unless Mr. Hoover fathered the child through sexual intercourse with Mrs. Templeton, which he does not claim to have done, there is no way in my mind that he can prove the child is his. Even if, and I submit the 'if' is a mighty big one, even if reincarnation could be proved to be a viable theory, all it would show is that she may have formerly been Hoover's child, but is not presently. This document is the only certified legal instrument attesting to the child's parentage, and nothing Elliot Hoover claims or believes can ever change that."

A certain strength returned to the judge's face as he eagerly perused the birth certificate. This was something he could grapple with, something tangible, of legal import.

Holding it before Brice Mack like a cudgel, he asked, "What about it, counselor, can the defendant render a like document to the court proving his legal right to claim the child as being his?"

Brice Mack's eyes sought the floor as a small, tolerant smile formed on his lips. It was a smile that Judge Langley could not abide. It smacked of arrogance, smart, slick Jewboy arrogance, born of assurance, know-how, and the need to make it.

"Your Honor"—the smile spoke—"there is no doubt, nor is the defense contending to the contrary, that the child was produced at the time and place and to the person that the birth certificate attests to. But just because there is the physical act of a baby coming out of a womb, it can't be assumed ipso facto that the baby necessarily belongs to that person."

About to answer, Judge Langley was cut short as Brice Mack stood up and slammed a half dollar down on his desk with a ringing clatter.

"If you were to swallow my half dollar, Your Honor, and it passed through your system and was finally ejected by you, would you say that that half dollar was then necessarily your property?"

Again Judge Langley, about to speak, was overridden by Mack. "I say to you that Janice Templeton's body may only have been a conduit to pass Elliot Hoover's child on from a past life into a present life."

Both Velie and Judge Langley waited for Brice Mack to continue, as it seemed he would since he remained standing, but it gradually became evident that he had finished what he had to say and was awaiting the judge's response.

"Sit down, Mr. Mack," Judge Langley said icily. "I'm not used to looking up to people in my own office."

The little smile never left Brice Mack's face as he slowly resumed his seat and hunched forward in an attitude of rapt attention.

"To begin with, young man," the judge continued, "if I were made to straddle a commode and strain out a fifty-cent piece, it damn well would be my property."

Brice Mack joined Scott Velie in a small chuckle, a salute to the judge's nimble sense of humor.

"Secondly," the old man went on, "the defense you are proposing, that of establishing the truth of reincarnation as a means of substantiating your client's innocence, even if successful, will not let your client off the hook unless you are also able to prove the kidnapped girl was in fact the defendant's reincarnated daughter. Your witnesses, as I now understand it, have no relationship to the defendant or to the crime he is accused of committing—they are to appear in court merely for the purpose of arguing and expounding on concepts of a philosophical and religious character, which arguments, may I say, would seem to me to be more fittingly heard in a seminary and not in a court of law. In short, Mr. Mack, you are proposing a defense that is highly irregular, highly unorthodox, and one which fills me with grave misgivings."

"Precisely, sir." The warm, knowing smile again. "As well it should, for the very nature of this case is highly irregular and highly unorthodox. As I explained to the jury, it is a case that is unique in the annals of Anglo-Saxon jurisprudence and one that will be studied, discussed, written about, and forever chronicled in the histories and record books detailing man's advent on earth."

He was courting him. Judge Langley knew the bastard was courting him—dangling the carrot fame in front of his nose, appealing to his baser instincts in order to jockey him into position. There were no ends these Hebes wouldn't go to in order to get what they wanted, he thought sourly. And yet the point was well made; there was no denying that. There'd be a hell of a press on this baby. For a change, Part Seven would find itself bustling and glittering under the glare of lights, cameras, boob-tube lenses, hallway press conferences, the whole ball of wax. They had never thrown the big ones his way. Fuller, Kararian, Pletchkow, Tanner, they got the cream of the cases. And left the dregs for him. The family squabbles. The junkie busts. The crap. Well, maybe the time had come to drag his ass out of the sewer they had consigned him to and step up into the light of day. It would mean letting his guard down, leaving himself open to possible criticism and ridicule. But what the hell? So what? How much longer did he have left anyway? Damn heart rumbling around inside his chest like an old motorboat. Be nice being followed around for a change. Asked questions. Made a fuss over. Yeah, it'd be nice for a change.

". . . and I submit, Your Honor, that if you deny the defense the right to develop a full understanding of what reincarnation consists of, a belief that is shared by millions upon millions of people in this world, you will be denying the defendant his constitutional right to plead his case and defend himself in the only possible manner left him. Furthermore, the defense is prepared to submit evidence supporting the defendant's claim that the girl is his reincarnated daughter."

Velie caught something in the judge's look, a slight slackening of the skin around the mouth, a wandering of focus in the eyes, that set off warning bells clanging in his brain. Langley was going for it! He was buying the bullshit! Goddamn!

"Your Honor," Velie quickly interposed, but even as he spoke, he knew it was too late. "Your Honor, this is beyond belief. Such a defense is totally unknown in Western courts. Reincarnation is believed in a portion of the world, true, but that world is not our world here. Are you going to impose another culture on our culture? You cannot do that, for then it will defy the laws that our legislature in its wisdom has passed down for the benefit of our society."

Judge Langley's tongue carefully moistened his lips before they opened to speak.

"You may be absolutely right, Mr. Velie, and I'm not saying you are wrong. However, I feel there is some merit in Mr. Mack's assessment of the situation. Since kidnapping is such a serious charge, I don't feel I can deprive the defendant of any defense he chooses to engage in that has some semblance of possibility for him."

Brice Mack remained immobile, scarcely breathing, as Scott Velie shot to his feet and, flushed with anger, turned upon the old judge.

"Judge Langley," he said, pronouncing the name as he would a malediction, "I plead with you to reconsider a decision for which there is no legal precedent." His tone shifted subtly to a threatening register. "It may well open a Pandora's box you may find impossible to close."

"Your concern is appreciated, Mr. Velie," Langley said dryly. "Nevertheless, until you can cite me any authority that holds reincarnation is impossible, I am not disposed to close off any area of defense for the defendant, so I will allow this testimony to go in, subject to its being connected to the actual facts of the case."

And that was it.

Brice Mack had won.

16

By the time Judge Langley had returned to the bench and reconvened the court the room was more than three-quarters filled with spectators waiting breathlessly in an atmosphere charged with anticipation. How the news that something was about to break in Part Seven had managed to travel as quickly and reach as many people as it had was completely baffling to Janice. Even the press row was accommodated by an assortment of newspaper and radio people, slouching in their seats, quietly awaiting the recommencement of the proceedings with smiling interest.

The defense attorney began with a tightly puzzled expression on his face. "Now where were we," he softly queried, leaving unstated but strictly implied, "before we were so rudely interrupted?" The question and the way in which it was put clearly informed the jurors that he had won his point in chambers and was now able to pursue the ends of justice in a free manner. Janice noticed that several jurors smiled and that a number of them cast surreptitious glances at Scott Velie, who sat motionless with his back turned to the defense attorney. She also sensed Bill gradually sinking deeper and deeper into his seat as the message of Velie's defeat got through to him.

"Let me see," Mack continued, pretending to sort through the cobwebs of his mind for the correct point of departure, not only fully aware of exactly where he had left off but of the precise order and nuance of each word he was about to utter—written, rewritten, rehearsed, and performed for hours on end each night for the past month before the cracked mirror in his cheap roach-ridden flat on West 103rd Street.

"Oh, yes, I was saying that we will demonstrate that the most conclusive and strongest possible familial relationship does indeed exist between the defendant, Elliot Hoover, and the child known as Ivy Templeton. A relationship, ladies and gentlemen, based not on the laws of man, which are imperfect and changeable, but on the perfect and immutable laws of a God and a religion embraced by more than one billion people on earth today; laws which are adhered to, believed in, practiced, and utilized in their daily lives with the same conviction and faith that we, in this courtroom, that *you*, sitting in that jury box, ascribe to your own religion."

There was a soft rustling throughout the court as Brice Mack paused. The jury exchanged glances with one another. The reporters' pencils remained poised over their pads.

"In the course of testimony, you will hear learned men expound on this religion, this faith and belief. You will be made privy to its tenets, its beauty, its rules and conditions, and its rewards." Turning toward Hoover, Brice Mack extended a finger out to him in a gentle gesture. "You will hear a story from that man, from his own lips—a story that will shake you, grieve you, but that will in the end thrill you and uplift you. You will know of his child, his only child, Audrey Rose, aged five, and of her tragic and horrible end along with her mother in a fiery automobile accident. You will feel the keenness of Elliot Hoover's loss, the desperate loneliness of his life in the aftermath of that terrible tragedy; you will hear how, in his darkest moment, a power and insight were granted him, how a message came to him, from the other side of the grave, as it were, a message through the intercession of one of this nation's most honored and revered exponents of psychic phenomena, the late Erik Lloyd. A message that sent this honest, toiling, bedrock American, a man such as you and I," he emphasized, gazing pointedly at Mr. Fitzgerald, "on a journey to far and exotic lands in order to corroborate its authenticity, to rid himself of all skepticism and doubt before permitting himself to credit its contents. A journey lasting seven years, during which time he embraced not only a faith and religion theretofore totally unknown to him, but a people as well, living with them, sharing their lives, their joys, their hopes, their misfortunes, and all for the purpose of ascertaining the validity of that strange and wondrous message proffered him by Erik Lloyd. A message that, if inaccurate, could seriously injure, do irreparable damage to the lives of three innocent human beings, but a message that, if true, could well provide the answer to one of man's most ancient and unexplained mysteries; that would shed light on the very meaning and nature of life . . . and death.

"A message that said. . . ."

The graveyard silence in the courtroom sustained the perfect atmosphere for Brice Mack's next remark, which came with the force and fury of a thunderclap.

"SHE LIVES!" he shouted, and wheeled around from the jury box to face the audience, his right hand pointing dramatically toward heaven. "YOUR DAUGHTER LIVES! AUDREY ROSE LIVES!"

Janice felt the entire courtroom jump as the words rent the air. Even Judge Langley flinched. Only Bill, burrowed deeply in his seat, eyes shut, chin sunk into his collar, mired in liquor and his own despair, seemed out of it.

"She lives!" Mack crooned tremblingly, his voice filled with a child's awe. "Audrey Rose has returned! Her soul has crossed over the vale of darkness into a new earth life where it now resides in perfect harmony within the body of a child—a child who dwells in the city of New York and who is called Ivy."

A general breath was exhaled by the court, accompanied by scattered titters. The jurors' faces seemed stiff and unnatural, under constraint to maintain the proper degree of decorum under the circumstances; a losing battle in Juror Number Four, Mr. Potash, the accountant, who was smiling blatantly.

Judge Langley pounded his gavel for order but voiced no warning.

"Yes, folks," Brice Mack continued on a less histrionic note, "this is the message that Elliot Hoover received from Erik Lloyd. It said that his daughter was alive. That Audrey Rose had been reincarnated. And through subsequent investigations, he would learn that on August 4, 1964, at exactly eight twenty-seven in the morning, a few minutes after the car accident which took his child's life, she was reborn in New York Hospital to Mr. and Mrs. William Templeton and would in this earth life henceforth be known as Ivy."

Janice heard the woman reporter in front of her softly chuckle and say, "Oh, come now." Bill, deep in his seat beside her, made neither sound nor movement and seemed to be asleep or, Janice did not rule out the possibility, passed out.

Stepping back and with a wave of the arm that was all-inclusive, Brice Mack appealed, "Please, ladies and gentlemen, look into your hearts and consider well your attitudes to what I have just told you. Words such as 'incredible,' 'unbelievable,' and 'impossible' have a distinct place and utility in the earthly matters of men but—I'm sure you will allow—have no pertinence at all in the heavenly affairs of God. All things are possible with God. And on God's lofty plane do the basic issues in this case reside! For we are dealing here with a man's faith, belief, and a most deeply felt religious commitment. A commitment to a religious concept that was made only after long and anguished soul-searching and years and years of travel and study before the seed of a firm conviction and absolute faith could take root and blossom in his heart and mind."

Brice Mack had slowly retreated from the jury box to a point just parallel to Elliot Hoover, who was sitting stiffly upright, scribbling intensely on his pad. Scott Velie, Janice noticed, had turned about in his chair and was observing his adversary with the interest and curiosity of a scientist studying a bug on the end of a pin. Even the press had paused in their note taking and were watching the young attorney, transfixed.

"Only then, ladies and gentlemen, after nearly a decade away from home, did he allow himself the privilege of returning to this country in order to bring down the curtain on the final act of his long and desperate quest. Only then, firm in his belief of the verity of Erik Lloyd's message, did he dare approach the lives of the plaintiffs and seek to introduce himself to them. And how did he present himself? As a beggar? No. As a robber out to take that which was not legally his? Never! He presented himself simply as the man of honor and decency that he is, requesting their indulgence, their understanding, and perhaps even a crumb of kindness. As he himself stated it to me, wanting nothing more than they were prepared to give him. He expected their derision, and he got it. He expected their rejection and received it. He expected their absolute denial of his God-granted right to meet and to visit with the child, Ivy—the earthly embodiment of his daughter, Audrey Rose—and fully accepted the whiplash of their denial with grace and understanding and was prepared to turn away from their door, to step out of their lives and never return again, when—when something happened to stop him, ladies and gentlemen. An event so extraordinary as to cause Elliot Hoover to halt in his tracks—to cause him to reconsider his adamant resolve to escape that intolerable situation, an event that suddenly lent force and meaning to all the years of travel and study and dedication he had given to his untiring pursuit of truth."

The defense attorney selected this crucial moment to relieve his parched throat and cruelly lingered over each step of pouring, measuring, and sipping the water.

"And that event, ladies and gentlemen, occurred on the very first night Elliot Hoover visited the Templeton family, at their invitation by the way, at which time, as if God in heaven had heard his appeal, a miracle took place. Yes, a miracle. For that night, for the first time in ten years, Elliot Hoover heard the voice of his daughter, Audrey Rose, cry out to him in desperate appeal, 'Daddy, Daddy, help me, help me!'

"Now let me make myself perfectly clear. I'm not talking about a voice that came to him out of his own anguish, an imagined voice, a voice in his head, disembodied, oh, no! It was a voice that was heard by all present, a real, honest-to-God voice that belonged to the one person who had the right to transmit Audrey Rose's appeal to her father—the Templetons' own daughter, Ivy!"

There was a noticeable stirring in the courtroom as throats were cleared and looks exchanged. A kind of nervous questioning in the faces of press, jury, and spectators alike, as if seeking corroboration to credit what they were hearing. Janice saw Scott Velie bestir himself and thought he might be preparing to object, but noting the disbelief on the jurors' faces, he apparently decided not to do so. A smug smile appeared on his face, instead, which, if Janice read it correctly, seemed to say, "Go on, buster, you're doing fine."

"Yes, ladies and gentlemen," Mack continued doggedly, "Ivy Templeton, who, caught in the grip of a terrible nightmare and in the presence of four witnesses, cried out to Elliot Hoover. And her cry was the cry of a soul in torment, the soul of Audrey Rose, who, seared by the flames of the fire that had consumed her, was unable to find rest, to find surcease from that devastating horror until . . . until, ladies and gentlemen, that man, Elliot Hoover, her father, went to her and through his very presence and fatherly love was finally able to soothe her restless spirit and allay her terrors."

The attorney turned to the jury and shook his head in quick negative jerks.

"No, I will not go into greater detail at this time. But understand, there is a great deal you need to know. And before this trial is over, you shall know it all, I promise you." His eyes shifted toward Scott Velie. "A prima facie case on kidnapping in the first degree against the defendant has been somewhat sparingly suggested by the learned prosecutor. Before this trial is over, we shall present evidence to refute that charge in its entirety. We will show that Elliot Hoover, far from entering the lives of the Templetons as an interloper and villain, bent on evil and mischief, was instead their benefactor, a man of compassion and concern who alone could assuage the awful and devastating torments of their daughter, Ivy, and through her the spirit of his own daughter, Audrey Rose. We will demonstrate beyond all shadow of a doubt that Elliot Hoover did not go to visit the Templetons that fateful night for the purpose of assaulting their daughter, but to place his special and unique services at their disposal in the hope of alleviating the sufferings of a young and innocent child."

In one abrupt motion he spun around to Janice and fixed her with a hard and accusing look.

"You will hear how, upon entering the bedroom of the apartment, he found the child bruised and bloodied and tied, yes, TIED to the bedstead like an animal. You will come to understand and fully believe why Elliot Hoover needed to take Ivy Templeton to his own apartment —not to steal or sequester her for purposes illegal or illicit, but to help her, to save her, to calm her, to wash her wounds, to treat and care for her pained and injured body and to pacify and ease her restless and tormented soul: the soul of Audrey Rose."

Calmly and with assurance, he turned to the jury.

They were listening. They were hanging onto his last word, waiting for his next. Sure, there was doubt, disbelief on the faces of Three and Ten. Number Four, Potash, was grinning. But Mrs. Carbone was listening. And Harrison and Fitzgerald and Hall. They were hearing. They were hooked. Nice going for ten minutes' work.

"I'm certain you will all keep an open mind to the testimony of the expert witnesses I will bring into this courtroom to establish a firm basis for our contention that Elliot Hoover had a perfect right—a ward's right —to take that child from an atmosphere fraught with violence and peril and remove her to a place of peace and safety. I am equally certain that when the testimony is completed, you will render a verdict—a just and honorable verdict—that will clear Elliot Hoover of any taint of guilt in regard to the false and misleading charges brought against him by the State of New York."

Then, turning to the bench, Brice Mack effected a slight bow and said, "Thank you, Your Honor."

Judge Langley quickly banged his gavel.

"This court will stand in recess until nine o'clock tomorrow morning."

Even after the judge's departure, the entire courtroom remained silent as time hung suspended for seconds until reality took over. Then the silence was rent as a sudden hailstorm of voices deluged the room with a huge, formless wave of sound.

As Janice rose and joined the exodus, she noted the smiles on the jurors' faces as they filed out of their box and were taken back to the jury room. There was no sign of the judge, but Scott Velie had remained behind and was chatting and laughing with a reporter. Spotting Janice, Velie winked and smiled at her encouragingly.

Elliot Hoover and Brice Mack were standing, hands clasped, smiling amiably while the guard stood by, wearing a small grin as he waited to take the prisoner back to his cell. Smiles and laughter seemed to dominate the moment, forcing Janice into a well of merriment.

The case of the *People* v. *Elliot Hoover* had got off to a gay and happy start.

There were messages at the desk, mainly for Bill and mainly from his office; his secretary twice, Don Goetz four times, Mr. Simmons once, and two from a reporter named Hazard from AP. There was a message for Janice from Carole: "Would they care to join them for dinner that night, veal birds and fettucini casa linga? PLEASE!!" Janice would not at all have minded but knew that Bill would say no. She would call Carole later and thank her.

Bill thrust aside the messages and put through a call to Mount Carmel.

Janice hung up their coats, then went upstairs and picked up the extension in time to hear, "And please don't worry, Mr. Templeton, all the sisters and the teachers have been alerted to safeguard your child's privacy and tranquillity. You can depend on us."

"Thank you, Mother Veronica," Bill said huskily, then made several fatherly inquiries about Ivy's schoolwork, deportment, and state of health.

"She's a lovely child," the mother enthused, "and a very good student; alert, bright, and well liked by the other girls. She's at dinner now. Suppose I have her call you after evening prayers?"

"I'd be grateful, Mother."

The *omelette à fines herbes sec* which she whipped together with dried parsley and basil flakes was a disaster since there was neither butter nor oil in the house. The final result, poached in a bit of water, was limpid, mealy, and inedible.

Before Ivy's call came through at seven fifteen, they'd received two other calls, both for Bill. Don Goetz's call came first, a few minutes after they had given up on the omelet.

"Hey, guy, you're famous," Don chortled. His voice held a note of mild shock and hilarity. "You made page six of the *Post*."

"Yeah, I know," Bill lied with a matching laugh. "Crazy, isn't it?"

"Wow! Is it on the level?"

"Is what on the level?"

"What it says: THIS IS MY CHILD, KIDNAPPER CLAIMS, REINCARNATED."

Bill felt a lump take root inside his chest as Don chuckled his way through a couple of the choicer lines in the news story. "'. . . renowned psychic clued Hoover to reborn daughter's whereabouts . . . defendant heard cry of his daughter's soul issue from mouth of kidnapped girl . . . defense promises expert witnesses will substantiate claim. . . .' Jesus, man!" Don said in a high, strident voice. "Is this guy for real?"

There was no hint of levity in Pel Simmons' voice when he called a few minutes later. In fact, there was a decidedly funereal quality to their brief transaction as Bill filled Pel in on the essentials of the case and Pel, undoubtedly disturbed, expressed sympathy and support for Bill and his family.

"Don't worry about things at the office," Pel said in conclusion. "Don will stay on top of your accounts."

Bill felt the first vague and distant reverberations of the death knell in this last statement.

Ivy's call came through as Bill was wrapping up with Pel. Janice answered and was listening mutely and with concern to Ivy as Bill approached.

"What is it?" he asked, fearing the worst.

Janice covered the mouthpiece with her hand. "She's coughing. I think she's coming down with a cold."

"Oh," said Bill with a sigh of relief.

"Here's Daddy. He'd like to say hello." Janice handed the phone to Bill.

"Hi, Princess, what's this about a cold?"

"It's nothing, Daddy," Ivy said in between coughs. "All the girls have the sniffles."

"Well, be sure to bundle up good when you go out, and if it gets any worse, go see the nurse in the dispensary."

"I've already been," Ivy said agreeably. "She gave me some groovy cough medicine. Tastes like cherries, of course." Then, shifting subjects: "Daddy, you and Mommy *are* coming up this weekend, aren't you?"

"Try keeping us away." Bill grinned.

"You know Mina Dawson?"

"Yeah, sure—that pretty friend of yours."

"Right, she's really swell, and I was wondering, Daddy. You see, her mother won't be coming up this weekend." Her voice lowered to a whisper. "She's going to Florida to file for a divorce and"—she continued aloud—"since Mina is going to be terribly lonely, I wondered if we couldn't ask her to join us for dinner at the Clam Box Saturday night."

Janice saw a pleased, crooked smile spread over Bill's features as he chuckled and said, "We'd be delighted, Princess. Tell Mina to count on it."

They talked awhile longer; then Bill allowed Janice to say good-bye before taking the phone back for a final word.

"And if any of the kids there should say anything to you, Princess, anything at all that might sound strange and funny, promise me you won't listen to them, promise you'll tell them to bug off, okay?"

"Strange and funny like what?"

"Oh. . . ." Bill groped. "Like . . . your father's got two heads and a bushy tail, crazy, creepy things like that."

Ivy laughed. "The only girl here'd say anything like that is Jill O'Connor, but then she's a freak." Her voice lowered to a whisper. "Her left boob is twice as big as her right one."

After hanging up the receiver, Bill checked with the desk for messages. There were three, two from the man named Hazard and one from a girl in the news department of WNBC local. Bill told Ernie not to bother sending them up.

Later, after a long, relaxing bath, Bill put on his robe and joined Janice in the living room.

She was surprised to see him go to the television set and turn it on. He had pointedly avoided the six thirty news but now seemed almost eager to catch the ten o'clock summary.

It did not come until the really important issues of the day had been put aside and six commercial messages had been heard. It was only in the final minutes of the telecast that the worry lines in the newscaster's craggy face gradually relaxed, and the dark, brooding eyes displayed an unaccustomed glint of humor and mischief as he launched into the lighter side of the day's happenings.

"Shades of *The Exorcist* in Old Bailey," he intoned, forcing an ill-fitting smile onto his face. "The courtroom of Judge Harmon T. Langley was the scene of strange and eerie doings this day as a voice from the grave was offered as an extenuating circumstance by defense attorney Brice Mack during his opening remarks in the trial of Elliot Hoover, accused kidnapper of ten-year-old Ivy Templeton. It seems, or at least it says here in my script, that the kidnapped child was no stranger to Mr. Hoover, since she had shared his company in another lifetime—as his daughter, Audrey Rose, deceased these past ten years. More spectacular episodes in this occult thriller are promised in the days and weeks ahead as Judge Langley's caldron boils and bubbles while Mr. Mack toils and troubles to prevent his client's incarceration on the reasonable assumption of reincarnation."

At which point the newscaster, obviously caught unaware by the demented poesy his waggish writer had planted in the script, fell into a deep and rumbling fit of laughter from which he could not be retrieved. All his efforts to control himself failed, until finally the camera cut away from him and went to a commercial.

At the first eruption Janice laughed with him and, she was happy to see, so did Bill. Their laughter grew and intensified apace with the stricken newscaster's, and even after he had been ignominiously removed from the air, their laughter continued until their eyes watered and their throats grew hoarse. Then, weak and exhausted, they flopped onto the sofa and simply fell into each other's arms, their laughter trailing off as they wiped the tears from each other's faces. Both knew it was the first genuine contact between them in weeks, and each was afraid to spoil it.

"Oh, Bill." Janice breathed huskily and snuggled closer to him. His mouth smelled of mint, his skin of soap, aphrodisiac scents to Janice. Undoing the belt of his robe, her hand began to explore and fondle the body she loved. With a deep sigh, Bill's back sought the pillows, and he allowed the tender touches, first of hands, then of lips, to work their wondrous magic to restore his harmed and aching spirit. Once he raised her head from his lap and softly moaned, "Let's do it together," to which Janice replied, "Later," and hungrily bent to conclude her obeisant and purifying ritual.

17

As predicted and feared, the corridor outside the courtroom was a maze of wires, cables, and people. Spotlights on stands were nestled in clusters in out-of-the-way corners and niches, their accumulated light bathing the smiling figure of Brice Mack, caught in the center of a crush of news people from all media.

Emerging from the elevator, Bill and Janice surreptitiously edged around the periphery of the camera crew and succeeded in making it through the courtroom door without being recognized.

Unlike previous mornings, the courtroom was filled with a congregation of curious and excited spectators. Many of them wore turbans and flashing smiles on swarthy faces. Newspaper people, including some out-of-town press, filled the press row just behind the railing.

As they moved across the row to their seats, both Bill and Janice felt a deep hush and a soft buzz of recognition spread across the courtroom. Even the reporters filling the seats in front of them stopped what they were doing and looked around at them as they took their seats. The man immediately in front of Janice turned full around and smiled his acknowledgment of her arrival. It was then she noticed that he was not a conventional reporter, but an artist assigned to quick-sketch various aspects of the proceedings. His pad presently contained a remarkable likeness of Elliot Hoover sitting at the defense table, brooding over his doodles. The artist had perfectly captured the expression of saintly forbearance in the eyes.

Janice glanced over the rows of heads to where Hoover sat and was immediately sorry she had, for she found him looking straight at her. Worse still, she found it impossible to tear her eyes away from his eyes, which clung to hers with the intensity of a command, willing her to obey, to take note, to listen, then, seeing compliance, gradually softening as if beseeching her pardon, understanding, and forgiveness and expressing sadness for all that had happened and was about to happen. When Janice was at last released through the intervention of Judge Langley's arrival in the courtroom, she felt light-headed and dizzy as she rose and sat in obedience to the bailiff's command and heard her heart pounding in the grip of an emotion she could not define.

The proceedings against Elliot Hoover finally got under way as the parade of witnesses for the prosecution in response to the bailiff's admonishments to "tell the truth, the whole truth and nothing but the truth, so help you God," each added his or her small isolated piece of evidence to Scott Velie's intricately wrought case against the defendant.

In the next four days twelve persons, several of whom were totally unknown to Bill and Janice, would take the stand and tell what they knew from firsthand knowledge about the defendant and his actions near or about the vicinity of the Ethical Culture School, and the apartment house known variously as 1 West Sixty-seventh Street and by the sobriquet Des Artistes.

Three women, one a grandmotherly type, all of whom Janice only vaguely recognized as part of the group who waited daily in front of the school, followed one another in quick order. Each told approximately the same story of having seen a man with black mustache and sideburns hovering about the school steps each morning the children arrived and each afternoon at their departure. None, however, could actually identify the defendant as being that man.

Nor would the next two witnesses make that connection, as Ernesto Pucci and Dominick D'Allesandro, both looking decidedly uncomfortable and unfamiliar out of their burgundy and braid uniforms, took the stand and affirmed the fact that Elliot Hoover did enter the lobby of the plaintiff's abode on at least four occasions with the expressed intentions of "calling on the Templetons."

"Can you describe the defendant's demeanor on these occasions?" Velie asked Dominick.

"Demeanor?"

"How did he act? Did he seem upset, nervous?"

"Oh, yes, especially when they wouldn't let him up."

"All right, Mr. D'Allesandro," Velie continued. "Let's talk about the first time you saw the defendant. Describe what happened."

"Well, the first time he came, he was okay, I mean, he was calm because they let him up."

"And the following times?"

"In my opinion, he was definitely not happy about not getting to go up."

"Did you see the defendant on the morning of November 12th?"

"Yes."

"How did the defendant appear to you on that day?"

"He appeared happy again because he had sublet an apartment in the building, and now he could go up whenever he wanted. I mean, we can't keep tenants out of the elevators."

There was a brief spate of laughter and gavel rapping during which Scott Velie walked to his table to consult his notes.

"Now, then, Mr. D'Allesandro"—Velie's tone signified a shift to the crucial issue—"on the night of November 13, the night of the alleged kidnapping, will you tell the jury what you saw?"

Dominick nodded and launched into a detailed and obviously prepared recitation of his actions and observations. It was a fine, concise narrative of the night's events, told with operatic flair and fervor, Janice thought, feeling a surge of pride for Dominick.

When Scott Velie passed the witness to the defense, Brice Mack had a short series of questions for him.

"Think back, Mr. D'Allesandro, and take your time in doing so, but wasn't there one more time between the first and last times when Mr. Hoover was also happy? Or, at least, not unhappy?"

Dominick brooded over the question a long time before answering.

"There was another time between the first and last time when he got up. Mr. Templeton was away on a business trip, and Miz Templeton, she let him up."

"Right. And wasn't he happy at that time?"

"I couldn't say."

A few titters in the courtroom were brought under control by the gavel.

"You did say, did you not, that Mr. Hoover was definitely not happy about *not* getting to go up?"

"That's right."

"Well, when Mrs. Templeton did invite him up, did the defendant appear to be happy?"

"Yes, I guess so."

"That is all."

Bill felt Janice flinch at the mention of her name and saw the veiled wink of encouragement Velie flashed her just prior to excusing the witness. They knew the defense was banking heavily on Janice's testimony regarding the evening she had invited Hoover to the apartment and were prepared to "handle" it. Yet, with all of Scott Velie's assurances and displays of confidence in their ability to "handle" things, Janice dreaded the moment when she would have to rise and walk to the witness box and answer questions about that night.

The legal ceremony moved slowly and surely onward. Day after day, irrefutable items called facts were chipped from witnesses and presented to the jury to help them render a verdict that would be fair beyond a shadow of a doubt.

Hammering onward, the agile and resolute district attorney summoned Carole Federico to the stand to tell of the two harassing phone calls from Hoover which she had taken during Janice's absence and of her salty and somewhat abusive reprimand of his behavior, which drew a laugh from all precincts of the courtroom, including the bench.

The two arresting police officers were next to take the stand, followed by the Templetons' neighbors who had been witness to Elliot Hoover's assault on Bill in the hallway that evening two months before, and all, so help them God, told their version of the truth, which was filed and registered in the court record and in the jury's mind along with the rest of the "facts."

Brice Mack had few objections to offer and even fewer questions to ask of these witnesses, excusing all of them but one without stirring from his seat. Of Officer Noonan he wished confirmation of the fact that Elliot Hoover did open the door, albeit after some slight hesitation, but that he did ultimately open it at the officer's request.

"It wasn't a request, sir," Officer Noonan responded tautly. "It was an order. And he did it only upon threat of our sending for the riot squad."

"But he *did* voluntarily open that door, did he not?"

"Yes, sir," Noonan said wryly. "We persuaded him to open the door."

Pale and with fear in her eyes, Janice addressed herself to the comings and goings of the court's business those first four days in a state of suspended animation.

On the Friday before the weekend break, however, an event took place to bring Janice out of her self-imposed dream state.

It occurred just after they had returned from lunch and court was preparing to reconvene. Bill was conferring with Scott Velie at the railing. The morning's witness had been Dr. Kaplan, and there had been a controversy over the propriety of some of the questions Brice Mack had put to him on cross-examination and would continue to put to him, since Kaplan had not been excused. The defense attorney had sought to know the reason Kaplan had been summoned on the night in question and what the nature of Ivy's illness was. Velie had objected on the grounds that the questions were improper, that they went beyond the scope of direct examination, and they violated the doctor-patient privilege.

"Dr. Kaplan cannot testify to what treatments he gave the child or even the reason he was summoned to treat her."

Judge Langley sustained, whereupon Brice Mack asked permission to call Dr. Kaplan as a witness for the defense and further asked the court's permission to take the witness out of turn since his questions were indeed beyond the scope of direct examination and were pertinent to the defendant's case. After a moment's consideration, and some hesitation, Langley instructed Dr. Kaplan to remain available but said he would consider the defense's request to call Dr. Kaplan "out of turn" during the lunch recess.

Now they were back, and Bill and Scott Velie were plotting strategy to thwart the defense attorney's attempts to gain information from Kaplan regarding Ivy's nightmares should the judge grant Brice Mack's request.

A few minutes after Janice had taken her seat and was idly watching the artist putting the finishing touches on a full-figure sketch of Scott Velie rising to his feet to object, a newspaperman ambled down the press row and, his body shielding his actions from Bill's view, thrust a slip of paper into her hand. Before she could react or look up, he had turned and was walking rapidly back to his seat in the middle of the press row behind the defense table.

It took Janice some minutes to work up the courage to examine the slip of paper, and when she did, she did so covertly, stealthily. The paper had been torn from a yellow legal pad and was folded. She sensed it was from Hoover and was right; yet, opening it, she was surprised to see, instead of the expected mincing script, two lines of bold black letters, hand-printed at an arresting angle and with exclamation marks emphasizing the urgency of the message, "I AM AFRAID FOR THE CHILD!! IS SHE ALL RIGHT?? PLEASE, PLEASE LET ME KNOW!!! E. H."

Terse, pointed, terrifying, like a telegram from the Defense Department. Janice felt a shudder ripple over her, a trembling of the flesh as she crumpled the slip of paper into a nervous ball and allowed it to drop from her hand to the floor.

Slyly, surreptitiously, and with pounding heart, Janice dared a glance in Hoover's direction and saw his eyes boring across the courtroom at her. Once engaged, she was riveted by the compelling, beseeching, anguished intensity of his demand for an answer to his question.

At this moment Judge Langley decided to enter the courtroom, forcing all to rise. Their eyes continued to hold fast throughout half of the bailiff's litany, at which point Janice, fearing the imminence of Bill's return to his seat, allowed her face to soften into the semblance of a smile and, with a barely perceptible nod of her head, affirmed Ivy's well-being. Hoover sighed and immediately relaxed. Fear and concern drained from his face and were replaced by a look of gratitude and a smile of such ineffable sweetness that Janice was forced to look away lest she betray an emotion she would later regret.

The drone of Judge Langley's voice ruling on Brice Mack's request formed an unintelligible hum in the background of Janice's thoughts, still focused on the contents of Elliot Hoover's message. Some dire premonition must have prompted his sudden concern; of this she was sure. Too much had happened in their lives for her to start doubting him now. If some intuitive apprehension for Ivy's safety had telepathed itself to him, then she must honor and act upon it. Her first thought was that the dreams had come back, that Audrey Rose had once again succeeded in blasting through Ivy's subconscious and was crying out to her father sitting in a jail cell some fifty miles away. And that he had received the message. But if that were so, the school would certainly have got in touch with them. In any case, she must call Mount Carmel and speak to Ivy. Now!

Rising and leaving the courtroom during the judge's solemn oration would certainly draw attention to her, might even incur the judge's displeasure, but there was no help for it. She had to get to a phone. Shifting around in her seat, she hurriedly whispered to Bill that she wasn't feeling well and edged her way across to the side aisle. Judge Langley's voice hesitated in midsentence as a soft hum of whispers, like a distant drone of locusts, accompanied her progress to the door. A gentle rap of his gavel rebuked all and sundry for the unseemly interruption.

Janice found the public phones in a cul-de-sac between the men's and ladies' rest rooms at the very end of the long corridor. She was happy she had committed the school's phone number to memory and had kept her purse bulging with coins for just such an eventuality. Still, the transaction took close to five minutes before Ivy's voice sprang back at her through the receiver.

"Mom! How great! What gives?" The voice was joyful, exuberant, healthy, thank God!

"Nothing important, dear. Just lonely," said Janice with an inward sigh of relief. "How're things?"

"Great!"

"Sleeping okay?"

"Sure, except not enough. They wake you up at six for matins. By the way, guess what you interrupted?"

"What?" Janice tried to keep her voice casual.

"Algebra," Ivy said with disgust. "Sister Mary Margaret was just about to call on me. I could tell by the shifty looks she was giving me. . . ."

As Ivy chattered, Janice listened with the concentrated, intensive smile of a mother sharing a moment of joyful intimacy with her child, yet in actuality she was scarcely listening. Her mind flitted over other fields of concern. With the play the trial was getting in the press and on television, could it be that Ivy still knew nothing about it? True, the sisters had promised to do their best to shelter Ivy from its impact, but Mount Carmel was certainly no walled-in cloister observing the rule of silence. Certainly there was television, and most of the children owned transistor radios. How Ivy could have been kept innocent of what was going on for so long was a total mystery to Janice.

". . . and Sylvester's more than sixteen feet tall, and we're only up to his shoulders."

Ivy was talking with unrelieved enthusiasm when Janice tuned back in to her.

"Mina thinks he'll top twenty-three feet when we crown him, and that'll beat the school record. . . ."

Sylvester was the school snowman—a yearly tradition at Mount Carmel, weather permitting, the cooperative project of the entire student body.

"I'm happy to hear you've stopped coughing, dear," Janice interposed.

"I still do at night a little. Postnasal drip. Nothing serious, the nurse said." Her voice dropped to a whisper. "Jill O'Connor menstruates. At least that's what she told Mina. And she's only nine, Mom, do you believe it?"

"No, I don't." Janice laughed. "I think Jill O'Connor's a fibber."

"She's a *liar*," Ivy affirmed with sudden vehemence. "She's spreading the craziest stories about me around the school."

"What sort of stories?" Janice inquired with apprehension.

"She says I'm two people, that I'm some kind of freak and that it's all over the radio and TV."

Janice hesitated. "That's silly."

"I know," Ivy answered cheerfully. "Besides, there aren't any radios and TV's allowed here anymore. Mother Veronica Joseph outlawed them last week. The sisters had a shakedown inspection and collected every one of them."

Janice hesitated again.

"Daddy and I are looking forward to tomorrow," she said, forcing a cheery note into her voice.

"So are we. Mina and I've decided on pork chops and french fries for supper. We hardly ever get meat here."

There was no possible way to shield her from the truth forever. Sooner or later she would have to be told, and if Janice had her way, it would be sooner.

As soon as possible.

This weekend.

18

Sunk in a mood of agitated gloom, Janice forbore returning to the courtroom till the last possible moment, lingering in the ladies' room to sponge her face and repair her makeup until she felt her continued absence ran the danger of exciting Bill's curiosity. If she didn't return soon, she was certain a matron would be dispatched to search for her.

One hour and twenty-five minutes after she had left, she returned to the big double doors and, reaching out to the brass handle, felt the door push silently outward as the guard emerged. Smiling and nodding, the elderly man graciously held the door open for Janice to enter.

"Thank you," Janice whispered, and crossed the threshold.

The shock of what greeted her brought her to a full swaying stop. Holding onto the door handle, she found herself unable to move as she stood staring, in pained surprise, at Brice Mack battering questions at Bill, sitting grimly in the witness box. That Bill had been called to the stand as a witness was not what shocked Janice; it was that he had been called so soon. She had thought surely there would be several interim witnesses, Russ, Harold Yates, before it would be their turn. But for some reason, Scott Velie had put Bill on sooner, which meant that she would probably follow him. And probably today. It was still quite early. Janice was seized with panic. She had not counted on taking the stand today. She wasn't prepared to or at least hadn't fortified herself for the ordeal. She had banked on more time, the weekend at least, to think about it, to put her head in order, to get her act together. They had no right to rush her onto the stand like this.

Her return to her seat caused no stir among the spectators since all eyes and ears were firmly fixed on the witness box.

Brice Mack stood with his arms folded across his chest, shooting questions at Bill, who was sitting just inches away from him.

"You have declared under oath that the moment you ordered Mr. Hoover to leave, he seized you and flung you bodily over his head? Is that correct?"

"Yes."

"And that prior to this hostile act of his, you did nothing that could, in any way, be construed as having, either by movement, gesture, or direct physical contact, precipitated this harsh and seemingly arbitrary reaction of Mr. Hoover's?"

"I never laid a hand on him," Bill said resolutely, failing to add that he had been given no opportunity to do so.

The defense attorney was about to question Bill further on this point, had a change of mind, and asked instead, "After the neck-pinching episode, Mr. Templeton, during which time you were paralyzed, tell me again, if you don't mind, exactly what happened after Mr. Hoover released your carotid artery?"

"Well, as I said, my wife came out and helped pull him off me, at which point he turned and rushed into the apartment and locked himself inside."

"Yes, so you've said, but think back, Mr. Templeton. Was he not, in fact, requested to enter your apartment?"

"Requested?"

"Yes, requested—by Ivy!"

Bill hesitated. "I don't know what you mean."

"I mean, Mr. Templeton, that Ivy's pathetic cries and pleadings funneled down through the apartment and were heard and accepted by Mr. Hoover as a legitimate summons for his help, that's what I mean!"

Bill shook his head. "I didn't hear any cries or pleadings."

"Is it not a fact that Ivy, just shortly prior to Mr. Hoover's arrival, had experienced one of her nightmares—a nightmare from which she could not be awakened and of such a punishing nature as to require you and your wife to tie her to the bed?"

"Just a moment," Velie interrupted. "I object to the form of the question. It calls for a compound answer, and furthermore, it is objectionable because it goes beyond the scope of direct examination."

"The objection is sustained," Judge Langley ruled.

Brice Mack shrugged. Then, turning to Bill: "The witness is excused, but I will ask the court to instruct him to keep himself available to serve as a witness for the defense when we present our case."

"The witness is so instructed." Judge Langley looked toward Scott Velie. "Your next witness?"

Janice shut her eyes and tensed her body for the expected blow, but it failed to materialize. There was a slight delay as Scott Velie selected this moment to introduce Ivy's birth certificate into the record. Bill edged his way down the row to his seat as the attenuated ritual of entering the birth certificate in evidence as People's Exhibit Number One was ceremoniously performed.

Looking grim and baleful, Janice leaned over to Bill. "I'm not ready for this," she said in a high, choked whisper.

"It'll be all right," Bill whispered back, his hand gripping her knee, which he found was trembling.

"What happened to Russ and Harold Yates? Why didn't he put them on?"

"He's saving them as rebuttal witnesses after the defense has put on its case."

"I'm not ready for this," Janice reiterated. Her face was florid, unhealthily so.

"Proceed with your next witness," Judge Langley directed.

"My next witness," Velie announced, "is Mrs. William Templeton."

Janice pushed herself up from the seat and immediately began to feel worse. Her face, flushed and red a moment before, became pale as ashes, and she was sure she would collapse before reaching the witness stand.

An uncommon quiet settled over the courtroom as Janice awkwardly sidestepped her way to the aisle and, the blood surging and pounding in her head, mechanically made her way toward the gate in the railing, each step of her wavering progress seemingly energized by an inner force beyond her command or comprehension. It struck her that under just such a dissociated, yet irresistible compulsion must the French nobility have climbed the ladder to conclude their tête-à-tête with Madame La Guillotine.

At the witness stand Janice held up her right hand, took the oath, then sat, all at the bailiff's direction.

Scott Velie approached her with a mien of gentle warmth and compassion.

"Would you state your full name, please?"

"Janice Gilbert Templeton."

"You are the wife of William Templeton?"

"Yes."

"And the mother of Ivy Templeton?"

"Yes."

"She is your natural child?"

"Yes."

"Mrs. Templeton, describe the events that occurred between the date you first saw the defendant and the date he removed your daughter from your apartment and carried her to his apartment."

Janice swallowed, cleared her throat, and sought her voice. That she found it, and found it full-bodied, strong, and authoritative, was a further enigma in an afternoon of enigmas. The sound of her own voice was immediately reassuring to her, and soon she heard herself talking more rapidly.

It was with the confidence, assurance, and the practiced hand of a master that Scott Velie elicited the story he wished the jury to hear from Janice, permitting her no opportunity to flesh out, embellish, or develop any points or stray into areas that could in any way provide the defense with an opening wedge on cross-examination that would be detrimental to the people's case. Even Brice Mack had to admit it was an astonishing feat of legal legerdemain.

At last, Scott Velie turned to the defense attorney.

"Cross-examine," he said.

"Your Honor"—Brice Mack purposely kept the moment dangling, taking an obvious sadistic pleasure in tantalizing the frightened woman in the witness box—"may I say that as long as Mrs. Templeton is shielded by the rules of evidentiary procedure, there is little I can hope to learn in cross-examination. However, there is a great deal to be learned from this witness and from the witness preceding her, a great many truths that have been suppressed by my distinguished colleague's artful and inspired direct examination." His eyes fixed Janice with a cold, steely look of warning. "Truths that I fully intend to bring forth into the light of day. Therefore, I have no questions of the witness at this time, but I will certainly want her back as a witness for the defense."

"Very well," Judge Langley said as Brice Mack strode back to the defense table. "The witness is excused but instructed to keep herself available as a witness for the defense."

Turning to Scott Velie, who was heavily engaged in a strategy powwow with his associate, Judge Langley dryly registered his annoyance.

"Mr. Velie, if you will forgive the court's interruption, we are awaiting the calling of your next witness."

"If the court please," Velie said, rising with an apologetic smile, "that is my case. I have no further evidence to put on at this time."

"In that case," said Judge Langley with a solemn rap of his gavel, "we will continue the trial until Monday morning at nine o'clock. The defendant is remanded to custody."

Rising from her chair, moving unsurely and unsteadily toward Bill, Janice experienced the sense of elation, the delicious inertia of a person stumbling dazed but unscathed away from a plane crash.

The time for telling Ivy "all the facts" came the following evening just after they had returned from delivering Mina back to the school and had settled themselves into their family suite at the Candlemas Inn.

Bill and Janice had driven up earlier in the day, arriving just after lunch, in time to sit in on afternoon choir practice along with a number of other parents. Ivy's vivid blond beauty could be easily distinguished among the group of girls in the alto section. It was during Handel's *Kyrie Eleison* that Janice began to sense the first vague stirrings of interest and curiosity in the air—the secretive glances, smirks, and whisperings flitted about them like straws in a high wind.

Even more disturbing were the bright, darting glances they received from the girls as they bounded past them out of the chapel and into the snow-clad yard, where a headless Sylvester awaited their attention. Ivy and Mina brought up the rear, their hands clasped, moving slowly and indolently up to them, both wearing brave smiles in the presence of tragedy.

"Hi, Daddy. Hi, Mommy," Ivy said wanly. "You remember Mina."

"Sure, Princess." Bill smiled. "Hi, Mina."

"Hi, Mr. Templeton. Hi, Mrs. Templeton," Mina said, passing the ball to Janice.

"Hello, Mina," Janice said, completing the circle of greetings.

Bill bent to kiss Ivy and felt her flinch the slightest millimeter. Janice noticed and quickly asked, "Gonna go to work on Sylvester?"

"Not today, we don't feel like it."

"No," Mina repeated with distaste, "we don't feel like it."

"Well, then," Janice said with a surge of enthusiasm, "why don't you girls go and get ready for our little party?"

The prospect of dinner out brightened the moment for Mina at least. After they had left to shower and change into their prettiest dresses, permitted at Mount Carmel only on weekends or on family outings, Bill and Janice walked across the yard, past the towering snowman under construction, and entered the administration building.

"One of the girls smuggled newspapers into the dormitory. We think it was Jill O'Connor, but we are not sure of it."

Several copies of the Westport *Guardian* containing the front-page item "Jurors hear tape of principals in reincarnation-kidnapping case" were spread open on the mother superior's desk. Mother Veronica Joseph's eyes held the familiar note of pity and compassion, but the set of her face had altered, Bill thought; had hardened, become stern, even severe.

"I will talk to the parents collectively before they leave today and seek their cooperation in the matter. And I've asked Father Paul to speak to the children during mass in the morning."

Bill leaned anxiously forward in his chair. "We appreciate all you've done, Mother, to shield our daughter from this knowledge. Ivy told us about the ban on radios and TV."

Mother Veronica Joseph's face softened the slightest bit.

"While my heart and sympathy go out to Ivy and to both of you," she said in a hushed tone more suited to the confessional booth, "please understand what I am about to say. The rules I instituted and the things I did to suppress this story at Mount Carmel were not done for your entire benefit. What I did I did for all the children and for the sake of the school. There is no doubt that Ivy was the unwilling victim of a poor soul's delusion and deserved to be shielded from the attendant publicity. But an equal, if not greater, danger was that the school would find itself the unwilling victim of a celebrity in its midst, which now indeed has occurred and which, as you must know, is the kind of distraction few institutions of this order can long tolerate."

"Which," as Bill succinctly put it to Janice on their way to pick up Ivy and her friend, "simply means, start looking for another school for Ivy."

"That's not at all what she said," protested Janice.

"It's what she meant."

Yes, Janice thought, it was true, it was there in her voice, a clear warning to them to get the problem solved soon, or she would be forced to take action.

Dinner with the girls was a quiet, intense affair consisting of much eating and little talk. Ivy was withdrawn and remote but managed to finish her chops and french fries and even join Mina in a second dessert. Several times Bill caught her looking at him in a kind of lost, perplexed way, as if saying, "What does it all mean? What's happening?"

The burden of disclosure fell on Bill and took place in Janice's presence in the small sitting room which doubled as Ivy's bedroom. Propped up and bundled in the rollaway bed, Ivy listened intently as Bill told her all the facts with delicacy, understanding, and total candor, omitting only one—the nightmares.

"But is that possible?" Ivy asked. The words and her tone held a heady, breathless incredulity, as well as a tinge of excitement.

"No, Princess," Bill responded. "But Mr. Hoover seems to think so." Then, in a gentler voice: "Understand, Ivy, when a father loses someone he loves very dearly—in this case, his wife and daughter—his sadness and hurt can be so great as to cause his mind to refuse to believe what happened. It's at such times that a man is willing to believe anything just to keep himself going. Mr. Hoover is such a man. When he lost all he held dear, he could not accept the fact and went looking for other answers. And the saddest thing is that there were people, wicked people, who were waiting on the sidelines ready to give him the answers he wanted to hear. This is how he came to believe that his dead child was reborn in your body. So you see, Princess, it really wasn't his fault; he was just a victim of his own grief."

There was a long silence, during which Ivy heaved a long, woebegone sigh.

"How awfully sad," she said in a muffled voice. "I remember him at school. And the time he walked me home. He seemed so nice."

"Maybe he is nice, Princess. Maybe he's just misguided. Let's think that, shall we?"

Ivy nodded, then looked at Janice. "Isn't it funny that I don't remember a thing about it. I mean, his taking me out of bed and carrying me off like that?"

"You were asleep," Janice said.

"Wow!" said Ivy with a shake of the head and an amazed lift of the eyebrows. "No wonder all the girls are giving me the treatment. I really am a freak."

"You are not a freak, Ivy," Bill insisted. "As I explained, you are the victim of a man's hallucinations—a man whom the State of New York is going to send to jail for a good long time for what he has done. Whenever the girls look at you or say anything or snicker behind your back, just remember that, will you? You have nothing to fear and certainly nothing to be ashamed of." Bill's voice softened. "And if things get to be too difficult here, just let me know, and I'll come and take you home."

Ivy felt a sudden twinge of sadness. "I hope I'll be able to stay. I really like it here."

At three ten in the morning, Janice was awakened by sounds coming from Ivy's room—coughing sounds, high-pitched, racking.

Hurrying into the sitting room and quietly closing the door behind her so as not to waken Bill, Janice turned on the wall switch and gazed, stunned, at the sight of her child sitting up in bed, head hunched over her knees, coughing and wheezing into the blanket. Janice sped across to her side, quickly gathered her into her arms, and began to pat her back to stem the course of the spasms.

"Medicine's in my bag." Ivy managed to choke out the words between coughs.

The label read "To be taken as needed." Ivy swallowed some from the bottle as there was no spoon nearby. Whatever it contained worked rapidly, and soon the coughing spell was under control, leaving her limp and shaking.

"Wow," she squeaked. "That was something."

Her face was pure scarlet, and her eyes watered pitifully.

Janice was shocked by the force and fury of the attack.

"Does this happen every night?"

"Umm," affirmed Ivy. "Most nights this past week. Not as bad as this, though."

"I'll take you to a doctor in the morning."

"'Kay." Ivy swallowed. "Mom?"

Janice felt Ivy's head. It was cool.

"Yes, dear?"

"Wouldn't it be wonderful?"

"What?"

"If what Mr. Hoover believes is really true. That we all just keep on living and living and living forever and ever and never die?"

The question had a dreamlike quality that lulled Janice into a mood of somber contemplation in which the face of Elliot Hoover appeared to her: gentle, pained, distraught.

Drawing Ivy to her bosom and nestling her face into the soft blond hair, Janice whispered in a crooning, abject way, "Yes, darling, it would be wonderful. Really wonderful."

The two men faced each other across the metal table in the small, spare, windowless room. A panel of overhead fluorescent lights cast hard shadows over papers and file folders spread out between them, lending to each face the gaunt and bloodless aspect of a death mask. But for the steady hum of the ceiling air conditioner and their own subdued voices, the room preserved the dull, echoless silence of a vault.

Elliot Hoover had called for the meeting and had engineered its course for the past hour, requesting a full and thorough review of the defense's strategy in all its myriad details and complexities. At this, the eleventh hour, he was challenging witnesses, suggesting changes, and ordering reappraisals of evidence and testimony.

Sitting beneath the harsh light, mopping his face with a soggy ball of cloth, Brice Mack could only stare appalled at the cucumber-cool countenance of his client as he softly uttered his recommendations, which, if questioned or disputed, became orders.

The discussion had started with a further analysis of Gupta Pradesh, the renowned maharishi from Ghurni, who was currently ensconced at the Waldorf-Astoria Hotel and would be called to the stand as their first witness. Elliot Hoover did not know Pradesh personally, but was sufficiently acquainted with his background and works to consider him the ideal witness to inform the jury on some of the deeper philosophical aspects of the Hindu religion. However, because of the maharishi's undisputed saintliness and the extreme reverence he was held in by all his followers, the defense attorney was instructed to desist from any but the loftiest of inquisitions, eliminating any references or attempts to indulge in chitchat concerning the lay, or "bread-and-butter," aspects of reincarnation during his examination. Which dealt a severe blow to the solar plexus of Brice Mack's curtain raiser in the case.

"But he must know of actual cases of reincarnation," Brice Mack protested. "Specific instances that would help substantiate your position."

"There's no doubt he can cite such instances," Hoover blandly replied, "but it would be demeaning for him to discuss such matters in a public forum. Understand, the maharishi is a holy individual bound to the same oath of confidentiality as a Catholic priest, so you will accord him all the respect due a man of his station."

Brice Mack groped in his briefcase for Kleenex but found none.

There was no disagreement on the questioning of the second witness, who, like Gupta Pradesh, professed an expertise in Far Eastern religious concepts but, unlike the maharishi, was a pure-blooded American scholar—professor emeritus of religious studies in one of the country's leading citadels of learning—a man whose name conjured up every folksy image of early American history from the battle green of Lexington to the fog-shrouded perch of a Rocky Mountain rendezvous.

James Beardsley Hancock's testimony on the specific laws of Karma would, it was reasoned by Mack and his associates, weigh heavily with a jury not only because it came from a white, grass-roots, eminently credentialed American, but because it was also the faith he personally practiced and espoused.

As Hoover put it to Brice Mack, "He's on the inside looking out, which makes him our man."

The big wrangle came over the inclusion of the third "expert" witness, Marion Worthman, a latter-day Edgar Cayce, a psychic, self-professed witch, prophet, seer, and devoted proponent and interpreter of the Bible, a woman who could tune in telepathically on a person's mind and body and relate information regarding that person's present and past lives.

Although her adherents numbered in the tens of thousands, and her published works topped every best-seller list, Elliot Hoover fought against bringing her into the courtroom to render testimony in his behalf, fearing that she would bring to the proceedings the taint of a medicine show, which was precisely the reason Brice Mack fought for her inclusion.

Still, Hoover remained skeptical, feeling that their greatest source of help would be forthcoming from the Templetons and Carole Federico when Mack put them on the stand.

"They were there," Hoover stressed. "They were present during the nightmare and saw the child respond to my appeals to Audrey Rose. They know the truth and must be made to tell it."

"The truth?" Brice Mack said, suddenly weary. "What truth are you talking about? Your truth or theirs?"

"They're one and the same."

The attorney sighed pathetically.

"Did you ever hear the one about the three blind men who were each asked to describe an elephant? Each described what he felt as his hands explored the elephant's body, and each description was totally different. Yet they all told the truth."

Nonplussed, Hoover gazed at him.

"What I'm saying," Mack explained, "is that while four people witnessed the same event, in this case a child's nightmare, it doesn't necessarily mean they all saw the same thing. In fact, I'm willing to bet we'll get four different interpretations of what transpired in the bedroom that night."

"Janice Templeton knows the truth," Hoover quietly said. "She summoned me because she knew that I was the only one who could help the child."

"Fine," the attorney allowed. "And when I get her on the stand, I'll certainly explore that matter with her. But don't hold your breath about how much she's going to remember or admit that she remembers about that night."

There was a moment of silence during which Elliot Hoover regarded Brice Mack carefully.

"I take it you don't have much faith in the outcome of this case."

"Put it another way," Brice Mack said. "I don't have much faith in the Templetons' coming to your rescue. The case I have spent eight weeks and a good deal of your money preparing relies heavily on the testimony of our expert witnesses. If you'll permit me to handle them as I had planned to, I think we stand a good chance of selling reincarnation to even the most doubtful juror."

"Otherwise?"

Brice Mack decided to lay it on the line.

"Otherwise, I don't think your chances for acquittal are very good."

Hoover studied the attorney minutely.

"I appreciate your frankness, Mr. Mack," Hoover said in a voice edged with scorn. "Now let me be frank with you. I still insist, no matter what your opinion of the outcome of the case may be, that you conduct it with all possible taste and decorum. I realize how driven you are by personal ambition to succeed. Still, the determination of my guilt or innocence before man's bar of justice is not a platform to serve your egotism, nor will I permit it to become a base for your self-aggrandizement. It is my freedom that is at stake here, Mr. Mack, not your reputation. Therefore, I will be the one to decide each step we take in the course of this case. If you do not understand me or feel that you cannot respect my wishes to the letter, please tell me now, and I shall have you replaced."

"Sure, anything you say." Brice Mack's light, offhanded acceptance of Hoover's contempt was contrived to conceal his profound shock and surprise. The accuracy with which Hoover had hit the mark was devastating. Could it be he was always this transparent?

Leaving the stuffy environs of the Criminal Courts Building and stepping into the frigid, abandoned streets of late Sunday afternoon, Brice Mack sensed the exquisite irony of the bulging briefcase he was toting, filled with hopes, ambitions, and eight weeks of striving and planning which now, shorn of his power to function, represented a briefcase full of nothing.

The temptation to drop it in a litter bin as he searched in vain for a cab while sloughing his way toward the BMT on the corner of Foley Square was dissipated by a crescendo of confused noise rumbling beneath his feet as he approached the subway kiosk.

The trip home in the nearly empty car was made in the company of two frightened women and a vomiting black, which, all things considered, seemed the proper coda to cap off the day's dispiriting events.

Pressed against the corner of his quaking seat, enveloped by the clatter of wheels and groans and the overpowering stench, the young attorney observed the second hand of his wristwatch sweeping inexorably toward the morrow, producing the disquieting sensation of an unstoppable doom hurtling toward him. It was at this moment that Brice Mack thought of his mother and the night she was sped into the operating theater with less than a ten percent chance of making it back out alive. He smiled, remembering the brave smile on her face as she winked her encouragement at him, both knowing it would be the last physical gesture they would ever share together on this earth.

19

The first inkling of catastrophe greeted Brice Mack's arrival at the Criminal Courts Building the following morning.

The time was early enough to provide a calming and comforting vista of empty, slushy streets as his cab sluiced up the narrow canyons leading into Foley Square. Four chartered buses parked in front of the court building directly behind a television truck provided the first shiver of anxiety in the young attorney as he paid off the cabdriver and hurried up the freshly sanded steps.

Even in the sealed container of the elevator with its attendant hum, rhythmic sounds could be heard increasing in volume as the car approached the seventh floor, sounds that exploded into joyous chanting, "HARE KRISHNA! HARE KRISHNA! HARE KRISHNA!" as the doors slid open to a corridor packed solid with more than a hundred and fifty Children of Lord Krishna, who, he later learned, had arrived with the dawn from their *gurukula* in Bronxville to pay tribute to the venerable saint Gupta Pradesh, the first of Brice Mack's witnesses.

Girls and boys, ranging in ages from thirteen to eighteen, all dressed in saffron robes, the girls' foreheads daubed with paste, the boys' heads shaved except for the topknot enabling Krishna to yank them up to heaven at the proper time, were gathered in a six-deep phalanx down the length of the corridor, hopping up and down, beating drums, ringing bells, and chanting "Hare Krishna" over and over, transforming the bleak, sterile surroundings into a gay and vivid bazaar. All under the amazed and watchful eyes of a cordon of helmeted, club-wielding police officers who had been summoned to maintain order.

Brice Mack was literally stunned by the sight and the noise and wavered momentarily before plunging ahead into the mass of exotically scented bodies in a game attempt to reach the telephone at the other end of the corridor. It was important he reach Gupta Pradesh at the Waldorf and warn him to stay clear of the main elevators and to find his way into the building through the service entrance.

With the help of a policeman, who seemed to delight in roughly clearing a path for him through the dancing, swaying, happy mob, the attorney finally made it to the end of the hall where the telephones were situated. There he found the space in front of them occupied by an impeccably dressed and carnationed Judge Langley standing in the center of a barrage of lights, cameras, and questioning reporters, vainly attempting to add a brick or two to his own national image and reputation.

The reporters, however, seemed of a different mind, for instead of concentrating on the relevant issue of the moment, that of reincarnation, they peppered him with embarrassing questions concerning his Tammany days and his ascendancy in the O'Dwyer hierarchy, wanting particularly to know how he had managed to elude the tentacles of the Kefauver inquisition and, in general, prying and poking into the shadier corners of a past that the aged jurist would just as soon had lain dormant and forgotten.

Even as the carnation wilted under the extreme heat of the lights, so did Judge Langley's disposition and temper erode under the onslaught of punishing questions, until at last his replies and rejoinders descended to a brash, monosyllabic level better suited to the gutter than to the august environs of a courthouse corridor.

Finally, with a display of temper, Langley pushed his way past his inquisitors, shouting, "Out of my way, goddamn you," and, calling for a police escort, ordered him to clear a path through the mob of caterwauling children to his chambers.

The area cleared of paraphernalia, Brice Mack put through his call to the Waldorf and learned that the maharishi, in the company of Fred Hudson, had already left. Bullying his way through the Hare Krishnas to the elevators, the attorney hurried down to the main entrance to intercept his witness.

Tall, lean, ascetic, garbed in the simple orange-colored robe of one who has thrust aside the world of material delights, the Holy Maharishi Gupta Pradesh allowed Brice Mack and his assistant, Fred Hudson, to usher him through the dark and tortuous basement of the Criminal Courts Building to the service elevators, which they found stacked high with overflowing trash bins and with scarcely enough room for the operator. Only by huddling together in a tight knot, with their faces pressed through the grillwork of the elevator gate, were the three men able to make the slow trip up to the seventh floor.

Booming, rhythmic cadences from within the courtroom informed them that the Children of Krishna were inside, awaiting the appearance of their master.

At the first sight of Gupta Pradesh, a deep, reverent hush fell over the courtroom as all eyes strained to absorb the form and countenance of the saintly man. The purity and intensity of their consciousness of him flooded the courtroom so strongly that even Brice Mack could tangibly experience the high level of awareness the children radiated.

With a smile both serene and loving, Pradesh raised his hand in greeting toward the Children of Lord Krishna and then proceeded to the defense table and Elliot Hoover, who had risen and was awaiting him with outstretched hand.

Judge Langley remained speechless, his face contorted with incredulity as he silently observed the genteel passage of salutations between witness, audience, and defendant.

With a taut rap of his gavel and seething voice, he addressed the defense attorney.

"Mr. Mack, you have kept the court waiting a full five minutes, and I don't mind telling you we are fast losing our patience! When I say, 'Court will convene at a certain time,' I mean it, and I make a point of personally being in the courtroom at that time!"

"I apologize to the court for our tardiness, Your Honor," Brice Mack said with a small bow of the head. "With your permission, I am ready to call my first witness."

"All right, proceed."

As Brice Mack slowly turned around to the defense table, he quickly scanned the room, momentarily dwelling on the look of assured indifference on Scott Velie's face; noting that the reporters' row directly behind the railing was packed solid with an assortment of familiar and unfamiliar faces, including one Catholic priest and several dark, turbaned gentlemen probably representing some foreign or religious press; and also noting with some surprise the absence of Janice Templeton, her husband being the sole occupant of the witnesses' row.

Brice Mack cleared his throat and in a loud, clear voice trembling with chivalrous politeness declaimed, "It is my honor to call His Holiness Gupta Pradesh to the stand."

The silence in the courtroom deepened as the maharishi, who was still standing alongside Elliot Hoover and the guard, who had also risen and was attending his prisoner with a watchful eye, inclined his head toward the bench and slowly advanced to the witness stand at Brice Mack's direction.

The bailiff, Bible in hand, stood by the chair and waited patiently to administer the oath; however, upon seeing the book containing the revealed truth of the Christian faith, the old Hindu came to a sudden halt and, turning to Brice Mack, engaged him in a whispered conference.

After a few seconds of this, Judge Langley craned forward in annoyance and demanded, "What's wrong now?"

"It's the Bible, Your Honor," the attorney explained. "The maharishi informs me that he cannot swear an oath on the Christian Testaments."

"Well, does he possess his own Bible?"

"No, Your Honor, the Hindu faith subscribes to neither a founder nor a sacred book."

Judge Langley turned to the bailiff.

"Administer the substitute oath."

While the bailiff foraged through the back flap of the Bible for the correct slip of paper, Gupta Pradesh ceremoniously ascended the stand and turned to confront his audience. His long, curly hair encompassed a face of purest tranquillity. His eyes, which seemed to be gazing into eternity, brimmed over with warmth and compassion for all they beheld.

At last, the bailiff found the right passage.

"Do you solemnly affirm that the testimony you may give in the cause now pending before this court shall be the truth, the whole truth, and nothing but the truth, this you do under the pain and penalty of perjury?"

"To the extent that the power and the ability is given me to do so, I do solemnly affirm," intoned the maharishi, for the very first time lifting his deep-chorded English-accented voice to the heights and depths of the immense chamber, filling it so entirely as to produce an overflow of reverberations at the conclusion of his statement.

It was a voice that thrilled, that sent shivers even up Bill's spine, and that stimulated an immediate reaction in the Children of Lord Krishna, who rose from their seats as one and in perfect unison started to chant and hum and sway in an excess of joy.

"Order! Order!" Judge Langley's voice was a whisper in a hailstorm. "I'll have order in this courtroom!"

As Brice Mack stepped up to the railing and waved his arms in a desperate plea for silence, his face was as abject and distraught as Scott Velie's was filled with amusement and delight.

"Hare Krishna! HARE KRISHNA!" The bedlam of voices grew and built, setting up a vibration that caused the water glasses to rattle on their trays.

There seemed no way to bring the situation under control short of sending for the police, which Langley was about to do when, suddenly, in response to a gesture from the venerable Hindu, the mere raising of his hands to the Children of Krishna, the chanting immediately stopped.

"My children," appealed the maharishi in his melodious, commanding voice. "It is not necessary to visit and pay homage to my physical being when to find me you have only to look within your spiritual sight."

The statement, meant to calm them, only served to rekindle their ardor and bring on a new wave of chanting, different in sound and pattern from the previous one: a formless, seemingly wordless humming, "OM! OM! OM! OM!" producing a deep, bell-like vibration of ear-shattering power and intensity.

"Order," Judge Langley shouted, "or I'll have this courtroom cleared!"

"My children!" the maharishi beseeched, to no avail.

Then, as if obeying some wordless, inner-inspired signal, numbers of the Children began drawing out small pots of incense from within the folds of their robes and setting them aflame.

Judge Langley shot to his feet in a rage and spluttered his final warning. "There'll be no damn smoking in my court!" And turning to the bailiff, ordered: "Bailiff, I want this courtroom cleared! Send for the police, and eject these people from the building!" And with a final rap of the gavel: "Court will stand in recess until order has been restored!"

Pressing his way through the ranks of singing, laughing, chanting children, swaying amid clouds of incense, drumbeats, and recitations from the Bhagavad Gita, Bill hurried to outpace the reporters to the main door before the police arrived and the ensuing turmoil sealed off the route of escape. His single aim was to get to a phone and report the disaster to Janice, who had remained at the Candlemas Inn in Westport to care for Ivy.

The connection to their room made, he counted twelve rings before the desk clerk switched in to inform the operator that the party didn't answer and offered the message desk. Bill then asked to have Janice paged, as it was still early enough for them to be at breakfast, but with no success.

Hanging up the receiver, Bill retraced his steps to the courtroom in bewilderment, augmented by a tinge of anxiety. It was more than odd not to find Janice at the inn, not only because of Ivy's illness, which he felt Janice had been disposed to exaggerate, but because she knew the importance of staying close to the telephone. The decision for Janice to remain in Westport had been made with Scott Velie's knowledge and concurrence. His only warning was to keep herself available for any summons from the court since failure to appear at the defense's request would be construed as an act of contempt. Why would Janice have chosen to ignore Scott Velie's warning?

Perhaps, he reflected gloomily, Ivy had taken a turn for the worse.

It was ten twenty before peace and quiet was at last restored and court reconvened.

The spaces vacated by the Children of Krishna, who had been boisterously carried off in the four buses to their *gurukula* in Bronxville, were only partially filled as Brice Mack opened his examination of the badly rattled Hindu sage, commencing with a series of questions concerning the rudiments of his background, his name, place of birth, education, place of current abode, and the general character of his life's calling, and of the faith to which he had dedicated the sum and substance of his seventy-two years.

At Brice Mack's gentle proddings, the maharishi picked his way through the complex web of the Hindu faith, telling of the origin of the word "Hindu" itself, in the sixth century B.C., as it was applied by invading Persians to the Sanskrit-speaking people living by the Indus River.

In a flutelike voice, he sang of the sacred writings, or Vedas, composed well before the first millennium B.C., and of the catalogue of magical *yajnas*, sacrificial formulas, mantras, and rituals that the Vedic religion embodied, and of the many schools, sects, and religions that had developed through the centuries: Sankhya, Yoga, Vedanta, Vaishnavas, Shaivas, Shaktas, all of which were preached and practiced under the separate canopies of Buddhism, Jainism, and Sikhism, which in turn took their impetus from the original Vedic, changing and refining the basic precepts into a multiplicity of separate doctrines: *Karma, avatar, samsara, dharma, trimurti, bhakti, maya.*

For more than an hour, what people were in the courtroom seemed mesmerized by the singsong voice and the strange-sounding words, as the maharishi particularized the many gradations of beliefs, emphasizing the eclectic nature of the faith, which adhered to no particular belief, nor worshiped any particular prophet or God, such as the Christians' Jesus or Islam's Muhammad, but found expression in the worship of animals, ancestors, spirits, sages, and the entire world of nature. A religion as variable as the people who practiced it, yet with certain constants: the belief in holy pilgrimages, in bathing in sacred rivers, in the veneration of sages and gurus, and, above all, the belief in the reality of reincarnation.

Which was the cue Brice Mack had been waiting for, since the expression on Scott Velie's face presaged an objection about to erupt on several valid grounds.

"About reincarnation," the young attorney quickly interposed, veering the maharishi toward the relevant issue in the case. "You speak of it as a reality, as a functioning doctrine believed in and subscribed to by millions of your countrymen. Can you elaborate for the jury on the precise manifestation of reincarnation?"

The impudence of the question brought a smile to the elderly man's lips. From the casual tone of the young man, he might have been asking him to interpret the mechanics of a harvest combine instead of an eternal mystery vouchsafed to but a handful of saints. And yet, reasoned Pradesh to himself, he was in America, where machinery ruled, where the wonders of science were worshiped above faith, and only that which was explainable was viewed without suspicion and accepted as reality.

Delivering a primer on the dwelling place of the soul between its incarnations and the inner workings of the astral cosmos to an alien audience was tantamount to explaining the principles of atomic energy to a Bushman.

Turning to the oddly mixed faces of the twelve men and women sitting in the jury box, all of whom seemed to be observing him with varying degrees of doubt and skepticism, the elderly man began his discourse on the world between and beyond incarnations in a manner so childlike as to preclude misunderstanding by all but the densest of intelligences.

"The astral world," he began, "contains many planes, many levels, many spheres to receive souls as they pass out of the body at death. There are many astral planes teeming with astral beings who have come from the earth life to dwell in these different mansions in accordance with Karmic qualifications. By this I mean the soul of a gross person whose Karmic qualifications are of a low order dwells on a lower plane than those souls of more enriched substance. The gross person, whose main drives in the earth life were of a fleshly and material tendency, will reincarnate very shortly after death since there is little for such a soul to meditate over, as all its attractions and needs are of a material kind. These souls soon find their way back, for there is always a sufficient supply of new bodies among parents of like natures, which offer ideal opportunities in which to reincarnate."

As Gupta Pradesh continued to outline the rules and conditions of "life" in the astral world, Brice Mack's eyes flicked toward the jury for a quick assessment of their reactions and was happy to see more than half of them sitting in rapt attention, listening with keen interest. The maharishi's voice held a bell-like clarity as he joyously told of how souls occupying a higher plane were able to look down on the planes below them and how they were also able to visit friends and relatives on the lower planes, but that those living on the lower planes were unable to return the compliment as they could neither see nor hear the souls on a higher plane.

"As the earthbound needs of the material life decrease, so do the periods of spiritual existence between incarnations grow longer, some elevated and highly refined souls remaining in their state of rest for twenty thousand years or even more and returning to the earth life only when the need of their specialized services to enrich and improve the world is required. These are the leaders, the great philosophers, the great teachers, the great statesmen, men such as Abraham Lincoln, Luther Burbank, Albert Einstein, Mahatma Gandhi, men whose Karmic qualifications have approached the pinnacle of perfection and whose spiritual development has brought them to the very threshold of that state of bliss in the presence of the Divine One which is Nirvana, the place of final rest in the loftiest of spiritual realms."

Brice Mack's wandering eyes caught Juror Seven, Graser, yawning and Potash grinning like a loon. He'd had a feeling that Potash would be trouble and could kick himself for not having used a peremptory on him when he had the chance.

"But these perfect souls are few in number. The majority of souls occupy various lower levels of the astral world in which they wait and work and, through meditation, seek to clothe themselves in the higher spiritual garments and so achieve promotion from a lower to a higher plane. When a soul wishes to return to earth life, it allows itself to seek a rebirth, foraging about for the proper parents and circumstances in which to be reborn. Quite often, a returning soul may be accompanied by another soul, as, for example, the soul of a loved one, each selecting to be incarnated at the same time so as to enjoy a continuance of relationship on earth. None of the past, however, is remembered, and the new earth life manifests its own demands and conditions, sweeping the awakening child into the dizzying whirl of its own pace."

Gupta Pradesh suddenly paused and remained caught in a torpor of contemplation, his glazed eyes reflecting the vacuity of a man who has temporarily lost his way. A ripple of restlessness coursed throughout the courtroom. When, after a full minute of silence, he had still not picked up the thread of his discourse, Brice Mack gently prodded, "Is there anything more you wish to add, sir?"

The question penetrated the empty look and brought the return of awareness.

"Just this," the maharishi pronounced in a breathless, hushed tone and with a countenance suddenly revitalized. "A message from beyond. The journey is far. Progression is eternal. The end is good. There is nothing to fear. The power that rules on earth rules in the astral cosmos. And all is governed by law! All are blessed and watched over and protected, even to the final atom in the scale of being."

A supernal glow of inner faith shone forth from the maharishi's eyes and impinged upon Elliot Hoover, who sat mesmerized, a beatific smile on a face that radiated understanding, acceptance, and eternal gratitude. Neither tacit nor secret, but openly expressed, the communication between the two men did not pass the attention of the court. The jurors' eyes, Brice Mack noted, shifted back and forth between the witness stand and the defense table as though covering the progress of a tennis match. Judge Langley's crotchety face, hanging over the bench, wore an expression of perplexed irritation as a further spate of silence ensued, which finally provoked the nettled jurist caustically to demand of the defense attorney, "Any further questions of this witness, Mr. Mack?"

There were plenty of questions he desperately wanted to ask, basic, bedrock questions that would pull the maharishi off his lofty astral plane and bring him down to earth, but Hoover's strict admonition prevented him from doing so. With a small, pathetic sigh and shake of the head, the defense attorney turned from the witness and addressed the bench.

"No, Your Honor, no further questions."

The judge raised his eyes toward the prosecutor, who had already risen from his seat.

"Mr. Velie?"

"Yes, Your Honor, we have several questions we wish to ask the learned gentleman."

The maharishi, assured of the veneration that his followers accorded him, preserved a mien of gentle acceptance and tranquillity even in the face of this gross and callous man lumbering toward him, his teeth partially exposed in a twisted smile that bespoke a heart of stone and a mind filled with harmful intentions.

"This astral world, or cosmos, that you speak of—is it simply a metaphysical symbol, like heaven and hell, or is it an actual place?"

"It exists," replied the maharishi in a kindly and temperate voice.

"Have you ever been there? Seen it?"

"Many times throughout eternity." The maharishi smiled. "As have you."

"Well, I'm somewhat foggy on the physical details of the place; perhaps you can refresh my memory a bit."

The pale and limpid waters of the sage's eyes became like granite as Scott Velie continued.

"For example, this astral cosmos, teeming with astral beings, can you tell the jury what it looks like?"

"Looks like?"

"Yes. Is it like a big park with trees and shrubs and rocks, or is it rather like a desert, say, a barren wasteland, with no signs of vegetation?"

Gupta Pradesh moistened his lips with his tongue.

"The astral universe cannot be described in the same way one describes the material cosmos. The astral universe consists of subtler hues of light and color and numberless vibrations. In the astral world, all is beauty, purity, and perfection."

"Hmm." Scott Velie took a few seconds to consider the maharishi's words. "What you're saying is, it's no place like home?"

The quip brought a response of laughter from jurors and reporters alike and a smile to Judge Langley's face. Bill saw Brice Mack rise to object and Elliot Hoover's hand stop him from doing so.

The maharishi seemed impervious to the prosecutor's cynicism and calmly replied, "It is certainly not a home as we know it on earth; however, to the beings who dwell on the various levels of the astral universe, it is a home of infinite and shining beauty."

"Oh, yes—can you tell us about these beings who dwell there? Do they continue to take a human form, or are they just. . . . uh . . . you know, smoke and blobs?"

"Astral beings may manifest any forms they so desire, human, animal, even floral. There are no restrictions or limitations."

A mischievous grin appeared on Velie's face.

"Really?" His voice struggled to subdue laughter. "You don't say! You mean I could transform myself into a rose or a daisy if I wanted to?"

"Or, even more easily, a pig."

The maharishi's equanimity was supreme. Potash guffawed aloud, as did Carbone and Fitzgerald. Judge Langley, wreathed in smiles, banged his gavel halfheartedly as Velie, obviously chagrined, took the time to walk to his table and consult his notes.

"By the way," Velie asked in an offhanded manner, "are you aware of the defendant's belief that the victim in this case, the child, Ivy Templeton, is the reincarnation of his daughter, Audrey Rose?"

"I have been told that, yes."

"Do you subscribe to his belief?"

"Yes, I believe it."

Brice Mack was itching to object on a couple of legitimate grounds. The question assumed a fact not yet in evidence, and it certainly was not proper cross-examination since it went far beyond the scope of his direct examination; still, he restrained the impulse in the hope that Velie would lead the witness up the very channels that had been denied him by Elliot Hoover.

"Can you tell the jury your reasons for believing this to be true?" pursued the district attorney.

"Such occurrences are not uncommon in my land," the maharishi replied. "Presently working in my ashram is a young student who is the reincarnation of a former student of mine who died in the cholera epidemic of 1936."

The statement had a magical effect on the jury, Brice Mack noted; they all seemed to lean forward in their chairs in fascination.

The district attorney also noted the surge of sudden interest in the jury and quickly interposed, "Move to strike his answer as not responsive to my question."

"So moved," Judge Langley said. "The answer to the last question is stricken from the record, and the jury is instructed to disregard it."

Scott Velie continued. "Let me repeat, can you tell the jury your reason for believing this—and by 'this,' I mean the defendant's belief that the victim is the reincarnation of his daughter—to be true?"

The maharishi gazed across the courtroom at Elliot Hoover and graced him with a look that bespoke faith and confidence.

"I believe this to be true," he said simply, "because a man of truth told me it was so."

"I see," Velie said, smiling. "Would you believe anything this man of truth told you?"

The maharishi returned the prosecutor's smile.

"I would believe any truthful thing he told me."

Judge Langley looked down at Brice Mack. "Any objection from the defense?"

"No objection," Mack said. "I feel the state should have every opportunity to pursue the subject of reincarnation with the witness."

"Very well, proceed," the judge said to Scott Velie.

"Thank you, Your Honor," Velie said, as he pored through his notes and finally found what he was looking for. "Oh, yes, let me ask you, Mr. Pradesh. These trips that astral beings take from a higher plane to a lower one, how are they made?"

The question drew a blank stare from the maharishi.

"Do they fly?" Velie pressed. "Do they have wings?"

"No, they are not as the angels on the ceiling of the Sistine Chapel," replied the maharishi in all seriousness. "Communication and travel from one astral plane to another is accomplished through telepathic means and is faster than the speed of light."

"Really? Speaking of travel, may I ask how *you* got here?"

The maharishi's clear brow furrowed in puzzlement.

"How I got here?"

"Yes, how you came to America?"

"I do not understand—"

"It's a simple enough question. You certainly didn't make the trip by telepathic means—"

"No. I was flown in an aircraft."

"Precisely." Scott Velie thumbed down his page of notes. "Air India, to be exact. Flight Seventeen, departed Calcutta the evening of December 23, arrived Kennedy Airport on the following afternoon at three thirty-five, which was the day before Christmas. Round-trip first-class passage in the amount of two thousand, seven hundred, and twenty-eight dollars and fourteen cents was paid from a special legal account in the defendant's name at Chase Manhattan Bank, as were all your personal expenses during the past month, which to this date, including your one-hundred-and twenty-dollar-a-day suite at the Waldorf-Astoria Hotel, come to the tidy figure of six thousand, three hundred, and fifty dollars, or thereabouts." Velie lifted his eyes from his notes and fixed the witness with a cynical smile. "That's quite a heap of living for a man who's turned away from the gross and fleshly tendencies of the material world, wouldn't you say?"

Brice Mack jumped to his feet, shocked to discover that Elliot Hoover's bank records had been subpoenaed by the DA's office.

"Your Honor, I object to this spurious, argumentative, and demeaning attack against the character of the witness. It has never been a secret that the defense paid for the Reverend Pradesh's trip to America, as well as his expenses while he patiently stood by and awaited his day in court. The comforts provided His Holiness were never a request or condition of the maharishi but the generous gift of the defendant and, as such, are entirely proper, as the district attorney well knows."

Before Judge Langley had a chance to rule on the defense's objection, Scott Velie announced, "Your Honor, I will allow that the expenses incurred by Mr. Pradesh, while obviously excessive, may be deemed proper; however, since I was interrupted by defense counsel before the completion of my question, there is one more item that I wish to enter into the record."

"Very well, continue," Judge Langley said.

Consulting his notes, Velie dramatically dropped his bombshell.

"It is the item of a check drawn on the legal account of Elliot Hoover in the amount of twenty-five thousand dollars and made payable to Mr. Gupta Pradesh."

Bill noticed the look of stunned amazement on Brice Mack's face as he turned and rapidly conferred with his client. The sketch artist's pen worked furiously to catch the various reactions on paper: Hoover and his attorney huddled in head-to-head colloquy, Judge Langley's wide-eyed expression, Scott Velie lording triumphantly above the maharishi, whose eyes gazed up at the prosecutor with a serpentine malevolence.

"I now ask you, Mr. Pradesh," Velie demanded, "did you, in fact, receive such a check?"

"Yes, I did."

"And were you given that check in exchange for your testimony?"

"I object to this line of questioning," Brice Mack shouted, rising and facing the bench with an expression of helpless innocence. "I had no idea of the passage of money between the defendant and the witness, Your Honor; however, my client informs me that while the check *was* made in His Holiness' name, it was specifically earmarked for philanthropic uses of the highest possible order and was never intended for his personal use."

"Your Honor," Scott Velie quickly put in, "Mr. Mack is not a witness or under oath, and I asked the question of Mr. Pradesh and not defense counsel; therefore, I move that the defense counsel's remarks be stricken from the record as improper. It's immaterial to what uses the money is eventually put. What is material is that a witness for the defense had received payment from the defendant. I submit that twenty-five thousand dollars can buy a lot of cooperation, and that this witness' testimony has been bought and paid for."

"Your Honor," Brice Mack shouted, but was stopped from continuing by a hard hammerblow on the gavel.

"Just a minute," Judge Langley warned. "I will not grant Mr. Velie's motion to strike defense counsel's remarks from the record, but on my own motion I will strike all remarks made by both counsel from the record, and I will instruct the jury to disregard all arguments advanced by both counsel in connection with their opinions as to the reason the witness was given a twenty-five-thousand-dollar check."

Then, turning to Velie: "If you have any further questions to ask of this witness, do so."

"I am still waiting for an answer to my last question, Your Honor."

In the interests of accuracy and saving time, Judge Langley asked the court clerk to read the prosecutor's question to the witness.

"'And were you given that check in exchange for your testimony?'"

During the entire exchange between lawyers and bench, the maharishi had maintained the bland and imperturbable façade of a man who has mentally absented himself from a world he found both petty and vulgar. He seemed to Bill to be in a trance or, rather, in a different plane from the others and either failed to hear or chose to ignore the clerk's question.

"The witness will answer the question," Judge Langley sharply ordered.

Still the veil of apathy remained drawn across the maharishi's eyes.

With a gunshot rap on his gavel, Judge Langley leaned over to the witness and barked, "Does the witness hear me?"

The sudden harshness of the hammerblow caused the maharishi to jump and awareness to flood back into his eyes. He stared up at the judge in the disoriented manner of a man just awakened from a sound sleep.

"You must answer the question," the judge snapped.

"The question?" the maharishi repeated in a seeming daze.

The judge turned impatiently to the clerk. "Read the question again!"

"'And were you given that check in exchange for your testimony?'"

As the full significance of the question, barbed as it was with insult and innuendo, was finally absorbed by the maharishi, his eyes became deeply aggrieved, and his face tautened with rancor, hurt, and hostility. In one sudden motion, he rose from the witness stand and proceeded to stalk floatingly out of the courtroom.

There was a collective gasp from the audience. Judge Langley had trouble finding his voice and, jerking up to his feet, finally shouted after the departing witness, "Stop! You have not been dismissed!

Guard! Restrain that man! Seize him and return him to the witness stand!"

The maharishi was now through the gate railing and moving swiftly up the aisle toward the exit when the door guard sprinted toward him and collected his feather-light body in a powerful hug (later telling a reporter that it felt as if he were grabbing a bag of loose bones).

At the first wince of pain on the maharishi's face, Elliot Hoover jumped up from his seat and bounded to the old Hindu's rescue, clearing the railing in a sprightly jump, and, seizing the guard by the carotid artery, quickly separated the two men.

Bill, standing and watching with a helpless grin of amazement, felt a quick stab of pity for the guard, who immediately sank to the floor in a daze.

Judge Langley banged furiously with his gavel. "Order!" he shouted. "This is a court of justice! Guards, restrain the defendant!"

The two burly officers needed no admonition from the bench to join the fray and zeroed in on Hoover from opposite directions with their pistols drawn.

The reporters were all on their feet, as were the jurors—Mr. Fitzgerald, shaking his head in disbelief; Mrs. Carbone, hand at mouth, weeping in anguish and emotion, "Oh, my God! Oh, my God!"; Mr. Potash's ferocious metallic laughter rising above the din of insanity in peal after peal of mindless merriment.

It was at this juncture of the pandemonium that Brice Mack, seated at the defense table, lowered his head into his hands in an effort to blot out the specter of his own ignominious defeat. What had been planned as a tasteful inquiry into the esthetics and religion of a far-flung people had turned, instead, into a rough-and-tumble street brawl. How any jury could ever be brought back to a sober frame of mind after a debacle of this magnitude was a deep and impenetrable mystery to him, one he couldn't even bear to think of.

"I want handcuffs on the defendant!" the grating voice of Judge Langley cut through the darkness of Brice Mack's despair. "Return the witness to the stand and see that he doesn't leave it until he's excused!"

The clinking of metal handcuffs added its note to the general commotion.

"Order!" The judge's voice cracked with hysteria. "There will be order in the court or I will clear the courtroom! The spectators will be silent!"

Drawing his hands slowly from his face, the first sight to assail Mack was his client, sitting beside him in an attitude of stoic resignation, his left wrist cuffed to the chair arm, and a disheveled guard hovering vigilantly over him. Turning his gaze to the maharishi, Mack found the lean and stately form of the holy man hunched deeply into the witness chair, peering forlornly forth from a ball of rumpled saffron cloth. Two policemen stood threateningly on either side of the hapless Hindu's chair.

"Mr. Mack," growled Judge Langley, huffing and puffing as if he had just run a race, "I am going to hold you responsible for the actions of your witness and your client. If you cannot control them, not only will I have them bound and strapped to their chairs, but I will hold you in contempt of court. Is that understood?"

The whipped-dog expression on the young lawyer's face was committed to the artist's pad as he meekly replied, "Yes, Your Honor."

"Mr. Velie," Judge Langley continued in a strident, no-nonsense voice, *"you* will ask your question of the witness."

Scott Velie, who had been seated throughout most of the tumult and enjoying it, took his time in rising and then stood waiting for absolute silence before measuredly addressing the bench.

"Your Honor," he said, "I withdraw the question." And, fixing the witness with a look of monumental disdain, he added, "I have no further questions to ask the *Reverend* Pradesh!"

The courtroom sighed and recessed for lunch.

20

Brice Mack sat hunched over the platter of barbecued pork ribs, maintaining a sulky silence while his teeth tore at the fatty flesh, ripping cartilage from bone in quick, cruel bites. The need to tear into something, to rip and mutilate and deform was hard upon him, and Fred Hudson, the only member of the "team" to have joined him at the long table at Pinetta's this bitter hour—having quickly gauged the boss' manic mood—kept a wary and respectful distance between them.

Greasily sucking at a bone, Mack quietly observed Hudson and the empty chairs across and between them with eyes void of expression. He knew where the two lawyers were—still screwing around in the library, picking and scratching about in the books for precedential straws to grasp at, which at this point would be thoroughly useless. Professor Ahmanson, he knew, had gone to Washington Heights to collect James Beardsley Hancock, their next witness. Mack felt a small comfort that he'd had the foresight to order a limousine to cart the old boy down to the courthouse to ensure his getting there on time. One more foul-up at this point, and Langley would throw the book at him. He was itching to do it.

Only Brennigan was unaccountable for. His last contact with the Irish sot was on Friday, just after the lunch recess, when he showed up with half a bag on and whispered to Mack that he was on to something. "Something," he had cryptically added, "that'll loosen Velie's bowels, me boy."

Slowly chewing and swallowing the crispy, pungent pork, the young lawyer's thoughts veered back to James Beardsley Hancock, his last bright hope on a dismal and threatening horizon. Hoover's adamant refusal to allow Marion Worthman to take the stand in his behalf had been reinforced by the Pradesh fiasco. Now only Hancock was left to lend his expertise to their case, a fact which not only failed to discourage Brice Mack, but sent an odd surge of renewed optimism coursing through him.

Having met and interviewed the old man on six separate occasions, Mack had finally come to know and truly to believe that James Beardsley Hancock would make an imposing study on the witness stand. At times, his look was Olympian; at others, Lincolnesque. His head could have graced a Roman coin or a Yankee postage stamp. His bearing transmitted respect; his leather-hard face and eagle-bright eyes conveyed honor, truth, and a fearsome integrity. In the courtroom he would seem to belong where the judge was sitting.

Recalling bits and pieces of their first meeting in the graceful sun room of Hancock's house overlooking the Hudson River always had a tranquilizing effect on Brice Mack. It was a house that was bristling with historic markers and was reputed to have quartered George Washington and his staff during the Battle of Harlem Heights on the several occasions when his headquarters at Jumel Mansion was under British fire.

Mack had brought to that visit the inflexible mind of a skeptic in an attempt to test the old man's power of persuasion on a jury and was shocked to find himself, after an hour's worth of niggling questions and patient answers, completely taken in by Hancock's soft-spoken scholarship, plied with the most delicate of trowels, speaking neither up nor down to his guest, but capturing and keeping the spark of interest at a constant flash point. Mack not only was enraptured, but refused to believe that the morning had long gone and that they had talked clear through the lunch hour.

Reflecting back on the substance of that first meeting, the lawyer attempted to reconstruct those points in Hancock's talk that had so beguiled him. Instead of belaboring the issue of reincarnation with a scholar's cudgel, the wise old man had made a game of it, accepting Mack's skepticism and doubts and, on a number of occasions, seeming himself to be confounded, allowing Mack to help him with the answers.

At one point Mack had asked Hancock about proofs of reincarnation and whether or not he could cite specific examples to substantiate the concept that the soul had lived through many lifetimes. The old man gave the question serious thought before speaking.

"It's never happened to me, unfortunately, but many people have told me of experiencing fragmentary recollections of former lives—moments of sudden recognition of people or places they had never met or been to before and that yet seemed familiar to them."

Brice Mack had remembered several such events in his own lifetime and told Hancock how once, when he was a child, he had been sent to a free summer camp up in the Adirondacks and, one day, had become separated from his group during a woodland hike. Hopelessly lost, he had been forced to spend the night in this totally alien environment.

He remembered how he had wandered, in tears, through the darkness until sleep overcame him and how, with the coming of dawn, he had awakened cold, frightened, and hungry to a sight that immediately calmed his fears and restored his confidence. It was the sight of a rocky stream vaguely seen through a density of trees, but so familiar a sight as to seem an old friend to him. He was stunned by his firsthand knowledge of the place and was able to describe every rock, rill, and overhanging branch to himself, knowing for certain that somehow he had witnessed the same scene before and not in a picture or a painting, for the very atmosphere, scented with pine pitch and morning dew, was also a distinctly remembered smell.

"Yes, yes." The old man chuckled in delight. "You no doubt witnessed a scene that awakened memories of a past lying far back in the misty ages of a former lifetime. I am sure, too, that you were able to draw on that former experience to help you retrace your steps to safety?"

"That's the strangest part of all," admitted Mack. "At that point the whole woodland seemed familiar to me, and I was able to find my way back to camp without any trouble."

After a moment's sober reflection the old man had continued with a question: "Tell me, Brice, was your childhood a happy one?"

"Well—" the attorney grinned—"we were poor."

"Were your parents gifted or unique in any way?"

Brice shrugged. "Not especially. They weren't intellectuals, if that's what you mean. They came from a long line of peasants and were honest, hardworking people."

"The salt of the earth," added Hancock with undoubted sincerity. "Isn't it strange how often we see evidences of the 'prodigy,' the 'youthful genius' springing from such humble soil? Children possessing tastes, talents, predispositions, qualities that seem to spring from a deeper, richer loam than those of heredity and environment?"

Mack had felt himself blush. "Well," he allowed, "I'm no genius."

"And yet how certainly you seemed to gravitate toward a degree of intellectual achievement that neither heredity nor environment can account for. Reincarnationists would say that your work in this life had been preordained by the mental demands of a former life."

It was at this point in their conversation, Brice Mack recalled, that they had been interrupted by Hancock's housekeeper, a sprightly lady who seemed every bit as old as Hancock. It was time for his pills, four of them, placed on a freshly pressed linen napkin on a pewter tray alongside a crystal carafe of water and a glass. After she replenished

Mack's coffee cup and left the room with the tray, Mack was reminded of another case that he thought might interest Hancock.

It concerned the six-year-old son of a friend of his, a man he had known since childhood. Neither his friend nor his friend's wife possessed any particular artistic qualities to set them apart from the normal run of people, yet the boy, at age five, one day sat at a piano and began to play with a skill that was amazing, while he had never had a lesson.

"And what of Pascal," trilled the old man in a burst of uncontained joy, "who, at the age of twelve, mastered the greater part of plane geometry without instruction, drawing on the floor of his room all the figures in the First Book of Euclid? And Mozart, executing a sonata on the pianoforte with four-year-old fingers and composing an opera at the age of eight? And Rembrandt, drawing with masterly power before he could read? Can you doubt that these 'old souls' came to earth with remarkable powers acquired in a former existence?"

No, thought Mack, sucking at the marrow of a spare rib, and neither will the jury. The old boy's enthusiasm was infectious. He had a way with a word and a con man's gift for making the outlandish seem perfectly reasonable. The jury would listen to this man and believe him.

Mack glanced at his wristwatch. Twelve forty-seven. At this moment the limousine transporting the sum and substance of his case and the salvation of his professional reputation would be speeding down the southbound lanes of the West Side Drive en route to Foley Square. Gnawing at the rib, which was cold and greasy, Brice Mack reasoned that traffic would not be a problem at this early hour and that even now they might have arrived at their destination.

Had it been possible for the youthful and hopeful attorney to have known that at this very moment, instead of proceeding on a southward course, the limousine, with the aid of a police car's sirens to clear its path, was speeding westward toward the emergency room of Roosevelt Hospital containing the catatonic and moaning form of a very sick and very old man, certainly the porker whose ribs he had so rudely desecrated would have had its revenge, for Brice Mack would surely have choked on the last mouthful.

Janice got the news at three fifteen.

The phone was ringing as she and Ivy entered the suite at the Candlemas. Handed a number of messages at the desk—all from Bill and all marked "Call back. Urgent! 555-1461"—they had hurried up to the room to comply, but Bill got to them first.

"Where the hell have you been?" he shouted in a wild and hysterical petulance that Janice suspected was as much the result of alcohol as anger.

"Out," she replied, effecting a calm for Ivy's sake.

"Out? Damn it, Janice! You were told to stick by the phone!" His voice blasted in the receiver, causing static.

Janice felt an impulse to hang up but restrained it. Instead, she asked, "What's the matter?"

"What's the matter?" he mimicked. "Where the hell've you been, anyway? It's all over the radio and TV!"

Janice resisted asking, "What is," forcing Bill to continue.

"The defense's case has collapsed!" he shouted in a delirium of hostility and joy and proceeded to fill her in on the incredible happenings of the morning. And then—Bill's strident voice rose to a new height of emotion as he delivered the real bombshell—James Beardsley Hancock's sudden heart attack, the defense's key witness out of the picture, perhaps for good. . . .

"Congestive heart failure," Bill blurted out. "The hospital's last report has him deep in coma and critical. Brice Mack asked the court for a continuance till tomorrow morning in order to realign his witnesses, and damn it, Velie had to accede to his request because *you* weren't there and he was afraid Mack would want to bring you on next. . . ."

"Oh," Janice said.

"Velie's pissed, Janice, and so am I. We had them off-balance, on the run. This whole damn business could have been over by morning. Now the bastards have time to regroup and re-form their strategy."

"I'm sorry," Janice whispered.

"Damn it." Bill's voice lost its edge of shrillness. "We just can't go about doing as we damn please, Janice. We're not living a normal life. We're in a battle."

"I know." Janice's soft reply held just the right note of ambiguity. She could feel him weighing what she'd said. When he spoke next, he was decidedly calmer.

"How's Ivy?"

"She's here. Would you like to speak with her?"

"How is she, Janice?" Bill insisted.

"Okay . . . I think."

"You think? What does that mean? Is she sick or isn't she?"

"Her throat's better, and the cough is gone."

"Well then, bring her back to the city with you!"

Janice was taken unawares. "When?"

"Now. On the next train. It shouldn't take you long to check out of that place."

Janice hesitated. "She'd prefer to stay in school."

"And I'd prefer to have her home, where we can keep an eye on her."

Janice protested. "But we'll be in court all day."

"She'll be closer to us here than up there. I'll hire a sitter or a nurse, if you want. Pack her up and take her along, okay?"

A vein was throbbing in Janice's temple. Ivy must not return to the city. She mustn't give in to him on this point, and yet to raise the question of why she mustn't would only rekindle his anger and bring on a new wave of scorn and contempt for fears he considered not only foolish but traitorous.

"Janice?" Bill prodded after a too-lengthy pause. "I'll be expecting both of you down tonight, okay?"

Janice found herself stepping back warily from the receiver, not knowing how to answer him. Then, unexpectedly, surprising herself, she thrust the phone at Ivy and told her, "Here, darling, Daddy wants to say hello."

The happy and assured smile on her daughter's face brought a flush of guilt to Janice's cheeks. It was difficult to stand there quietly and to smile as Ivy chattered innocently and with total unawareness that she had been used as the stopgap in an irreconcilable situation.

". . . but I can't come home now," Ivy beseeched. "Tomorrow's the crowning, and I just can't miss it. We all worked so hard on Sylvester. Please, Daddy, please let me stay!"

Her pathetic pleas to remain gradually found a receptive ear, and soon Janice saw the clouds of gloom disperse and sunshine return to her face.

"Oh, thank you, Daddy," she cried. "And please don't worry, I'm really feeling much better. I haven't coughed once since we got to the room." Ivy's eyes flicked toward Janice. "Yes, she's here, I'll put her on. And, Daddy, I love you—"

Janice's grip tightened on the phone, and hearing Bill's breathing on the other end, she cleared her throat.

"Thanks," he said curtly. "Thanks a lot." His comment required no response, and she made none. "What's this crowning all about?"

"It's an every-year thing they do at the school, with the snowman."

There was a short space of silence.

"You feel all right about leaving her there?"

"Yes, I do," Janice said firmly.

His voice was downcast. "All right. Get down as soon as you can. I'll wait dinner for you."

"Fine."

Janice hung up the phone and turned to Ivy.

"We must pack quickly if we're going to get you back to school in time for dinner."

"I'm packed already," Ivy said a bit nervously. "Remember?"

Yes, Janice remembered. It was for an instant an effort to remember, principally because with memory returned the sickness in her heart, the feeling of dread that had relentlessly pursued her ever since Bill had left the night before. The things that had happened in—what?—less than twenty-four hours, things that Bill would surely have considered trifling and innocuous, were things which, step by step, had plunged her into a renewed state of panic and despair.

It began Sunday night, several hours after she and Ivy had gone to bed—Janice in the bedroom, Ivy next door in the sitting room. Janice had considered sharing the big bed with Ivy and would have if Ivy had wanted to, but since she didn't mention it, Janice didn't encourage it.

After calling out their last good-nights to each other in the darkness, Ivy had asked, "Mom, what's her name?"

The question troubled Janice, for she knew full well to whom Ivy was referring. Still, she had needlessly asked, "Who?"

"Mr. Hoover's little girl."

"Audrey Rose."

Janice could sense Ivy considering it.

"That's pretty."

After another moment of silence, Ivy moved a thought closer.

"Do you think she looked like me?"

"No," Janice answered abruptly.

"How do you know?"

"He showed us a picture of her. She had black hair and dark eyes, and her face didn't look anything like yours." Then, putting a cap on the conversation: "Shall we get some sleep now, darling?"

"Okay. Good night."

"Good night."

Later Janice was awakened by a slight disturbance. It was the soft creaking of the connecting door and the dying edge of a shaft of light as it closed.

Alerted by the possibility of illness, Janice quickly rose from the bed without turning on the lamp and quietly went to the door. She opened it a crack and saw that the light emerged from the bathroom at the far end of the sitting room. Ordinarily, she would have simply called out to Ivy and asked if anything was wrong, but some inner sense, vague and unspecific, stopped her from doing so. Instead, she silently padded across the ill-lit room to a point still some distance from the bathroom, but that afforded a clear view through the half-open door, whereupon she came to an abrupt stop.

Standing naked before the wall mirror, gazing transfixed at her own dimly reflected image, was Ivy. Her budding breasts pressed close to the glass, there was a strange, mad light in her eyes as they plumbed the eyes in the mirror, seeming to seek a route through the pale and glistening orbs and beyond, into the deep, impenetrable darkness that lay on the other side. For a moment, Janice thought it was the prelude to a nightmare—her proximity to the glass, the dazed, empty expression, her trancelike immobility all seemed to point in that direction—and she was about to enter when, all of a sudden, Ivy began to giggle: tinkling, high-pitched, girlish giggles directed at the image of herself in the mirror, at the eyes that returned the opaque, vacant gaze. Janice felt her knees trembling. The sight of her daughter's nakedness, the bizarre laughter that seemed both childishly innocent and hideously sinister were totally mesmerizing. Then the laughter stopped as abruptly as it had started, and in a soft, taunting voice, Ivy began to croon the name.

"Audrey Rose? Audrey Rose?"

Janice put a hand on the dresser to steady herself, then silently wheeled around and picked her way back to her own room, softly shutting the door behind her. Turning on the bed lamp, she consulted her watch. Twelve fifteen. The light from the lamp and the noises she purposely made alerted Ivy, and soon Janice heard the toilet flushing and her footsteps pattering across the floor back to bed. Janice waited a minute before opening the door and looking in on her. She lay on her side with her face to the wall and the blanket pulled tightly around her neck. Her pajamas were on the floor next to the bed.

"Are you all right?" Janice asked.

Ivy turned to her mother with a sleepy face of candid innocence and sweetness of youth.

"Umm." She smiled. "Had to go to the bathroom."

Sleep eluded Janice for what seemed hours. The fears, the terrors, the complexities, the tangles, the unhappy moments, the fevered pace of the past months pursued her toward dawn with a harpy's persistence.

She was awakened by a shaft of sunlight, hot and bright, digging into her eyes. For a split second she didn't know where she was, only that a light was burning her eyes and that a voice was shouting, "Mom! Mom!" She sat up.

"Yes—what is it?"

Struggling out of bed, she ran to the door and flung it open. And saw Ivy, standing in her pajamas in the center of the sitting room, shock and anguish splitting her face, her blond hair tousled.

"Mom, my things are gone. All my clothes—dresses, jeans, everything!"

"Gone? What do you mean, 'gone'?"

Janice automatically moved toward the closet.

"They've been stolen!" Ivy persisted. "Somebody must've stolen them! Hairbrush, toothpaste, shampoo, everything! Even my medicine!" At which point she coughed reflexively.

"That's impossible—"

"Well, look for yourself," Ivy chided and, pointing to a chair overflowing with clothing, added, "The only things they didn't take are what I wore yesterday. And my hat and coat."

Janice opened the closet door and saw the row of divested wire hangers. Her eyes drifted down to the floor, which was barren of shoes and boots. She felt a clammy perspiration on her forehead and strove to contain her anxiety so as not to upset Ivy further. Turning to the dresser, she casually opened each drawer to assure herself they were empty.

Ivy's lips drew into a grim line.

"Robbers must've come while we slept, Mom."

Janice forced herself to smile.

"What would robbers want with your clothes?"

Even before she finished the sentence, she noticed the suitcase peeking out from under the rollaway.

"They didn't seem to want your suitcase," Janice idly commented, dragging it out onto the floor and finding it heavy. Releasing the clasps, the lid practically exploded under the pressure of clothes, bottles, brushes, boots, shoes, all beautifully and expertly packed.

Turning to Ivy to question her about it, Janice was stopped by the look of stunned amazement on her daughter's face, a look that was completely genuine and spontaneous, a look no actor could have simulated.

"Who did that?" Ivy said in a tiny, stricken voice.

"One of us must have," Janice said lightly.

"I didn't!" Ivy exclaimed, putting all the force she could manage into the denial.

There was no doubt in Janice's mind that Ivy had some time during the night packed the suitcase, just as certainly as there was no doubt that she had no idea she had done so.

Later, at breakfast, Ivy suggested that Bill might have packed the bag before leaving for the city.

"You know how much he wants me back home. He really doesn't like my being up here. Maybe it was his way of saying so."

"You mean, like a hint?"

"It's possible, isn't it?"

"It's possible," Janice managed, putting down her coffee cup which was slopping over the sides from the trembling of her hand.

The time was not quite seven, and they were alone in the breakfast room. Outside was one of those infrequent mornings in midwinter when the sun seems to shed a warm and kindly light over the whole world. Ivy thought it would be fun having a picnic on the beach, and though it meant deserting her post at the telephone, Janice was quick to agree, hopeful that the therapy of salt air and sun-baked sands would help to calm her flesh and spirit. Her mind was a tempest of thoughts and conjectures, a whirling confusion of half-formed fears centering on the eye of a single fact: Ivy had packed her bag without realizing it. Why? What did it mean? If the act was beyond Ivy's control, then Audrey Rose must have been the motivating force behind it. If so, was it merely a symbolic statement, or did it have a practical application? A packed bag could mean but one thing. A trip. Was Audrey Rose pushing Ivy back to the city? Back to home—and Hoover? Was this her scheme? If so, how had she thought to accomplish it? A girl of ten—alone—with no money and no real knowledge of travel? The questions dizzied her, bringing a shocked, curling smile to her lips and a look of dumbstruck wonderment to her eyes. If Bill were privy to her fears, he would certainly have her locked up.

Her fears were to be confirmed later that morning.

There were gray clouds and stinging gusts of wind at the beach. Janice was sitting on the blanket, watching Ivy at the shoreline pitching shells into the boiling surf, when a sudden strong gust blew a speck of sand into her eye causing it to water furiously. Her hand felt its way to her tote bag for Kleenex, and after groping about and finding none, she looked down and discovered she was rummaging about in Ivy's tote bag by accident.

She came upon the train schedule almost at once—a printed leaflet offered by the New York, New Haven and Hartford, listing train arrivals and departures between New York and Westport. The pain in her eye forgotten, Janice hurriedly continued to go through the tote bag, darting surreptitious glances at Ivy still at the water's edge with her back turned, and drew out the blue satin hand-painted purse. She found the ten-dollar bill in a plastic folder tucked between two pictures, one of Janice and one of Bill.

An aura of doom closed around her as she conveyed both money and train schedule to her own purse, bringing a darkening pall to the lemon-bright day.

Janice knew that her daughter had taken both items from her purse, by her own conscious act or as the unconscious instrument of Audrey Rose's desperate need to return to the city.

There was a way to find out, and when Ivy came walking toward her, her face ivory-pale, her eyes downcast, introspective, Janice casually asked, "Shall we go home, darling?"

"To the hotel?"

"No, to the city, to Daddy."

"Do I have to?"

"Wouldn't you like to?"

"No, not now, please!" she cried in a burst of passion that was obviously sincere. "I *must* go back to school. There are so many things happening right now that I can't miss. Tomorrow's the crowning, and afterward there'll be a party in the rec room. It's all we've talked about for weeks! Please, Mom, don't take me back!"

She had slowly descended to her knees, bringing her tearful, beseeching face in close proximity to Janice's.

"Okay, okay," Janice soothed, reaching out to wipe a tear from the pale and worried face. "Of course, you can stay."

Gazing into the blue eyes that met hers so candidly, the serious, yet tender mouth, she could feel no doubt at all about who the thief had been—and *why*.

Janice arrived in Grand Central Station on the seven five and quickly found a cab outside the loading ramp on Vanderbilt Avenue.

Having bought a late-edition *Post* in the station, she scanned the headlines, finding, in the rising and falling light of streetlamps and shopwindows, nothing of interest on the front page.

The story, however, filled page three, continued on pages thirty-seven and eight, and was replete with sketches covering the highlights of the morning's mayhem.

A small box in the center of the page told of James Beardsley Hancock's heart attack and contained a quotation from Dr. John Whiting, a cardiologist in the intensive care unit at Roosevelt Hospital. "His condition is critical, but he seems to be holding his own. The next twelve hours will tell."

Entering the lobby of Des Artistes, Janice had the feeling of having been away for months. Mario's greeting was effusive, as was Dominick's as they rode up the elevator. There was a flush of victory in the air, the kind of jubilant delirium that follows a war's end.

She even found Bill sparkling, flushed with the day's success and in a celebrating mood, which was totally unexpected. She had prepared herself for a sullen and quarrelsome evening and was, instead, greeted with festive gaiety and lingering kisses. After her trials of the past twenty-four hours this was precisely what she needed.

The bridge table had been lovingly set for two before the fireplace, crackling and sputtering and exuding a pine-scented warmth. A magnum of Taittinger was icing frostily in the bucket. Large red apples, a wheel of Brie, and a crispy cold roast duck in foil tray garnished with minted greens awaited their appetites. Janice was overcome.

"How lovely," she said.

Bill grinned and twirled the bottle in its bucket. He seemed sober, which meant he had slept since they talked. He was dressed in pajamas and robe and was gazing at her longingly.

"Hurry down," he said, with a meaning that didn't escape her.

Bill timed it so that the cork popped as Janice, fresh and scented and in filmy, flowing peignoir, descended the staircase.

Their first toast was to success.

"Pel Simmons called," he told her, chuckling. "The old boy was really fractured by the day's events—couldn't stop laughing—kept congratulating me over and over, as if I'd had anything to do with it. Good to hear, though," he added, draining his glass. "Restores the faith."

He topped off their glasses. The second toast was to health—theirs and Ivy's.

"We've all been through a hell of a lot," he said, his expression hardening, "too damn much. But it'll be over soon. The seven o'clock news had Hancock sinking fast, poor old guy."

The tragic face he affected failed to camouflage the note of exultation in his voice.

"The defense is scrambling for cover. Velie tells me two lawyers spent the afternoon down at the hospital trying to con the doctors into allowing them to set up a deposition, but Hancock's on 'critical,' and chances are they never will." Bill grinned. "Desperation time."

He refilled his own glass.

"It *will* be over, you know," he assured Janice. "All we have to do now is sit tight and keep our cool. Mack's run out of time and people. Velie said that Hoover rejected his last *expert* witness—you know the one, that woman on the talk shows—the witch." Bill laughed. "Can't say I blame the nut. Probably the best decision he's made so far. With their luck she'd probably put a hex on the court—turn Langley into a goddamn bat—he's half bats already—"

Janice maintained a careful noncommittal smile that she hoped would conceal her shock at the callousness of his remarks.

"By this time tomorrow it'll all be over but the shouting," he went on thickly, putting down his glass and approaching her. "And when it finally is, there's a hell of a lot of making up I'm gonna have to do to you. I know what I've been, Janice. And what I haven't been."

Janice felt herself stiffen in his arms as he kissed her, and she tried to repress it, tried to relax, but failed. Bill either didn't sense it or didn't care.

They made love on the rug, unsatisfactorily, then ate in silence and went to bed.

Bill fell asleep before Janice.

At three o'clock in the afternoon of that same day Brice Mack, laden down with hat, overcoat, and bulging briefcase, left the interviewing room and began to walk down the long Spartan corridor toward the elevators. His gait was sluggish as his head was aching, and the glaring fluorescents reflecting hot and bright off the enameled walls hurt his eyes. His underclothing clung damply to his skin, and his face felt clammy and feverish. He was suffering all the usual symptoms of another claustrophobic bout with Hoover; only this time, instead of dissipating, the symptoms seemed to linger and escalate. He smiled wanly and reflected on what his blood pressure must be at this moment and decided he wouldn't care to know.

The meeting had been a normal one—predictable and totally bizarre. He knew in advance there would be no way to make his client understand the direness of their situation, that they were down to the wire and would lose the case unless they acted with boldness and daring.

"You don't seem to understand," insisted Mack anxiously. "There's nobody left. By the time Professor Ahmanson finds a replacement for Hancock, it'll be too late—unless we bring in Marion Worthman as a stopgap. I can keep her going for days."

Hoover's eyes narrowed to cynical slits, minutely studying the perspiring attorney.

"Don't worry so much, lawyer," he said imperiously, then added cryptically, "this case won't be won by Mrs. Worthman's presence, nor will it be lost by her absence. Whether you believe it or not, the verdict is already in. It was written long before you entered the case."

The remark had literally flabbergasted Brice Mack. For a moment he thought he would burst out laughing. It could not be said that life till now with Elliot Hoover had been entirely logical or sane, but this—this was pure, unadulterated, looney-bin talk.

"I wouldn't know about that, Mr. Hoover," Mack had replied. "I don't try my cases with a crystal ball. I'm forced to rely on the plain, ordinary, everyday methods prescribed by Sir William Blackstone."

Hoover was neither impressed nor offended by the remark and, seeming to dismiss it entirely, hunched forward across the table with an arch smile and softly confided to Mack, "A great man once said, 'Coincidence, traced back far enough, becomes the inevitable.' What happened today, for example, the gross and shameful degradation of a saint; the sudden illness of a key witness—these were not simply arbitrary occurrences, but necessary steps in a larger and infinitely complex movement of events that will inevitably lead to a predetermined conclusion, the nature of which will ultimately be revealed to us in its own good time. There is nothing you or I can do to alter its course. It is clear to me now that the case you so carefully planned and structured was always doomed to fail. In other words, you have tried to manipulate the unmanipulatable. Goaded on by personal ambition, you have tinkered with the workings of a force far beyond the scope of your knowledge and have been soundly repudiated. There is no further need for you to ponder, plan, or toil in my behalf. All matters will attend to themselves, so just sit back and relax. The machine purrs smoothly under its own management. Even now, as we sit and chat, forces are aligning themselves to feed its forward momentum and bring about those events and those people who will bear witness to my innocence and render justice in my behalf."

A wacky, though comforting philosophy, Mack reflected while waiting for the elevator to arrive. Yes, a comforting philosophy until one pinned it down to just who "those people" were. It sure as hell wouldn't be the Templetons, even allowing Hoover's boy scout faith in the basic honesty and integrity of Janice Templeton. Nor would his salvation descend on him like a bolt of lightning from a smiling sky. The attorney found himself chuckling. Miracles yet! If such things were possible, who'd need lawyers? Sit back and relax, he'd said. Sure, in the poorhouse, because they'd all be out of jobs.

While at the time these thoughts were simply an exercise in frustration, they would remain in the lawyer's memory the rest of his life, for just as one elevator arrived, so did a second one, discharging Reggie Brennigan. Later Mack would puzzle deeply over the coincidence of the two cars arriving at precisely the same time and of the detective stepping out of one just as he stepped into the other, each failing to see the other until Mack turned and caught a fleeting glimpse of frayed coat collar, stained and battered hat, and thick red neck through the closing slit of his elevator door. Later he would ponder over the split-second decision to thrust his arm through the narrowing breach.

"Ah! There you are, me boy." The old cop exuded a stale, winy breath into Mack's face.

"Where the hell've you been?" the lawyer grumbled in distaste and nausea.

"Places," wheezed Brennigan with a sly grin, and tapped his coat pocket significantly. Then, pointing toward the men's room at the end of the corridor, he added, "Shall we step into the presidential suite?" His pale and watery eyes attempted a twinkle and failed.

A few minutes later Mack found himself inside a toilet booth behind a locked door, reluctantly sitting on the commode with his trousers lowered, all at Brennigan's insistence, "for the sake of appearances, you know. . . ." The detective occupied the adjoining booth, sitting similarly, and only after carefully judging that the coast was clear, did he slip his find to Brice Mack through the space at the bottom of the separating wall.

The several dozen photo blow-ups were of such poor quality that the lawyer could hardly make them out in the poorly lit stall. They were photographs of documents, to be sure, written in a quick, scratchy hand that, under the best of circumstances, would have been difficult to read. Riffling through the batch, Mack paused at one and felt his heart skip a beat. It was a photograph of a manila file folder with the name "Templeton" printed boldly across the tab.

During the next five minutes, the lawyer, having forced his perceptions beyond the limit of their powers, was able to wring enough data out of the documents to convince him that herein lay the bulwark of his case: the much-needed missing element.

His face was hot and flushed, and his voice cracked when finally he spoke to Brennigan.

"Is this stuff legitimate?"

The detective chortled hollowly back through the wall separating them.

"Is a pig's pussy pork?"

"Jesus! Where'd you find it?"

"Where it's been sitting these seven years—in the file room of the Park East Psychiatric Clinic on One Hundred Sixth Street and Fifth Avenue."

"Jesus!" The excitement in Brice Mack's voice was beyond restraint. "How the hell did you get in? I mean . . . how'd you get these photos?"

"Do you really want to know?"

"No," the lawyer said quickly, and heard Brennigan laugh, and then heard a small slurping sound as the detective swallowed something from a bottle. "Did you talk to this Dr. Vassar?"

"No, she's dead. I spoke with a doctor named Perez, a young talkative spic who used to assist her. Knows all about the case."

"Jesus—" was all Mack could say.

At this point, someone came into the men's room and noisily entered a stall at the far end. During the five minutes of enforced silence, Brice Mack's emotions ran the gamut from delirious enthusiasm to numbing despondency. After the interloper had flushed, washed, combed, whistled a strain from "You'll Never Walk Alone," and left, the lawyer unloaded his despair onto the old cop.

"We'll never be able to get this into the evidence. It's a privileged communication."

A soft, wheezing laugh which, at first, the lawyer mistook for a strained and flaccid fart preceded the appearance at the base of the wall of still another batch of documents, which, incredibly, turned out to be a Xeroxed copy of a 1040 form for the year 1967—the joint return of William P. and Janice Templeton.

Mack's amazement was unbounded.

"Don't tell me you also broke into the Treasury Department!"

"I'll tell you all about it one day." The detective chuckled, then instructed: "Turn to the clipped page."

Mack's fumbling fingers found the clip and turned to a page of medical deductions, a long and detailed list that only gradually revealed its secret. And there it was—on two separate lines—the lead to the Park East Psychiatric Clinic and, immediately below it, the item that blew their privilege.

It was too much for the attorney's bruised and battered mind to handle all at once. Too goddamn much to think about while sitting on a crapper with his pants on the floor in the heart of the citadel of justice.

Brice Mack shook his aching head in a weary but happy way and tried to lean back against the wall but was prevented from doing so by a complication of pipes and knobs which dug into his back and which started him laughing. A laughter soon joined in by the old, lovely, besotted, beet-faced ex-cop in the stall adjoining. Mack could envision the dying eyes staring out of the pickled face, and the pathos of the image suddenly struck at his heart roots, and his laughter eased as memory took over. The memory of something his father had once said to him—long ago—after a bum had come to their door for a handout and, for good reason, was politely refused.

"My pity, I could not help him," Max had said in Yiddish, weeping. "He is a man, a creature made in God's image, with a mind and a spirit that might have been the salvation of the world. It is my pity that I could not help him."

A humble smile came to Brice Mack's lips as he thought about all the avenues that Reggie Brennigan—this creature in God's image—had opened to him. And then he thought of what Elliot Hoover had said, and the smile became fixed. The machine purred smoothly forward under its own power—aligning forces, creating events, introducing people. . . .

Could it be?

Was it really possible?

21

The sight of the lean olive-skinned man, soberly dressed in dark suit and carrying a slim briefcase, stepping through the door into the courtroom at 8:55 A.M. on Tuesday, triggered a sudden *déjà vu* in Bill Templeton. Somewhere, recently, he had seen this man, had seen the face in close proximity thrust before his own in a fleeting encounter. He couldn't be certain where, only that the face was familiar and that his instinctive reaction was one of panic.

Bill's eyes fastened blatantly on the man's face as he walked through the rail gate and took a seat at the end of their row.

It was at this weak and anxious moment that the identity of the man came to him in a sudden flash. They had met at the Park East Psychiatric Clinic. They had almost collided in the hallway that day he went to examine Dr. Vassar's notebook.

Bill felt a cold sweat sprout on his face as Judge Langley, cross and tired, entered the courtroom and hurriedly convened the court. Bill's memory of the man's name was soon refreshed by Brice Mack, who stood and, in a voice both bright and eager, said, "I call as my next witness Dr. Gregory Alonzo Perez."

Even before Perez stood up, Janice saw the quick, puzzled expression leap into Scott Velie's eyes as he turned to the courtroom, studying first the witness moving through the gate, then Bill, with a gaze that was intensely questioning. Bill's only response was to sigh deeply and shake his head in an abject way.

The news-hungry press leaned forward in their seats as the witness took the stand and was sworn in by the bailiff. A polite silence ensued while Brice Mack allowed Perez to make himself comfortable.

"Would you state your full name, please?" he asked in a soft, friendly voice.

"Gregory Alonzo Federico Perez."

"And what is your profession?"

"I am a Doctor of Psychiatry."

Bill recalled the thin Spanish-accented voice from their phone conversation of more than two months before.

"Are you licensed to practice in this city?"

"Yes."

"And at what address do you practice?"

"I hold a clinical appointment at the Park East Psychiatric Clinic at 1010 Fifth Avenue."

An expression of fear passed over Janice's face at the mention of the clinic.

"Will you tell the jury when you first received your appointment at the Park East Clinic?"

"Immediately after completing my training at the Sheppard and Enoch Pratt Hospital in Towson, Maryland, I arrived at Park East and served my internship there. The year was 1966."

"At that time were you brought into contact with Dr. Ellen Vassar?"

Scott Velie's lips pursed as if to speak, but he restrained himself.

"Yes, I worked closely with Dr. Vassar as her assistant for six years, until her death in 1972."

"Would I be correct in assuming that during that time you were familiar with most of Dr. Vassar's cases?"

"Yes. All her cases."

"Are you familiar with a case involving a patient named Ivy Templeton, who received treatment from Dr. Vassar during the period commencing December 12, 1966, and extending through September 23, 1967?"

Scott Velie rose slowly, his brow furrowed pensively, and in a flat, undramatic voice, said, "This is privileged information, Your Honor. Defense is getting into the question of a doctor-patient relationship, and this is privileged, and we object to it on that basis."

Mack, with an eye on the jury, quickly interposed, "There's no question that the privilege exists, Your Honor; however, in this case there has been a waiver of the privilege by the child's parents."

"At no time," Velie lashed back, "have the parents of Ivy Templeton waived the privilege, Your Honor. I contend the question violates the doctor-patient privilege rule and is objectionable, and I—"

Judge Langley had begun to bang his gavel and cut in with: "Just a second here." Then, turning a questioning face toward Brice Mack: "Are you prepared to make an offer of proof to support your claim of waiver?"

Mack, savoring this moment, said, "I am prepared to introduce into evidence three documents that clearly establish a waiver by the parents of Ivy Templeton of the doctor-patient privilege. One, the claim filed by Mr. and Mrs. Templeton with the Mutual Insurance Company of Manhattan. Two, the insurance claim form of the Mutual Insurance

Company of Manhattan, completed by Dr. Vassar and submitted to the insurance company. And three, the written supplementary statement concerning Ivy Templeton's mental disturbances, prepared by Dr. Vassar and submitted to the Mutual Insurance Company of Manhattan, all at the request of and with the authorization of Mr. and Mrs. Templeton."

Velie shouted, "That's not really a true waiver! It was only made for the purpose of collecting insurance money and wasn't intended to reveal the nature and contents of the child's illness!"

Judge Langley banged the gavel.

"They can't have their cake and eat it," he admonished the prosecutor. "They wanted to get reimbursed, and they had no objection to submitting information on the child's illness to a third party—namely, the insurance company's file clerks, typists, claim adjusters, and so forth. You can't claim privilege here, Mr. Velie. I deem it's been waived. Objection overruled."

Brice Mack turned back to the witness, wearing the smile of a victor. "Once again, Dr. Perez, are you familiar with a case involving a patient named Ivy Templeton, who received treatment from Dr. Vassar during the period commencing December 12, 1966, and extending through September 23, 1967?"

"Yes."

Brice Mack next addressed the bench. "Your Honor, in view of Dr. Perez's answer I ask your indulgence to have him step down from the stand. I'd like to put another witness on the stand out of order so as to lay a foundation for the introduction into evidence of the three documents I've just mentioned to you."

"Proceed," Judge Langley said.

Dr. Perez resumed his seat in the witness row while Frank Tallman, custodian of records for the Mutual Insurance Company of Manhattan, was called to the stand and sworn in.

During the transaction, Brice Mack glanced briefly at the Templetons and was not surprised to see them both slumped deeply in their seats, wearing expressions of shock, fear, and self-recrimination.

In total command of himself and greatly relishing the moment, the defense attorney quickly ascertained from the custodian of records his name, function, and the nature and contents of the record room over which he held custodianship. Brice Mack then asked him to identify the file which he had been subpoenaed to produce in court. Taking a folder from his briefcase, Tallman described it as a file concerning the claim of Mr. and Mrs. Templeton for reimbursement of medical expenses incurred by their daughter during the period of December 12, 1966, and September 23, 1967.

Selecting the three documents he had previously referred to from the file, Brice Mack offered them into evidence as Defense Exhibits One, Two, and Three, captioned "Templeton" and as identified by the witness.

Whereupon Scott Velie rose and, putting a good face on a bad situation, not only agreed to their admission, but insisted, "Your Honor, I think the entire file ought to go into the evidence." And further to demonstrate his utter lack of concern over their introduction into evidence, he even declined the right and privilege to examine the exhibits.

It was all over and done with in less than five minutes, at which point Frank Tallman returned the witness chair to Dr. Perez.

Brice Mack's smile went out to him like a soft embrace.

"Dr. Perez, will you tell the court something about the reputation Dr. Vassar enjoyed as a psychiatrist?"

"Certainly. She was an acknowledged leader in her field, being that of child psychiatry. She was in great demand as a lecturer, and she published frequently. Her papers are considered definitive by most psychiatrists even today. She was a brilliant woman."

"Thank you. Now, you said you worked in close association with Dr. Vassar until the time of her death?"

"Yes."

"And that you were privy to all her cases?"

"Yes."

"Dr. Perez, the subpoena served upon you required that you produce a file of Dr. Vassar's concerning her patient, Ivy Templeton. Have you produced those records?"

"Yes."

"Do you have them with you?"

"Yes."

"May I see them?"

With a nod, the witness unzipped his briefcase and removed the file folder that was immediately recognizable to Bill and Janice.

Accepting the folder, Brice Mack held it up to the witness.

"I show you a file folder, dated December 12, 1966, to September 23, 1967, and bearing the caption Templeton. Can you identify it?"

"Yes. It is the file containing the records of the examination and interviews and conclusions concerning a patient named Ivy Templeton, who, at two and a half years of age, came under the psychiatric care of Dr. Vassar during the period of those dates."

Turning to the bench, Mack said, "Your Honor, I offer this entire file into evidence as Defense Exhibit Number Four and ask that its entire contents be read into the record."

Velie stood. "Your Honor, defendant's attorney hasn't even shown me the common courtesy to permit me to examine this file before showing it to the witness. I ask that before the file is accepted into evidence, I be allowed to examine it."

"Granted." Judge Langley rose. "Court will take a thirty-minute recess."

"What do you think?" Bill asked.

Velie's hand lifted tenuously to ward off distraction as he continued flipping through the pages, dwelling at great length on the final entry, which referred to Jungian archetypes as a possible explanation for the nightmares. At last Velie shut the small book with a thump and sighed deeply.

"Well, I haven't found any material I think I can exclude on the basis of hearsay." He looked at Bill starkly. "It certainly opens a door for them."

"They didn't have this file yesterday," Bill said hotly.

Noting Bill's hunched-over, hangdog expression, the district attorney smiled and said equably, "He's opened a door, Bill, but let's not commit suicide till we find out what he thinks there is on the other side of it."

When court reconvened at ten forty, Brice Mack quickly renewed his motion to introduce the file into evidence. No objection was made by the district attorney, and the court ordered it marked as Defense Exhibit Four. At that point Brice Mack again asked the court's permission to read the entire file into the record.

Scott Velie came to his feet, pouting. "Your Honor, it's a voluminous file. The jury will have the opportunity to take the file into the jury room for assistance in its deliberations if it so chooses, and we strongly feel that it would be an unnecessary abuse of the court's time to permit the reading of the entire file into the evidence."

"Your Honor," Mack sighed with a maddening indolence—"I do ask the court's indulgence to read the entire file into the evidence, for I believe that it will assist the jury in intelligently evaluating the testimony that will be forthcoming in the trial if they have heard its contents."

Judge Langley, who seemed more than interested in hearing the entire contents of the file himself, quickly decided in favor of the defense.

The balance of the morning was spent in reading its contents into the record. Brice Mack identified each page of the notebook by page count and slowly enunciated each entry, struggling over the pronunciation of the more complex psychiatric terms and often being forced to spell a word into the record.

When the reading came to an end, a hushed expectancy hovered over the courtroom while Judge Langley considered his next move, which, although it was twenty minutes shy of twelve o'clock, was to declare the noon break.

Janice skipped lunch at Pinetta's on the pretext of some fictional errands. There was nothing ambiguous in the looks Bill had been sending her throughout the morning session, and her innate sense of danger ahead had sent up enough warning signals to convince her that his company was to be avoided at all costs. With a couple of martinis inside him, the short fuse on a temper that was boiling murderously close to the surface was sure to erupt, especially if she was there to ignite it.

Getting a call through to Ivy at Mount Carmel was an equally urgent reason for missing lunch. She had planned to call that morning; but Bill had routed her out of the apartment too early, and the courtroom pressures of the morning session had also prevented her from doing so.

Having lost three of her dimes, Janice trudged up and down icy streets in a biting wind, seeking a telephone booth with a working phone, and finally found one in the warm and aromatic precincts of an Optimo cigar store.

The woman who answered her call was a secular teacher named Miss Halderman, or Alderman, an assistant art teacher who supervised the lower grades. Her sprightly voice informed Janice that the girls had just finished lunch and were happily engaged in preparing Sylvester for the crowning and melting ceremonies that were due to commence at four fifteen sharp. Yes, Ivy was fine; in fact, Miss Alderman could spot her through the office window—at least, the lovely blond hair seemed to be Ivy's—in the midst of a group of girls who were helping Mr. Calitri, the school custodian, pile the boxes. Did Janice want her to go fetch Ivy?

"No, it's all right," Janice said, feeling a sudden unaccountable chill in the oven-warm booth. "I don't want to bother her. I just called to see how she is."

On the walk back to the Criminal Courts Building, Janice went into a pharmacy to buy some aspirin. Her head felt light, and the chill persisted.

Inside the lobby, she stopped at a fountain and took three aspirin. As she rose from the water spout, a wave of dizziness seized her, forcing her to grab onto the porcelain basin to keep from falling. She was trembling. Uncontrollably. Dear God, what was wrong? What was happening to her? It had started after the phone call. Actually, during it. Something in their conversation. Something Miss Alderman had said caused her to suddenly feel ill. But what?

"Dr. Perez, tell me. . . ."

Janice heard Brice Mack's voice as if through a filter. The trembling had stopped, but the chill persisted. That, and the empty hollow feeling of encroaching doom, which seemed to be moving now at a swifter pace.

A dry cough from Bill beside her caused her to open her eyes and steal a glance at him. He seemed blessedly out of it all—eyes shut, body slumped down in his seat, totally relaxed in a deep alcoholic euphoria. She was alone. The thought struck her in a painful way. *She was alone.* Bill's withdrawal into bitterness and his deepening self-absorption had made any real communication between them impossible. He had shown himself to be incapable of understanding not only her, but all that was truly happening in their lives. Yes, she was alone.

". . . and you say that Dr. Vassar took you into her confidence on all of her cases, including this one?"

"We worked very closely on every case, and especially this one."

"Why especially this one?"

"Because it was unusual, unique. It defied categorizing. Dr. Vassar had never before encountered such a case."

"And you and she discussed it at great length?"

"At great length and in great detail."

Brice Mack referred to a page in the notebook.

"I want to call to your attention certain language in Dr. Vassar's notebook, Dr. Perez. Certain language that requires interpretation."

Turning slightly toward the jury, the lawyer read in a clear voice:

"In the entry dated January 18, 1967, she says: '[the child] tries to climb over the back of a chair—and succeeds! Appears well coordinated and shows a degree of muscular coordination and skill of an older child. (Test subject's ability to climb over chair during wakened state.)'"

Flipping to a clipped section in the notebook, he continued:

"And in the entry dated February 20, 1967, she says, 'results of chair-climbing test during wakened state disclosed subject unable to climb over chair successfully without falling . . . but within dream state is able to climb over chair and appears to show much greater creative muscular skill and coordination than one would expect in a child of two and a half. . . .'" Mack looked up at the witness. "How do you interpret this observation that the child seemed 'older' during her dream state?"

"It didn't make sense to either of us. Because a person in a somnambulistic state may enact an event that happened at an earlier time, but in that case the person would appear younger. And yet here she was, enacting some prior event in a somnambulistic state in which she appeared to be actually older."

"So in your discussions with Dr. Vassar, what conclusions did you reach in regard to this phenomenal behavior?"

"We could reach none. It was completely unexplainable."

"Dr. Perez, what do you mean by the word 'unexplainable'?"

"I mean, there was no explanation for the child's behavior that we could give with any degree of medical certainty."

The lawyer hesitated. He weighed the wisdom of getting into the matter of Jungian archetypes at this point. Even though Vassar had suggested this as a possibility in her final entry, he finally decided to forgo raising the issue at all. It was possible that Dr. Vassar might have been more amenable to Jungian theory than Dr. Perez would be. Besides, the first rule in questioning any witness is: Never ask a question if you are not sure what the answer will be. He moved on to the next entry.

"On April twenty-first, there is an entry which reads: 'the window seems to be her main goal . . . the glass pane presenting a barrier of prodigious heat . . . the fires of hell? . . . attempts to approach glass unsuccessfully as heat too intense . . . stumbles back, falls, weeps. . . .' Did you have discussions with Dr. Vassar about this particular entry?"

"Yes, indeed. Many discussions."

"Did you and she discuss the significance of this behavior?"

"Yes, we did."

"And did you come to any conclusions?"

"We both felt there may have been a memory of an incident in which the child was trapped in some sort of enclosure and sought to escape, but the escape route was painful. So there was this contradiction of moving in a direction and being repelled by it at the same time."

"Were the child's parents questioned to determine whether or not such an incident existed in the child's past that would account for such a memory?"

"The file indicates that the matter was discussed with the parents and with the obstetrician who delivered Ivy, but none knew of any event in the child's past to account for such a memory."

Assuming an air of grave concentration, Brice Mack continued in a carefully measured voice. "Dr. Perez, assume that a child was trapped in a burning automobile, but the windows were closed and the fire blocked that avenue of escape. Do you have a medical opinion as to whether this set of circumstances might produce a similar reaction to the one you observed in the case of Ivy Templeton?"

"Yes, conceivably, that would account for such behavior."

"And to your knowledge, the patient, Ivy Templeton, had no history of having suffered the experience of being trapped in a burning automobile?"

"Yes, that's correct."

Brice Mack turned to the prosecutor.

"Cross-examine."

Scott Velie rose with exaggerated slowness. His voice seemed tired, his manner sleepy.

He said, "As I understand it, you joined the Park East Clinic in 1966, is that right?"

"Yes."

"The same year that the parents of Ivy Templeton sought help for their child?"

"Yes, it was in 1966."

"What month did you arrive at the clinic?"

"It was in November."

"Early November? Late November?"

"It was after Thanksgiving."

"I see." Velie pondered this a moment. "So that, in actuality, you commenced your internship only a few weeks before Ivy Templeton became a patient of Dr. Vassar's?"

"Yes."

"And yet new as you were to the psychiatric profession, you maintain that Dr. Vassar took you into her complete confidence on a case so *unusual* and *unique* that it *defied categorizing?*"

Dr. Perez licked his lips.

"Yes, that is correct."

"Is it customary in the psychiatric field for psychiatrists to consult with their interns on cases of behavior so complex as to be, and I quote you, 'unexplainable with any medical certainty'?"

"Dr. Vassar did so," Perez answered simply. "She was a remarkable woman."

"Well, how much did you actually participate with her on this case?"

"As I said before, we worked together very closely on it."

"How?"

"After each session we would review the substance of what happened and what was said and discuss it."

"And together arrive at conclusions?"

"Sometimes, when it was possible to do so."

"Did you sit in on these sessions with the child?"

"No."

"Were you with her at the apartment?"

"No."

"Did you ever observe the child during one of her nightmares?"

"No."

"Therefore you relied on what Dr. Vassar told you she had observed?"

"Yes."

"Then, when you say you came to conclusions with her, you're basing your conclusions only on what Dr. Vassar told you she heard or saw?"

"Yes."

The district attorney studied some notes and, after the full impact of his witness' testimony had been absorbed by the jury, renewed his questioning.

"Tell me, Doctor, this matter of the child 'appearing' older during her seizures, of performing functions and displaying greater muscular skill and coordination than a child her age normally would—is there not a circumstance under which such behavior may be seen to occur, a circumstance which you as a psychiatrist should be quite familiar with?"

Seeing the perplexed look on the witness' face, Velie went on, helpfully: "Is not hypnosis a fairly commonplace psychiatric tool in usage today among people in your profession?"

"Well, yes—"

"And is it not true that under a hypnotic trance a subject may be induced by suggestion to perform physical feats well beyond his normal capabilities during the wakened state?"

"Yes, but—"

"Thank you," Velie interrupted. "You have answered my question."

Brice Mack was watching the district attorney like a hawk, ready to strike, ready to ask Judge Langley to instruct Mr. Velie to permit the witness to give his questions the deliberate and careful consideration the jury required of an expert witness, but he held back, allowing the prosecutor to pluck half answers from the witness and preferring to await his own moment on redirect to fully explore the issues being raised.

Velie, meanwhile, had picked up Dr. Vassar's notebook and was flipping through its pages.

"Turning now to the matter of the child's groping motions toward the window . . ." He found the entry he was looking for. "'. . . the window *seems* to be her main goal . . . the glass pane presenting a barrier of prodigious heat . . . stumbles back, falls, weeps . . .' and so forth. I put it to you, Dr. Perez, isn't it conceivable that if someone is trapped in a building during a blizzard and is seeking to escape through that window but is unable to touch it because the window was so *cold* as to hurt his hand, that this, too, might account for the kind of behavior described here by Dr. Vassar?"

"Well, you see. . . ."

"I'm only after a simple yes or no. Is it or is it not possible?"

"Well, it's possible . . ."

"Thank you." Velie flipped to the back of the book. "This final entry of Dr. Vassar's, which, by the way"—Velie's voice became pointed—"counsel for the defense seemed disposed to bypass, deals with Dr. Jung's archetypes as a possible answer to account for the child's behavior. What is the significance of her reference to Dr. Jung's archetypes, Dr. Perez?"

Doctor Perez took his time about answering.

"It would be hard for me to say. I don't really subscribe to that theory myself."

"The theory being?"

"The theory she refers to is one that suggests that there is, within the human mind, the capacity to have memory of events that a person had not experienced. Events that are experiences of the human race, but not experiences of the individual. Dr. Vassar, because she studied at the Burghölzli, probably was influenced by Jungian theory and may have reached for that conclusion. Dr. Vassar was not herself actually a Jungian, but it may have been her only way to explain this behavior, since there is no way to explain the reenactment of events a person had not experienced in life unless, of course, you believe in reincarnation."

There, it was said, Janice thought. For the first time that day, the word was actually said. And strangely, the first to bring it up was the man of science.

"In your opinion, does Jungian theory extend toward reincarnation?"

"No, I don't really think so. What I think Jung believed was that the experience of generations of prior individuals created a kind of inheritance of memory. Just as earlier experiences leave genetic traces physically, he believed they left genetic traces on the memory. But I don't think he believed that individuals literally had a prior existence."

"What do *you* believe, Dr. Perez?"

"What?"

"Do you believe in reincarnation?"

A startled laugh escaped from the witness.

"No," he said. "I do not."

Brice Mack's confident smile successfully shielded the concern he felt at hearing the tenor of Perez's answer and noting the jurors' smiling faces. Still, there would be moments of high drama aplenty soon to come, he was certain, that would bring the jury back to his table.

Velie continued.

"Dr. Perez, are there many people in the world today, to your knowledge, who believe in the supernatural?"

"Yes, of course."

"From a psychiatrist's point of view, what is the basis of this belief in the supernatural?"

"Well," Perez said soberly, "we are most of us terrified at the thought of death, the sense of finality of death. And if one is religious, one may avoid accepting death as final by believing in afterlife. But the fear of death and the fear of not existing lead many people to try to find something that will give them a feeling of continuity. That is one aspect. Another aspect is that there is so much about human behavior that is mysterious, unexplainable, that presumably has some rational explanation, but that we can't explain now. And people, just by the nature of human curiosity, are driven to try to find explanations for things that are mysterious and supernatural to them. But I as a scientist assume there is no such thing as the supernatural, only things about nature we as yet do not know."

"But you do not think that reincarnation is one of those things?"

"No, I personally do not."

"Thank you. That is all."

Brice Mack, rising, bowed his head to Scott Velie and approached the witness.

"Just a few more questions, Dr. Perez, if you don't mind. I believe you were prevented from amplifying on your answers to several of Mr. Velie's questions. Specifically, the one concerning hypnosis as a means of inducing a subject to perform feats beyond his normal capabilities. In your opinion, does this suggestion, in any way, apply to, or explain, the behavior of Ivy Templeton as reported in the entries on January 18 and February 20, 1967?"

"No, of course not. I was going to say that the nature and conditions of a hypnotic trance and a somnambulistic form of hysteria are entirely different. Under hypnosis a subject is entirely under the control and is responsive to the examiner who is conducting the experiment. In a hypnotic trance a subject will make an overwhelming effort to obey all commands given by the examiner and even display physical dexterities that go beyond a subject's skill during the wakened state, but only on command of the examiner. In the somnambulistic state, however, a subject is under no such influence and is either recapitulating or expressing behavior of an earlier, deeply repressed traumatic experience. In each case, the conditions are entirely different."

Brice Mack accepted his explanation soberly, then steered the witness toward the issue of reincarnation.

"Although you expressed a disbelief in reincarnation, Dr. Perez, to your knowledge, are there scientists who do believe in reincarnation?"

"Yes, I suppose there are."

"Do you suppose there are qualified doctors, psychiatrists, who believe in reincarnation?"

"Yes, there probably are some."

"And is it possible, notwithstanding your opinion, that they are right and you are wrong?"

Dr. Perez shrugged.

"I guess that's a possibility."

Mack sent a sweeping glance along the jury box before turning back to the notebook.

"Oh, yes. . . . Dr. Perez, you previously testified that it was possible that the coldness of a window during a blizzard might be sufficient to hurt a person's hand and might account for the kind of behavior described by Dr. Vassar. I now ask you, in your opinion, is that likely?"

"No, the reaction of the child, the quick, reflexive drawing back from the glass pane, indicates that the magnitude of the painful experience was greater than ice could produce. This, plus her word-stream babbling of 'hothothothot,' suggests to me conclusively that it was a fire situation."

"Thank you, Dr. Perez. That is all."

As the witness started to rise, Velie swiveled about in his chair and his head jerked around.

"Just a second, Dr. Perez, you're not through yet."

Perez turned a languid look on Velie as he sat back down.

"Was Dr. Vassar a hypnotist?" he loudly asked from a seated position.

The crude manner in which the question was put seemed momentarily to fluster the witness. A droll and skeptical smile came to his lips.

"Dr. Vassar was a psychiatrist. She was adept in the use of hypnosis as a therapeutic tool, as are most psychiatrists today, including myself."

"I see," Velie said. "Then she *was* a hypnotist. Thank you."

The objection from Brice Mack came in a swift, businesslike way.

"I move that Mr. Velie's remark 'Then she *was* a hypnotist' be stricken from the record, Your Honor, since he's characterizing the answer of the witness. It is no more true that a person who's adept in hypnosis is a hypnotist than a man who's adept with a hammer is a carpenter."

"Objection sustained."

There was a momentary impasse during which Dr. Perez remained seated, not knowing whether he was to leave the stand or not.

Assuming his most weary expression, Judge Langley asked both attorneys if they were finally finished with the witness.

"For the time being, Your Honor," Velie said. "I'll probably want to ask him more questions later, however."

Judge Langley instructed Dr. Perez to keep himself available for possible recall and excused him. As the psychiatrist hurriedly escaped the courtroom, Judge Langley turned to Brice Mack and told him to call his next witness.

All eyes in the courtroom shifted expectantly to the door. However, Mary Lou Sides did not appear through the door but rose instead from a seat in the middle of the courtroom and walked down the aisle to the witness stand, causing a light flurry of nervous giggles among the spectators who had been taken unawares.

Janice stared at the big, heavyset, seemingly shy girl who couldn't have been more than twenty-five, as she raised her right hand and was sworn in by the bailiff. Looking at the straight cornsilk hair and the well-scrubbed, smiling face flushed with health, Janice was reminded of the Swiss milkmaid on the Baker's Chocolate boxes. Shifting her gaze to Hoover, she discovered that he, too, was staring at the girl and was smiling and that Mary Lou Sides returned his smile as she sat, which meant that they were probably acquainted.

The jury, reporters, spectators, and members of the court were not kept wondering long about the purpose of Mary Lou Sides' presence on the witness stand, for Brice Mack, after eliciting from the soft-spoken girl her name, age (she was thirty-one), and home address, which was in an outer suburb of Pittsburgh, launched immediately into the crux of her testimony.

"On the morning of August 4, 1964, Miss Sides, were you involved in a car accident on the Pennsylvania Turnpike?"

"Yes."

"Is it true that the car you were driving collided with a car being driven by Sylvia Flora Hoover?"

"Yes."

"Were you alone in your car?"

"No, I was with my girlfriend."

"And was Mrs. Hoover alone in her car?"

"No." Here the witness' voice faltered slightly, and her eyes seemed to cloud. "Her daughter was in the car with her."

"What was the name of Mrs. Hoover's daughter?"

"Audrey Rose."

"Will you tell the jury, Miss Sides, to the best of your recollection, just what happened as you observed it on the morning of August 4, 1964, at about eight thirty?"

"Yes." Miss Sides took a second to compose her thoughts, to place them back and fix her mind on that moment more than ten years before.

"I was driving on the Turnpike, on my way to work, traveling east. I was with a friend. We both worked for the Forsythe Insurance Company, whose main office building was about twenty miles outside Pittsburgh, and were due in the office at nine o'clock." She paused a moment. "It was a hot morning, but the sky was dark. It was going to storm, and I hoped I'd get to work before it started to rain. I always hate driving in the rain." The courtroom tensed as her voice, calm and expressionless till now, began to change pitch as she started reliving the next episodes.

"About five miles from work the storm broke. It was terrible. Hailstones as big as eggs. I thought they were going to break my windows. I could hardly see through the windshield and was thinking of pulling off to the side, when this car . . . this car. . . ." Her voice broke perceptibly. Press and jury strained forward in anticipation. "This car came skidding past me on my left . . . a big sedan, skidding and twisting in the road, and I tried to stop, but I couldn't and . . . I started skidding too, and I could see we were going to crash into each other. . . ." Her voice broke again. "I tried to control the car, but I couldn't, the wheel just twisted around in my hands . . . and then we hit each other . . . we crashed. . . ." A sob escaped her throat. "We crashed. . . ." Overcome by tears, she paused.

"Are you able to go on, Miss Sides?"

"Yes, I am."

The words came out in a rush now, punctuated with anguished cries and tears.

"We crashed and both cars went into the guardrail, but at the time I couldn't see what I'd hit or what stopped my car from going over the cliff because of the hailstorm, but it was a guardrail, and that stopped us, but it didn't stop the other car. It went over the guardrail and down this steep embankment." She paused here to control herself. "I don't know how long I remained in the car, but my girlfriend was unconscious, and I felt wet stuff on my face, which turned out to be blood, because I'd hit my head against the windshield, since I didn't have a safety belt on, and neither did my girlfriend, but she was unconscious." She paused, her eyes widening. "And then, all of a sudden, the storm ended, and the sun came out very bright. I remember getting out of the car and seeing the road lined with cars that had stopped, and people standing at the edge of the road, looking down the embankment at the other car, which was upside down. It was smoking, and one of the back wheels was still turning, and then I saw . . . I saw the face of a girl . . . a little girl . . . looking out of the window inside the car . . . and screaming. . . ."

The witness broke down here and sobbed openly as she tried to go on.

"Men were trying to climb down the steep embankment to rescue her, but it was hard at this point because it was too steep. Some other men drove down the road about a quarter of a mile to a place where it wasn't so steep, and I could see them coming far in the distance. But they never got there, because just then . . . there was an explosion . . .

not loud . . . like a puff . . . and all at once the car was swallowed up in flames. . . . It was just horrible. I could still see the little girl screaming and screaming and beating her hands against the window. . . . I could see her through the flames as the car was melting all around the window . . . the paint of the car melting and pouring down over the window. . . ."

Janice's heart was pounding. Her body was trembling.

". . . as she screamed and screamed and tried to get out of the car and kept. . . ."

The paint of the car melting and pouring. . . .

". . . beating her hands against the window. . . ."

Melting! The melting! The crowning and melting ceremonies, the woman had said. . . .

". . . which was slowly being covered over by the melting paint. . . ."

Dear God in heaven!

Janice's eyes darted to the wall clock. Four twenty. It was happening! *It was happening! Now!* Her eyes shot across at Hoover.

He was standing.

The two guards standing nervously behind him.

His face was wet, florid.

His eyes were ablaze—

—seeming to search a distance beyond the sobbing girl on the stand, beyond the memory of that distant horror freshly revived, to a time and place where future sounds were struggling to be heard, where winds whipped cold and children laughed and sheets of snow, pouring white on black, came melting down in a hiss of flame. . . .

Watching from her window, Mother Veronica Joseph felt the acrid taste of fear rising in her throat. As it did every year on this day.

Pagan, unchristian, she thought anxiously, watching the rapt and intense faces of one hundred and twenty-seven virgins observing their sacrificial effigy—a labor of weeks—succumb to the all-consuming flames. Homage to Moloch, pagan god of fire. Heathen gambols on consecrated soil. Why did she permit it? Each year she vowed to eliminate it from the school program, and each year she hesitated doing so. Why?

The flames were gathering force now—licking and hissing against the snowman's lower extremities—eroding his strength, vanquishing his pride, devouring his crowned glory. Creation. Adulation. Destruction. A primitive rite. Unthinkable.

And yet somewhere in Mount Carmel's Christian past, it had started. With the Franciscan Brothers, the old custodian, Calitri, had once told her. In the time when Mount Carmel was a school for boys. Before the conversion. In the days when her own name was not Veronica Joseph, but Adele Fiore. Yes, it was the brothers. They had put flame to the very first effigy—the first of what would become a yearly tradition at Mount Carmel—a yearly event so rooted in the minds of each succeeding class as to become a fixed and immutable part of the school, like the very ivy that cloaked its stained and ancient walls. . . .

Ivy? Was that the Templeton girl? She was much too close to the fire. . . .

Yes, the brothers. Respectable, honorable men, who doubtless were ignorant of what they had started, were responsible for the desecration that assaulted her vision and her senses.

Observing the leaping flames eating away at the mammoth snowman, Mother Veronica Joseph felt a small consolation in the thought that it would soon be over; that soon the effigy would come toppling down in a steaming, hissing mountain of blackened snow and the tradition would be done for another year. Yes, Mother Veronica Joseph vowed, this would be the final year. The haulage and cleaning charges alone were enough reason to bring the tradition to an end. . . .

The nun's eyes suddenly sharpened.

What was that child doing? Moving slowly toward the fire? Were all so fascinated by the flames they didn't see her?

Yes, fire fascinates. She had not understood its power until this moment. Fire! Man's age-old enemy! Satan's pillow! The licking flames, like demon eyes, beckoning, beguiling—

Now she's down on all fours! Moving ahead! Does no one see her?

"Stop!" shouted the nun, with a stuttering heart, but knew her voice was swallowed by the silences of the thick-skinned chancellery. Her fists beat at the leaded panes; she tried to budge the ancient windows but the rusted hinges held.

Dear God, dear Mary, the child was nearly into the flames, and still nobody noticed! Were they dreaming? Were they all mesmerized by the flickering flames? Seduced by the warmly inviting tongues of Satan's fiery embrace?

"Stop! *Stop her!*" screamed the nun, seizing a chalice and smashing the diamond-shaped panes of glass, inviting plumes of frigid air to batter her face and send her veil billowing behind her.

Dear Mary, Mother of God . . . . she's into the flames!

"THE CHILD!" shrieked the nun in the teeth of the blasting wind. "THE CHILD! STOP HER! STOP HER!"
Dear Mary, Mother of God, pray for us sinners, now and at the hour of our death. . . .

22

They arrived at the hospital outside Darien in the uncertain gray of twilight. It was bitter cold, and it seemed to both of them that there would be snow, but they did not discuss it.

They were met in the reception lounge just inside the main doors. Mother Veronica Joseph began talking even before Bill and Janice came to a stop, as did an elderly doctor—Dr. Webster—who quickly assuaged the pale and stricken parents in a calm, professional voice. Each went on talking animatedly, Bill and Janice trying to follow two streams of thought at once as they walked down the broad corridor, passing occasional nurses and other family groups clustered before half-open doors. The first dealt with what had happened—Mother Veronica Joseph's low, stunned voice re-creating, in detail, her eyewitness account of the accident, which had erupted without expectation and which, but for the quick action of Mr. Calitri, might have ended in real tragedy. The other was more complex a stream, dealing with the extent and prognosis of Ivy's injuries, which, they were assured, were mainly first- and second-degree burns, producing only a mild shock with no indication of a developing toxemia or septicemia.

"Lucky she was so well bundled and there was all that snow around," Dr. Webster encouraged. "Her body was completely untouched. Her face took some heat; however, there's no indication of respiratory tract damage; we don't see singed nasal hair, she's not coughing, and her throat doesn't seem hoarse. No expectoration of blood or carbon particles associated with inhalation of fire cases, just some transient facial swelling, redness on the left cheek, singed eyebrows and a few small developing blisters. . . ." He chuckled. "Nothing permanent to mar her good looks."

Janice, walking well ahead of them, strained to hear their conversation, but the distance and Mother Veronica Joseph's constant prattle made it impossible.

". . . I don't mind your knowing, Mrs. Templeton," the nun murmured softly and with a trace of self-righteousness, "that while nothing like this has ever happened before at Mount Carmel, it needn't have happened this time. What I'm saying is that it was no accident. Your daughter literally walked, then crawled into that fire."

Janice flinched. Then, with a shake of her head, she replied inadequately and with no conviction, "You must be mistaken. Why would she do a thing like that?"

"That I cannot answer, Mrs. Templeton. But I am not mistaken about what I saw. Understand, I am not saying that she was aware of what she was doing, only that it was no accident."

Ivy was sitting up in bed, perusing a magazine somberly. Her face, beneath the glistening medication, seemed lightly sunburned. Her long blond hair was singed in a ragged bob. The sight of Janice and Bill stirred her bruised senses, and unwilled tears rushed to her eyes. Bill and Janice hurried to her bedside but were cautioned by Dr. Webster to desist from embracing her.

"It's all right, baby," Bill soothed, kneeling at her side and clutching her hand.

Sitting on the edge of the bed, Janice held her other hand. For a time, Ivy could only look at her parents, back and forth at each face, in a lost, abject way and sob.

"What happened to me anyway?" she cried in a delirium of anguish. "What made me do such a thing?"

"It was an accident, baby," Bill said in a soft, relaxing voice.

"No, Daddy, I did it on purpose. They say I walked into the fire, and I don't remember anything about it."

Bill's expression tightened. "Who says you did that?"

Ivy's eyes sought the stately black-cloaked form standing at the foot of the bed. "Mother did," she said, weeping.

Bill ran a finger between his neck and his shirt collar.

"She's wrong," he said, then turned a hard, brutal face on Mother Veronica Joseph. "What do you build fires for anyway?" he rasped. "What kind of business is that in a convent? We send our children to you for peace and protection, and you build fires."

In receipt of Bill's anger, Mother Veronica Joseph made no reply. Silence quivered in the room until the old nun, her lips a thin, grim line, forced herself to speak.

"I'll wait outside," she said quietly, clutching her beads, and left.

Dr. Webster coughed and in a hushed voice conferred with the nurse who was in the room, attentive and constant, yet so unobtrusive as to have escaped Janice's notice.

"What's happening to me anyway?" Ivy repeated in a continuing moaning lament. "What's happening to me?"

Janice considered the question—a question unanswerable to all but herself—and one other person. There was never a doubt in her mind about who had been behind this murderous escapade, as there now was no doubt about Audrey Rose's ultimate intentions. As Elliot Hoover had warned, "*She will keep pushing Ivy back to the source of the problem; she'll be trying to get back to that moment and will be leading Ivy into dangers as tormenting and destructive as the fire that took her life. . . .*" Yes, Audrey Rose clearly had no compunction about showing her hand and would continue to have none. The consideration of how easily they could lose Ivy made her shudder. "*Audrey will continue to abuse Ivy's body until her soul is set free. . . .*" There was nothing to hold her, nothing to make her even hesitate. Unless—

Janice sat stunned by her own thought. Sitting erect, almost wooden, listening to the soft and mending sounds of Bill's voice gradually restore and calm their fear-stricken child, she gravely hesitated to pursue the thought, knowing with certainty that there could be only one possible result from such an act. Had the answer come to her too quickly? It was, in its way, a bizarre and capricious answer; still, it blazed in her head, for it seemed the only right answer. Tread lightly, a voice within her warned. Consider deeply. The next moves are fraught with peril. The decisions of the next twelve hours could blow up your world.

They didn't leave the hospital till nine fifteen. Neither was surprised to find that Mother Veronica Joseph had not waited. They encountered Dr. Webster in the reception lounge, chatting intimately with an elderly patient in a wheelchair.

Upon seeing the Templetons, he excused himself and joined them at the door. He reiterated his confidence that Ivy would be fine and would probably be discharged by the weekend. Janice asked if Nurse Baylor might be told to stay with Ivy through the night.

"She's off duty at twelve," the doctor said.

"Isn't there someone who replaces her?" Janice asked.

"Just the floor nurse, but there's nothing to be concerned about, her TV monitor covers each room."

Janice frowned. "Can't you get someone to stay with her?"

Bill flashed her a quick look, then turned to the doctor.

"Yes," he agreed. "We'd be willing to pay for a private nurse, of course."

Dr. Webster thought a moment. There was an urgency in the request he felt he couldn't ignore.

"I'll see what I can do," he finally said.

Outside, the snow had stopped and only a misty drizzle fell. Bill drove south on the Boston Post Road in search of a restaurant that wasn't crowded and found one with a few cars parked in front, just south of Stamford.

The dining room was nearly empty. A waiter led the way to a table against the wall, apart from the ones that were occupied. Drinks were brought them, after which they ordered and consumed an unusually large dinner.

They did not talk until the steak plates were removed and their drinks refilled. And then it was Bill who did the talking, not Janice. The things he said were pleasantly irrelevant, taxing neither her mind nor her emotions, which were deeply embedded in her own private turmoil. She was grateful for Bill's unwillingness to discuss the subject uppermost in both their minds. His attack on Mother Veronica Joseph had left no doubt about his feelings on the matter and was clearly intended as a warning to Janice as well.

To Bill, it was an accident. Nothing more. To suggest anything different would only fan the flames of his anger, unleash the full torrent of his scorn and ridicule. No useful purpose could be served in confiding her thoughts and feelings to Bill. Not now or ever. Her fears for Ivy's safety—for her life—would be her own private business.

She deliberately put from her mind all thoughts of Bill and, against the backdrop of his innocuous ramblings, plunged into the total consideration of the decision she must make before morning.

He noticed her absence and said harshly, "Where the hell are you anyway?"

His comment startled her. "What?"

"Up flittin' about with the spooks and goblins?"

There was an ugly twist to his grin. He drained his glass and ordered another. Janice's failure to answer further intrigued him.

"I suppose you agree with Reverend Mother?" And without waiting for her reply, added: "Well, it doesn't matter who you agree with or what you think. Hoover's had it. That little display in the courtroom this afternoon was their full salvo, and it didn't mean a goddamn thing. Velie said they've run out of witnesses. They've no place to go but us." He chuckled with grim pleasure. "Nobody left but us chickens. Unless they decide to put on Hoover or fly in some other gooney bird from Timbuktu." This idea made him laugh. "Gunga Din," he said, rounding out the thought. His drink came. He drank it while he settled the bill.

Nothing more was said until the drive south on the Merritt Parkway.

It was a cold ride since the car heater was faulty, a fact which had a decidedly sobering effect on Bill.

As they approached the Henry Hudson Parkway, he said without rancor, "We should do something for Mr. Calitri—to show our appreciation. A nice gift or a check."

Janice agreed.

Later, walking home from the Hertz garage, the two of them bent into the chill January wind which bore against them, he shouted to her, "I'd ask Harold Yates to look into a possible lawsuit for incompetence or negligence, but how the fuck do you sue the Catholic Church?"

It was near midnight when they entered the apartment.

Bill took a cold beer out of the refrigerator and poured himself a double bourbon. He seemed distant and sulky again and carried the drinks unsteadily to the staircase, where he paused. After some trouble balancing his nightcap, he managed to flick on the light switch with his elbow, illuminating the upstairs hallway. Before ascending, he stepped aside to allow Janice to precede him.

"Coming to bed?"

Janice said cautiously, "In a while."

He nodded sagely and with infinite wisdom. "Good night," he said, and raised his shot glass in a toast. "Pleasant dreams."

His scorn of her fears, which he had easily fathomed, was definitive, as was his amusement at her cowardice in expressing them.

Janice watched him ascend the stairs with a dazed stillness—not for his taunting ridicule of her, but for the barrier he had erected between them which now separated them irrevocably.

By one forty-five the apartment was silent.

Sitting in the rocker, Janice's expression was calm except for two pinched lines at the corners of her mouth. Her eyes traversed the living room—the only real world she ever knew and loved: the white stuccoed walls that encompassed it, the darkly stained pegged floor that supported it, the glorious ceiling that crowned it. She lingered over each cherished part of it, each pillow and piece of furniture, each painting, lamp, and oddment of bric-a-brac, each item invested with a sweet and gentle memory of a shared, beloved moment in their lives.

A sudden panic gripped her at the thought of all she was risking. She'd lose him. She'd surely lose Bill. She'd lose it all. His love. Their marriage. Their perfect life in their perfect apartment. She felt faint at the thought, and her senses battled against the reality of a life without

Bill—a life alone—one more member of that vast unloved, unwanted set, poking about on the fringes of other people's lives, outside looking in.

Her eyes filled with tears. She wiped them away with her hand and focused her blurred vision down at the worn and scuffed leather cover of the diary resting on her lap.

Hoover's diary.

She had taken it down from the closet for a reason—a reason that seemed urgent at the time, but that now was vague and incomprehensible.

Why had she taken it down? Was it simply an exercise to while away the sleepless hours ahead? Her need for a companion, a hand to hold through the dark and waiting night?

Or—her face grew stark—were there still things she had to know about this man before she could take her awesome step? All the scraps and pieces of his past, his thoughts and feelings, hopes and dreams, the deep and intimate confidences that lovers convey to each other during courtship.

Yes. That was it—reaching for the diary was a further step in their courtship. A further getting to know the man to whom she was about to consign her family's future.

Her trembling fingers sought the center page of the bulging diary, and pulling it open, she found herself in a section crammed with small, what seemed to be hieroglyphics—tiny pencil scrawlings in a language that was probably Hindi or Sanskrit. Page after page was filled with these writings; strange, nubby intense words that, although incomprehensible, purveyed a sense of deep passion in their very design and outpouring. The pages continued in this vein until Janice wondered if the tragedy of Prana and her family and Hoover's loss of faith in the aftermath of their deaths had not caused him to forsake the English language entirely. And then, turning a page, she was startled to see a paragraph written in the same chatty, informational Baedeker-English she remembered reading in the earlier part of the diary.

> I am in Mysore. I want to be here because it has been inhabited, I understand, as long as any place on earth. It is the size of New England, which seems almost nonexistent to me now. Are we really all under the same sky?
>
> Good roads. Hotels with formal gardens and fountains. Palaces across the river. But I am looking for animals and trees, not temples. Let me see if there is any majesty inside me.

The next two pages were in Sanskrit, followed by a page in English.

> Village life. Get me out of here. I see the same sweet women filling water jugs at the central fountain and the men, once again with their simple dignity as they move with the buffalo and the plows. Thousands of years old. The huts are skimpier than I am used to, and all the beds are outside. I never used to look at something and visualize catastrophe at the same time. But all I can think of is monsoon. Son of a bitch. In Benares I thought I was testing India. The sky opened; the tables turned. India tested me.

After a few more pages of Sanskrit, she came upon:

> I walk fast but keep hearing shouts of "Khedda! Khedda!" and eventually follow throngs—in India there are only throngs—hoping they will lead me out of the more civilized parts of Mysore.
> Now it's becoming clear to me what Sesh meant when he explained why the monks get off by themselves. He compared it to an artist during the act of creation. Stopping life to produce life. The artist who will give up all else when involved in creation. I've seen men give up food, sex, money, all because of a picture they have to paint. What feeds them is the love of the object and the desire to see it born. Stopping life to produce life. And in the center, the plan toward perfection. The work.

Janice's fingers flipped through the clipped weeks and months, through prayers and comments and observations, pausing now and again to read an entry that particularly caught her interest.

> I walk every day. In order to watch life happen. What I want to see is process, rather than the changes once they've happened.
> I don't seek beliefs or religion or divine inspiration here. I seek the quality of silence. I must hear that part of myself that is the most quiet. It is the bridge of my past, present, and future—offering the potential to make past, present, and future all one.

And later:

> The birth of a wild elephant baby. A circle is formed around the mother made up of all the members of the herd who face outward to ward off danger. The leader circles around, inspecting, guarding.
>
> Circles. Ritualistic circles. Cycles. The freedom here to watch night and day happen. To watch myself happen. The cycles that I am. I look inside myself and cannot find where I start or stop for there is motion. I think that's good. And yet, with no ends or beginnings, there is a center in me. Me, me, me, me, me! I'm connecting that funny center in ME to all I'm perceiving outside of ME. INFINITY. INDIA. INSIDE. All these words begin with IN.
>
> INCARNATION.

The barely legible script swam before Janice's vision, and she shut her eyes to rest them. She could hear, in the stillness of the apartment, the whir of the refrigerator and felt an overwhelming despair as she contemplated the coming day. For a long time she sat unmoving, listening for some sound of Bill's presence upstairs, but could hear nothing. She glanced down at the open diary and, with a nagging conscience, riffled through its remaining pages. There was so much left to read, so many words, so many years of wanderings and thoughts. Pausing at a page toward the end of the diary, she read:

> My walnut skin turns white. An icicle hardens on the tip of my nose. I breathe out warm air, and my nose tickles as the icicle melts. Something changes. Something remains. I laugh, and in my giggle there is a roar. Do I sound cocky? That's the thing with awareness. It just turns into greater awareness. Truth constructs truth.
>
> *Tabe Asi, Himalayas.* How that confused me when I first heard it. In Bengali, "good-bye," but literally, "then I come." Nothing ends. Everything evolves.
>
> India, my friend, my lover, my teacher, I leave you. Yet, we shall always hold hands. Prana, "breath of life" as they named you, within my pulse is the melody you sang that first day. I can open my eyes and close them. It is the same thing. A sense of what I am and all that I have learned, that energy we all share, I can now embrace and set into worthy action.

Soon my physical environment will be very different. But I shall still have the height of the sun to strive for. What is necessary is to connect all daily activity to my ultimate purpose.

To know, to love, to do.

That is the potent gift of life.

And the very final entry, written in pen and in a bolder hand:

Today, I am in Dharmsala. In a week I shall be in New York. I shall trade my *kata* for a business suit, put on shoes of leather, and move in the panic of cars and subways. Ham and eggs will be my breakfast and not the *moo-moo* I have become accustomed to. After seven years, a strange and frightening prospect. Yet I leave with a mind that hopes and a heart that leaps, for soon I shall be privileged to take the final step in my quest for truth, a step so Godlike as to be granted to only saints and deities. For given the knowledge and the faith and the belief I now possess, I must set my life's course on a trajectory that will intercept the progress of my daughter's soul. I must discover its abode and offer myself to its service, to pray and do good works in atonement for the lacks and errors of the past.

Janice shut the diary.

Outside, the January wind whistled shrilly and knifed in through the window cracks, bringing a chill to the room and causing her to shiver.

Words kept tumbling about in her head in random bursts. Hoover's words, repeated from close and distant corridors of memory.

. . . to know, to love, to do—I must intercept . . . my daughter's soul. . . .

He had come to their door to offer himself to the service of his daughter's soul—to pray for it and do good works for it—and they had him thrown into jail.

"*Your daughter's health is an illusion. As long as her body shelters a soul that is unprepared to accept its Karmic responsibilities of earth life, there can be no health, not for the body of Ivy or the soul of Audrey Rose. Both are in peril!*"

He had warned them, fully and correctly, and they had had him locked up in a cell.

"We must form a bond . . . a bond that is so tight and so filled with all the love you have, and all the love that I have, that we can carefully mend her, patch her—so that Audrey Rose's soul may be put to rest once again. . . ."

He had offered them the only possible solution, and they had rejected it, had him put behind bars, and were now striving to make it permanent.

"We are all part of this child. We have all had to do with the making of her, and only we can help her. . . ."

He was right. They were all part of her. All had to do with her making, and now only they, together, could help her.

It was the only way.

If Ivy was to live.

It was just nearing daybreak when he arrived at Foley Square. He had asked the cabdriver to let him off at Fourteenth Street and had been walking for the past hour and a half. He had stopped once briefly in one of those small, bad-smelling all-night hole-in-the-wall eateries for a cup of coffee, which he drank without sugar or cream—not his usual habit—but a necessary act of self-mortification in this, his hour of grief.

Sipping its scalding bitterness, Brice Mack remembered how his mother had sat *shivah* after his father's death. A neighbor had brought her an orange crate, rough and splintered, upon which she sat for the seven days and nights, her face unwashed, her hair unkempt, her clothes rent, drinking the bitterest of teas, rocking quietly backward and forward, moaning softly from the depths of her soul, putting her anguish on public display in memory of the husband she had lost, the man she had loved and whose son she had borne, lamenting in expiation for all she had not said and not done for him—the lapses and lacks and wifely duties she had failed to perform in life and would no longer have opportunity to correct in death.

The morning air was cold and damp, and spumes of steam filtered up through manhole covers in the empty streets surrounding Foley Square.

Yes, Brice Mack reflected solemnly, running his tongue over his teeth, cleansing them of the acrid taste of coffee, Momma sat *shivah* for Poppa, as he had sat *shivah* for Momma. But who was there to sit *shivah* for James Beardsley Hancock? Who was there to moan and rock from side to side and for seven days mount the rough and bruising crate of anguish for him?

There would be a *Times* obituary for him, one of considerable length and detail, no doubt, but possessing none of the passion and rending torment of a *shivah* to mark his passage from life. His would be a simple service—a brief, pallid, goyish exercise totally lacking in power and meaning. And here was a man whose splendid, exemplary, and beautiful life warranted—no, demanded!—the full outcry, the full spectacle of human grief and suffering to mourn its loss properly. There was no justice. Had he been born a Jew, he would have got the full treatment. Now, unfortunately, there was only Brice Mack, a miserable, unworthy substitute for the real thing, to cry for him.

He had been with James Beardsley Hancock at the end. Sitting at his bedside. At one ten there had been no forewarning that at one eleven it would be the end. They had been conversing—that is, Hancock had been talking, softly and eloquently, on the very subject of death when it came stealing into the room on tiptoes to claim him.

Mack had spent most of the evening at the hospital, not exclusively to pay a sick call, but to confer with the doctors to ascertain whether Hancock would be in a condition improved enough to enable a deposition to be taken or, provided Mack could persuade the court to come up to the hospital with the jury, whether Hancock would be physically able to subject himself to what might be a grueling examination and cross-examination.

Despite the day's stunning success with his witnesses, whose combined testimony forged an absolute link between Audrey Rose's gruesome death and the substance of Ivy Templeton's nightmares, Brice Mack knew that unless he could make a strong and convincing case for reincarnation, he was still a long way from home. With the Pradesh mess, Hancock's heart attack, and Hoover's rejection of Marion Worthman, his case for reincarnation at this point was practically nonexistent. Unless and until a full exposure of the subject could be placed before the jury by a person of consummate skill and unimpeachable scholarship and integrity, there would be little point in bringing Hoover or even the Templetons to the stand since their testimony would be heard in the absence of any real understanding of the basic issue in the case. It was essential their next witness be an expert on the level of Hancock.

At eight twenty that evening the doctors were sufficiently encouraged by Hancock's improvement to hold out a vague hope that Hancock might be able to testify *intra muros* on the following day. Which was sufficiently encouraging to Brice Mack to permit him to leave the hospital and keep a nine o'clock dinner appointment with Professor Ahmanson and a man named Robert Vanable, a possible substitute expert whom Ahmanson had met in a Scientology meeting hall.

Himself a "clear," a term applied to those who had achieved the apex of Scientological perfection and were moving up the OT Levels on which one attains abilities which are God-given and God-like, Robert Vanable instructed Mack through dessert on the true nature of life beyond death as revealed to L.R.H., the initials of L. Ron Hubbard, founder of the Church of Scientology, and as expressed by him in his famous lecture to the Eighteenth American Advanced Clinical Course back in 1957.

"L.R.H. was the first to cognate what really happens when a thetan splits the scene, and to postulate it," enthused Vanable, sipping his Irish coffee. "A thetan exteriorizes fast from a body when it kicks the bucket. There's plenty of confusion, too, and it has a terrible time until it can locate another body and get going again. Meanwhile, it's totally cognizant. Knows who it was and who its friends were. All it's suffered is the loss of mass. The mind remains. The Christian misconceptions of heaven, hell, purgatory—that's all baloney. A thetan's proving ground is still good ol' terra firma.

"Forgettingness doesn't start till the pickup of the new body, at which point the memory valve shuts off, but not before some interesting prayers and dedications are said to insure a happy is-ness in the next life. . . ." And more.

After leaving the restaurant, Brice Mack returned to Roosevelt Hospital to check on Hancock's condition.

The time was twelve twenty-seven when he entered the anteroom of the intensive care unit. A nurse informed him that Dr. Pignatelli, Hancock's personal physician, was with the patient now. At twelve forty Dr. Pignatelli emerged and, flashing the lawyer a quick smile, briefly conferred with the nurse before turning to the lawyer. He told him that Hancock's prognosis was good, his vital signs were improved, and barring a setback, he seemed to be making excellent progress. It was still too soon to tell when he would be able to authorize the heavy program of activity Brice Mack had earlier outlined since Hancock wasn't off the critical list as yet.

Brice Mack felt fatigue press down on him. What Pignatelli was saying was that Hancock wouldn't be well enough to testify in the morning. Which left Mack with the tricky problem of having to vamp till the old boy was ready. That meant bringing on other witnesses—but who? Not Hoover. Not now. Not ever, if he could help it. Nor the

Templetons. Maybe the doctor—Dr. Kaplan—he'd be good for a morning. And Carole Federico. He might be able to string them out for a day or so. . . .

"Would you care to see him?" Dr. Pignatelli's voice cut in on the lawyer's somber musings.

"Is it allowed?"

Pignatelli laughed. "It'll do him good. He's just awakened from a long nap, and he's bored to distraction."

It wasn't difficult to pick out James Beardsley Hancock in the large, brightly lit, antiseptic room. Every other patient was enclosed within the inviolate privacy of screens and curtains. James Beardsley Hancock was fully exposed to view, sitting rigidly up, with the mattress raised to its highest position, like an enthroned king, imperiously surveying his domain through eagle-bright eyes.

The old man stared straight at the lawyer coming across the room toward him, and a smile spread across his face, a smile that seemed genuinely glad and fiercely self-assured, a smile that said, "Look! I'm still here. I have not left this earth life, not quite yet."

Encompassed by gurgling bottles and TV monitors, each reporting a phase of his illness, and hampered as he was by tubes and wires that seemed to sprout from every orifice of his body including his mouth, which held a thermometer, James Beardsley Hancock could not say a word, or offer Brice Mack his hand, or even wave him into a chair. He could only express his pleasure at seeing his guest with eyes that glowed and a head that gently nodded.

"Well, sir, this is a pleasure," Brice Mack said, pulling up a white metal chair to the bedside and sitting down. "I didn't expect to be let in."

A nurse arrived to take the thermometer out of Hancock's mouth and to register its reading on a chart at the head of the bed. Before leaving, she carefully checked the tubes and wires attached to his body and critically studied the TV monitors.

Hancock sighed. "That's better."

His voice was strong, resonant and, as always for Brice Mack, a pleasure to listen to. For a long space of time they sat in silence, smiling at each other, and then the lawyer saw a look of sorrow come over the hard, bony face and a mistiness cloud his eyes.

"I must apologize to you, Brice, and to Mr. Hoover, for my"—the flicker of a smile returned—"my unscheduled truancy."

The lawyer grinned and made a demurring gesture with his hand.

"Tell me," Hancock continued, "how is the case going for him?"

"It's going." The lawyer shrugged. "It'll be all right." He laughed rather nervously. "Once we get you up there, we've got it made."

Hancock nodded sagely and reached for a slim book which was on the bed a few inches away from his right hand.

"I'm boning up for my part." He smiled and ran his thumb along the side of the pages. "Louis Fiquier. French philosopher. Makes a good case for reincarnation. Good for our case." His smile broadened. "Convince the skeptics." His fingers opened the book at a page marked by a tiny folded corner. "Read here, Brice," he said, and pushed the book slightly toward the lawyer.

Mack rose and, reaching out for the book, found his hand suddenly enclosed by Hancock's in a strong grip. Startled, he raised his eyes to Hancock's eyes and found a twinkling mischief in them.

"Maybe even convince the most stubborn of skeptics," Hancock said pointedly.

Brice returned his smile and gently disengaged his hand from Hancock's. Sitting back in his chair, he opened the book, which was entitled *The Tomorrow of Death*, to the indicated page and began to read. After a moment of silence, Hancock's deep voice ordered, "Aloud, please."

Brice Mack cleared his throat and, in a voice soft enough so as not to disturb nearby patients but loud enough to be heard above the cacophony of beeps and squeaks of the heart machines and pacemakers, read.

"'Some men are endowed with all the benefits of mind; others, on the contrary, are devoid of intelligence, penetration and memory. They stumble at every step in their rough life-paths. They can succeed in nothing, and Fate seems to have chosen them for the constant objects of its most deadly blows. Why are they here on earth? God would be unjust and wicked if He imposed so miserable an existence upon beings who had done nothing to incur it, and have not asked for it. But God is not unjust or wicked; the opposite qualities belong to his perfect essence. Therefore the unequal distribution of evil on our globe must remain unexplained, unless we admit the plurality of human existences and reincarnation—that is, the passage of the same soul through several bodies—then all is made wonderfully clear. We have a soul that we must purify, improve, and ennoble during our stay on earth, or, having already completed an imperfect and wicked life, we are compelled to begin a new one, and thus strive to rise to the level of those who have passed on to higher planes. . . .'"

When Brice Mack looked up, he was certain that Hancock had fallen asleep. His eyes were closed; a soft, peaceful stillness was upon his face. About to rise and leave, the lawyer was stopped by Hancock's voice.

"You see, Brice," he said in the quietly modulated, wandering way of a person on the edge of sleep, "without the doctrine of reincarnation, it is not possible to justify the ways of God."

His voice trailed off, and again he seemed to drift off into a drowse. Mack remained seated, waiting to see if sleep had indeed overcome him. His eyes flickered down to his wristwatch. It was one ten. Apparently, even this slightest movement alerted Hancock, for his eyes fluttered open and remained watchful, seeking the intruder who had disturbed his slumber. There ensued a passage of time—no more than a few seconds—during which the old man re-formed his senses, reestablishing the time and place of the space he occupied, and, finding it, relaxed again in the security of its knowledge.

"It's all right," he whispered scarcely audibly. "We all experience levels of dying in our daily lives. . . . We're just so used to life and death being opposites . . . that we don't allow ourselves to have these thoughts. . . ."

His speech was so low that Brice Mack could hardly distinguish his words.

"And yet just drifting off into sleep, that twilight hour, is a different level of consciousness and very much . . . what part of death . . . is like. . . ."

Hancock's eyes suddenly snapped open. He seemed at first to be staring at Mack, then through Mack, and beyond him, beyond the walls of the room, into some vast ethereal infinity beyond the spatial confines of the known world, wherein was revealed to him a vision which brought a radiance to his face, a surprised and wondrous look of utter joy and longing and needing and finally, at the end, an expression of bliss so intensive and absorbing as to cause his whole body to vibrate in its divine totality. His mouth opened, and in his last gurgling breath, he choked out the words "Oh, my!"

What happened in the next minutes—the perfunctory, professional reaction to the beeper's strident warning signals, drawing nurses and doctors from all parts of the room like a swarm of locusts around a crust of bread, and their concerted attempts to restore Hancock to life, their quick, definitive moves with hypodermics, oxygen equipment, and finally their very fists pounding on his chest as one would pound on a door, hoping to encourage the sleeper to awaken—was scarcely apprehended by Brice Mack. His gaze remained firmly fixed on Hancock's face, on the eyes casually closed, the mouth that was smiling, the nostrils flared, the sense of peace, of perfected joy, suffusing the noble countenance.

"He's dead," somebody murmured, and gradually the group retreated, in stages, first the doctors, then the nurses, all but one nurse, who stayed behind to disconnect the tubes and wires, roll down the mattress, and gently pull the sheet over the still-strong and energetic face.

For a very long time Brice Mack remained rooted, gazing entranced at the draped quiescent form on the bed, till he became aware that tears were running down his face. Their wetness snapped him back to awareness of the life struggles going on all around him and sent him stumbling from the room in a daze. The nurse in the anteroom said something to him which he didn't quite get but which sounded like an expression of sympathy as he plowed through the double doors and into the corridor leading to the exit doors.

It was a little after two o'clock when he left the hospital and began to walk eastward on Fifty-seventh Street, across the entire width of the island, until he came to the East River. The night was dark and freezing, and a sharp wind at his back propelled him forward on his aimless course.

At Sutton Terrace he leaned over the railing and gazed into the stirring waters. The rumbling of speeding traffic coursing up and down the East Side Drive made the pavement quiver beneath his feet.

For a time, his mind remained void of thought, caught in the hums and vibrations of the surrounding night, until the very quality of the sounds became blurred and distorted, taking on the gurgling sound of speech, of words, *"Oh, my!,"* the parting words of Hancock, *"Oh, my!,"* while in the middle of the dark, swirling waters, his eyes found the fragmented image of the dead man's face, reflected in a thousand flickering lights.

Tears sprang to his eyes, and his throat clutched as he fought to subdue the deep sob of anguish which came to it.

What am I doing? he berated himself. Crying over a dead man I hardly knew. It makes no sense. Especially when you consider it's what he wanted . . . what he's looked forward to all his life.

"Bullshit!" He spit out the word into the wind gusts whipping off the river. "Bullshit!" he repeated, seeming to find comfort in its sound. Dead is dead! he told himself angrily. When the lights go out, they stay out, and those who believe different are crappin' themselves, and that includes Hancock and Hoover and all the pathetic bastards who can't stand to face the—how did the shrink put it?—"The finality of death."

He was right. Perez was right. We're so scared shitless of death that we're ready to buy anybody's bullshit theory. And yet— And yet, an implacable voice within him cautioned, there was that look on Hancock's face . . . that expression of pure ecstasy? Yeah, ecstasy, that was it. The old boy was really seeing something, and feeling something.

Swirling lights? Beckoning hands? Siren songs? The lush, inviting vulva of the astral womb? Or was it simply as Mel Stern, his doctor, once told him, that the body orgasms at death? Yeah, that would account for the look of ecstasy. Especially in a man of eighty-four.

Who knew? Who really knew anything? The only thing *he* knew for certain was that Hancock was dead, departed, gone, of no further use to himself or to Mack or the case or anything or anybody, ever again, and that save for the icing tears which were beginning to itch his cheeks, there would be few, if any, to cry for the old man and properly mourn his passing.

With considerable surprise, Brice Mack discovered he was standing on the corner of Fifty-ninth Street and Second Avenue. He had no memory of having left the railing overlooking the East River and walking the distance. What made him aware of it now was the lone cab cruising down the broad avenue which, devoid of traffic, seemed elegantly spacious. He frantically waved the cab down.

Entering from the bitter cold, he found the heat inside the cab oppressive and stifling. The extreme contrast of temperatures made his skin flow with rivulets of perspiration that even the removal of his coat and the loosening of his tie failed to stanch.

At Fourteenth Street he paid off the cab and walked the rest of the way to Foley Square in the solitude of his thoughts and in the company of Hancock's face imprinted on his mind in that final instant of life, alert, vital, every inch the man he was and in that first instant of death, shocked, surprised, wondrous, his faculties at their fullest stretch, and the gurgling breath, "*Oh, my!*," and then nothing.

The first person Brice Mack saw, upon making his weary entrance into the courtroom at eight forty, was Elliot Hoover, already seated at the defense table. There was a worn and haggard look on Hoover's upraised face, and the bloodshot eyes staring vacantly off into space clearly told of an anxiety-ridden and sleepless night. Had he learned about Hancock's death? If not, he must inform him at once and try to impress on him their weakened position and the need to bring on Marion Worthman and keep her on until Ahmanson came through with somebody else. This was no time to fret over taste and decorum and other such niceties, not now, and not in a court of law, especially when the charge was kidnapping in the first degree. He must make him realize that the waters in Part Seven were shark-infested and highly dangerous, even murderous.

The spectators' section was fully occupied and the reporters had begun to file in as Brice Mack, wearing his most serious and worried face, walked up to Elliot Hoover. About to engage him in what he knew would be a one-sided, probably useless discussion, the lawyer's attention was suddenly diverted by a noticeable lull, more a hush, in the otherwise noisy chamber, followed by an electric ripple of excitement. Glancing up to the center aisle, he saw Janice Templeton, her face pale, drawn, yet animated by a luminous intensity, striding purposefully down to the witness row well in advance of her husband, who seemed his typical, hung-over self. It was the quality of Janice Templeton's bearing—the stick-straight, ramrod, resolute way in which she carried herself—that caught the lawyer's interest and, apparently, the interest of the spectators and reporters as well, for the room was abuzz with whispers and aflutter with covert side glances.

Janice Templeton seemed a different woman this morning.

Something had happened.

With his eyes firmly fixed on Janice Templeton, Brice Mack failed to notice that Elliot Hoover had risen to his feet and was standing and facing the spectators' section, facing the witness row and, particularly, facing Janice Templeton—not until he saw Janice Templeton, still a couple of steps from her seat, suddenly stop and turn and stare back at Elliot Hoover.

It was in this one stricken moment of frank and open exchange, in this deep and intimate silent communication between plaintiff and defendant, in the subtle passage of looks of affirmation, the bestowal and acceptance of each other's trust and confidence—there for all the court to see, including her husband, whose expression of utter confusion had frozen on his face, and in light of the fearful, darting looks that were being exchanged at the DA's table—that Brice Mack realized that whatever had happened to Janice Templeton was good for their case.

Through some special grace, the machine continued to purr smoothly under its own management and had, once again, provided him with his next witness.

23

NEW YORK, NEW YORK, WEDNESDAY, JANUARY 29, 1975, 9:00 A.M.

JANICE TEMPLETON

called as a witness by the defendant herein, having been sworn, testified as follows:

DIRECT EXAMINATION

BY MR. MACK:

Q Mrs. Templeton, you said in your earlier testimony that the birth of your daughter was entirely normal?
A Yes.
Q And the child was normal and healthy in every respect?
A Oh, yes. She was healthy and beautiful.
Q So that when the nightmares occurred two and a half years later, you did not attribute them to some possible malfunction at birth?
A No, not at all.
Q As a result of the nightmares, did you seek the services of a psychiatrist?
A Yes.
Q What was the name of the psychiatrist?
A Dr. Ellen Vassar.
Q Did Dr. Vassar observe your daughter during her nightmares?
A Yes, during many of them.
Q Were you present on each occasion that Dr. Vassar observed your daughter undergoing a nightmare?
A Yes.
Q Mrs. Templeton, were you in court when Dr. Perez testified and described Dr. Vassar's eyewitness account of the nature and content of the nightmares?
A Yes.

Q Does your eyewitness account of the nightmares differ from that of Dr. Vassar's?
A No.
Q How often did these nightmares happen?
A The first few weeks they came about every third night, then increased as time went on. By the time we went to see Dr. Vassar they were happening every night.
Q Did the nightmares ever vary in nature or content?
A No, they pretty much duplicated each other.
Q So that in each nightmare the child was running around the room, sobbing and babbling, "Hothothot?"
A Yes.
Q And in each nightmare she was attempting to touch the window with her hands and recoiling as if in pain?
A Yes.
Q How long did this first episode of nightmares continue?
A Through the winter and spring of '67. They became less and less frequent under Dr. Vassar's therapy. By summer they had stopped.
Q At the time did you attribute their lessening frequency to something Dr. Vassar was doing in her therapy?
A Yes, of course.
Q So that when they finally stopped, you credited Dr. Vassar with having brought about their end?
A Yes.
Q Did Dr. Vassar ever discuss with you her opinion as to what triggered the nightmares?
A She said that Ivy was expressing some special fears of separation from me and that she appeared to have mastered them.
Q Then she never once confided to you any of the thoughts and suspicions she put down in her notebook?
A No.
Q Let's move forward from the 1967 series of nightmares to the time when Ivy next experienced a nightmare. Am I correct in placing the date at October 22, 1974?
A Yes.
Q Please relate the circumstances of what happened on that night, to the best of your recollection.
A Yes. We sent Ivy to spend the night with a neighbor. We were expecting Mr. Hoover. He was coming to visit us, and we thought it best that Ivy not be around since—well, you know—because of the things he was claiming and the way he was acting.

Q Will you explain what you mean by "the things he was claiming and the way he was acting?"

A Well, he was claiming that Ivy was the reincarnation of his daughter, Audrey Rose. And he was very persistent in his claims, very assured of himself. Of course, we thought his claims outlandish and that possibly he was a mental case. That's why my husband and I didn't want Ivy around when he showed up. We didn't know what he might do or say.

Q When did you first learn that Ivy was having a nightmare that evening?

A About an hour after Mr. Hoover arrived. Carole—Mrs. Federico—phoned us, terribly upset. She said that Ivy was having a fit and was running around the room, screaming and babbling, and that she couldn't waken her. Naturally, my husband and I knew what that meant.

Q And you rushed down to the Federico apartment?

A Yes.

Q And what did you find?

A Ivy was in the midst of a nightmare. It had returned.

Q And this nightmare was similar in nature and content to the ones she suffered seven years before?

A Identical. Even her speech and movements were those of a much younger child.

Q So that during the first episode of nightmares, whereas she seemed to be duplicating the speech and displaying the muscular coordination of an older child, during *this* nightmare, she seemed to be duplicating the speech and muscular coordination of a younger child?

A Yes, it seemed that way.

Q What happened next?

A The same conditions prevailed. She was running about the room, falling over furniture, sobbing and pleading and babbling those words, "hothothot," and trying to get to the window, but not being able to.

Q And as before, you could do nothing to help her?

A Yes. It was the same as before. We could only stand by and watch. Until—

Q Yes?

A Mr. Hoover came into the room.

Q What happened then?

A He said, "My God." He seemed staggered by what he was seeing, and he said, "My God," as if he suddenly realized the truth of what was happening.

Q And what did he do?
A He went to Ivy—she was near the window, sobbing and screaming terribly—and he called to her.
Q By name?
A Yes.
Q What name?
A Audrey Rose.
Q And did she respond to him?
A Not at first. It took some time. He continued to call to her and tried to break through her nightmare. He'd say, "Come to me! Come, Audrey Rose! It's Daddy, I'm here! Come!"
Q And did she finally go to him?
A Yes. It was incredible. All at once, she seemed released from the nightmare, and she went to him.
Q How did she go to him?
A She ran to him. And threw her arms around him.
Q And then?
A He held her. And he comforted her. And soon she fell asleep. Peacefully.
Q What was your reaction to what you were seeing?
A I didn't know what to think. I was amazed.
Q Did you discuss it with your husband?
A Yes, later.
Q What did he say?
A Bill thought he was some kind of hypnotist. That he had somehow cast a spell on Ivy and influenced her into doing what she did.
Q Did you agree with him?
A Yes.
Q Let us move on to the following night, Mrs. Templeton. The night of the twenty-third. Did the nightmare recur on that night?
A Yes.
Q Describe what happened on that night, to the best of your recollection?
A The same things happened. The screaming, running around, babbling—it was a duplication of what happened the night before, except Mr. Hoover wasn't there to stop it. The nightmare continued for hours until the doctor arrived and gave her a sedative.
Q That would be Dr. Kaplan?
A Yes. He's Ivy's pediatrician. He's taken care of her since she was born.

Q Let us move on to the night of the twenty-fourth. Your husband was out of town, I believe, and you were alone with Ivy?
A Yes.
Q Tell the jury what happened on that night.
A The nightmare started at about ten o'clock, and it was the most terrifying of them all. In trying to phone Dr. Kaplan, I accidentally left the bedroom door open and she got out. She fell down the stairs and hurt herself. She was bleeding, and there was nothing I could do to help her. She kept running away from me every time I'd approach. I'd never seen her so desperate and hysterical. She kept running around the living room from window to window, lunging at them and then pulling away, seeking to get out. I was terrified that she might accidentally go through one of them.
Q Did you have a visitor that night?
A Yes. Mr. Hoover. He came to the apartment house at about eleven.
Q Did you ask him up?
A Yes.
Q Why did you ask him up?
A Because I needed help.
Q But wasn't the doctor coming?
A I needed help immediately.
Q Then why didn't you call the police or send for one of the men on duty in the apartment house?
A *I needed Mr. Hoover's help!*
MR. VELIE: Your Honor, if the court please, it has come to my attention that Mrs. Templeton suffered a severe trauma yesterday brought about by the injury of her daughter in an accident. Mrs. Templeton is in a highly agitated and emotional state, and I feel she should be spared the burden of testifying at this time.
MR. MACK: Your Honor, this is patently a device by the prosecution to prevent this witness from testifying because the witness' testimony will destroy the prosecution's case.
MR. VELIE: I'm sure the defense joins the prosecution in wanting to get to the truth of this matter; therefore, it is important that the testimony being presented be given in the absence of disturbing emotional influences. I believe that a recess until tomorrow morning in order to give the witness an opportunity to calm herself so that she may answer questions with some degree of responsibility is in order. I believe it not only is the humanitarian thing to do but will best serve the ends of justice.

Mr. Mack: It is because the defense wants the truth to come out that it believes this witness should be permitted to testify here and now, and I object to Mr. Velie's statements concerning Mrs. Templeton's condition and state of mind which imply that she is incapable of testifying honestly and truthfully at this time, and I request that his statements be stricken from the record and that the jury be instructed to disregard them.

The Court: I won't strike the remarks from the record, but I will instruct the jury that arguments made by either side are not to be considered as evidence. Mrs. Templeton, are you able to continue?

Mrs. Templeton: Yes, I'm all right. I want to continue.

The Court: Proceed, Mr. Mack.

Q by Mr. Mack: You said you needed Mr. Hoover's help, Mrs. Templeton. What help did you need from Mr. Hoover?

A I needed him to help stop my daughter's nightmare, to bring it to an end, as he did before.

Q And did you ask Mr. Hoover to help you?

A I didn't have to. He came into the apartment and immediately began saying those things to her.

Q What things?

A You know, calling to her, telling her he was here now, and that everything was all right. He said, "Audrey Rose! It's Daddy! Here, darling! I'm here!"

Q Did that help your daughter?

A Yes, almost at once. She seemed to recognize him, as she did on the previous night, and rushed into his arms, and then, as he was comforting her, she just fell asleep. Peacefully.

Q What happened after he calmed your daughter?

A He carried her upstairs, and he washed her wounds and then dressed them. And he put her to bed.

Q Was this done with your consent?

A Yes.

Q Did you have a discussion with Mr. Hoover at that time?

A Yes.

Q What did he say to you?

A He said that Ivy was in danger. That his daughter's soul—that is, Audrey Rose's soul—was crying out to him for help through Ivy's nightmares. That Audrey Rose was very unhappy and was seeking to escape this earth life, and because of that, she would be pushing Ivy into dangerous moments.

Q Did he say anything else?

A He said that since her soul was crying out for help, he must take an active part in providing it with the help it needed, that we would have to form a bond between us, a bond so tight with all the love I had and all the love that he had that together we might mend and patch it and put the soul of Audrey Rose to rest again.

Q Did you believe what he was telling you?

A No. I just couldn't comprehend this kind of thinking. It was foreign to my upbringing and religious training. I just couldn't believe it.

Q Mrs. Templeton, is your belief as to what Mr. Hoover told you the same today as it was that night?

A No.

Q Tell us what way your belief has changed?

A (Answer unclear)

THE COURT: Will the witness please speak up?

A I said, I believe now in Mr. Hoover and what he is claiming.

MR. VELIE: Your Honor. I object.

THE COURT: Yes, Mr. Velie? What is your objection?

MR. VELIE: I've changed my mind. I withdraw the objection.

THE COURT: Continue.

Q BY MR. MACK: Are there any reasons, Mrs. Templeton, that you can describe that have caused you to change your opinion of Elliot Hoover?

A Yes, a number of events have happened recently to convince me that Mr. Hoover's fears were justified.

Q What, specifically?

A Well, my husband and I made the decision to send Ivy to a boarding school out of the city for at least while the trial lasted. I thought she would be safe there, away from the influence of Mr. Hoover. I thought that Audrey Rose, if indeed she were the force that triggered the nightmares, would remain subdued away from Mr. Hoover's close proximity. And indeed the nightmares did stop, but other things started happening. Subtle things.

Q For example?

A Well, she caught a cold. Most of the girls at the school had colds, but Ivy's cold developed into a severe bronchial infection. She was up half the night—that was this past Saturday night—having terrible coughing spasms. And she had a fever. I didn't have a thermometer, but I could feel her head all flushed and feverish. I don't know how we managed to get through the night it was so terrible, and the next morning Bill suggested we take her back to the city to see Dr. Kaplan. But I was afraid to take her back to the city, because of Mr. Hoover's being there, so we took her to United Hospital in Port Chester instead, since it was Sunday, and the few doctors we called in Westport were unable to see her. Well, when we got to the hospital, the fever was gone, and so was the bronchial infection. The cough had completely subsided, and the doctor who examined her found her perfectly normal, except for a slight redness in her throat.

Q And what greater significance did you place in this, other than your daughter had suffered a slight cold?

A Well, I saw the whole thing as a ploy to get Ivy back to the city. The coughing spasms and fever were meant to frighten us into taking Ivy down to see Dr. Kaplan. And it almost worked.

Q You say, "a ploy to get Ivy back to the city," Mrs. Templeton. Who was behind this ploy?

A Audrey Rose, of course.

Mr. Velie: Objection. The witness' answer is unbelievable. Her reference to a mythical Audrey Rose is compelling proof that she is under such an emotional strain as to be incapable of giving competent testimony.

The Court: Objection sustained.

Q by Mr. Mack: Did anything else happen?

A That same night, Sunday night, I remained in Westport with Ivy while Bill returned to the city. Well, that night I was awakened by a noise coming from Ivy's room. When I went to investigate, I found Ivy in the bathroom, standing naked in front of the mirror, looking at herself and giggling and whispering, "Audrey Rose," as if she were calling to her, as if Audrey Rose were hiding somewhere inside her body and Ivy were trying to reach her.

Q Did your daughter know about Audrey Rose at this time?

A Oh, yes, we had told her everything the night before. Some of the girls at the school found out what was going on down here and quickly spread the word around, so we thought it best to tell Ivy everything.

Q How did your daughter accept the news?

A Amazement. Disbelief. But all in all, she took it pretty well. In fact, the more she thought about it, the more romantic and appealing she found the whole notion. She particularly loved the idea of living on and on and never dying.

Q And what significance did you place in her behavior in front of the mirror?

A At first, I thought it was simply little girl curiosity, but the nakedness seemed to suggest something more.

Q What was that?
A She was displaying herself, showing her body, it seemed to me, on someone else's command.
Q On whose command?
A Audrey Rose's.
Mr. Velie: Objection, Your Honor. Move to strike the answer as referring to a mythical person. There has been no evidence that such a person exists.
The Court: Objection sustained.
Q by Mr. Mack: Did anything else happen that night?
A That night Ivy packed her suitcase and in the morning didn't realize she had done it. Sometime during the night she arose in her sleep and quietly, neatly packed all her things. It was a clear sign to me of Audrey Rose's desperate need to get back to the city; however, I didn't know how she hoped to accomplish it, since Ivy had no money and knew nothing about train travel. Later that day, however, I found a train schedule and a ten-dollar bill in Ivy's tote bag. Both had been stolen from my purse.
Q Stolen by Ivy?
A Of course not. By Audrey Rose.
Mr. Velie: Objection on the grounds that there has been no evidence that Audrey Rose is a living person.
The Court: Sustained.
Q by Mr. Mack: Do you know why Audrey Rose was so desperate to get back to the city?
Mr. Velie: Objection, Your Honor. The question assumes a fact not in evidence; that there is such a person named Audrey Rose.
The Court: Objection sustained.
Q by Mr. Mack: Do you know why your daughter was so desperate to get back to the city?
A To be close to her father.
Q Her father being?
A Mr. Hoover.
Q You mean Mr. Templeton, don't you?
A No, I mean Ivy was being driven to reach Mr. Hoover.
Q Did anything else happen?
A Yes, she tried to kill Ivy.
Q Who tried to kill her?
A Audrey Rose.
Mr. Velie: Objection on the same grounds previously stated, Your

Honor. There has been no evidence that such a person as Audrey Rose exists.

THE COURT: Objection sustained.

Q BY MR. MACK: When was there an attempt to kill Ivy?

A Yesterday afternoon. All the girls at the school had built this huge snowman and they were having what they call a crowning and melting ceremony. That is, they had built a fire around it and were melting it down, destroying it; it's a ritual they do every year. And while it was burning, Ivy, Ivy started to walk into the fire. It wasn't accidental; she did it purposely; Mother Superior told me that. She said that Ivy literally walked and then crawled into the fire, and if it hadn't been for the custodian, Mr. Calitri, who rushed in after her and pulled her out, she would have been killed.

Q You mean, your daughter purposely tried to kill herself?

A Oh, no! It wasn't Ivy. It was Audrey Rose who tried to kill her. Don't you see, she was thwarted? Unable to get back to the city, she was seeking to escape this earth life by forcing Ivy to walk into the fire. (Witness overcome by tears)

MR. VELIE: Your Honor, I have refrained from objecting to the last two answers given by Mrs. Templeton, although I believe there are ample grounds to have her answers stricken from the record as hearsay, because I believed that it would soon become apparent to this court that Mrs. Templeton is so distraught, because of the near miss that her daughter had with death yesterday, that she cannot possibly be responsible for the answers that she's giving and I, again, most urgently, suggest that it would be appropriate to recess this court until such time as the witness has been able to calm and collect herself.

THE COURT: Do you feel able to continue, Mrs. Templeton?

MRS. TEMPLETON: Yes, yes. I want to continue. I want to tell it all.

THE COURT: There seems no reason, in my opinion, to grant a recess at this time, Mr. Velie. Mrs. Templeton seems to have recovered sufficiently to continue. However, I will strike the witness' last two answers from the record and direct the jury to disregard them.

Q BY MR. MACK: Mrs. Templeton, do you believe in reincarnation?

A Yes. I do.

Q Mrs. Templeton, do you believe that your daughter, Ivy, is the reincarnation of Mr. Hoover's daughter, Audrey Rose?

A Yes, I do.

Q Mrs. Templeton, do you believe that Mr. Hoover kidnapped your daughter?

A No, I do not. I believe he was doing a humanitarian thing and had every right to go to her bedroom that night to help her, to see to her, to take care of her, because I believe that what he says is true. I believe that the only help my child will ever get on this earth will be through Mr. Hoover. The only chance she has of living is if this man is released from jail. (Witness overcome by tears)

Mr. Velie: I object to the question, Your Honor, as calling for a conclusion of law, and I move that the witness' answer be stricken in its entirety. It's for the jury to make that judgment.

The Court: Sustained. Strike the entire answer of the witness from the record, and the jury is instructed to disregard the witness' answer. Continue, Mr. Mack.

Mr. Mack: Your Honor, I have no further questions.

The Court: Mr. Velie, you may cross-examine.

Mr. Velie: Your Honor, this woman is in such a highly charged and emotional state, in my opinion, I do not believe that the answers she has given to the questions addressed to her by defense counsel bear any relation to the truth in the matter, and I would feel that any cross-examination I might subject her to at this point would also elicit answers that would be based on her highly distraught condition. Therefore, I will not ask her any questions.

Mr. Mack: Your Honor, I move that all of Mr. Velie's remarks be stricken from the record as being argument and that the jury be instructed to disregard them.

The Court: Motion sustained. The court reporter will strike the entire last statement by Mr. Velie from the record, and the jury is instructed to disregard it. You may call your next witness, Mr. Mack.

Mr. Mack: I have no further witnesses at this time, Your Honor. The defense rests.

The Court: Are you prepared for rebuttal, Mr. Velie?

Mr. Velie: Your Honor, in the light of Mrs. Templeton's testimony and in the light of the fact that I have determined that I am unable to cross-examine her because of her condition, I do require additional time to prepare my rebuttal portion of the case. I therefore request a recess until tomorrow morning.

The Court: Very well. Court will reconvene at nine o'clock in the morning.

(Whereupon the above proceedings were concluded)

Judge Langley's hammer shot on the gavel brought down the curtain on the performance. In this heightened moment the audience was held in the grip of a tomblike hush, lightly punctuated by the soft aftersobs of the witness. In the next moment the air was rent by what seemed a thunderous ovation—a dramatic and explosive outburst of surprise, delight, approval, and amusement as spectators scrambled noisily to their feet and reporters launched a wild gallop to the doors.

In the midst of pandemonium, Janice Templeton remained seated in the witness chair, her stricken face lowered into her hands, blotting out the scene, taking deep, even breaths to control the tears and the chill in her bones. She could sense the hot flickerings of a thousand eyes upon her, including Bill's eyes—oh, God, what hatred must be in them!—yet she felt cleansed, relieved, the anxiety that had been eating at her these past months suddenly gone.

All at once, she became aware that the courtroom noise had diminished—were they all staring at her in silence?—which caused her to open her eyes and look up. The first face to swim before her blurred vision was Elliot Hoover's, hovering in the forefront of the clearing courtroom, surrounded by smiles and sparkles of curiosity as far as the eye could see. Flanked by two guards, Hoover had purposely remained behind, waiting for Janice to look up, insisting on his right to thank her, to relay to her his gratitude for all she had said, for all she had risked in his behalf. Her vision clearing somewhat, she saw that tears had formed in his eyes, too, and that he was smiling at her and nodding his head in a gesture that said, "I know, I know."

Janice wanted to look away but dared not shift her gaze to the side of the room where Bill was sitting. It was too soon to confront him; she was too weak to cope with all the problems that awaited her in that quarter.

What finally brought her attention around was the sound of her name, spoken in a low, throbbing voice by Scott Velie.

"Mrs. Templeton," he said dully, "we're having a meeting in my office after lunch. Can you be there?"

He looked as he sounded, empty.

"Can you be there?" he repeated.

She felt her head nod and saw him turn away and walk briskly to the door.

It was at this moment that she worked up the nerve to face Bill and, when she did, discovered that his seat was empty.

Scott Velie, senior deputy district attorney of the City of New York, sat alone in his office.

His eyes scanned the somber shelves of lawbooks rising to the ceiling on each wall, found its darkly stained, lemon-oiled atmosphere and soft resonances conducive to thought, restful to spirit. It was his think tank, hall of memories, and phone booth, all rolled in one. It fitted his moods and temperaments like an old leather glove, calming him during troubled times, energizing him when weariness threatened to clog his brain, and gently stroking him when the depressions struck.

Why had his instinct failed him this time?

Normally, he would have sensed that Mrs. Templeton was on the edge. He had seen the signs in her darting looks, her too-quick smile, in the hundred little mannerisms she employed to camouflage her fears and guilts. All the signposts had been up. She had all but screamed to him that she was ready to crack. Why had he failed to see it?

Velie knew that his instinct, that rare and delicate instrument, had gone wrong. At age sixty-three, after years of service, it had failed him.

In thirty-two years he had seen the full pageant of human misery walk through his door—all ages, sexes, colors, shapes, sizes, and with every kink in the book: junkies, pushers, prosties, pimps, thieves, kooks, killers, you name it. He had felt sorry for many of them, especially the ones stamped for misery at birth, the professional losers, who, even in this great land of opportunity, never seemed to find their way. He knew about these people. They formed the backdrop of his own youth and still lurked in the corners of his memory. Sometimes, standing across his desk, he'd recognize his own face in the hopeless, fear-ravaged visage of a young felon and wonder how he'd managed to escape a similar fate. Sometimes he'd see himself so clearly he'd allow himself to be plea-bargained by some green-behind-the-ears attorney and not feel he had abused his trust.

Then there were the Hoovers—the ivory-white Hoovers flushed with all the benefits of a doting society, the people of intelligence and position who slid through life plucking up the breaks as they dropped in their laps—who had nothing better to do with their lives than indulge their fantasies with harebrained schemes and crackpot notions and then feel they had the legal right to inflict their sick delusions on decent, law-abiding people. Janice Templeton's testimony was proof of Hoover's contaminating influence on the helpless, the good people. She wanted so desperately for her child to be spared the pain and suffering of mental illness she was willing to buy any crackpot theory. She had accepted Hoover's reincarnation claims as a terminal patient accepts a phony cancer cure—out of desperation. Hoover not only had buffaloed her, but had surely destroyed a good marriage.

Velie could see that it was all over between the Templetons from the way they sat and looked away from each other during their meeting. They were like strangers. Worse, like enemies. She couldn't face him, and he couldn't bear to look at her. From her cool, bland expression, she seemed to be in another world—on an astral plane of her own. The only time she reacted was when Velie made his suggestion. Her face became like chalk. The husband, on the other hand, seemed to grow a couple of feet. He really sparked to the notion. Especially when he saw his wife's reaction, when he saw the color drain from her face and her expression turn lunatic. It was his wife's stunned reaction that made him rise to Velie's bait; not because he thought that much of it, but to punish his wife. Velie had never seen such venom in a smile of pleasure. Yes, Hoover did a great job on those two. Brought out their finest instincts.

When Velie sprang his gimmick on them, he never expected either of them to agree to it. He hardly expected himself to agree to it. It was pure hokum, the kind of horseshit Mack would fling and totally alien to his own nature. Yet this was the kind of arena he was in, the kind of game they were playing, and if they start throwing horseshit at you, you throw horseshit back. Sometimes it was the only way to deal with the Brice Macks—the horseshit throwers. Well, he knew his way around this sort of arena, too. He knew enough about horseshit to be able to throw it back at the best of them.

Scott Velie rose and walked to the window. The late-afternoon sky was blue for a change. Maybe the weather would hold out through the weekend. He had promised Ted and Virginia that he'd spend the weekend with them at their lodge in Pennsylvania and was looking forward to it. It would be good seeing them again, spending a few days with old friends. Since Harriet died, that's all he had now, all he could depend on—the kindness of old friends.

When he saw the slim figure of Janice Templeton descending the courthouse steps six stories below, Scott Velie knew why he had come to the window. He was curious to know if they would leave the building together. Seeing her now descending the steps alone and walking to the hack stand, the prosecutor began to wonder if perhaps he hadn't been as much to blame for their breakup as Hoover.

What had she said to Bill, with that lost, haunted look? "You'd really subject your own child to a terrible thing like that?" And how had he answered her? Grinning? "It's no worse than what you're willing to subject her to."

Scott Velie saw the cab with Janice Templeton in it pull away from the curb. A few seconds later he saw Bill Templeton descend the steps and head in the direction of Pinetta's.

Velie heard himself sigh. There'd be a cold and lonely bed in the Templeton household this night.

Velie knew about cold and lonely beds. The last five years qualified him as an expert.

Judge Langley entered his courtroom determinedly for a change, with a jaunty step and a flourish of robes. Settling himself onto his elevated perch, he silently contemplated his constituency. Another packed house, he was pleased to see. Another day in which Part Seven would fulfill its sacred trust to render justice fairly, impartially, and judiciously and uphold the public's right to know—the public's inalienable right to gawk, titter, whisper, and express their oohs and ahs at the drama unfolding before their eyes. That's what it was, by God! A drama! A goddamn spectacular. A whizbang meller with more thrills, spills, and chills than a three-ring circus.

A note of awe entered the judge's thoughts. A lawsuit like this one came but once, if ever, in a jurist's lifetime, and though it was tardy in making its appearance in his own lifetime, it had finally come, and he vowed, by God, to make the most of it. Having his picture taken, having his expert opinion constantly sought after by the press, and, just last evening, being offered that contract by one of the country's most exclusive and important lecture agencies gave Harmon T. Langley the gloriously buoyant feeling of having at last arrived.

A sudden hush and sense of expectancy in his courtroom encroached on the judge's daydreams of the good life that lay ahead and caused him reluctantly to wrest his mind back to the day's order of business.

"If you are ready, you may proceed with your rebuttal, Mr. Velie," said the judge, his eyes shifting between the battle stations of the opposing attorneys, while, to himself, adding the silent prayer, "And please, God, for my sake, grant them the wisdom to keep the ol' pot boiling."

Velie rose and smiled stiffly.

"Thank you, Your Honor. I recall Dr. Gregory Perez to the witness stand."

At the defendant's table Brice Mack sat relaxed and comfortable, letting a weary smile indicate his lack of concern over the prosecution's recall of his own witness. Shortly, however, his smile would become frozen as the import of Velie's questions gradually unfolded.

"Dr. Perez," began Velie, approaching the witness with quiet deference, "I understood you to say earlier that hypnosis is a therapeutic tool utilized by most psychiatrists, including yourself, is that correct?"

"Yes. Many psychiatrists employ hypnotic techniques in their therapy."

"And is one of the techniques used by psychiatrists called hypnotic age regression?"

Perez looked at Velie impassively.

"Yes."

"What exactly is meant by hypnotic age regression?"

"It is the process by which an individual under hypnosis is brought back to an earlier time in his life and then can reexperience feelings, memories, thoughts, behavior that were characteristic of that period. A person who has been regressed under hypnosis will behave just as though he were literally back at that time."

As the question was being answered, the prosecutor slowly turned toward the jury box, so that he was now fully facing the defendant's twelve peers as he put his next question to Dr. Perez.

"How far back can a person be regressed hypnotically?"

"Theoretically, there isn't any limit, except that one would not use age regression to bring a person back to a time before that person could speak." The doctor's voice trailed behind Velie as he began a slow walk toward the jury box. "Theoretically, one could take a person back to infancy, but since he couldn't speak in infancy, he couldn't report to you what he was experiencing, so that, normally, when we take a person back under age regression, we usually do it to young childhood in order to recapture memories of events that took place and are now repressed but that may be causing an effect on the adult's behavior and feelings. In order to try to remove those things that produce neurotic behavior now, we try to recapture the earlier, 'hidden' memories through age regression."

Velie paused at the jury railing.

"But it *is* possible to regress a person to infancy?"

"Yes."

"Is it possible to regress a person to a time prior to infancy? To some stage, say, of fetal development in his mother's womb?"

Perez hesitated.

"It's theoretically possible to do so, provided there is consciousness and awareness, but again, there would be nothing one could learn since a fetus cannot relate its thoughts and feelings."

Velie gripped the jury railing, pressed his body forward dramatically, and clearly enunciated, "Dr. Perez, is it possible through hypnotic age regression to take a person back beyond the fetal age, beyond the barrier of a current existence, and into a past existence?"

The question elicited a burst of nervous laughter from the doctor.

"Well, there are those who have claimed to be able not only to regress patients back prior to their birth but actually to regress them back to different personalities." His words tumbled forth in rapid staccato. "They have had patients claim, under hypnosis, that they had lived before, at another time and with other identities and who, in the hypnotic state, had spoken languages that they did not know in the awakened state. To answer your question, is it possible to do this, I would have to say, theoretically, yes, it is possible. It is believed by some and disbelieved by others. It's a controversial issue, but there are people who have claimed to be able to regress patients into other existences."

Velie's eyes made a circuit of the arena, covertly studying the reactions of reporters, spectators, and, particularly, the defendant and his attorney, who were engaged in a subdued, yet energetic discussion. It seemed to Velie that Hoover was restraining Brice Mack from objecting, and he was pleased to see the noxious effect his questions were having on his youthful opponent, who seemed ready to jump out of his skin at suddenly finding himself on the receiving end of his own horseshit.

"Dr. Perez," said Velie, turning back to the witness, "if this court asked you to attempt it, would it be possible for you to regress a subject back beyond the barrier of this life and into a prior existence, if indeed such a thing exists?"

Perez shrugged nervously.

"I have never attempted such a thing."

"Would you be willing to try?"

Perez stirred restively.

"I would be willing if the court wanted me to."

Brice Mack, incapable of further restraint, exploded from his seat.

"Objection, Your Honor," he shouted. "This is pure speculation! It is obvious what the district attorney is leading up to, and I register my strongest possible objection. It is not only highly irregular, but a cheap and tawdry attempt on the part of Mr. Velie to influence and inflame the jury!"

A hum of excitement swept across the courtroom. A light tap of the gavel quickly restored order, whereupon Judge Langley addressed himself to the defense's objection.

"You are probably right, Mr. Mack," said the judge courteously. "The questions do call for speculation on the part of the witness, but insofar as he is an expert witness, I'm inclined to permit the district attorney to continue this line of questioning until *I* see where it's leading."

Velie picked up on the judge's ruling swiftly.

"Your Honor," said the prosecutor soberly, "I have what may be an unusual request to make of the court, but I think this is a most unusual case. It's a case that has excited national and even world attention, and I think that in the interest of seeing justice done, and to try all possible means of arriving at the truth in this matter, Your Honor should authorize the conducting of an experiment whereby Ivy Templeton is put under regressive hypnosis by Dr. Perez to ascertain whether or not, in fact, she had a prior life and, if so, whether or not that prior life conforms with the defendant's claims and whether the hypnosis will reveal it. I further propose that the experiment be conducted under controlled conditions in the hospital in Darien, Connecticut, where Ivy Templeton is presently recovering from injuries sustained a few days ago. I have taken the liberty of calling the hospital and ascertaining what facilities it has. It can provide this court with a large room in its psychiatric wing that is normally used as an observation theater to permit doctors and students the opportunity of studying cases from an unseen vantage point. The room contains a substantial viewing space behind one-way glass which can comfortably seat the jury, defendant, all the lawyers, the court reporter, and this court. I have been assured by the doctors attending Ivy Templeton that she is physically able to withstand the hypnosis, and they foresee no problems arising from such an experiment. With the understanding, Your Honor, that this test be conducted under rules that you promulgate to make sure it is fair to both sides." A stiff smile formed on Velie's face. "I'm sure the defense will welcome this experiment if, in fact, the defendant believes in reincarnation as fully and completely as he says he does."

Brice Mack had remained standing throughout Velie's proposal, his face a mime show of shock and incredulity. His voice, after he had struggled to find it, was held to the level of a stunned whisper.

"Your Honor, this is unbelievable."

"Is defense objecting?" Langley inquired.

"Yes. Defense objects most emphatically on the basis that such a test could not possibly be conclusive. There is no way such a test could be conducted with any guarantee of accuracy." A helpless note of amusement entered his voice. "Look, Your Honor, if the hypnotist is unable to bring Ivy back beyond her birth, that won't prove that reincarnation doesn't exist. All it would prove is that he's not a very successful hypnotist."

Velie smiled derisively.

"It was not the prosecution who introduced Dr. Perez as a qualified and trustworthy expert in his field, but the defense. And now the defense is seeking to impugn the professional credibility of his own witness."

Judge Langley swiveled about to consider the position, but in truth, his decision had been reached the moment Scott Velie propounded the motion. Moving the entire court into a hospital theater with all those juicy little dramatic touches—the one-way glass, hypnotizing a child, the search for a former lifetime conducted under the hard, uncompromising scrutiny of both science and the law—offered just the right dash of spice to round out his coming lecture tour, even though, as the defense rightly contended, such a test could not possibly provide evidence of a conclusive or substantive nature.

The softening, almost sensual drifting of the eyes and the slack, succumbing expression on the judge's face, an expression whose meaning both attorneys had come to know, communicated itself to them simultaneously and brought an immediate roaring objection from Brice Mack.

"I reiterate my objection most strongly, Your Honor! This test is not only highly irregular, but—"

"I do not object, Your Honor," shouted Hoover, overpowering his attorney's objection and springing lightly to his feet, which quickly brought the guards to their feet. "I want it done and give my permission!"

The suddenness of Hoover's countermanding statement brought several reporters to their feet and a heightened atmosphere to the courtroom.

Brice Mack glanced grimly at his client.

"I will not withdraw my objection, Your Honor," he said coldly and defiantly.

"And I *insist* on the experiment," said Hoover tightly.

Chairs squealed as spectators in the rear stood up to gain a clearer, less encumbered view of the action.

"Sit down, Mr. Hoover," ordered Judge Langley wearily. "You have a lawyer representing you, and you're not permitted to speak."

Anger flooded Hoover's sallow cheeks.

"Then I discharge my lawyer, Your Honor."

Brice Mack went white. "May I have a few minutes, Your Honor?" he said.

"Granted," said Judge Langley.

Startled into wariness, the attorney approached his distraught client and began a low-voiced conversation at the defense table. The court waited patiently as the two men engaged in vigorous discussion with much hand waving and head shaking. Finally, Brice Mack stood up and faced the bench, striving to maintain an air of command over a bad situation.

"I withdraw my objection, Your Honor," he said firmly. "My client is most anxious that this test be conducted, as he feels he will be vindicated by it."

Sunk down on his spine, Bill Templeton stared fixedly and with enjoyment at the ignominy of Brice Mack's disgrace. It was a comeuppance the young cock richly rated.

"I see no reason why this court should not permit this test," said the judge with unusual mildness. "After all, this *is* a case of truly unique dimensions and, as Mr. Velie so rightly pointed out, of international concern. Since I have permitted the defendant a wide latitude in presenting his defense, I do not feel that I can now place arbitrary restrictions on the prosecution's right to seek its own path to the truth. However, I do demand that there be some specifications of how the test will be conducted and what safeguards can be provided to insure that it's being conducted properly, that it's doing a fair and unbiased job of seeking a true result, and that the person or persons conducting the test are highly qualified to do so."

Judge Langley addressed his next remarks to the district attorney.

"In the light of the defense's objection, Mr. Velie, I have decided that in addition to Dr. Perez, two other psychiatrists be selected to participate in the test, both of whom have used hypnosis in the treatment of their patients. The court will name the two experts and will seek to retain the most highly qualified people it can find."

The courtroom remained tensely quiet as Judge Langley made a notation on his pad, then looked blandly up at the sea of expectant faces, and said, "If there are no further questions, we will recess the case till Monday morning, which should give the court enough time to arrange for the additional psychiatrists and the procedures for testing. The defendant is remanded to custody."

Janice heard about it over the bedroom radio.
The noon news report confirmed her defeat.

Not only was the court willing to permit the barbarity to take place, but according to the newscaster, Elliot Hoover had unqualifiedly endorsed the test.

Janice stood stunned in the middle of the bedroom, listening to the high-pitched, eager voice punch across the grisly details.

It would take place on Monday morning. At the hospital in Darien. The entire court would be transported there. Jury, judge, lawyers, and defendant would observe from a hidden room. Three psychiatrists would preside. The public would be excluded. A special room with TV closed circuit would accommodate the press.

Janice turned off the radio, hurried to the telephone, and dialed information. Bill might still be at the court building. And if not Bill, Scott Velie or Judge Langley. She had to reach one of them, had to stop this test from happening. She would deny her consent. After all, she was Ivy's mother—she had some rights. . . .

Paged, Bill Templeton did not respond. Scott Velie had just left, would be out of town for the weekend, someone thought. Judge Langley might still be in his chamber, however, hold on, please—

The voice that returned was masculine, elderly, but not Langley's.

"Who is calling?" it asked.

"This is Janice Templeton."

"Oh, Mrs. Templeton, this is John Cartright, the court bailiff."

"I must speak to Judge Langley, Mr. Cartright. It's urgent."

"The judge isn't here at present, Mrs. Templeton. Can I help?"

"It's about my daughter. About the test. I do not want it to take place. I refuse to give my permission."

"I'll try to get your message to Judge Langley."

Fingers of terror seemed to be reaching toward her, seeking to grip her as she quickly showered and packed enough clothing for a lengthy stay. Her hands moved automatically—she was scarcely aware she was directing them—while her mind raced. She must get to Ivy. She must stay with her. Be with her. Somehow she'd stop the test.

Her head reeled sickeningly as she lifted the heavy suitcase and dragged it down the narrow staircase to the living room.

She went out into the hallway and rang for the elevator. While Ernie went inside to fetch the suitcase, Janice remained at the door, looking wistfully back into the living room—a long, piercing, unmoving look—thinking of all she was leaving, and wondering if it would ever be the same again, if she and Bill and Ivy would ever again share the sweet and beautiful life they had made for themselves.

"Dear God, let it not be the end," Janice cried to herself as tears bit at her eyes and she squeezed them shut against the thought of the terrible deprivation. "Don't let it be the end," she prayed, while, at the same time, deep, deep in her heart knowing, as she had known all along, from the very beginning, from that very first day in front of the school and the man with the sideburns and mustache, in that moment of instant prescience, that one day the final act would have to be played out, on its own terms, finding its own way to its own ending.

PART FOUR

Audrey Rose

24

"GOOD morning. My name is Steven F. Lipscomb. I'm a Doctor of Psychiatry and have been chosen to lead the team of three psychiatrists selected by the court to conduct this test."

The slight, forward hunch of his body and the few remaining strands of gray hair put him somewhere in his sixties, though he might have been younger. The crow's-feet at the corners of his weary, patient eyes, his calmness of manner and intelligence, coupled with an almost humorless sincerity, affirmed his place in the ranks of the medical profession.

"After consultation with my colleagues Dr. Nathan Kaufman and Dr. Gregory Perez, we have decided to approach the testing of the subject individually, in succeeding shifts, Dr. Kaufman to succeed me, Dr. Perez to succeed him, should the testing fail to achieve results after a predetermined length of time."

He was standing in a room that was calm, softly lit, barren of decor, and, save for a leather couch and a hard-backed chair, devoid of furnishings. The walls were an impersonal buff, which lent an added dimension to the somewhat limited space.

"There is no special reason why I was selected to start the testing. It was a purely arbitrary decision and in no way is meant to imply that I am either better qualified or more experienced in hypnotic techniques than my colleagues."

He stood by the chair in the center of the windowless examining room and seemed to address his own image reflected in a rectangular mirror constituting an entire wall. He knew, however, that he was not talking to himself, but to a tightly packed group of people who were exercising their legal right and mandate to watch him and listen to him from the other side of the looking glass.

"You have all received personal and professional data sheets on each member of the examining team which should amply acquaint you with our medical backgrounds and credentials. If further information is required, we will be happy to furnish it at the conclusion of the test."

He knew that his voice was reaching the principals in this trial through a speaker and that they were probably totally absorbed in what he was saying, displaying neither the restlessness nor the lassitude his lectures ordinarily evoked in his students at the university. But even if there were some shifting about, some clearing of throats and coughing, he would not be aware of it since, like the one-way glass, the room was additionally soundproofed to preserve further the myth of seclusion and privacy.

"Before bringing in the subject of this test, I'd like to say a few words about what we are endeavoring to do here this morning. Hypnosis is neither mysterious nor uncommon and is in wide use today among psychiatrists as a therapeutic means of alleviating the symptoms of certain mental disorders. Hypnosis is the term applied to a state of heightened suggestibility induced by another person."

He was also aware that his image, as well as his voice, was being transmitted to the recreation hall on the third floor via a small, innocuous TV camera implanted in the upper part of the room above the mirror. Having earlier assessed the rec hall, he knew that more than a hundred people, some from distant parts of the world, were at this very moment hunched over their pads committing his every word to paper.

"Before bringing the subject in, I'd like to add a few words about hypnotic age regression and the level of trance that will be necessary to induce a vivid flow of memories from her earlier life."

Nineteen people were crammed into a space designed to hold ten. The jury had been given the best seats and were crushed together against the glass, with Judge Langley nestled ceremoniously in their midst. The DA and the defense attorney had the dubious pleasure of sharing a bench in the upper left quarter of the cubicle, directly behind the court reporter, whose steno machine and table took up the space of a person. Hoover, with guard in attendance, sat directly in front of Bill —a proximity that was more than disconcerting to him.

"And after the subject is sufficiently relaxed and reassured that nothing harmful will occur to her, I will use. . . ."

Janice had excluded herself from the ringside proceedings, electing to join the reporters in the rec hall instead. Her decision, Bill reflected with the same hopeless repetition of grief he felt whenever Janice entered his thoughts now, was clearly motivated by her need to avoid him. She had been successful at doing so ever since he had arrived at the hospital earlier that morning.

". . . and once I have determined that the suggestions are working, I will test her to ascertain the depth of her trance. Once that has been satisfactorily established, I will commence to regress her into her past life."

He should have got to the hospital sooner, Bill knew, but when he had learned from Dominick that Miz Templeton had left in a cab with a heavy suitcase, all he could think about was tying one on. It was a bruising beaut that left him limp and trembling and with a terrifying headache that wouldn't quit. Even now he felt as if a shaft of hot steel were running through his head from the left ear to the right.

"Oftentime the regression will release a flow of free associations that frequently arouse memories of early emotional events of a traumatic nature. The subject may express feelings of pain or profound melancholy and may even cry out or display bizarre personality changes. I will attempt to keep her away from these painful moments, but understand, this is normal and to be expected in age regression and will not prove harmful or injurious to the child in any permanent way. Also, I will be able to awaken her and bring her out of trance at any point I wish."

He could have called Janice, Bill thought. Even drunk, he could have at least done that. Displayed some small vestige of parental concern. It had occurred to him of course, but somehow he couldn't bring himself to a telephone. He knew the things she'd say, which was more than he could face.

"What we are attempting this morning is unique in the annals of psychiatry. To regress a subject to a time of early infancy and, even beyond that, to a prenatal period, while it has been achieved in experimental studies, is certainly uncommon enough, but to attempt to take a subject beyond a present life into a former lifetime has never, to my knowledge, fallen within the purview of serious psychiatric inquiry."

They had talked, briefly, in the hospital cafeteria earlier. The place was packed with reporters, and a carnival atmosphere prevailed. He saw her sitting at a table, alone, drinking coffee. When she saw him, she rose and hurried to leave. He had intercepted her at the door and had said, "Janice, trust me for once, I know what I'm doing." She had seemed so tired, beaten, her face drawn and empty, her gaze averted from his. "No, you don't," she had replied in a helpless voice, bereft of hope or accusation. "But even if you did, it wouldn't matter. It really wouldn't matter."

"In agreeing to conduct this test, I do so with no pretense of a belief or faith in its ultimate success. I am here at the behest of a government agency to perform a function I have been trained and am licensed to perform."

Bill's clothing clung to his skin. The room was like a pressure cooker. Why was the garrulous old bastard going on so? Why couldn't he shut up and get the damn show on the road—get the damn thing over with?

"An hour ago I met with the defendant, Mr. Hoover. He has told me five facts about his daughter's life. Details of events of a special, intimate nature that made a memorable impression on Audrey Rose and that are known only to Mr. Hoover, myself, and my colleagues. If we indeed achieve our purpose here this morning, I will ask the subject to recall these events. Her ability to do so, or not to do so, might well prove conclusive."

It would be over—soon. Soon the issue would be settled—once and for all. Soon they'd all be together again. And once it was over and behind them, they'd find their way back to each other. There would be a distance, a strain for a time, but in the end there'd be forgiveness. Their love would help Janice stretch to forgiveness—in time.

"I will now bring in the subject."

All was silent in the recreation hall, as more than a hundred pairs of eyes unblinkingly fixed on one of three strategically placed television monitors, each purveying the same angle of Dr. Lipscomb as he walked to the examining-room door and opened it to admit Ivy.

The contact between eyes and screens was palpable, like a high-tension electrical current, Janice thought, fighting to concentrate on the technical aspects of the test. She had conditioned her mind to accept the test as the next inevitable step in a progression that was unstoppable. She would not cry, she had counseled herself. Tears would serve no purpose now, would be of no use to Ivy or to herself. It was too late for tears. But the sight of Ivy on the screen, entering the room and allowing the doctor to lead her by the hand to the couch, so shy, so trusting, so vulnerable, caused Janice to catch her breath. For an instant, she feared panic would overwhelm her, and she had to struggle to suppress it.

Ivy's lovely blond hair had been bobbed to a feather cut by Janice, and her facial skin still bore the high color of her recent injury, and yet, even over the coarse black and white transmission which reduced everything to indiscriminate shades of gray, her beauty remained undiminished.

Sitting back comfortably on the couch with one foot tucked under her, Ivy betrayed no nervousness and seemed in total control of herself.

"Relax, Ivy," Dr. Lipscomb said in a softly insinuating monotone. "Relax and allow every muscle in your body to become limp and loose. As we discussed the other day, you will not be harmed in any way, but simply feel very tired, very tired, so tired that you will wish to fall asleep for a while. Nothing harmful, nothing bad is going to happen to you. You will not mind falling asleep for a while, for soon you will begin to feel so tired, so tired that you will not mind falling asleep. Will you mind falling asleep, Ivy?"

"No, it's all right," Ivy replied, wide awake. "I won't mind."

No, Ivy wouldn't mind, Janice thought. Although the psychiatrists in all their smug wisdom thought her a child and easily deceived, Ivy had quickly fathomed the purpose of the test and had confided it to Janice.

"They want to hypnotize me to find out if Audrey Rose is making me do all those crazy things."

"You don't have to go through with it," Janice had told her. "Nobody can be hypnotized against her will."

"But I *want* to," she had replied with eyes grave and anxious. "I have to know what's wrong with me. I can't stand being the way I am."

It was truly amazing, Janice had thought, how Ivy too had become a willing part of Audrey Rose's conspiracy. First, Scott Velie, then Bill, then Hoover, then Judge Langley, and now the victim herself, all being whipped into a unity of purpose by a force incomprehensible to them. Was it possible that only she, Janice, knew what was going on, that only she had divined the meaning and intent behind Audrey Rose's latest ploy?

It surely seemed so. At every turn Janice had been rebuffed.

All through the long weekend she had tried to get through to *somebody*, made countless calls to the apartment in the hope that Bill had finally decided to go home, but he never did. Scott Velie had been unlocatable. She'd tried to coerce the operator into divulging Judge Langley's unlisted phone number—claiming it was a matter of life and death, which it was—but all her passionate pleadings had been met with softly courteous refusals, first by the operator and then, maddeningly, by her supervisor.

When she did finally get to Langley early this morning after waiting two hours in the frigid, wind-whipped hospital parking lot for his rented limousine to arrive and did, at last, get to register her objections to the test in her strongest, most earnest, yet respectful tone, his response, rattled off to her as they sprinted across the treacherously slick parking lot, had all the spontaneity and sincerity of a prepared statement committed to memory.

"Madam, I understand your objections, and I feel very deeply about them. You have every right to make your feelings known, and under normal circumstances, I would give every consideration to your wishes. However, your husband and the defense both have equal rights of consent in this matter and, I am told by Dr. Lipscomb, your daughter has also consented and not only is willing to undergo the test but wishes very strongly to do so. What we are doing is, no doubt, highly unusual, but this is a criminal case. The charge is a very serious one, and should the defendant be found guilty, he will be subject to very severe penalties. In the consideration of that and in the interest of justice, I must deny your request. But rest assured, we have taken every precaution to ensure the safety of your child. We have brought in the best psychiatrists, and the test will be conducted as if in the privacy of a hospital room."

Langley had been her last rational hope.

Her only option left was the irrational.

The test was scheduled to start at ten. At nine five, she'd sought out Dr. Webster. Found him in the lobby. Talking with reporters. Freshly starched smock, shining stethoscope around his neck, fully prepared for the occasion. Janice caught his eye. He joined her in the vestibule, which was cold and deserted.

Was Ivy well enough to go home? she'd casually inquired.

"Sure," he'd agreed. "Soon as this test is over."

Her next stop was Ivy's room. She'd found her sitting on the bed, chatting amiably with the three psychiatrists. Their conversation was light and general, no doubt a calming exercise. Relaxing the patient before the operation. They'd hardly noticed Janice. She'd waited patiently for them to leave. When, after two or three minutes, they didn't, she'd interrupted with a slightly hysterical "May I please have a few moments alone with my daughter?" The psychiatrists eyed her with professional interest and silently left.

Pulling Ivy's overnight bag out of the closet, she'd quickly started to pack. Ivy watched her with suspicion. Finally asked, "What are you doing?"

"Get your coat," Janice ordered. "We're getting out of here."

"What?" said Ivy, in shock.

"I'm not letting you go through with this thing!"

"Mom!" The word exploded in a rush of tears. "Mom, I've got to! I've got to! Don't you understand?" she cried in panic. "I've got to do it! Please! Please! Please!" Her voice dissolved into great heaving sobs.

Janice went to her, frightened. "Easy, baby, easy—" and tried to take her hand, but Ivy jerked it away and gripped the sides of the bed.

"I won't let you take me away! I won't!" she shouted, her reddening face consumed with anguish. "I won't! I won't! I won't!"

The door opened. Nurse Baylor stuck her head in.

"Can I help?"

Janice remained standing by the bedside, staring blindly down at the tearstained, contorted face, unable to speak, paralyzed by the aching effort it cost her mind to absorb the fact that there *was* no help for Ivy, no possibility of mortal help left for her child—that Audrey Rose was not to be stopped. That now *her* will would prevail.

"I want you to relax," continued Dr. Lipscomb in the soothing, regular voice. "I want you to relax. Let yourself fully relax. Lean back and be very comfortable."

The friction of pens against paper, of charcoal against sketchboard formed a counterpoint of sound to Dr. Lipscomb's voice as he produced a pencil flashlight and gradually held its beam aloft in his right hand.

"Look at the light now, Ivy. Look up and keep watching the light. Keep watching it. Keep watching. Now, as you're watching the light, you're beginning to feel your eyes growing heavy. Your eyelids are getting heavier and heavier, and you're finding it harder and harder and harder to keep them open. Finding it harder and harder to keep watching the light. Harder and harder. . . . And slowly your eyelids are feeling so heavy that they want to close . . . want to close. And slowly your eyelids are feeling so heavy that they begin to close . . . begin to close. . . ."

The position of the light, well above her level of vision, was so placed to cause her eyelids gradually to feel heavier and heavier from the strain of constantly looking up, and the suggestibility of the repetitive, metronomic voice slowly worked its effect on Ivy.

"Your eyelids are beginning to get so heavy, so heavy, they're getting heavier and heavier . . . so heavy that you cannot keep them open at all . . . and your eyes are beginning to close, beginning to close, even though you don't want them to, they're beginning to close . . . so heavy you must close them, must close them, close them, close them. . . ."

Janice heard her own pounding heart join the counterpoint of sound as she watched her daughter gradually relinquish her will to this stranger spiriting her off into an endless night.

"Your eyelids are so heavy now, so heavy, that they must close and remain closed, remain closed. Now your eyes are closed. They're closed so tightly that you cannot open them. You cannot open them. Even if you want to, and try your hardest, you cannot open them. Try! Try to open them, Ivy!"

The television camera zoomed into Ivy's face as she tried to open her eyes, strained hard to open them, but could not.

The view from the observation booth was not so fortunate. Not only was the one-way glass an impeding factor, but Dr. Lipscomb's chair had been imprudently placed at an angle so that his body blocked more than half the subject. The people on Bill's side of the room got only a partial view of Ivy. Those on the other side got no view of her at all. Which caused Judge Langley to testily demand that someone go tell the doctor to move aside.

"Patience," Scott Velie's voice counseled respectfully. "Wait till she's fully under."

"There, you cannot open your eyes, they're so tired, so tired, they simply must stay closed. Just relax, Ivy, relax—nothing bad is going to happen to you. You are safe and snug and fully asleep now. Fully asleep. And now your right arm is beginning to feel lighter and lighter. It's feeling so light that it wants to lift away from the couch. So light it just seems to want to float in the air."

It did.

"And now your arm is beginning to feel heavy again, so heavy that it wants to fall back onto the couch, fall back onto the couch and rest itself."

It obeyed.

"You are fully asleep now. Fully asleep. If I wish to awaken you, I will count to five. At the count of five, I will say, 'Awaken, Ivy!' and you will awaken promptly. Do you understand?"

"Yes." Her voice was weak, pallid.

"At my command, you will awaken, and you will feel rested and well, as if you had taken a nap. Do you understand?"

"Yes."

The scraping of a chair, followed by a stumbling footstep, preceded the appearance of Scott Velie's silhouette at the window. He tapped lightly on the glass and caught the attention of the doctor, who, turning about nervously, quickly grasped the problem and obliged by shifting himself and chair off to a side, permitting the court an unencumbered view of the subject. The slight disturbance in no way seemed to affect or elicit a reaction from the sleeping child, and once settled, Dr. Lipscomb renewed the hypnosis.

"Now, as your eyes are closed, and you are deeply asleep, and you are completely relaxed, you're gradually moving back in time. Back, back, Ivy . . . back in time. You're moving back in time to your eighth birthday. All right, Ivy, I will count to three, and you will be at your eighth birthday party. You will remember every detail of your eighth birthday party. One, two, three. . . ."

In the next instant, an expression of joy appeared on Ivy's face—an inner, contained joy that seemed pure and natural and genuine.

"You are now at the party, among your friends. Do you see your friends, Ivy?"

She nodded, still smiling.

"Tell me about them, Ivy. Who is at the party?"

"Bettina, Carrie. Mary Ellen. The twins. Peter."

"Tell me about your presents. Do you love your presents?"

"Oh, yes. I love my Terry doll with travel wardrobe. And the game of Clue that Bettina bought me. And the roller skates. . . ."

Janice winced inwardly when the roller skates were recalled. The memory of the ear-shattering, head-splitting sound of Ivy clopping around the apartment on them in tears after falling every third step, and Janice's decision to bury them away in a closet and pretend that they had either been lost or stolen, came crashing back in alternating waves of guilt and sadness, knowing that the skates, still haunting that closet, would remain there now, unused, forever.

"Now we will leave this birthday and go back in time to an earlier birthday. Just relax and move back in time to your fourth birthday party, Ivy. I will count to three, and you will be at your fourth birthday party. Ready! One . . . two . . . three. . . ."

Her look turned suddenly grave, taking on the plaintive expression of a much younger child, a child who has just sustained a keen and humiliating disappointment.

"You are now at your fourth birthday party. Your friends have brought you presents, Ivy. Do you see your presents, Ivy?"

Her cheeks flamed with hurt and resentment. She turned petulantly away from the doctor's question, chin quivering.

Noting her reaction to this area of remembrance, Dr. Lipscomb gently led her away from it.

"What a grand birthday cake your parents bought. It's got four lovely candles for you to blow out and make a wish on, Ivy."

"Five candles," she sullenly corrected. "Didn't buy it. Too offenspif. Mommy made it from a magzadine, and I helped her."

Tears sprang to Janice's eyes at the sound of the voice, the sweet, simple voice of her four-year-old, making all those charming mistakes in pronunciation. "Offenspif" for "expensive," "magzadine" for "magazine"—wistfully recalling the times she had hesitated to correct her, waging war with the years to preserve her exquisite naïveté, reluctant to let go of the child.

Janice's mind was suddenly wrenched back to the present by the sound of sobbing, as she watched Ivy, huddled in the couch, hands covering her face, surrender herself to heartbreak in wave after wave of sobs so intense as to cause her body to shudder. *Why was she crying?* Janice asked herself, probing her memory for some clue to her grief. It had been a joyous birthday, hadn't it? And then Janice remembered. There had been a moment, a terrible moment when that boy—what was his name?—

"He broke it!" Ivy sobbed. "Stuart broke my monkey!"

Yes, Stuart—that was it—the wind-up toy—a monkey on a tricycle. Stuart Cowan, a boy from the nursery school Ivy attended, had wound it up so tightly that the spring broke.

"Damn rotten little boy!" Ivy wailed.

Bill swallowed as the scene shot vividly back to him. *It was a melee. Ivy screaming. Stuart laughing. Bill mollifying, telling her that Stuart was just a damn rotten little boy.*

"Damn rotten little boy!" Ivy repeated in a singsong of sobs.

"It's all right, Ivy," soothed Dr. Lipscomb. "It's all right. You're going to move away from that bad memory. You'll leave it now and move back in time even farther. You'll move back in time to your third birthday. One . . . two . . . three. . . . You are now at your third birthday party, Ivy. . . ."

The tears stopped. The expression became remote, then softened. A smile hovered at her lips, followed by a tinkling, childish giggling, which then exploded into a burst of laughter—harsh, raucous.

"I win! I win! I win!" she screeched in the wild, hysterical manner of a three-year-old. "I win! I win and you lose! You all lose 'cept me!"

"Very good, Ivy," praised the doctor. "Very good. Now, move back in time a little bit farther. A little farther back in time. You're two and a half, and you're having trouble sleeping. Go back to the night when the bad dreams began. You're dreaming now the same dream you had on that night. . . ."

Her expression gradually tightened. She began to fret and tremble. Her breath came in quick, shallow bursts. The whimpering came next. "Mommydaddymommydaddyhothothot—" And began to build.

Bill heard sharp intakes of breaths and a general nervous stirring in the observation room.

Janice sensed a deep hush around her as pencils paused above pads and attentions riveted on the screens.

"DaddydaddydaddyhothotHOTHOT—"

"All right, Ivy! Leave the bad dream!" Dr. Lipscomb commanded. "Leave the bad dream! It's morning, and the dream is over!"

The whimpering abated. The face lost its tension, began to relax.

"Good, Ivy, good. . . . Now just relax, relax, calm. I want you to slip back farther and farther in time now. Go way back in time, Ivy. Way back to a time when you can see and hear and feel and think but you cannot say things. You're a little baby in Mommy's arms now, and Mommy's putting you in your carriage. . . ."

Once again, tears rushed to Janice's eyes as Ivy began to chortle and smile and express the small, scattered discomforts and pleasures of early infancy. The utter sweetness of this recollection came back in full force, bringing with it the very feel and smell of the tiny bundled body in her arms and a stab of pain to her heart for all those treasured, precious moments forever gone, forever lost to her, some even beyond the rescue of memory.

"Very good, Ivy," Dr. Lipscomb told her, his voice so soft, so caressing in its gentleness. "And now, we are going even farther back in time . . . farther back . . . farther back to a time before you were born . . . before you were born . . . before you were born. . . ."

The repetition, the insinuating cadence, the firm, indomitable note of command gradually began to manifest an overwhelming lethargy in the child. Eyes tightly shut, head reposing on a shoulder, her hands slowly clasped together as if in prayer, and her knees gradually drew up to her chest in a startling approximation of a fetal ball, whereupon she remained rigidly still, neither moving nor flinching nor seeming even to draw breath, in effect, duplicating the perfect in-limbo attitude of a fetus floating in the womb's juices.

The moment was electric.

"My God," Janice heard someone behind her whisper, "she's in her mother's womb."

In the observation booth, not a ripple of sound disturbed the steaming, fetid stillness as nineteen people were held captive by the incredible performance.

His face bathed in sweat, his eyes blurring from the room's closeness and the strain he was subjecting them to, Bill could only stare along with the rest of them, uncertainty giving way to incredulity, as the weird behavior of his child, his own little princess, unfolded before his stunned scrutiny. *It was impossible,* he thought. *She was playacting. Had to be playacting. Wasn't asleep at all. Just putting the old duffer on. Had a good memory of her birthdays, that was it. But—how did she know about things like fetuses? And what they looked like? Books? Bettina probably. She was pretty damned advanced. And yet—it was weird, how still she remained, how deathly still—like one of those things in jars you sometimes see in doctors' offices. Weird.* His struggles and his doubts were now showing plainly on his face. And his fear. If this was on the level, it was wrong. All wrong. . . . ?

"Back, back, back in time," the verbal metronome continued, urging, pleading, pushing, "back in time, back farther and farther to the time before you existed as yourself. Back to the time when you were not Ivy, not Ivy, not Ivy, back to the time when you were somebody else, somebody else, not Ivy, but somebody else."

This was wrong. Bad. The way she sat there, not moving, hardly breathing, suspended in space, floating. What the hell was he doing to her? Where was he taking her? Was it possible he was really taking her back to another life? Crazy. Impossible. And yet—

". . . not Ivy, but somebody else, somebody else, back in time, back in time, back in time . . . back in time until you can remember, until you can remember, remember, remember, remember . . . remember the very next thing, the very next thing, remember, remember . . . you are not Ivy but somebody else . . . somebody else . . . not Ivy, not Ivy . . . but . . . who are you? Who are you? WHO ARE YOU?"

He'd stop it! Dammit, he'd stop it! This was wrong. Bad. He'd stop it now!

"WHO ARE YOU?"

"I want this test stopped, Mr. Velie!" Bill had risen to his feet and was swaying uncertainly. His head felt ready to burst.

"WHO ARE YOU?"

"I want it stopped!" he demanded in a quavering voice, clutching the chair to keep from falling. "God damn it, do you hear me?"

"WHO ARE YOU?"

"Stop this test!" he shouted. "Mr. Velie, Judge Langley—do you hear me?"

But even if they heard, which was doubtful, none could act, for all sat mesmerized, shocked into silence by the specter that was slowly materializing on the other side of the mirror. For now the child was sitting bolt upright on the couch, eyes wide open and staring, body rigid, expression startled, hovering between terror and amusement, warily seeking a persona just beyond reach, moving tentatively, cautiously, toward the brink of some startling discovery.

"WHO ARE YOU?" the voice pursued relentlessly, pushing, thrusting, projecting her forward on her course.

Trembling, Bill tried to steady himself but collapsed into the chair, unable to speak, hardly able to breathe. He tried to close his eyes to blot out the scene but could not. *He'd have to look. This was his doing—his goddamn doing—now, he'd have to watch it—all of it!*

"WHO ARE YOU?"

Suddenly, her face froze. Her eyes—bright, expectant—grew even wider, beseeching some distant memory which now appeared to be at hand, within reach. Her breath quickened. The lines of tension around her mouth relaxed into a gradual smile, spreading softly, suffusing the face with a light of such shimmering joy, radiating a warmth of expression so tender, so grateful as to be unmistakably that of a homecoming. She had arrived—at last. After long and weary wanderings, she had finally come home.

"Mommy?" the child's voice rang out, clear and sharp. "Mommy!" She laughed, in peal after peal of rapture and delight. "Mommy! Mommy, Mommy, Mommy!"

It was at this moment of arrival, of laughter and reunion, that Janice Templeton shut her eyes and began to softly recite the Prayer for the Dead.

"*O God, Whose property is always to have mercy and to spare, we humbly beseech thee for the soul of thy servant, Ivy Templeton, which thou hast this day commanded to depart out of this world. . . .*"

"Mommy, Mommy, Mommy!" the childish voice repeated in an unabating litany, but the tone underwent a subtle change. What had been gay, joyous, charged with a fervor of jubilation and rejoicing, gradually began to take on a note of anxiety and hysteria. "Mommy, Mommy, Mommy!" the voice shrieked, graduating up the scale, in a rising glissando, from fear to fright to strident horror.

"*. . . that thou wouldst not deliver her into the hands of the enemy, nor forget her unto the end, but wouldst command her to be received by the holy angels. . . .*"

"Mommy-eeeeee!"

In the observation booth there was shocked silence. No one moved.

Bill peered feverishly through the murky glass, his eyes locked on the distant face, hardly able to focus. *What the hell was happening to her? She was laughing one minute, and now—* It was changing. The voice—the face—was changing. *It was breaking apart—fragmenting into panels and lines of fear . . . terror—breathless, welling terror . . . like kids wear on their faces coming down a roller coaster. That was it, she was swaying back and forth like she was moving—no, like the world around her was moving—like the couch was moving and the world was rushing by her. . . .*

"Mommy-eeeeee!" The word got swallowed up in a scream so high-pitched and intense that the wall speaker crackled and popped.

"My God," someone in the room whispered as the screams sustained a strident peak and the swaying became more pronounced—back and forth, from side to side, forcing her hands to cling to the arms of the couch and her body to fight to stay upright, to fight this power that seemed determined to send her reeling through the air. . . .

"It's all right, Ivy!" Dr. Lipscomb said nervously.

"*Eeeeeeeeeee!*"

"It's all right, Ivy!" he repeated, his voice rising, mustering sternness. "You will leave this memory now! You will move farther back in time away from this memory! Farther back in time, Ivy!"

"*Mommy-eeeee!*" shrieked the voice as her body swayed and teetered to and fro, wildly now, the muscles of her face drawn into knots, her head zigzagging from side to side, her fingers desperately clutching the fabric of the couch to keep from being hurled into space.

"You will move away from this memory, Ivy! When I count to three, you will move back in time. One . . . two . . . three!"

"*Mommmm-eee! Crash-crash-crash-crash!*"

"One . . . two . . . three! Do you understand me, Ivy!"

"Not Ivy!" a voice in the observation room whispered hoarsely. A voice that was Elliot Hoover's. "She's not Ivy!"

"*Moooommmm-eeeee! Crash-crash-crash-crash!*"

Her scream, rising to decibels of a stridency that overloaded speakers and eardrums alike, pierced the air in a single sustained note as her body, incapable of longer resisting its own violent, turbulent oscillations, thrust itself upward from the couch as if impelled by some irresistible power, sending her staggering to her feet and holding her suspended in space momentarily—arms outstretched, eyes bulging, the scream dying in her throat—before dropping her to the floor with a shocking suddenness and force that could be heard through the speakers. Head striking first, her body tumbled over in a bruising somersault, whereupon she remained in a crumpled ball, writhing and trembling in what seemed only partial consciousness—eyes half closed, a line of blood trickling from her mouth, and muted, pained moans of a terribly injured person rising and falling in her throat.

The effect upon the audience was staggering and unmistakable.

". . . *it was smoking, and one of the back wheels was still turning.* . . ."

All around Janice, chairs scraped. People rose. A deathly silence held as all awaited the terrible aftermath.

"O Lord, deliver her from the rigor of thy justice. O Lord, deliver her from long-enduring sorrow. . . ."

Dr. Lipscomb, stunned into speechlessness along with the others, recovered his professional presence and, dropping to his knees, placed his trembling fingers on the child's pulse. His face mirrored concern. His voice ratified it.

"You will now awaken, Ivy!" he commanded in a tone that wavered with uncertainty. "When I count to five, you will awaken and feel rested and well. One . . . two . . . three . . . four . . . five. . . . Awaken, Ivy!"

The child lay on her back, eyes closed, breathing hard, writhing, moaning.

"You will obey me, Ivy! At the count of five, you will awaken!"

"Not Ivy, not Ivy," Hoover muttered in a fever of anxiety.

"One . . . two . . . three . . . four. . . ."

"O Lord, deliver her from the cruel flames—"

". . . five!"

Her eyes popped open. She sat bolt upright. Weak. Exhausted. Panting. Intensely alert. Senses keened. Eyes widening with alarm. Nostrils flaring. Smelling. Head twisting about, rubber-necking, startled, bird-like, sensing an imminent danger. Face contorting in a kaleidoscope of expressions—fear, dismay, panic, horror—

". . . then . . . there was an explosion . . . not loud . . . like a puff . . . and all at once the car was swallowed up in flames. . . ."

The scream burst forth like a gunshot, built to an incredible crescendo, and sustained.

Behind the mirror, bodies flinched and breaths expelled to melt the inner tension.

Bill was on his feet, not knowing it, drawing the sight into his stunned mind. He felt something tightening in his chest.

"One . . . two . . . three . . . four . . . five! Awaken, Ivy!"

"She's not Ivy, damn you!" shouted Hoover, jumping to his feet, bringing the guard up with him.

"One . . . two . . . three. . . ."

The strung-out scream maintained its steady, piercing shrillness, mindless of the doctor's importunings. Her body twisted away from his outstretched hands, slithering then crawling from their grasp.

". . . four . . . five! Awaken, Ivy!"

Stumbling to her feet, her eyes darted frantically about for a path of escape and, seeing the mirror, she quickly scampered toward the reflected image of her own fear-ravaged face, rushing to meet it, her scream suddenly fading, replaced by choking gasps which then erupted into the quick, explosive sobs and whimperings, "Mommydaddymommydaddyhothothot!"

"O Lord, deliver her from dreadful weeping and wailing, through thine admirable conception!"

A sudden hum of rising voices and a shuffling of footsteps forced Janice to open her eyes. Everybody was standing, watching the screens, pressing forward to get a better view of the picture, which, Janice saw, had lost the images of Ivy and Dr. Lipscomb, though their voices, rising in opposition, were clearly heard.

"Mommydaddymommydaddydaddydaddyhothothot!"

"One . . . two . . . three. . . ."

Janice took a deep breath, knowing that they must be at the window now, out of camera range.

A wailing shriek coming through the speakers, half of pain, half of horror, started the exodus from the recreation hall as the reporters gave up on the TV and hurried to the stairway.

Janice rose. It was time for her to go, too. She would neither hurry nor linger but descend the three floors at a normal rate of speed. It would take her just under two minutes to get there. She had timed it earlier. By then it would be over.

In the observation booth, all eyes clung to the scene being played just beyond the length of the glass—

—The figure of the child, blurred, ethereal, rushing back and forth across the length of the glass—

—Her hands beckoning toward it, withdrawing, weeping, "hothothothot—"

—The doctor, ". . . four . . . five! Awaken, Ivy!" moving toward her, reaching out—

—The child screaming, struggling violently, furiously, eluding him—

—Her face wild, her breathing heavy, her eyes reflecting coruscating glints of panic, her senses sharpened now by the encroaching peril—

—Her fists balled into hard knots, mustering the energy of despair—

"*It was just horrible. I could still see the little girl screaming and beating her hands against the window. . . .*"

—Pounding the glass and sobbing, "Hothothothothot!"

"*I could see her through the flames as the car was melting all around the window. . . .*"

—A loud, shrill scream bursting suddenly from her throat, causing the line of jurors at the glass to jerk back in their chairs—

—"You will obey me, Ivy!"—
—Hoover shouting shudderingly, "AUDREY ROSE."
—"One . . . two. . . ."—
—"They can't hear you," Velie explaining. "Room's soundproof."—
—". . . three . . . four. . . ."—
—Langley watching openmouthed—his mind refusing to comprehend what was happening—
". . . . five! Awaken, Ivy!"—
—"AUDREY ROSE!"—
—Panting, gasping for breath, helpless prey to a whirl of emotions beyond her control, clawing, beating against the glass, screaming, "Daddydaddydaddyhothothot!"—
—Hoover shouting, "I'm here!" and plunging over chairs and bodies, stumbling down to the window—
—The guard withdrawing his revolver, indecisively—
—Velie shouting, "Put it away, Tim!" decisively—
—"Daddydaddydaddy!"—
—Hoover's body splayed against the glass, hands outstretched—
—"Hothothothot!"—
—". . . *she screamed and screamed and tried to get out of the car. . . .*"—
—Bill frozen, staring mutely, a crazed and awful guilt in his eyes—
—". . . *and kept beating her hands against the window. . . .*"—
—"HOTHOTHOT!"—
—Dr. Lipscomb, grim-faced in defeat, speaking up at the mirror. "I'll have to give her a sedative, Your Honor," then hurrying in helpless frustration to his medical bag—
—"Hothothot . . . Daddy . . . hot . . . hot. . . ."—
—Her voice, scarcely sane, growing feeble, the pallor of her face reddening, taking on a ghastly hue—
—"Hot . . . hot . . . hot. . . ."—
—Coughing, choking, the words dying in her throat—
—". . . hot. . . ."—
—Clutching her throat, collapsing to her knees, her eyes disappearing upward into her head—
—Mrs. Carbone shrieking, "Oh, God, she's dying!" extending her arms to the suffering child struggling to survive on the other side of the glass. "She's choking to death!" rising, pleading. "Somebody help her! SHE'S DYING!"—
—"DADDY-EEEEE!" the agony in her soul bursting forth in one long and final scream of anguish—

—Mrs. Carbone shouting at Hoover, pummeling his arm, "You're her father! Help her! HELP HER!"—

—Hoover turning to his assailant, eyes widening, body tensing, his movements measured, deliberate, seizing Mrs. Carbone's chair and, with a sharp cry, "AUDREY!" swinging it in a powerful arc against the far end of the glass, shattering it into a hailstorm of shimmering splinters—

The corridor outside the observation theater was clogged with reporters. Two tight-lipped Connecticut highway patrolmen stood guard before the closed door, indifferent to the litany of questions battering them from all sides.

"Please let me through," Janice asked at the outer fringes of the gathering.

Upon seeing who she was, a hush fell in a gradual wave across the assembled group, and a path was cleared for her.

"She's the child's mother," someone informed the patrolmen, who immediately opened the door just wide enough for her slim body to slip through.

The dimly lit room enveloped her in its suffocating closeness, offering her its quiet murmurings and air of deep, unredeemable gloom.

The floor was gritty with powdered glass, causing her footsteps to announce her presence as she slowly approached the men and women gathered in a semicircle, their bodies shielding an object of intense concern from her view. They were faces she had come to know well: Scott Velie, Brice Mack, Judge Langley, the court clerk (she never did know his name), Hoover's guard (Finchley or Findley, she had once read), the twelve jurors, each face reflecting sensations of sadness, awe, and disbelief. Mrs. Carbone weeping into a handkerchief, people from the courtroom, people from the hospital, the three psychiatrists standing shoulder to shoulder, ludicrously, Janice thought, seeing no evil, hearing no evil, speaking no evil. And Bill—finally Bill—alone in the observation booth, sitting with his back pressed against the wall, dramatically framed by jagged splinters of glass, staring sightless into space, shaking his head from side to side as people whose burdens in life are too great often do.

"Mrs. Templeton—" The gentle hand, the kindly voice were Dr. Webster's. His expression combined disillusion and grief equally. His stethoscope, still in place around his neck, glittered like a jewel. "It

". . . it happened so fast . . . we tried . . . I can't tell you how. . . ." His voice faltered, the words too painful to express.

Heads turned. A channel parted. Janice pushed through and for a panicked moment felt her breath stop, saw a wavering opaqueness begin to draw across her vision.

Someone's hand gripped her arm. Steadied her. Forced her back to consciousness. Forced her to look down toward the floor at her child, at her own sweet Ivy, lying now so still and breathless in the arms of Elliot Hoover. Her eyes were open, reflecting a luster that seemed to radiate life; her pale lips were slightly parted, as if about to speak.

But it was Hoover who spoke for her.

"It's all right," he said, rocking the body gently back and forth in his arms. "She's at peace now." His voice was depleted, yet tranquil and strangely reassuring. Looking up at Janice, and in the half-light, his face seemed worn, scarred by the marks of a long and grueling battle, yet at peace.

"It's all right now," he repeated, offering her the strength and comfort of his belief like a legacy from God to His beleaguered children, lending the words an emphasis and finality of a conviction so powerful as to be indisputable, while clutching the still and lifeless form of—

—*their child.*

END PAPERS

35493

CORONER'S INVESTIGATION and POST MORTEM REPORTS

Over the Remains of

Ivy TEMPLETON

Filed   FEB 3 1975   , 19

RALPH W. EPPERS
                                    Clerk

By *Wm. McCauley*
                              Deputy Clerk

CASE No. 88990

Exhibit
People's #2
Date Feb 4, 1975
By C. Briggs
County Clerk

OFFICE OF SHERIFF-CORONER

POST MORTEM RECORD

Name TEMPLETON, Ivy   Age 10
Sex Female   Race Caucasian   Height 59"   Weight 70 (est.)
Date and Time of Death 2-3-75 at 10:43 A.M.   Autopsy: Place: SJGH
                        7:05 P.M.   Date: 2-3-75   Time: 4:25 P.M.

INSPECTION

1. Marks of Identification: Coroner's identification wrist-band Ivy Templeton.

2. Eyes Gray   3. Ears Not remarkable   4. Mouth Not remarkable
5. Rigor Mortis Light, generalized
6. Wounds and General Remarks Well developed, well nourished caucasian female appearing
stated age. Evidence of healing 4 day old 2nd degree burns on face. Healed old
burn scars on hands (remote). No other skin lesions. No other remarkable external
abnormalities.

AUTOPSY

No abnormalities of upper respiratory tract. Neck shows no evidence of trauma
or induced strangulation. The larynx shows mild edema but no internal obstruction
or other abnormality. The plural surfaces show numerous small petechial hemorrhages
probably due to anoxia. The lungs appeared completely normal. There were no
abnormalities of the cardiovascular system. No gross or microscopic of abdominal
organs. Central nervous system: brain appeared normal showing no evidence of
tumor, hemorrhage, edema or vascular lesions.
Toxicological Exam: Complete and exhaustive studies reveal no abnormalities.

We, the undersigned, having made the above examination, find the cause of death to have been due to
ASPHYXIATION DUE TO LARYNGOSPASM - PROBABLY CAUSED BY PSYCHOGENIC FACTORS

1. Specimens taken (results): A. Blood x
Taken by: R.F. Shad   Date: 2-3   Time: 10:30 A.M.
B. Stomach Contents
C. Tissue x General-fixative-storage
D. Other urine, bile-toxicology
Taken for: Alcohol content x   Typing   Tox: - barb,
Taken by: R.F. Shad   Date: 2-3   Time: 10:30 A.M.   morphine & gen. screen
Delivered to: SJGH Laboratory

                                    R. F. Shad, M.D.
                                    Sheriff-Coroner

(UPI—FEBRUARY 4, 1975) AFTER A FULL MORNING OF FINAL ARGUMENTS, THE JURY RECEIVED INSTRUCTIONS ON THE LAW AND BEGAN ITS DELIBERATIONS IN THE TRIAL OF ELLIOT S. HOOVER THIS AFTERNOON AT 1407 HOURS. JUDGE HARMON T. LANGLEY, IN AN ALMOST ONE-HOUR EXPLANATION OF THE LAW TO THE JURY, TOLD THEM IN PART: "IT IS FOR YOU TO DECIDE WHAT EVIDENCE IS CREDIBLE IN THIS TRIAL. YOU THE JURORS ARE THE SOLE JUDGE OF THE CREDIBILITY OF THE WITNESSES AND OF THE EVENTS THAT HAVE TAKEN PLACE IN THIS VERY UNUSUAL CASE. YOUR FUNCTION IS TO CONSIDER THE FACTS AND TO DETERMINE THE FACTS." LESS THAN 30 MINUTES AFTER IT RETIRED TO CONSIDER ITS VERDICT THE JURY SENT WORD THAT IT HAD REACHED A DECISION. THE VERDICT, ANNOUNCED BY FOREMAN HERMAN M. POTASH, FOUND ELLIOT HOOVER NOT GUILTY OF ALL CHARGES, WHEREUPON JUDGE LANGLEY THANKED THE JURY AND ORDERED THE DEFENDANT RELEASED. ENDS. FINAL FEBRUARY 4 1604N UPI.

New York Times, February 6, 1975

VITAL RECORDS

DEATHS

Funeral Announcements

TEMPLETON, Ivy, beloved daughter of William P., & Janice Templeton. Private inurnment at Mt. Canaan Mausoleum, Valhalla, N.Y., under the direction of Boyce & Logan, Co., funeral directors, New York City.

IN MEMORIAM

In loving memory
AUDREY ROSE HOOVER
Private memorial services 7:30 p.m., February 7, at Hompa Hongwanji Buddhist Temple, 14 Christopher Place, N.Y.

I.T.

Mr. E. S. Hoover
c/o Mr. Sesh Mehrotra
Benares Hindu University
Benares, U.P.
India

New York City
March 24, 1975

Dear Mr. Hoover:

   Thank you for your beautiful letter. Knowing you are there, doing all the things you must for the peace and purification of our daughter's soul, helps to ease the burden of our sadness. I include Bill in my thanks, even though he is as yet unable to accept what he knows in his heart to be true. Bill is not the type to change his way of thinking easily. Especially since he blames himself utterly for Ivy's death, believing that had he not lent his support to the test she would still be alive today. His grief, reinforced by guilt, makes it difficult for him to understand that what happened to Ivy was inevitable and totally beyond his or anybody's control. I must confess that till that last morning at the hospital I found it hard to accept myself.

   The loss of the physical being of Ivy is to Bill the loss of a cherished possession, which is what children are to most parents. One day, I am sure, Bill will come to understand, as I have, that we cannot think of our children as possessions, or try to possess them — that they are only lent to us for a brief time. We may support them and help mold them somewhat, but in the end they must be their own persons, fulfilling whatever destiny they have come to earth to fulfill, no matter how full or empty, how lengthy or brief, how beautiful or tragic it may be. In permitting you to take Ivy's ashes to India, I believe that Bill has taken the first step toward this understanding.

Ivy's death has left an unrelenting vacuum in our lives. The sudden separation that death brings to every family is truly unbearable, and I can only pray that God gives us the strength and understanding to live with our loss. The apartment rings with Ivy's presence and now that it is Spring again, and the park is budding with reminders of our happiest days, the city has become unendurable. We have put the apartment up for sale and are considering a move to Portland, Oregon. It was my home, originally, and Bill doesn't seem to mind where we try to pick up our lives.

Know that I add my prayers to yours for our daughter's soul to mend itself, and find the peace and fulfillment in heaven that it was denied in its earth-life, and that the day will come when it will feel free and able to continue its cyclic journey toward perfection, and that when it does, she will select parents who are generous, understanding, and who will love her as we all loved her.

Take Asi
Janice Templeton

EPILOGUE

He had not come to the cemetery since his mother's funeral more than three years before. He was not sure why he had come today. What had started out as a directionless Sunday spin in the new Camaro had somehow turned into a purposeful trip down U.S. 1 to Woodbridge, New Jersey. He had given it no prior thought. It was really the last place he cared to be on this warm, breezy, peaceful May afternoon.

To Brice Mack, cemeteries were not places of peace, but of turmoil. Of abrupt endings and dreams unresolved. Of bones and spirits linked together in an outcry of rage against a fate that is snappish, arbitrary and rude, heedlessly interrupting deeds in middoing, thoughts in midflight, words in midsentence.

Driving through the main gates and up the winding road to the crest of Beth Israel Cemetery, he brought the car to a sudden stop as he saw below him a wilderness of headstones stretching out as far as the eye could see. In three years the cemetery's population had truly exploded. Had at least quadrupled. My God, he thought, so many in so short a time.

Easing up on the brake, he allowed the Camaro to inch its way down the hill into Beth Israel's granite densities, heading not for the part set aside for individual plots, but for the substantial section apportioned into small communities, each one representing a lodge, society, or brotherhood from a city, township, or hamlet in the old country, permitting families, relatives, and friends to live together in death as they had lived in life, huddled in their tiny ghettos, *landsmen* forever.

The car moved slowly along the narrow street, flanked on either side by these settlements, each one fronted by elaborate posterns proudly bearing the town names. "RAWICZ INDEPENDENT BROTHERHOOD," "THE CHILDREN OF CZERSK," "PAUSZKOW LODGE 121," "BOYS OF KRAJENSKIE," were some of the names Brice Mack remembered passing on the two other occasions he had come to the cemetery. It surprised him to discover how surely he knew the route to the "STANISLAWOWER INDEPENDENT SO-

CIETY," named for the Polish village where his parents were born, raised, were married, and from which they emigrated.

The marble gateposts prominently featured the names of the long-deceased first president, Jacob Gilbert; the vice-president, Oscar Goldfeder; the treasurer, Morris Pinkus; and the sergeant-at-arms, Max Ladner. Beneath the executives' names were listed those of the membership in order of demise, Max Marmorstein's preceding Sadie's by seventeen names. The list had grown long in three years, Brice Mack sadly reflected. The membership had died off, seemingly all at once, choking the settlement with tombstones.

It was no hardship locating his mother and father's plot. Denied of care, it stood out among its neighbors like a small patch of desert in a rich and fertile valley—abandoned, forgotten.

A sense of shame filled Mack as he bent down and tried to pull a dead weed from the dry, powdery soil near the stone, but its roots were deep and stubborn and resisted his strongest efforts. He rose to his feet, panting, resolving to stop by the office and order "Care" for his parents' grave on the way out. At the very least, he could do that for them. Restore their pride. Allow them to hold up their heads again before their *landsmen*.

He felt a sting at his eyes, and tears begin to blur the names on the double headstone. How little they had asked of him and how little he had given.

Still, they would be proud of him today. Momma especially. His future was assured now. It's what she had always wanted for him—a future free of the doubts and uncertainties that had plagued her own life.

Well, Sadie would be pleased to know that from where he was standing now, the future looked mighty bright for her boy. The case of the decade won. A partnership in a firm with a Fifth Avenue address secured. A duplex apartment in Greenwich Village rented. New clothes bought. New car leased. Even the boss' Bryn Mawr daughter, Cynthia, a serious romantic possibility. It was a Horatio Alger script, a delicious fantasy come true.

Whether or not he had earned it was immaterial. Though the case had not been won entirely by his own hand, there was no denying he had been the winner's representative and the rightful beneficiary of a good part of the glory. Judge Langley was certainly making hay, stomping the countryside, indulging in a lot of bragging, name-dropping rhetoric, part the jurist, part the Buddhist monk. Even Scott Velie, the loser, had had his shot on the *Johnny Carson Show*.

And still—whenever the peculiar facts in the case came rushing back in the dead of a sleepless night, contradicting and distorting his carefully developed daytime explanations and rationales, he would have to admit that he didn't really know what had happened and what the hell it had all been about. It was crazy, was all he knew for sure—the whole case was crazy, from its nutty start to its deadly finish.

A breeze rolled across the cemetery, rustling leaves and bending bushes. Brice Mack's face reflected feelings too complex to disentangle. It happened whenever he thought of the little girl behind the mirror, choking, gasping for breath, dying—just as that other little girl had died in the car crash. He had known, even before Hoover's Valkyrian windup, as everybody in that room must have known, that there was no hope of rescue for her—that all the doctors and needles and tubes down the throat would not alter her destiny, that her death had been preordained from the very beginning, from that very moment of dawning consciousness she had so graphically described to them during the hypnosis. It was this memory of the girl, the memory of her floating in her mother's womb, that came stealing back at unsuspecting moments to taunt his skepticism and erode his confidence—and that would continue to do so, he knew, for the rest of his life.

Brice Mack sighed deeply and shook his head. Who knew? Who knew anything? Reincarnation. Rebirth. Another life. A thousand lives. An eternity of lives. Back and forth. Here and there. Was it true? Could it be? Were Max and Sadie watching him from some astral plane even now, shaking their heads and smiling reassurances down at him? Or were they already reborn, kicking up a fuss in a couple of Long Island baby carriages? Who knew? Who knew what was true? What was true was what was here before him—now. A Sunday in May. A warm breeze. A present that was real. A future that was potent, wholesome, and intact.

"Excuse, please—"

The man had approached from behind so that Brice Mack did not see him until he felt the soft touch of his hand on his own and heard the gentle voice.

"You want I should say a Yiskor for Max and Sadie?"

He was one of the men, Brice Mack remembered, who spent their days at cemeteries, plying God's word at gravesides for a consideration. Hatted and frocked in unseasonable woolens, the pale eyes shone out of a face that was pure, unlined, and lightly bearded with silken hair.

"You want?" he prodded, smiling.

"Yeah, sure," Brice Mack mumbled, seeking his billfold while the man produced a paper yarmulke and gave it to him to cover his head.

Brice took out a ten-dollar bill, then as an afterthought, made it twenty, and quickly wrote three names down on the back of a card. Handing the money and card over to the man, he said, "Include them in, too."

The man scrutinized the names for a long moment in a puzzled way, silently saying the surnames to himself before asking, "They're Jewish?"

"No," Brice Mack replied. "Does it matter?"

The man thought a moment, then shrugged and smiled. "It can't hurt," he assured and, lowering his head, began to read from a slip of paper the Kaddish, the Jewish prayer for the dead.

"*Yiskor elohim nishmos ovi ve'imi, skeynay,* Max, *u'skeynosay,* Sadie, *es nishmas,* James Beardsley Hancock, Ivy Templeton, Audrey Rose Hoover, *baavur sheanee nodeir zdokoh baadom, bischar zeh tihyeno nafshosom zruros bizror hachayim im nishmos Avrohom, Yizchok ve' Yaakov, Soroh, Rivkoh, Rocheil ve'Leyo, v'im sh'or zadikim vezidkonios sheb'gan Edne, venomar omain.*"